A Spell on the Water

SWEETWATER FICTION: ORIGINALS

TITLES IN THE SERIES:

Where No Gods Came
by Sheila O'Connor

The Goat Bridge
by T. M. McNally

Greetings from Cutler County
by Travis Mulhauser

How Like an Angel
by Jack Driscoll

One Mile Past Dangerous Curve
by Darrell Spencer

The Most Beautiful Girl in the World
by Judy Doenges

Grand River and Joy
by Susan Messer

A Spell on the Water
by Marjorie Kowalski Cole

A Spell on the Water

MARJORIE KOWALSKI COLE

The University of Michigan Press · Ann Arbor

Published in the United States of America by
The University of Michigan Press
Manufactured in the United States of America
⊗ Printed on acid-free paper

2014 2013 2012 2011 4 3 2 1

A CIP catalog record for this book is available from the British Library.

Library of Congress Cataloging-in-Publication Data

Cole, Marjorie Kowalski.
A spell on the water / Marjorie Kowalski Cole.
p. cm. — (Sweetwater fiction)
ISBN 978-0-472-03463-5 (cloth : alk. paper) — ISBN 978-0-472-02756-9 (ebk.)
1. Life change events—Fiction. 2. Widows—Fiction. 3. Country life—Michigan—Fiction. 4. Mother and child—Fiction. 5. Fatherless families—Fiction. I. Title.
PS3603.O429S64 2011
813'.6—dc22 2011007257

This book is dedicated to my sisters and my brother,

MARIE, MARTHA KAREN, HENRY PAUL, & LOUISE,

fellow travelers and none better,

with incredible memories and all my love.

Menelaus harangued them to get organized—
time to ride home on the sea's broad back, he said.

—*The Odyssey,* Book III,
translated by Robert Fitzgerald

For sometimes, when the world is not our home
Nor have we any home elsewhere, but all
Things look to leave us naked, hungry, cold,
We suddenly may seem in paradise
Again, in ignorance and emptiness
Blessed beyond all that we thought to know:
Then on sweet waters echoes the loon's cry.

—Howard Nemerov, "The Loon's Cry"

Sometimes you don't really decide, you just move forward, and that is what I did—moved forward blindly and mindlessly into a new and unknown life.

—Katherine Graham, *A Personal History*

1

On a hot afternoon in August of 1955, Mary Ashton Leader stepped up onto the wooden porch of Howie's Marine and Bait, consumed with many errands besides the shopping list in her skirt pocket. On the shaded porch, next to the drinks cooler, a teenage girl in a bathing suit bent to smooth white, smelly suntan lotion on her legs. Two boys leaning against the porch rail grew wide-eyed as she twisted to reach behind her knees. Mary caught the whiff of Sea & Ski. She would afterward associate that smell with this day, this moment. She would never buy that brand again.

These loafing teenagers were summer people, just like Mary's family, but Mary's family didn't have time to decorate the porch of Howie's all afternoon, or pose for each other on the deck of a Chris Craft. Mary's family came up from Chicago to Northern Michigan to run a small resort, and the chores of maintaining their half-mile of lakeshore with five small rental cabins made their summers on Achill Lake possible and kept them busy at the same time. When she saw kids loafing like these three she thought, I'd rather do it our way. It can't be healthy growing up with everything done for you. Without a care in the world, as though the people living here just exist to make your leisure possible. Huh! It's not going to be this way for my children!

The screen door whomped behind her as she walked into the store, and she went straight to the rope. Two coils of nylon rope, one package of salmon eggs, and one tall yellow can of powdered pyrethium flowers to burn at night when the gnats and flies were at their worst. She set these on the counter, greeted Howie's son at the cash register, and pulled out her shopping list to see what she might be forgetting.

The teenagers on the porch stopped ogling each other to stare at the deputy sheriff who drew up a few minutes after Mary, left his patrol car right there in the road, and came up the steps two at a time. He didn't look at the kids as he crossed the porch. They moved to the door after him, curious.

He walked up the aisle toward the cash register, touched Mary on the shoulder, and told her that her husband, Dr. Jim Leader, had just been taken to Miltonia Hospital. To make sure she understood, he said, "I mean as a patient this time. You probably want to head on over."

Mary took three steps toward the door, and then her legs buckled. She put a hand on the counter and saw herself trying to drive the station wagon over ten miles of farming country toward Miltonia and turned back toward the deputy sheriff.

"You'll have to drive me," she told him, and shook her head. She felt surprised, even puzzled, to ask such a favor from a man not her husband. "I don't think I can drive." But her arms and legs were not working right. Something about the way he talked. She recognized that guarded speech. Mary was a nurse; she'd heard that tone plenty.

The teenagers backed away from the door as Mary and the deputy came out, fast, and he opened the door of the car for her.

Miltonia Hospital, a five-story oblong that angled away from the back of the Catholic elementary school, was thirty years old, and the linoleum floor in the main hallway rippled under her feet, seemed to throw her forward as she ran toward the emergency room. Jim had privileges here; they knew her. The doctor's face, the nurses' faces had that awful void look, telling her nothing.

"Where is he!"

Dr. Jim had passed away five minutes earlier. A blood clot, the doctor told her, trotting alongside her because Mary started to run as soon as he spoke. She bent over her husband and put her hands on the sides of his head and stared at him in disbelief. Without life in his face his features were sharp, craggy.

"Jim," she said. "Oh, Jim." Wanting to add, stop this. Stop it! We have things to do, she thought, tonight even. Melina's birthday party. The youngest of their five children, Melina turned two years old today. Who's going to tell the kids you won't be there?

Mary's face suddenly reddened, and she was flooded with the reality of this day. This butchery of her life. She stared at her handsome husband who would never hold her again, this face that would never light up at the sight of her. She stroked his bare arms that would never again lift the eighteen-foot Grumman canoe to his shoulders, stretch along the gunwales, grip the hands of a small child who wanted to walk up Daddy's torso, never fling a fishing line over the still water, support one of the kids in the backfloat position all the way to the raft. She touched his hands that would never repair another birth defect at Cook County. Or come to her own desperately hungry skin.

"No!" she cried. "Jim, don't you do this to me! Don't do this to me!" She tried to wake him, pounding his chest, shaking his shoulders. She sank her hands into his hair and shook his head. "Don't you do this!" She was screaming when a very tall nurse took Mary in her arms, and a priest appeared, started touching Jim's forehead and mumbling in Latin. Lickety-split, like it had to be done fast. Mary stared from the nurse's arms. Mary had never known a woman with arms like that, arms like a farmer's, like the ash rails of a fence. She didn't get a look at the nurse's face, and later she didn't know if they ever saw one another again. She remembered those arms, later, like she remembered the smell of Sea & Ski, but with some wonder, even gratitude.

Within days, with her five children, her brother, and Jim's family, she stood wide-eyed at the grave site in Chicago. The coffin looked like a king's, like a hero's, draped with a flag because Jim was a veteran and the veterans were helping pay for all this. But then some men lifted the flag, folded it into a wedge, and handed it to her. The coffin became a plain, ugly box, and they wanted her to take this flag? Why do I want this? she started to ask. And they were lowering the plain box into the ground, and unbelievably, everyone started to turn away. The funeral was over. It was time to go. Jim in that box and everyone turning away, herself caught up in a crowd of alien family and friends. They knew nothing. People expected her to turn away from Jim, never see him again?

She screamed and broke from the pressure of her sister-in-law and her brother and went after Jim one more time. Maybe she would have jumped in with him. Someone pulled her away, and that's when a new pain started just below her breastbone. The numbness ended entirely and left her with a spur of pain inside her chest. At that moment she could see that her grief, even for her beloved husband, was going to be inappropriate from now on, needed to be reined in, would always be outsized compared to the concerns of people around her. No one understood it or shared it. Except for Grandma Leader. To lose a child, that would be worse.

Someone had given the flag to six-year-old Sean, she noticed when they all got into her brother's Packard. She realized that Sean had not spoken much in the past week. Had he spoken at all? She wasn't sure. Now he held the flag closely, almost proudly. Melina, on Aunt Tony's lap in the backseat, took her bottle of milk out of her mouth, and patted the flag with her right hand. Her soft, pink lips came together in an expression of satisfaction and pleasure. Those stripes pleased her. Melina looked up at her mother, who was twisted around in the front seat.

"Hello there," she said to Mary. "Hello there."

Melina's face was unaffected, happy, clean of sorrow. Her broad forehead and wide cheekbones were Jim's, and that cowlick in the middle of her hairline. But not those multicolored eyes, one startling green, one green-and-brown. Big, wide-set multicolored eyes.

"Hello there," said Mary. "Okay. Sean, Melina, we're going home now." She turned back, facing forward, and took Grandma's gloved hand in hers.

"Home now," Melina repeated to her brother. Sean didn't answer.

Mary held Grandma's hand gently in both of her own. She wanted to squeeze someone's hand, but she didn't dare press Grandma's, bony and arthritic with painful-looking lumps on the knuckles. Mary's brother Nat started the car and inched it forward on the narrow lane between the manicured, flag-trimmed slopes. Mary and Grandma closed their eyes, and Mary put her head against Grandma's while that awful thing, that spur of pain, rotated in her chest so that she had to breathe around it. She couldn't believe that physical pain like this came with grief. No one had ever told her it happened this way.

The very next week she started making decisions, because if she didn't, someone else might get the idea they could make them for her. She was going to need a full-time job, fast. Thank God the veterans helped with the funeral because Jim's life insurance didn't amount to much at all. There would be one Social Security payment, and there'd be a little Social Security for each child, too, at age eighteen. Seed money for college, and that was that. Welfare, someone advised her: apply to Aid to Dependent Children, because you can't head off to work and leave those five little children with someone else.

Mary was horrified. What a ghastly idea; make a bad situation worse? I didn't go to nursing school, at a huge sacrifice during the Depression, just to go on welfare. She had been working part-time in the polio ward at the children's hospital. She put in for full-time work.

And Pinestead Resort, ten hours' drive to the north, that little bit of Eden she and Jim had sunk their savings into so that the kids could escape Chicago in the summer, and paying guests would help cover expenses for the resort—what to do about that? The caretaker, Chris Olivet, was handling things right now. Would they go back? Could she handle a place like that on her own?

Aunt Tony, Jim's oldest sister, had been all set to make her big career move out to Seattle, Washington. The insurance company where she typed had promoted her to administration in the Seattle office. But Tony changed her mind. She announced that she would stay in Chicago because she couldn't possibly leave Grandma and Mary right now. An instant distaste, rebellion at the news, rose in Mary. She kept her mouth shut; it was none of her business, but she knew she was watching someone take the wrong road at a fork. What could she say? How could she venture an opinion on someone else's decision with so many of her own looming up, her own crossroads so crowded with lives to sort out. Don't anyone think you can decide things for me, she thought.

She telephoned Chris Olivet at Pinestead.

He listed the September chores that he'd begun. As he talked, she remembered the sound of the lake water lapping at the stones, the winds sighing through the pines and cedars. She asked him about the mergansers and the loons that nested down the shore. The mama merganser had adopted some motherless ducklings; a brood of eleven or twelve rode the waves near the dock morning and night. They weren't big enough to fly south, she thought. Chris complained about the raccoons, and suddenly her body craved the soft, rich darkness, untroubled by streetlights. No fireflies like in North Carolina where she herself grew up. Stumbling in the pitch dark from dock to cottage, daring yourself not to use a flashlight because you knew the terrain so well, and it was beautifully dark like an enveloping sweater except for the thick stars. Thick as sand on the beach almost, those stars north of Chicago, stars in the still water if you canoed on a quiet night.

And if you did cave in and flick on the flashlight, chances are you'd catch the great-eyed stare of a startled raccoon on top of the cistern.

How she missed the dark suddenly. Above all else. What's the matter with me, she thought, to crave the pitch-black night? But wouldn't that be a comfort right now?

Will we ever go back? If I sell the place it sure will help. I'm going to need to hire someone, to help clean, and to watch Melina while I'm at work. Alexandra and Sharon and Becky and I can't do it alone, they're only ten and nine and seven, they have a ways to go. And Sean and Melina, what a handful, they need attention. It'll be a while before these kids can look after themselves.

Jim smiled at her. As she walked toward him, across the living room, he smiled but didn't reach for her. It surprised her that he kept his arms at his sides. When she came near it even hurt her feelings that he kept air space between them, despite a broad smile. Then he reached for the front door.

"Jim, don't leave," she said. She was stunned. He was stepping through the door. "You can't go. What will I do with all these children?"

Jim walked out, then poked his head back, still grinning. "Frankly, my dear," he said, "I don't give a damn."

Mary woke up, stared at the ceiling. Streetlights crept under the shade. She was revolted by her dream, treating loss like a pratfall, but something told her to reach after the dream just the same—there's something there. It'll help. Don't let this dream get away! Something in that dream could relieve her pain a little bit—what was it?

Gone with the Wind, now why was she dreaming about that? The memories of poverty? The terror of having nothing, of losing her chance to go to college back in 1933, everything collapsing. That vacuum, that nightmare of poverty.

Eighteen years old, waiting tables at Chapel Hill, a sophomore, she wrote home from the university begging her mother, though it humiliated both of them, for twelve dollars. Twelve dollars would keep her in the boardinghouse at school until Christmas. But her mom and dad didn't have it. Mary had to drop out and go home.

The Ashtons ran country hotels until her dad's drinking got them in trouble, sent them packing, looking for another inn to manage, each one smaller than the one before. Her mother turned the kitchen into a factory making skin cream out of Georgia clay and baking frosted coconut cakes for the bigger hotels in Asheville. Mary came home and found work at the front counter of the Bee Laundry, spent two grim years handing salesmen their dry-cleaning and starched collars and writing up invoices for the hotel bedsheets and curtains and tablecloths that two heavy sweating Negro women ran through the mangle in back.

Then Dad went to look at land in Miami and won five hundred dollars for catching a giant grouper in the fishing derby. He came back and put Mary on the train to nursing school in Ann Arbor. "I'll make it hard for you to quit this time," he said. That was the second time her daddy saved her life.

I'll make it hard for you to quit this time. He had died of appendicitis the first year she was married, or she might go home now, see if he could rescue her again. Drinker or not, he was the one who saved her life, once when she was dying of osteomyelitis as a six-year-old, and everyone else was ready to give up. He took her to the brand-new children's orthopedic hospital in Gastonia. And she didn't die. She wore a plaster cast for six months, but she didn't die; she came out of there determined to be a nurse and save lives herself. And a second time he saved her life, when she was in despair at the laundry. He didn't drink it away or even give her mother first crack at that derby money; he gave three hundred dollars and a train ticket to Mary.

Maybe she ought to go back home. It was cheaper to live by far, down there in the South, than in Chicago. Half as much. Everything was cheaper.

But there are reasons why I never quit, why I never went back after 1940.

That poor kid murdered in Mississippi last week, Emmett Till. Beaten and drowned because they said he was fresh to a white woman. It isn't a lynching, Grandma Leader said, it's a crime that two men carried out, there's no need to call it a lynching. Of course it was a lynching, they wouldn't have done it for any other reason! Grandma didn't know! She didn't grow up in the South, but Mary did. Under the surface, all the time, that violence.

She liked to tell herself North Carolina was never as bad as Mississippi, but how much comfort would that be if it was your son or daughter or husband singled out for brutality?

She was plenty shocked back in 1940, to find herself next to a Negro on the city bus in Ann Arbor, or that first time pushing through a revolving door at the department store with a Negro family. She even wrote home about it. It's true, they really do let darkies in the theaters with you, she wrote to her own mother. But then she got used to it, so fast she was astounded. When she talked to Negro people they sometimes smiled at her accent, asked where home was. It made her happy.

Now a few Negro families from Benton Harbor sometimes rented at Pinestead. Mr. Duquesne, an engineer at the Whirlpool plant, and his tall, skinny wife, a switchboard operator, were regulars, renting a cottage every August, ignoring the stares of other guests and locals, so few Negro people vacationed up north. Negroes mostly came up to Achill to work as maids, and they kept to themselves.

No, she would not go home to North Carolina. It was awful enough her few visits back there, for her parents' funerals and her brother's wedding, not to get upset at things they said. And North Carolina's heat, and the insects, and all that heavy food, she was tired of that. Going back home was like going back to the past, your own past, the one with its sticky suckers out to trap you all the time, always reaching out to draw you in. You don't ever want to go back. It was hard being on the move at first. She reeled from homesickness, that first year away, but she got over it. She grew to love the feeling of being on the move, free of her hometown.

She and Jim had plans. Chicago was only the first stop. Maybe, someday, they'd go out west. To Seattle, Washington, the saltwater and the mountains out there. Maybe all the way to Alaska! Clint Geoghan, a hired man who worked the farm behind Pinestead, once prospected for gold in Alaska. He told wonderful stories. Someday, they were going to visit Alaska. Maybe move there!

Instead, Jim walked out the door. Frankly, my dear, you counted on the wrong man.

Grandma was saying her rosary in the living room when Mary came downstairs for coffee. She or Tony stayed over to help with the kids while Mary filled her early-morning shift at the hospital. The background murmur of the rosary calmed Mary, pleased her, but she herself was having a damned hard time finding any solace on her own from the church. At least the Holy Mother knew how it felt.

You'd think the church would be more help at times like this. But God was the one who invented a beautiful human body that failed at age thirty-nine without any warning after fathering five children and promising his wife the moon and everything else, convincing someone that companionship for all its hard work and all its failures was still better than loneliness, God invented this crazy system. It was enough to make you turn your back on God. Of course she wouldn't do that. Too many other people to consider. And children need the sacraments, children need to know the church is there for them. If there is a contradiction here, Mary thought, best just not to think about it. It's not meant to be thought about too much. I don't have time.

What's going on in me has nothing to do with the church. That dream, now, there's something salvational in that dream, if I can hang onto the way Jim laughed at me, leered at me even, walking out the door. A pratfall, a joke, and this time on me. Not that I deserved it. I did nothing to deserve this. That's why it's a joke, maybe, a very bad joke the universe plays on everyone sooner or later. On every free person. If you get it, you're on your way to feeling less pain.

Try explaining this to a priest. Try getting help understanding this part of it from that chain-smoking Father Cox, with the punishing, stale odor of his cigarettes coming right off his cassock through the confessional at her, his mild penances as though he hadn't even heard the gravity of her sins. (I was rude to my mother-in-law, sometimes I doubt the Resurrection, I had two cups of coffee before communion, I don't think it's God's will that children are in iron lungs and I told someone that and they started to cry and I realized that I'd taken away their last bit of comfort, and what right have I to do that? And the sins she wouldn't confess: Jim used a rubber last night, Father, though I didn't want him to, still I enjoyed myself. I actually liked it better than him withdrawing early, though we do that a lot, too. Which is the more grievous sin, Father?)

When they met at age twenty-six they were way overdue for being together; they weren't to marry for three years, but that didn't stop them. They had no reason to wait. What on earth would they wait for, a good income? They'd still be waiting! Sleeping together was no sin, it awoke feelings more like generosity and gratitude than guilt. You'd know if it was a sin. Her conscience was clear, and private, shared with no one but Jim.

It occurred to her to go out to Holy Rood Cemetery that afternoon, and visit Jim. She would ask him what to do, she would ask him about the dream. She wouldn't tell anybody. A private visit. She was trembling with eagerness that afternoon on the bus, ran up the slope to his grave.

What did she expect? That he would speak, embrace her?

As bad as it was, she went back in a few days, and again a week later.

Alex and Sharon did remember, in later years, their mother coming home after these visits sopping wet, because she had curled up to get closer to him, even in the rain.

The only way to make up her mind about Pinestead would be to go back, go over the books and talk with Chris Olivet, the caretaker. In mid-September she planned a trip of four or five days, without the children. Grandma and Tony would watch the girls, and she'd take Sean as far north as Uncle Stan's cabin in Manistee, Michigan, let him fish to his heart's content there. This was complicated, accounting for everybody. It was hard to pry Melina's arms from around her neck, listening to that sobbing even though she knew it always stopped the minute Mommy's car pulled away.

The first big change in plans came at Uncle Stan's. When she said goodbye to Sean, he suddenly looked traumatized. This was new. His brown eyes were enormous, his small pale face startled. She thought, but you have to be with men, Sean, and you love fishing all day! I can't fish with you! She forced herself to wave cheerfully and drive away. Twenty miles up Highway 31 she stopped and telephoned.

"It's not going well," said Uncle Stan.

"I'm coming right back to get him," she said. "It's too soon for this. I'll be right there. You can tell him."

Am I caving in? she wondered. But when Sean climbed into the front seat, happy and restored, with a glimmer of the old Sean in his face—that carefree little boy—she wondered if maybe she had just barely by the skin of her teeth made the right choice at a crossroads she hadn't seen coming.

"I'm going to need your help up north," she said. "I musta been crazy thinking I wouldn't need your help! You and me, we've got work to do." He nodded, warming to his role. Mary turned her head to the window so that he couldn't see the broad smile that once she would have exchanged with Jim. Their eyes meeting above the heads of the children said everything. It was one of the unexpected good parts of being parents together—sharing that amusement. For a minute she wasn't hurting anymore. She needn't deny herself the pleasure of her own boy's company.

At the village of Itara she stopped for a suppertime snack, intending to buy a can of Vienna sausages and fruit from the grocery store. Instead, seeing the German bakery open, she let Sean choose two Bismarcks to eat in the car.

He was asleep a few minutes later, flecks of frosting and cream on his lips and his t-shirt, his suspenders slipping, his hands unclenched.

At a bluff over Lake Michigan, about forty-five minutes south of

Pinestead, she stopped for the sunset. The fiery disc sank in five minutes, highlighting the hidden shapes of clouds. A path across the water turned red. Yes, she was unprepared, she didn't know why Sean was so happy, tonight, for the first time in weeks. She hoped he didn't think that his daddy would be waiting for him. How would she ever know the next direction to take with him, with the girls, though somehow she wondered if it might be hardest on him. She knew that it was unfair, this intuition that somehow the girls were going to be able to handle their grief better. It wasn't fair, but there it was.

She realized that for an hour, or more, she had been free of that rotating spur of pain. As she thought about it, the pain started up again, started to flutter beneath her breastbone.

"Oh, please," she said. "Stop it." She reached across to Sean and touched his hair, let her hand fall on his leg.

"Are we there, Mom?" he mumbled. "How many miles?"

"Eight," she said, making something up. "Eight. Go back to sleep."

2

She woke to a glass-blue, sparkling morning, and when she checked the face of the lake she saw a light chop rushing down the center—a wind from the north. When she opened the bedroom closet to find a sweater she caught a whiff of Jim's shirts. They hung next to her own, along with his plaid corduroy jacket. She put her face into his shirts and breathed a smell that sometimes clung to Jim, that unmistakable smell of clothes that overwinter in a pine-board closet. She put the corduroy jacket on and rolled the cuffs over her wrists.

With the first, perfect cup of coffee she walked outside, across pale, bristly grass—it had been dry these past few weeks—down to the dock. The waves were picking up, turning to whitecaps. Jim liked to take the canoe out in water like this. Any kind of water, come to think of it, wild or smooth as a mirror.

She walked to the end of the dock, and there he was. Fleshy, immortal, just about to laugh, but a ghost. A ghost about to laugh at her.

Jim standing fifty feet out from shore in water that came to his ribs, so she could see his powerful arms and pectorals, his long-waisted torso beginning to add fat—that layer of fat over muscle that made him impervious to the cold water. Unless the day was scorching hot, Mary would always have to swim vigorously or find herself shivering, but he played games with the kids, dared them to swamp the canoe, taught them to swim. She could see him as clearly this morning as if his figure were revealed in a hole cut out of a celluloid sky. He laughed outright and dared her to come on in.

Too late. Never again. We're too late for each other, Jim. Something happened.

She stared across the water at him for several minutes, stunned. Why stay here, then, if it was going to hurt like this? And yet Pinestead was the best of Jim. These were the best reminders or would be, someday. Back in Chicago it was Jim with his mind on work, whenever she saw him, or falling asleep in the big chair in front of the fire with a bottle of beer in his hand so she'd come over and remove it before it toppled and maybe finish it herself. The kids playing around him, happy enough to have him in the same room, if that was all they were going to get, and usually it was.

And the city was so full of things that were no good in his absence. Jim had made things tolerable, shared the hardship. Jesus Mary and Joseph, that was the worst, no Jim to complain to, the week's bills coming to her eyes alone, no one to help her understand the day's news. She couldn't ask him to help her make sense of this world where some terrible things kept happening, and no one else wanted to talk about them.

Summer days she walked into a room filled with iron lungs at the Children's Hospital, a child stricken with polio in each one. She couldn't shout, "Oh, Jim, look at what's going on! Help me live with this!"

Or the story of Emmett Till, beaten and dumped in a river down in Mississippi after he winked at the white woman behind the cash register in a country store. Mary could just see that young woman, not much older than Emmett Till, poor and ignorant and no one to lord it over but the Negro sharecroppers. When they found his body, weighted with the rusty fan from a cotton gin, they sent it back to Chicago, and his mother took one look at her son's face and screamed and collapsed right there at the train station.

When Mary looked at those pictures and read the story she wanted to scream, she wanted at least to talk to someone. A dietician at the hospital, Miriam Huley, brought in the *Chicago Defender*, the Negro paper, that ran a photograph of the boy's face. The *Tribune* did not run the same picture; the *Tribune* kept the worst out. And Grandma and Tony pretty much did the same thing, wouldn't talk about it. Just "Oh dear, Mary. Oh dear, it's a terrible crime, it's no more than that. Why talk about a terrible crime?" They acted like if you talked about difficult things you made them worse. Drove her mad.

Jim always recognized her mix of feelings. He could talk to her. He could talk to how she felt.

Everywhere you go, Mary reminded herself, he'll be there.

Find something to do.

Pinestead's better than Chicago, anyway. In Chicago they expect you to pull yourself together. No one sees me here. She drained her coffee and counted the merganser ducklings, as they followed their mother up the lakeshore. Only nine—the mom had lost a few.

"You did your best, momma duck," she called softly, and started back to the house for a second cup. She walked slowly, looking down at her own feet, and discovered that she liked the sight of these faded sneakers, once red, now pink, with no laces, that she wore around the place. She liked to see her feet crossing the grass, the right sneaker frayed at the toe. As she passed a cedar tree, a drop of sap landed on her arm. This happened a lot, people always wondered if it was raining, looked puzzled, mentioned it only when it happened a second or third time.

The sneakers, the dry grass, sap dropping from the cedar trees. This coffee mug, with pheasants painted on it and a shaped rim that fit so nicely against her lips. The mergansers coming out from under the dock. Here in Michigan certain familiar things didn't bring her pain.

Maybe, the first time she saw things, from now on, she'd see Jim—she'd look at his little office inside the house, she'd look in the closet at his creel and his plaid shirts, she'd reach for the green-handled canoe paddle he always used, and she'd see him, but just the first time. Then after that maybe it would start to be okay. Because really, this physical pain, this was not supposed to happen. No one ever told her about this part. They didn't tell you much. The truth of it was, this physical pain was getting to her, a gear with teeth turning and turning under her breastbone. Find something to do.

Start by getting this hair up off her neck. She went into the bathroom and lifted a brush. Neglected these past weeks, this hair desperately needed a beauty salon and a hot curling iron. She brushed it hard, the long, thick wad of it back, back, until her face hurt. Once she'd been proud of her hair. But it was so thick and straight. Years ago she'd attempted curls, but they were so much trouble. Would she ever do that again? Sit in a beauty parlor bored half out of her mind with those hot steel rollers against her head? Listening to those trite conversations women had with each other, agreeing with each other. Laughter with a touch of coarseness in it.

Mary found a comb, ploughed it through her hair, divided her hair in half, and braided each chunk. She hadn't worn braids in twenty years. There, she thought. You don't lose the knack. Almost forty—am I too old for braids? She took the bandanna out of her pocket and tied it over her head. A compromise. Bandannaed head with two braids escaping underneath. The Michigan resort owner.

All right now. What's next?

She found Sean in the kitchen, looking for juice. To her pleasure Sean seemed a bit more vigorous and independent up here than he had seemed in Chicago. While she got out flour and eggs for pancakes, he asked if he could play with Yolanda Quillen. The Quillens always stayed late at their summer place, down the lakeshore. Dr. Quillen was a renowned snake expert at the University of Cincinnati. They seemed to have a lot of money, which couldn't have come just from herpetology. She telephoned them and found them in. "Of course," said Bonnie Quillen, "we'd love to have him. We're running an errand up that way; we'll pick him up."

Mary poured half a bottle of beer in the pancake batter to make them rise, and though it wasn't ten A.M. yet, she drank the other half herself at the same time to wash down one of the phenobarbitals she'd found in Jim's medical bag. There were only three left. She would like to get some more. Who'd write her a prescription? She'd have to start going to doctors. God almighty, going to doctors!

After the Quillens left with Sean, exhaustion and the pill slammed into her, and she fell back into bed for a nap. She was asleep almost immediately and didn't wake for two hours. At one in the afternoon she came back to life. Let's try again, Miss Mary, she told herself, in the voice of Sister Peter back in Gastonia. Sister Peter could handle a situation like this, she could handle anything. Sister had a grip almost as strong as that nurse in Miltonia Hospital, arms like a man's. Maybe Sister Peter had wanted to be a man, when she was little. And why couldn't Sister Peter live a man's life, if she wanted to?

But of course then I wouldn't have had her as my Sister Peter for seven years. Second through eighth grade, I was her favorite. First communion through confirmation. Let's try again, Miss Mary. Mary Ashton was Sister's pet. You better believe it.

In the cubbyhole office under the stairwell, Mary opened the book with next summer's reservations, and whistled through the gap in her front teeth. They were doing all right! Families were scheduled for every single month. The Duquesnes and the Wilsons were coming in August—and another family for two weeks in September! Not bad, Jim, she thought. They'd never had so many, a year in advance, before. Pinestead's got a decent reputation. Repeat visitors—everyone said that was the key to solvency around here. All the way into September 1956! Mostly fishermen, but a few deer hunters, foliage seekers, bird watchers. At any rate, the property taxes might get paid next year after all. So what do I do, write and advise these people to forget it because I don't know what's happening with the place, or hope to transfer these reservations to a new owner, or . . . oh, Lord. What do I do?

The local insurance man, Dean Holbus, always said to take a good inventory once a year. It's time to close, but when somebody gets here next May, what needs to be done? And who will that somebody be, Chris Olivet? No time in the spring for engine repair, it's a madhouse at Howie's and everywhere else, has to be done now. Chris will take care of that. And he's got to finish the roofs. Cottages and house too. We lost shingles in the storm last winter and didn't do a thing about it this summer.

I've got to walk through the cottages and see what people lost, or stole, or accidentally took with them . . . why are people the way they are? Sometimes so kind and steady. But then, surprises. Walking off with towels and bottle openers, even the cute little wall plaques I found at the Nifty Thrifty, for the love of God. They don't know my husband's gone and died, they have to make it worse by going off with the percolator. Jesus Mary and Joseph.

When she heard Chris Olivet's Studebaker pickup on the driveway, she went outside to meet him. The sky had darkened with clouds, and the waves had turned grayish blue. Maybe a squall coming. Chris stepped out of the truck and came slowly over to her, with his head ducked down and to the side, as always, and surprised her when he swung out a sympathetic hand to touch her shoulder. Because he acknowledged her loss so quickly, grief surged up again inside her, right into her throat, like a solid object. She couldn't speak.

"I'm sorry," he murmured to the ground.

As they stood there, she thought of how much he and Jim had enjoyed doing things together, fishing, repairing things—it was not her idea of a close friendship, but she was wrong. They had enjoyed each other's expertise and love of this country. Now it was no longer available to Chris.

"I know you . . ." she began, "and Jim enjoyed doing things together."

"A real good person," he said in a sudden rush. Silence fell. She couldn't say anything more. Chris met her eyes briefly. He rarely looked directly at people, out of either shyness or disinterest; she had never known or cared which. His face was severely scarred by acne, so much so she had never looked closely at him, she didn't even know what color his eyes were. Green? Brown? Both, like her youngest daughter, Melina, who had one eye sea green, the other half green, half brown with yellow specks.

He said he should probably take a couple of the outboards away with him, to another shop, where a guy who knew small engines could look them over. "Lemme get that taken care of, get the right ones into the truck. Yeah, the roofs'll need attention. And that pine in front of the south cottage, my thought is take that one out."

"Cut the tree?"

"Winter storms. You don't want it coming down on the place."

"It's that bad?"

"They're kinda shallow rooted, I'm afraid. Bad situation in this sandy ground around here. Your . . . Jim and I . . . we talked about it."

Shallow rooted.

"The cedars now," he said, "are doing really well. The whole row is in a nice spot, not going to take the brunt of any storm off the lake."

She stared at him a minute, absorbing this new information about Chris—that he knew about trees. A man with opinions about what he saw: not indifferent.

But she did not want to know these things about people, not alone she didn't. Jim was supposed to absorb some of this. Her big, fleshy Jim. That little bit of fat over his muscle. Skin softer than hers. Information was one more thing that never hurt him. Nothing hurt him. Except black flies and poison ivy, once or twice too damn much to drink, and some things he must have seen during the buildup to the war in Korea but never talked about with her. She knew things he saw in Korea upset him, because he'd get surly with her, surly and quiet that first year after he came back. But that went away. And then one day an embolism.

"I'm going to go down on the dock for a second," she said.

"You bet, Mrs."

She would look back at the whole place from there. The patchy, stained roof, the pine trees, the paint peeling off the fronts of the cottages in the path of the afternoon sun. Holy Mary, a paint job lasted for one summer around here!

She slid down the steep, short grassy slope to the dock and walked out on the weathered gray planks. The wind's battering slapped her awake. Water was flung up in wild pyramids. Jim had always loved this face of the lake. It was not cold, just gloriously windy. This could happen: a summer day turn wild, with no prelude. Sometimes you'd look out at the lake and see the squall coming at you. Rush around and batten the windows. Gosh, it was fun, they'd had some good times, the wind and the lake putting on an incredible show, and the rain would come, slamming the ground, slamming the ironwork lawn chairs, breaking cedar boughs. And you always looked for people who had stayed too long out there in a boat and might be in serious trouble.

This wasn't going to be that kind of squall. It was a fierce afternoon wind, but no more. A roar of wind, the slap of waves against the rocks and the wooden standards of the old dock, the groan, almost scream, of the metal hoist that usually held the big motorboat. Chris had already put the boat in storage last week. The empty hoist made a strange but consoling keening in the wind. And the raft out on the water, planks attached to empty fifty-gallon drums, lifted on the waves, then settled down on the hollow drums and made a wonderful, deep boom like tympani. On a windy night, that was often the only noise you'd hear, from the bedroom—that faint boom, over and over.

In all this noise, she felt like shouting, too. She flung her head back as if to scream, and that's when she saw the first hawk.

It rode against the wind over the roof of the boathouse. Breast to the wind. Like the way canvas pressed out when Jim would mount a sail on the canoe. As she stared at the bird, she saw another and another. She counted five, to her amazement. She had never seen hawks so low, a group of them, pushing against the wind or riding the wind.

Chris looked down at her from the top of the lawn, his arms filled with an outboard motor. Had she shouted? She waved at him and then again, trying to gesture that he should come here quick and see this. He set the motor on the grass and skidded down the slope, ran out on the dock. She waved toward the sky. He couldn't see anything at first, and then more hawks appeared over the ridgeline of the boathouse. One, two more; there were seven altogether! Chris's knees bent suddenly as if the sight were enough to knock him down.

"I've never seen anything like that," he said when he caught up to her. They stared up until the hawks rode the wind east, as if sliding sideways on the wind itself, over the roof of the boathouse. Chris and Mary looked at each other.

"Heard you calling, I thought something was wrong," he said.

"Well, of course something is wrong. Things couldn't be more wrong."

"Yes, of course. I didn't mean . . ."

The wind whipped at his open flannel shirt, and she noticed that the t-shirt he wore underneath was spattered with colorful paint. House paint and paint from his own easel; Chris did oil painting as a hobby. Wolves and Indians, Jim said. Chris could be part Ojibwa, for all she knew. She'd never seen his paintings. She also noticed, by the way his t-shirt wrinkled across his chest and was crammed into his jeans, that his torso was lean and even attractive. Maybe he was younger than he looked, with that dark, intense face, always looking down at the ground, and those scars. Did the scars give him a look of intensity he might not really deserve? The right girlfriend would modify all that. He needed a girlfriend. She had always thought so. "Leave him be," Jim used to say.

Mary rubbed her neck where it ached from ogling the hawks.

"Well, we should carry on. I need to make a list for this fall and for next spring, or maybe not," she said. Maybe it won't be my place next spring.

"You can see that bad section of roof from here, between the gable and the ridgeline, looks like a checkerboard, where the shingles come off. Oh, Mrs., they're back!" He pressed her forearm, to get her to look up. This time she nearly fell over as she flung her head back in amazement. The seven hawks were much lower. They had turned and powered back for another ride. The dark terrifying shape of their wings floated almost directly above her. No one had ever seen anything like this. Their wings sliced into the wind like rudders, just enough to keep the birds pointed the way they wanted, angled into the wind. Because they wanted to.

The strangeness of it made her shudder, and yet it was a good, a wonderful feeling. They could block the sun. If there were enough of them. It was as weird a thing as death, almost, because it had nothing to do with humans. Nothing to do with us! But how many people have watched, so closely, the underside of hawks?

"Never seen that before," said Chris again. Even though he grew up here. They stared until the wind carried the birds over the ridgeline of the boathouse, away from the lake. "You never know what you might see in these woods," said Chris. "I never get tired of it. Different all the time."

"What's it like in winter?"

"Last year one time when the lake froze over before it snowed, we were out skating, could look down six feet into that clear ice. Down the lagoon you can see painted turtles under the ice, swimmin' along, lookin' for a place to settle in. Where are the rich people now? we said to each other. Don't mean you, Mrs."

Mrs.? she thought, tickled. It had a sweet, familiar sort of sound to it.

"No, Chris. I am not rich. Don't know what I'm going to do. This resort was our way to be able to afford to come north in the summer. Get away from the city. Jim loved the woods, you know. Jim and I. Wanted to see it all."

"Yeah, I know that."

Chris would know. He took Jim fishing often enough. Down the Manistee, the Lebanon, the Sandy, up to the UP, all through the chain of lakes. Mary stopped going fishing about the time of the third baby. She declared her independence from those horrible early dawns, all that sitting. She liked camping, having something to do, but not getting up at a hellish hour just to wait in one place for a bite. Good grief. Those men in the bass boats at dawn. They made a pretty silhouette on the lake, but how could they stand it?

But to be outside most of the day. That was the best.

"I wonder, Chris, if my family could live here year-round."

"Take some work, I'd say, to be comfortable."

"But we got this place. Why should we turn our backs on it, go back to where we are really at a disadvantage in so many ways? One parent trying to do everything, down in the city. And us dependent on Grandma Leader just to hold things together. I mean, Grandma loves to do it, but dear God." Why was she talking to him like this? Mary was a private person, she didn't ask others for advice, never had. But I need a green light, she thought. I need some direction.

"I'd never be able to live in a city," he said. "Especially a big city like Chicago."

"I live for summers up here," she said. "But maybe kids need more than what this place offers. I suppose the isolation here in the winter isn't good for kids."

Chris looked at her directly and repeated her words. "Not good for kids?"

She stared at him, and suddenly saw the two of them standing on a dock in a lake in upstate Michigan—standing between the storm and the cottage—and unexpectedly, she laughed. What don't kids love about this?

"But they also need," she tried again, "schools, and so on."

"Schools up here, Mrs. I went to Miltonia High School. There's a real good private school couple hours south."

"Well, yes, but other things."

"I guess Dr. Leader needed to be near the big hospitals."

And what other things, she thought, do kids need? To be with their own kind? What kind are we, now that Jim's gone?

Who are we?

Chicagoans. The barrel of a killer wind coming at you, five o'clock on a winter night, and I'm sitting on a wheezing gasping city bus in Wicker Park trying to get home to the kids.

Or, give them this.

Either way, she thought, they've had a loss. Don't kid yourself. Neither way is the best way. But I get to choose, just the same. Standing right here, I don't hurt. Damn, I don't hurt!

"Chris, what does the big house need, if we stayed here all winter?"

"If you wanted to keep the place open all year, try to keep warm and dry . . . that's a bit of work. Roof repaired. Boiler and chimney inspected. And firewood."

"Where do I get firewood around here?"

"But Mrs., you'll need more than firewood. That fireplace in there is not much more than decoration. It'll heat the one room, but you need to get the furnace taken care of. And more insulation in the place, I'm sure a that. Gets cold enough to freeze canned food."

"Let's see what that will cost. The furnace. Some insulation. What kind of a mother would I be, not to give them this? This place, this—this wildness." She thought, this is almost equal to our loss. Nature is. The surprise of it.

You died, Jim, left everything to me, you don't get a say anymore. What am I supposed to do, limp ahead in the life we planned even though you aren't here? So much hard work here, the hard work itself will help me raise the kids. Keep them busy. Something almost equal to our loss.

"For this winter?" said Chris. He made it sound almost too real. He seemed to think it was possible, that she was serious. And maybe she was.

"Well, I don't know, Chris. Let's just get started. Let's say next winter. I don't want them to freeze to death, but you know what? More and more, I think it's a good idea. I feel like it's . . ."

"It's a big decision."

Mary stared at him again. His eyes were actually an indeterminate color, like the ground itself, the color of the forest floor. A big decision, huh? So not one to be made impulsively, you impulsive, emotional woman, you. Is that what he thought?

"Yes," she said.

For the first time in her life, she felt just that way—impulsive. People criticized her growing up for being too matter-of-fact, too ambitious, too cool in a storm, for knowing her own mind. It was unfeminine, even unattractive in a woman. Aloof, they used to call her, just because she was by nature reserved. That little Mary Ashton keeps a tight lid on, they said. Not feminine. Dear, don't you want to catch a man?

Well, she must be plenty attractive now, all woman, all emotion and impulse.

When you come to a fork in the road, quit the place. That used to be her motto. Don't dally at the crossing place going oooh, oooooh. Well, by God, she was not so grief stricken she didn't recognize a crossroads when she stood in one, and this place belonged to her, as much as the house in Chicago, and those kids were her responsibility, not Grandma Leader's or the Welfare Board's. Three people, count them, three people in Chicago had assumed she would apply for welfare, even advised her to get right on it! So she could be at home for her kids!

Go on welfare? Make a bad situation worse?

Living in Chicago without Jim was making a lonely situation even worse.

Maybe it was just a matter of preference. Maybe she ought to do what she wanted.

She said, "I'm going to go put coffee on. Help me figure out where I stand." She almost asked him to come in and have a cup, but then she remembered—Chris never came in the house. He didn't want to. Jim had told her before, always take a cup right on out to him, he doesn't want to come in. Some people up here are like that.

"I'll bring you out a cup of coffee," she said, and walked down the dock, across the grass, up to her front door. For the first time in weeks, her chest expanded with enough air. What an idea, moving up here, but there you are. She was thrust out into freedom, further than she'd ever been before. So this is how people move on, she thought, doing new stuff before you even have enough air in your lungs to take the first step. You got to do some things even without enough air. Without knowing exactly how it will all turn out. I mean, if you waited, if you waited for strength, when would it come?

All I have to do is keep an eye on the kids, be there for them, not let them drown or fall out of a tree. Don't even think like that, Mary. Way to get over Jim is to do something he never did, spend the winter here. One winter, at least. Start with just one.

The pain below her breastbone fluttered. No, I won't get over Jim, don't think like that, Mary. Every time you have a thought like that the pain comes back, like some kinda punishment. That's the wrong thought to have. Don't have that thought.

But she did like the idea of sailing into a new season, one she'd never experienced before here at Pinestead. Watching new things happen outdoors. She liked that thought very much. Shallow-rooted or not. Gastonia to Ann Arbor to Boston for Jim's residency to Portland, Maine, for another residency, home to Chicago, and now Northern Michigan. Maybe someday Alaska. Was Mary Leader "kinda shallow rooted" too? Could be an advantage to that, somehow.

Having an idea like this, having a new plan, made her smile that night as she and Sean finished supper. And he delighted her by smiling back. A good day with his friend Yolanda in a place he loved, or just being back at Pinestead among the familiar objects and routines of summer which were not, as it turned out, in a shambles. They were still here, the good routines, in the chores, in the land, in the water. If a five-year-old can find his daddy's presence in these things—in the canoe, the fishing tackle, the outboards stored in the boathouse for the winter, the incinerator needing to be raked clean of ash, the small dusty office with its battered green filing cabinet—maybe it will help. Time is on Sean's side in this, she thought. And this half mile of lakeshore is on our side, too.

3

They'd made the drive many times, but never quite like this.

Mary took two last pictures—one of Grandma and Tony together on the sidewalk, and another of the loaded station wagon, with Becky, Alex, Sharon, Sean, and Melina and the dogs, Klondy and Yukon, crowding out of car windows, the kids waving over each other's heads and around each other's shoulders. Then she put the camera in its bag, handed the bag to Sharon in the front passenger's seat, and sat behind the wheel. She waved and blew more kisses and started the car, driving slowly down to the corner. When I turn left, she thought, I'll really be on my way. I'll never come back here the same person. We're doing it.

It comforted her that Grandma and Tony would come up to Pinestead in August, just like in past years. She was already counting on their help, babysitting and cooking. But Mary wouldn't be coming back here.

It took almost a year, but she'd talked herself and everyone around her into the move. She'd cleaned, painted, and rented the house in Wicker Park, sorted everything they owned, packed up the essentials into the Mercury and a little green rented U-Haul trailer and tied an army tarp over it. And this crystal-clear early morning in June of 1956, loaded with food for an army, they drove away from Wicker Park. The kids kept shouting goodbyes back at Grandma and Tony on the sidewalk. Mary looked in the mirror one more time at the two women, and turned the car and trailer slowly toward the shore of Lake Michigan and the road north. Wonder and high seriousness took possession of her. This boat is under way!

After that day last September when the seven hawks had come out over the lake to ride the storm, she had not stopped thinking about moving north. The dream had kept her going all winter. Keep things simple, whip the books into shape, squeeze every penny more than you ever did before, if that's possible. She bought the kids' school shoes at St. Vincent de Paul. Don't even darken the doorway of Sears Roebuck, she reminded herself, don't even window shop. Used is good enough. Used is just fine! She turned their trips to St. Vincent's into family outings, and the kids would race each other to the free table. Sean found a wire rack from a nut company, five deep coated-wire bins welded together in an open stack. She knew it would be perfect for sorting clothes. A bin for each kid. A metal plaque on the top wire said, "Nuts to you, by Heck!"

Without this adventure, this change, to dream on, she might have despaired, going through this winter without Jim. She did despair at times, face it. Sometimes she wanted to load all five kids into the train and hurl herself back to North Carolina, let her bustling and sweet-talking women relatives take over her life, just for a few days or maybe forever. But Mary had seen something of the world since 1940. She could no more go back home than Miriam Huley, the Negro dietician at the hospital, who also came from North Carolina, could go back to live there.

One time when Mary came into the cafeteria at three for a late lunch, Miriam came out from the kitchen with two extra-large helpings of bread pudding.

"Let me sit down with you, Mary, ruin our suppers together," she said. A huge dish of bread pudding was the last thing Mary thought she wanted, but it was delicious, it was as if Mary hadn't eaten in weeks. She didn't mean to eat it all. There was enough in that bowl for six hungry nurses. But her spoon kept going into it. She wanted to cry in gratitude, do more than squeeze Miriam's arm.

Pinning her ridiculous cap back onto her head, saying goodbye, she blurted out, "I can't believe how different things are!"

They stared at each other. Mary in her uniform that looked to be cut out of tin, it was that crisp from the laundry, and Miriam in a grimy blue dress and hairnet, holding the two empty bowls, sticky with pudding. How can I complain to her? Mary thought. But I want her to take this pain away from me. I almost feel she could do it.

"Makes a person want to go home," Miriam said at last.

"Can't do that," Mary said. "Can't ever go back there."

"Yeah," said Miriam. "I didn't mean North Carolina. No. I guess what I meant . . . you wish you could. Even at my age I can't believe there isn't someplace I could lay it all down. That's what home is. Sure ain't Chicago."

"I'm hoping I'll find something like that up north."

"Mary, lamb, you got your work cut out."

"Maybe you'll get up that way sometime. Take a week off."

"Might happen," Miriam said cheerfully. "We got family in Grand Rapids. For me I can't contemplate a move right now, my son on probation. We can't run from what he's been up to. Doesn't feel like a true and honest strategy for him."

"I can't see very far ahead. It scares me."

"Well, you take it slow and easy, because if you all right, then the children will have what they need. If their sky is serene. And you, Mary, you are that sky, now."

Serenity. Mary chuckled; she couldn't help it. Serenity seemed as far away as North Carolina, as the Sistine Chapel for that matter. As unlikely as having one of those Renoirs at the Art Institute hanging in her own dining room. Some things weren't possible. Serenity—what was there to be serene about? But slow and easy—there was a nice sound to that. There was real charity in Miriam's words. She wanted to take those sticky bowls from Miriam's hands and give her a hug. But she hesitated too long. The moment passed.

She was almost happy now, by Heck, driving northeast through Gary. Up to Michigan City, and then they'd have smooth sailing all the way up the lake. Sean with his now perpetual frown had squirreled into a nest in the far back of the station wagon, among duffel bags and laundry baskets, clutching his cast-iron farm set, an old toy of Jim's that Sean was too old to play with anymore but always kept near him. Becky and Alex surrounded Melina and the dogs in the backseat. Next to Mary, in front, Sharon recaptured her own special place. Jim always made Sharon his copilot when they used to get up early for the drive north. Sharon might be the only one awake, helping Jim navigate, the road a black promise and Sharon his little glowworm. And they'd sing to each other: "Glow and glimmer, swim through the sea of night, little swimmer."

Mary liked it too, drowsing behind them, relaxed finally after all the work of packing, one daughter in her arms and another against her shoulder. Away from it all. Jim to herself for three weeks, then he'd have to leave for a week or two, come and go for the rest of the summer. She never missed Chicago. She wouldn't this time, either.

She loved her mother-in-law, but she wouldn't miss Grandma and Aunt Tony's assumptions, trying to enlist her in their campaign of decency. They were going to keep the family safe from ugly talk. They couldn't bear the outrage that filled Chicago after Emmett Till's death and the other stories that came out. A white woman had died of appendicitis after she was turned away from a hospital because of her Negro husband and kids. Grandma said, "I don't believe it, a doctor wouldn't do that, my son was a doctor and that's not what Jim would do."

Mary brought home the *Chicago Defender*, with its picture of Emmett Till's beaten, eyeless head, swollen and mangled like a picture from Jim's medical textbook of elephantiasis. She showed it to Grandma, who turned away, shaking her head.

"Mother! It wasn't an accident, it was a lynching, with the collusion of a whole town. A whole country. They couldn't have gotten away with it otherwise!" Mary wanted to fan these flames, she wanted the truth to burst out. Grandma shook her head and insisted on calling it a terrible misunderstanding. Did she really have no inkling? Mary wondered. The men who did this got off scot-free. They weren't considered criminals. They went to church every Sunday. They claimed to be Christians.

"A church is a place where you are supposed to be getting an education out of the greatest book ever written, or so they claim, but they did this? Mother, how else do you get people's attention at a time like this but publishing the truth?"

"Dear," said Grandma, "you'll frighten the children. You're turning from your own work to someone else's. This is not what you have in front of you to do." It was the hurt look in her eyes that made Mary drop the subject. Like a child whose innocence was threatened. I might as well have slapped her face, Mary thought. Grandma's been through her own hell, sure enough. If Jim was here, what would he say?

It's not that I'm wrong, it's that I shouted.

"I'm sorry for being short," she said. "Please forgive me." This was no time to take the high ground, not with the last person on earth who loved Jim as much as Mary did. They were two of a kind, she and Grandma, ripped open inside.

No, she wouldn't miss them, but she'd miss having family around. Other adults. After Easter dinner, after all the cleaning and the games, when the younger kids went to bed, Tony took out a bottle of whiskey and poured three glasses. "It's not good to drink without eating, Jim always said," she announced, and brought the turkey carcass and the ham out of the refrigerator. The ham was like candy, a Smithfield with so much flavor you couldn't stop nibbling. They sat around the table sipping the whiskey and eating slices of meat right off the bone, four of them. Alex had joined the impromptu party.

Alex was Mary's right hand these days, no question, a true lieutenant. Right now she was wrapped up in one of the silk kimonos that Jim had brought home from Korea in 1948. Splashes of purple, yellow, and orange on black silk.

They ate and drank with a powerful sense of having washed up on a shore of respite. What the three women were sad for, and what was left to them, was held in the glowing kitchen that Easter night: no men left to cook for, and an unlikely, unasked-for freedom. Only Alex was perfectly happy, they could see it in her face. To Alex that moment was like being out on the foredeck of a ship heading to new places. To be included with the grown-ups, to sample maturity, to be taking part in this unscheduled, ungirdled moment. Eating late at night was not something they normally did. Something made it sacramental tonight.

Mary dipped a sliver of turkey breast into a dollop of bleu cheese salad dressing. She loved the sharp, rich flavor against the smoky savor of the whiskey. Alex, across the table, chewed a turkey sandwich and drank a glass of Ovaltine. On the plump side, almost eleven years old, with small but lively mouse-brown eyes and a big forehead just like Jim's. Always listening intently to the grown-ups, and everything she heard, she could spit right back at you too with her own editorial slant. Mary had heard her entertaining her sisters. A straight-A student with a big heart and a spirit like rubber, she didn't sit on her grief, that one.

Unlike Sean, so quiet lately. He'd taken over Jim's workbench in the basement and covered it with Scouting projects, leathercraft, and a birdhouse for the lake. He wouldn't ask for help. The projects seemed to be too much for him. It hurt to see him struggle, but he refused to let anyone touch anything.

Grandma and Tony still didn't concede that she was moving.

"At least," Grandma said, "I'm glad you are not selling the resort. In years to come it'll be like a gift to Sean from his daddy. They loved it so, the two of them."

Mary said, "Yes, we all do." She thought, I've just turned forty! Why are we already leaving it to Sean? Is my life over? But don't argue, Mary, let this day come to an end without a fight, without more grief, for a change. Try it for a change.

"You never run out of surprises up there, Mother," she said. "Never. Nature . . . it's like a teacher, a really incredible teacher. Here's how I think of it." She sipped her second inch of Scotch, grateful for its wallop, and dipped another piece of turkey into salad dressing. "I think of it like this," she repeated, struggling to find the exact right place to start, struggling against the whiskey which now said to her, relax and surrender, even while it freed her tongue. "Nature is equal to our loss."

Grandma frowned and shook her head.

"Almost," Mary said. "In a way I need to explain, a different way. It's not yet equal, not yet, for me not ever maybe, but when you experience all that nature provides for us, you know it's true even if you yourself can't quite measure up, can't get over your grief. It's like God's love, Mother. You know it's there, in big and small ways both."

"Oh dear," said Tony.

"My parents came over from Belgium with my older brothers," Grandma said at last. "If they did it, Mary, so young and with small children, then I guess you can do it too. Even without a husband to help you. It's a man's world up there. But after all, it won't be the first time we've handled things alone." They all looked quickly at her. She almost smiled. "Sometimes, even, we manage quite well without their best ideas."

"Oh, during the war we had to," Tony rushed in, breathless.

Mary smiled at Grandma. "Your blessing means so much to me."

"But you'll need help," Tony said.

"I can hire help, and I will. Chris Olivet, we can rely on him, he knows just what to do like it's his own place. And I'm trying to tell you, the routine will help. The seasons of the year. I'm convinced that it is worth a try."

She looked around at the yellow-painted walls and trimmed cupboards, the daisy-printed curtains, Alex's kimono, the checkered oilcloth on the table. Everything glowed with the bright coziness of a manmade world. This was a warm, glowing cave built by men, lit and tended by women's fussing. Men built clubhouses, and women decorated them and made them livable. But what I'm hungry for, Mary thought, is out there. You can't find it in Chicago. It's out on the black empty lake. If she could follow that black, empty water north, away from the skyline, her heart would find solace. That place to set things down, she would find that place. The loon would call morning and night, welcoming her home.

They stopped in Whitehall, Manistee, and Itara, and then put on the gas to beat the sunset.

"How much farther?" Becky and Sean yelped. "Eight," Mary hollered back. Her standard answer, which meant change the subject, I'm not humoring you anymore. She usually called out "Eight" when she was tired, but tonight it was making everyone laugh, including Mary.

They spilled out onto the lawn at Pinestead after ten hours of driving, and the lake, with a bare shimmer of wind on its surface, filled their eyes. The kids, well trained after years of summer vacations, promptly began hauling things into the house; they wouldn't even run from car to house without their arms full of duffel bags.

"Come quick!" Mary called from the dock. "Sunset!"

Clouds in the west, above the rugged, dark line of hills, emerged from the shadows as the setting sun flamed at their edges. A red stripe poured across the lake right at Pinestead and made the surface glow. Like someone had laid a sheet of hammered silver, hammered to transparency, on top of the water. She felt crucified between wanting to stare and wanting to retrieve her camera. Wanting the sunset to prove the rightness of her decision. After ten minutes, when she turned away, Alex was staring at her. Watching her mother instead of the lake. Alex, Mary realized, was growing up. She might remember this night her whole life, the night we came back to Pinestead, the choice we made.

4

Becky and Melina followed her everywhere.

Becky took on the physical world with vigor; she'd swum out to the raft unaided at five, earlier than her older sisters. And yet she tended to cling, to both her baby sister and her mother. They dragged their dolls to Mary's side wherever she went. It was fine. Mary wanted to keep an eye on them, but she was surprised. Now they watched her pin up the first load of bedsheets and towels on the line among the maple trees.

Up the lakeshore from the cabins, in a clearing hidden from the driveway and the beach by a few skinny maples, the clothesline was her personal delight. Laundry hanging from a line made no great advertisement for a resort, but the freshness of sun-dried sheets pleased Mary. It was sunlight that helped save her life as a child, she thought. They didn't have any antibiotics at the Children's Orthopedic Hospital in 1922; they put the kids out in the sun, every day. Sunlight helped kill infection, they told her. She loved to press her face into new-folded, sweet-smelling sheets. It sure beat using a tumble dryer, but now they'd have to get one for winter. No question. She hadn't thought of that until now.

"Mom," said Becky. "Why aren't you smiling?"

Like a warning dart: am I heading into some kind of a funk? Mary turned and smiled at Becky and said, "Oh, just remembering this and that. Let's get out that big old hammock, shall we? I'm gonna stay where you loaf all day, where they boil in oil the inventors of toil, on the big rock candy mountain. Remember that song? Is it time to loaf? Let's go get it." The hammock where she and Jim had pressed into each other from tip to toe, one afternoon years ago.

After three years of marriage, Mary had admitted to herself that sex might be losing its glory. She even found herself crying sometimes as she lay next to Jim in bed, that it wasn't like it used to be. Good, yes, but not like it used to be. Her incredible abundance of physical reactions to Jim Leader's attentions seemed to be fading away. The first two years they were together, he had only to hold her hand as they walked from the dining commons toward her boardinghouse in Ann Arbor, and things would happen to her. She'd swell and open up just when his hand touched hers. She'd even wet herself thinking about him. She wanted to leap on him behind the nearest hydrangea bush; she couldn't wait till they were alone together.

As the years went by, something changed. In order to have a good time, she had to work at it. Produce it in herself. Surely the tears on her cheeks that night were foolish. How dare she weep for this, for sex losing its newness—and anyway, who knows, maybe it was just advancing age. Inevitable.

But at times, almost like a miracle, it would be right there again, that effortless, unasked-for astonishment. Oh yes you do love him, the angels would cry.

Like the day he put this very hammock up between the two maples. They stared at it like two kids and then climbed in, of one mind. Sandy and Sharon, their two babies, were napping.

A hammock, what a joke that turned out to be in later years, whoever had time for a hammock? In later years the kids turned it into a swing, then a way of initiating cousins into life at Pinestead. A competition. How many rotations could you stand before begging for it to stop, maybe tumbling out and having the wind knocked out of you? They thought she didn't know what they were doing. But she had an ear out, always, in case it went too far.

Still, that first day.

Jim and Mary gazed at it, the clean white canvas and the blond yokes at each end, swinging between their maple trees, and as one they climbed in. Their bodies pressed together, and her head came to his chin, her slight, taut figure lost itself in his. High overhead, waving leaves gentled the sun's ovenlike force, made it tender. Then his hand dove between her legs, and she flung her leg over his hips, and he pulled her against him. Inside herself she moved in response. Her breath almost stopped. He pulled her blouse out of her jeans, touched her bare skin.

"Why do they say beauty is only skin deep?" he said. "Isn't that deep enough?"

"What do you mean?"

"I'm saying that I love your surface."

She wanted to say, "Listen to the plastic surgeon talking," but she didn't because she would have meant it as an endearment—I love that about you, Jim—and he would have taken it as a criticism. She criticized him too much. She knew that. She liked it that Jim appreciated surfaces, and she knew that when he said "skin," he meant "and its contents, your contents, your skin, all of Mary, everything you do in order to look pretty." The skin is the organ most like the brain, he used to say. Instead of speaking, she looked into his eyes as he shifted his body against hers, and she felt the thrill of expectation and the joy of waiting. It possessed her again.

He unzipped her jeans, and his fingers touched her belly and moved down, and she had never in her life felt so ready. She pushed up against him to make it easier, squeezed her eyes shut. All of her being rushed to meet his touch. The secret, enveloped tip of Mary leaped to meet Jim's hand, and she cried out, "I'm so glad!"

She meant, "I'm so glad to have a body!" At the height of her joy, she didn't complete her sentence, but she held the rest of it.

This memory was pain free. She came to herself and got back to work. Becky was trying to hoist Melina into the hammock. Mary watched them, and suddenly thought of the refrigerator behind her, in the garage, with its case of Drewrys beer. One of those would be nice right now.

Or maybe she was making a habit of that—a cold beer every afternoon after lunch. It would be nothing if others were drinking around her. Something a little funny about having one alone. And then having another one.

The hammock after seven years had turned from white to gray, but its thick rope was still not frayed. Was it one of those "attractive nuisances" people warned her about, like abandoned Frigidaires? She would have to take extreme care to avoid attractive nuisances, now that she was on her own, or somebody might get hurt. There was no more leeway. "One mistake could bring everything down," someone said to her last winter in Chicago, trying to dissuade her from moving up here. One mistake, is it? she thought scornfully. But now she remembered those words, with a little more sobriety. No harm in a little extra caution. But for Christ's sake. One mistake, anywhere, could bring it all down around you; you can't live in fear.

I feel sorry, she thought, for people who think they need the city around them, in order to be safe.

Becky climbed in with Melina and held on to her.

"Swing us!" she begged.

She always wanted to know where her mother was, but Becky was still the bravest of the girls, the one who wanted to try everything: waterskiing, roller-skating, capsizing the canoe to see what would happen. As long as Mary or Jim were nearby. What a contradiction. What a set of opposites in one child.

Mary laughed and set to pumping the hammock, gently at first, then a little harder. It felt good to hear her children shriek with joy, to control the speed of their adventure with her own strong right arm.

"Makes my palate jump for joy!" Mary cried, as she and Alex leaned over the kitchen sink to finish sugar-glazed cherry pockets, juice dripping down their chins and fingers. Grandma's specialty. It was August, and Grandma's cooking transformed the household, once again.

Chris Olivet, in his quiet and steady way, had set about remodeling the north end of the house, adding a bedroom and insulation and enlarging the little office off the back porch. Someone, Mary or Grandma, took Chris a cup of coffee and a baked goody midmorning every day.

"Oh," he'd say, as if astonished. "Oh, thank you, that's nice," and he'd go wash his hands in cold spring water at the outside spigot. The progress on the house fascinated Mary, so incremental, so many details of planning and structure underlying each improvement. It pleased her to see a young, pleasant-looking man about the place. Sometimes you'd forget about him, he was that quiet, unless he used a power tool or his hammer, and it could be spooky to round the corner of the house and run into him. On hot days his ragged, color-spattered t-shirts clung damply to his arms and back. She liked to see him lift a one-by-ten board off the table saw and hike it up the ladder. The length of his back, his arms, pleased her. Guess I'm not dead yet, she thought. But why doesn't he have someone in his life? Why is such an able, attractive man alone at his age?

Grandma and Tony's presence warmed the house like a big old fireplace, and the kids were inspired by the reassuring ratio of grown-ups to children. Sharon, Alex, Becky, and Sean showed off their helpfulness and gloried in a new audience for their swimming, canoeing, and bonfire-tending skills. It was good this way. It would only be for a month, but a month could sustain you, Mary guessed, even through tough times.

But new problems haunted her. Public Health had hired her to give polio shots in schools all through Northern Michigan this fall. She needed to go down to Ann Arbor for a week for education about the brand-new vaccine, and it tore at her to think of leaving, even just for those few days. Not that she wouldn't enjoy the company of other nurses for a while. Not that she needed to be with her own kids every minute. But the unsettled feeling inside, the feeling of being torn apart because you have responsibilities in two places and can't be in both—that hurt. It bothered her; she couldn't relax, she could never put that anxiety to bed.

And come the school year, who was going to look after Melina all day, with the kids in school, Grandma back in Chicago?

This baby girl was so bright, full of mischief, and frankly so demanding. She'd get lonely without the noise and chaos and constant hugging, kissing, teasing from her siblings. To go from this scene of steady physical affection to being alone with a stranger all day? Mary couldn't bear the thought. She could just see Melina climbing experimentally into someone's lap, distressed inside by the silence around her, with that deep, expectant gaze out of multicolored eyes, one brown, one green and brown, that made you want to say, What is it? What's going on with you?

Much better for Melina to be surrounded by other children at a preschool, but the only good place was almost an hour each way by bus. Mary had interviewed the teacher, heard all about the benefits of early childhood education, but couldn't make the discomfort inside go away. Still, no doubt, this was the lesser of two evils. It's such a long way to go and to be without family all day—but we'll be here, when she gets home. What else can I do, hire some local woman, some stranger, to come here and be alone with her all day long? Why don't I trust that idea?

Should I buy a TV, like some people recommended, to keep the kids glued together in one room when I'm gone? That thought repulsed Mary. It felt like it would be giving up, to do such a thing—giving up on her own kids. Those strangers' voices rattling the walls, those silly, grotesque advertisements for cleaners, cigarettes, beer, new cars. What was a home for, if not to keep those ugly, shrill, indifferent voices out?

It was confusing last year at the hospital, when the nurses were invited into the doctors' lounge to watch Edward R. Murrow interview Jonas Salk. The excitement of watching the show together was palpable. That was a good thing about television. It burned in all of them, the thrill of witnessing this advance in public health, this victory. Salk and Murrow were heroes to her. You could read all about the vaccine in *Life* and *Look* and *JAMA*, but it seemed like TV helped you share the excitement with other people. Still, that wasn't enough reason to buy one.

Mary finally decided on the private preschool for Melina, and public school for the others, despite harangues from the pulpit about sending your kids to Catholic schools, to the grade school at St. Mary's of the Lake. No, sir, she thought. My kids need to mix with their peers. They don't need daily tutoring in sin and shame. Saturday catechism classes will do just fine. Once a week, that's enough.

If it was up to me, I'd sure throw some of that religious training out the door, anyway. Replace it with training in health. Don't tell me God put us here to feel bad about our bodies. These wonderful machines! Our jaws should drop to the floor at what bodies can do. And how beautiful we are, muscles under the skin, everything with a function. Everything, every part of us. Maybe not the appendix, but there you are.

She thought of the time when she was twelve and curious about her own body, asking her mother, "What is sex?" and her mother whirled on her and said, "Never, never again use that word!" Her mother's reaction was so extreme that Mary went off with her cousins to giggle hysterically. She still laughed about it. Someday she'd tell Alex and Sharon this story and let them know that she herself was more open-minded, they could ask her anything. But that day's a way off. We're a long way off.

The polio vaccine class in Ann Arbor would take place the very same week that the Duquesnes would arrive from Benton Harbor. Grandma and Tony would have to welcome them, offer a plate of cookies and pot of coffee the first day. She went over the procedure carefully with them. But she didn't tell them other things, like how Mrs. Wilgosch across the highway had become alarmed when she saw the Duquesnes arrive that first time; how she had phoned Mary and offered to call the police, just because she saw a Negro family driving into Pinestead.

"Mr. Duquesne'll be out fishing, four A.M. to noon, every day," she told Grandma. "And his wife, she'll sleep late and read and play in the lake with their little girl, Armonica. She's Melina's age. Sharon and Alex like to play with the little girl, and they can watch Melina too. They'll all have fun together, but it's up to you. You do whatever you like."

"That's all right, dear."

"It is indeed, Mother. Sharon and Alex look forward to it. Four summers already they've been here. Repeat customers are our bread and butter. The cabin's all ready, and please remind them that the Inn at Glacier Point holds a big chicken dinner for resorters Sunday. They won't go, they never do, but no reason not to invite them."

"Now you don't worry about a thing," said Grandma. "Except drive carefully, and I hope you won't pick up any hitchhikers, Mary. It's not safe as it used to be. You're softhearted that way, but I'm afraid of who's out there, these days, all that distance."

"I won't, Mother," Mary said, surprised at the warning. She used to hitchhike all the time, she and Jim, during the war. They thought Grandma never knew about that. But did she?

"And Chris Olivet will be here every day, so be sure to take him a cup of coffee every morning. Just take it outside to him. Don't wait for him to ask or invite him inside, he'd rather have it outside. That's what Jim used to say. Some people up here are like that."

"I will, honey."

Grandma was in for a penny, in for a pound. She said she'd do something, she'd do it.

The second day in Ann Arbor the nurses were examining and talking with a dozen children called Polio Pioneers, who had received their vaccinations a year before. There was a sudden profound stirring, a vibration around her, and everyone looked up at a slight, dark, handsome man in a lab coat, moving among them. His dark hair, dark eyes, and small, elegant hands were familiar from *Time* and *Life* and the television news. Jonas Salk himself. Greeting the children, looking at their arms, chatting with them, meeting the nurses who would be delivering his vaccine to thousands of children next year!

Her mouth hung open. And she wasn't the only one.

"Carry on," someone was murmuring to the nurses, and Dr. Salk moved through the room greeting all of them one at a time. He was small, slightly nervous, and so appealing. Mary recognized something in him. Jim had it. It was the unmistakable self-possession of someone who spends most of each day doing just what he wants to do, what he was put on this earth to do. Consumed by a project. Meeting people like he was doing now—it was just coming up for air. Like athletes who shower and put on a suit and tie and mingle for a short time with others, his real life was elsewhere, and it showed in that glow and intensity. That heat.

Pick your jaw up off the floor, Mary Ashton Leader, she said to herself.

"This is Mrs. Leader from Northern Michigan," said the chief nurse. Dr. Salk looked her directly in the eyes and smiled and nodded, and they looked together at the slight rash on the arm of the little boy between them. Oh my God, Mary thought. My husband was like you, she wanted to say. Then he was about to move away. She had to say something. Not for her own sake.

"My husband wanted to meet you," she blurted. "He was real interested in tissue culture. We read your article in *JAMA*. He wanted to use neonatal skin to help burn patients."

The head nurse stared at her. Dr. Salk looked back. Such dark, interested eyes. Like Jim, he could go from relaxed to back-in-action just like that. She wanted to say, I recognize you!

"How you were able to use human tissue cells to build your samples, my husband was so excited about that, about Dr. Enders's work. He thought that was promising. He told me this two years ago, that maybe the youngest skin cells could grow tissue for burn grafts. That's what he did, pediatric plastic surgery."

"Dr. Enders's work was a breakthrough," Dr. Salk said. "I see the thinking, yes, though that is an entirely different field for me." He nodded. "Yes, I see it. But you say, he 'did' plastic surgery?"

"Well, he passed away last year." For a second she couldn't talk or think or breathe. Get away from this subject. "I know, I know they are different things, burns and viral research. Isn't it amazing where they have something in common."

"Was he able to pursue this?"

"No, no. But it was an idea he had."

"He was on the right track. The youngest tissue, clean and strong, a miracle of rejuvenation could be possible."

"Yes," she said.

"I'm sorry for your loss."

She put a hand on her waist. "Thank you."

And then, after a minute, neither one speaking again, he held out his hand.

"Good to speak with you."

She stared after him. She wanted to tell him Jim's name. She pressed her hand into her waistband, trying to stimulate her diaphragm. Move, damn it, I need to breathe.

By the time they were dismissed for the day, she was flying. The team of nurses was ecstatic after Dr. Salk's visit. Walking back to the boardinghouse, one of them suggested a quick drink at the A-Squared Tavern. Mary ordered a bourbon and water and hardly realized that she was gulping it. After fifteen minutes, while the others worked on their old fashioneds, she ordered a second. She went over and over the conversation, taking pleasure in each word. If only she'd told him Jim's name. Maybe he'd heard of Jim.

Because Jim would have been just like that, his fingers so gentle on a small boy's arm, his smile so ready, looking directly at you. All that's best in medicine, that was Jonas Salk. And that was Jim.

"Mary sure had a nice conversation with him," someone was saying.

"Ah," she smiled and shook her head.

"Well you sure did, Mary. I don't know what you were saying, but he seemed interested."

"He seemed interested in everything. He's interested in life, period," someone said.

"They say he has a finger in every part of it. That he can do any part of the work, oversees it all."

"Here's to making history!"

Mary raised her glass with the others. They were, in fact, making history, but there was something more to it. Seeing Dr. Salk had reminded her so powerfully of Jim's work and Jim's presence, the future that she had once trusted would be her own, through Jim. She had picked up from today's adventure the tangible, huge reality that was the life of an optimistic doctor exploring new ways to solve problems. But her own life had changed. She had to go down a different road now. Navigate a whole different set of hurdles, alone.

Victory over polio was breathtaking. But even though the head nurse called them "ground troops," Mary knew that she herself was way back in the lines. She was going to be a public health nurse, run a resort, and take care of her own kids. Whiskey warm in her brain, that almost seemed good enough. She needed to get out of this uniform now, out of this girdle that didn't expand with her waistline, and get back home to her half mile of wooded shoreline and the five people most precious to her in the world.

She'd gained weight this month, working so hard and eating Grandma's cherry pockets. Her girdle was way too tight. And a couple of beers every day, that was too many calories. What would Jim think of her now, forty and pudgy, stuffed into this uniform looking like a big old larva, and acting like a stage-door Johnny with a thumping heart. Good God almighty.

A woman who struck up a conversation with Jonas Salk was no blubbery heap. She would manage. Before she'd ever met Jim Leader, in fact, she'd moved north on her own, made it into nursing school. She'd have to do it again. Get going, do what was in front of her to do, get over one hurdle at a time. Move blindly if she had to. It wasn't like she had a choice. You pick up your pallet and go.

5

With no white crystals to give back the starlight or moonlight, the darkness was winning. Mary drove home every night in increasing desperation.

Oncoming winter seemed to be forming a tunnel around her struggling family. November passed and December darkened around them, still without snow. Half the time it felt colder inside the house than out as the dark, bitter mornings and evenings wrapped around them, circumscribed the day and every move they made. Mary would wake up at five, sometimes four, every morning with a sense of alarm, facing a day that wouldn't even get light for a few hours. Her eyes wide as the Nancy cartoon in the Sunday comics, she'd stare across the empty bed from where she pressed against the wall.

The two new rooms that Chris Olivet had created out of one small office and a sleeping porch were now the best-insulated rooms in the house. They were meant to be Mary's office and bedroom, but on cold evenings she hated to send Becky and Melina upstairs. So she handed one room over to the two of them. Sharon and Alex were thrilled to share the second floor with Sean and have their own rooms for the first time in their lives. Becky and Melina took over the double bed, and into the other room, facing the lake—her new office—Mary brought her dresser and a narrow pallet from the small stock of roll-away cots kept for the cottages. The cots themselves with their swaying springs hurt her back, but the floor made a perfectly adequate bedboard. Make me a pallet on your floor, someone used to sing back home. Now she could sleep, comforted by the rise of the wall against her body, like she had taken comfort in Jim next to her. When she came awake she'd see the limbs of the beech and maple trees outside the window, welcoming her back to the land of the living.

Never mind that it made no sense, but she liked thinking, too, that she could roll up that pallet and hit the road, anytime. Anytime wanderlust called. Not that she'd ever do such a thing. Who could say why it comforted her to look down at her thin little bedroll and sense that she was just camping. Maybe it was a way of not feeling these chains that actually did weigh heavy. This life of hers. She could no more walk away from it than she could walk away from her own self, or her last name, nor would she. Not ever.

Saturday-afternoon naps were her happy moments. She'd slide into sleep with the help of a couple of phenobarbs and a beer chaser or two. That feeling of everyone safely accounted for and nothing pressing to do—that was sheer heaven. She took one pill every weekday afternoon and every night, but two on Saturdays after lunch. She hadn't planned it, to include pills and beer in her life . . . but the hours facing her . . . dear God, those hard hours recommended the phenobarb and a lager or two. Calories or no. Once she had her hand around that bottle of beer, Saturday afternoon became a gift—something peaceful, blissful, private. She would set out the week's laundry for the kids to sort into the wire bin that said Nuts to you, by Heck! She'd put a box of socks to mate on the living room floor, and a pile of empty shoeboxes for Becky and Melina to make into villages—a game they never tired of: building stores, barbershops, libraries, a nostalgic world as real to them as the towns of Miltonia or Itara. Sometimes she could hear Alex organizing her sisters into a housework brigade as she drifted off.

But by the middle of December, the hours of darkness and cold were too much. She hadn't anticipated this. She missed the streetlights of Chicago. Except for their own porch light, there were no outside lights at all around here! Rarely a green light moved up the lake—a fisherman heading north.

The kids stumbled downstairs to dress for school over the heating grates. Becky and Melina even stood atop one in the corner of the dining room as they swallowed their cream of rice, sharing twelve inches of heat without fighting.

The heaps of leaves all over, like frozen surf, had long since faded in color, from flaming orange and yellow to a dull, rosy brown. Oak leaves went from a rich butterscotch that made you salivate to look at them to dull, drab heaps.

The gray trunks of beech trees had been so lovely in November, pale gray pillars touched here and there with the bright orange or yellow of remaining leaves. Becky, Melina, and Sean with his toy bow and arrow became Hiawatha and his band. The edge of the lake turned milky with new ice. She would have to find money for six pairs of ice skates. Mergansers and wood ducks surprised her on the still dark water like migrants who had missed their train. Why were they still here?

But as the weeks went by and the nights lengthened, this long stretch with no snow unnerved her. People were talking about snow, anticipating snow, eyeballing her like she was some kind of neophyte. She didn't know what to expect.

"Goin' into winter wi' them tires, Lady? I wouldn't," said a mechanic in Petoskey one day in November, when she left the Mercury for winterization while she gave shots all day up at the school just six blocks away.

"I have chains," she said.

"Chains," he repeated, and looked around as if for someone to bounce an eyeshot off. Listen to the lady talk about chains. "These here tires gonna send you in the wrong direction any day now. There's a glaze on the road wit' or wit'out snow. Lady, I hate to see you drive outta here on these. Hasn't anyone else told you so?"

"Well, yes, but . . ." He thinks he's found an easy mark, she thought, gonna get me to spend a week's salary right now.

"You think about it, you call me up today and give me the go ahead."

"But what difference does it make when you have chains?"

"You want to find out or you want me to tell you?"

She stared back at him. If you knew what I had to deal with you wouldn't talk to me this way.

"Treads is gone on your front tires and just about on your rear ones," he went on with an exaggerated patience. "You don't wanna plane all over the road like a speedboat when it's wet and icy. All's you got to do ask anyone, ask your husband."

"I don't think so, not today," she said, but then she started worrying. She stopped in a day later at her insurance man's office in Miltonia, Dean Holbus. He came outside and bent to look the tires over: a short, bald man in a white shirt and tie, wearing steel-rimmed glasses, he was infinitely comforting somehow. It amazed her that he didn't put on a coat to come outside; she found the cold so painful.

"There's no question, Mary," he said, standing up from a crouch next to her front tire. Three minutes outside, and his skin had turned blotchy in the cold. "This is something you have to do, Mary. You know what? I wouldn't wait another day, either. Those kids of yours . . . Where your precious cargo meets the road, you need to have a decent grip. That's one of the most important parts of the vehicle."

Almost a week's salary for new tires. She wanted to cry, there was a weight behind her eyes, but Mary Ashton Leader had stopped crying a while ago. She couldn't cry anymore; she just had to let things hurt. She had to let things build up. There was no way to let it out. But phenobarb and a beer would make it go away for a while.

Saturday mornings, after dropping the four oldest children off at catechism classes, she and Melina would go to the Lake Michigan shore, and something wonderful would happen. Wrapping a scarf around her face against the wind, chasing or piggybacking Melina up and down the shore, discovering odd things like a small surprising heap of bones, fur, or feathers where two animals had fought for survival, she felt alive in a different way. Never anyone else there, except sometimes a hunter in an orange or red jacket would come out of the woods and stare at her, his shotgun broken over his arm or slung on his shoulder.

The novelist of Alaska, Rex Beach, came from around here somewhere. This was a place that nourished daydreamers. Last summer Sean kept two painted turtles in an old washtub and named them Rex and Lucky, after Rex Beach who was lucky enough to go to Alaska. All the big kids were entranced by the stories the old hired man, Clint Geoghan, told of Alaska.

Melina was a daydreamer, too. As she rode her mother's shoulders in the wind, she would tell the story of Paddle-to-the-Sea and his spiraling journey down the length of Lake Michigan. She almost had that book memorized, Sharon had read it to her so many times. What a joy to have bright children. Mary had five, and this one—her zest for life was untroubled, though her father was gone and her mother distracted.

"I can't carry you anymore, let's run," she would say.

"Carry!"

"No, let's run!" and Mary would lope ahead. "Come on!"

And they ran until she threw herself against a broken dune or a drift log, and Melina sat next to her to draw in the sand, to wave a stick at the great gray lake and shout, "Where's Paddle?"

She might do all right after all, with those big green-and-brown eyes.

Heterochromia iridium, Jim said when she was a baby, but Mary said, "Her eyes are like jewels. Don't try and scare me with your fancy words."

"I didn't scare you, and you know it," he said. "This baby's perfect. All my children are."

While Melina played, Mary would stare at the water and try to hold the whole lake in her mind's eye for just a fraction of a fraction of a second. And she could always succeed in this. Invariably it made her stomach drop, like being in an elevator. It made her feel icy but alive inside. She loved it—the way she could get the outside to match the inside, for just that tiny bit of time. That was enough, too. Enough was enough. A puzzling sense of gratitude tore at her heart.

Then they'd stop at the new IGA, if there was time, and pack a shopping cart: a case of beer, five pounds of lean ground meat or slabs of round steak (don't let the kids eat too much animal fat, Jim used to say, it's bad for the blood). The lean meat was more expensive, but she bought it anyway. At least what you paid for didn't melt away into liquid fat you just had to pour out. Just like those new tires, protein was something you had to pay for. Tomato soup and canned tuna, canned peaches and plums, eggs, lettuce and canned corn, celery and carrots, bags of dried garbanzos or pea beans, bags of noodles and rice, toilet paper and vinegar and Bon Ami scouring powder. A carton of buttermilk—to remind her of home. It made her mouth feel so fresh and clean. A bag of Gravy Train. That would be it, almost every week. Sometimes they'd run by the day-old bakery for cartons of bread and cupcakes, or Lily Dairy for a fifty-pound sack of powdered milk. The back of the car loaded up, they'd pick up the older kids. The week's work was done, at that point. Finally done. In some ways that moment, coming back home with a station wagon full of kids and food, everyone's work done, was the best part of the week.

Mary always had big plans for Saturday afternoon. She'd do this or that, and then she'd take her nap. But it didn't work out that way. Lunch of BLTs or grilled cheese sandwiches, get the laundry going, and then her eyelids got heavy, and she'd say, "I'm going to work on bills for a minute," and finally she stopped saying even that. She'd just go into her office and shut the door, shut out the noise. Let sleep come.

They went down on the train at Christmas to be with Grandma and Tony, though Mary's heart pulled both ways—to stay at Pinestead and hope for snow or to be snug in the comfort of family. In Grand Rapids, where they changed trains, she made the kids stand in a circle around the luggage, holding hands, while she ran to buy tickets for the next leg. Mortified, Sharon and Alex glowered and refused to forgive her all the way to Chicago. They ate Vienna sausage from the can for dinner. It was a nightmare, not at all the adventure she had hoped for, but, she told herself in Chicago, over and over again: worth it, this one more time.

They arrived back home to a bare landscape. No snow into January.

On a Sunday morning, two weeks after school had started up again, she opened her eyes in the darkness, climbed out of the army surplus sleeping bag she had added to her blankets, looked at her watch. Seven—she had slept late. She wrapped up in her bathrobe and went out to put the coffee on. She had to open a new can of Hills Brothers. There was a gasp of air as she pried off the lid and broke the vacuum, and a heavenly smell greeted her, even better than the coffee was going to be. The first cup was the best moment of the day. Her own mother would never have coffee before Holy Communion, not even take an aspirin for her arthritis. She curved a spoon into the beautiful, brown surface, lifted it to the aluminum basket of the percolator. Her feet, even in ragg wool socks, curled on the cold linoleum. She lit the gas and set the percolator on the flame and looked out the window. In the darkness something moved.

Mary looked closer. Just within the light cast by the kitchen window, she saw falling snow. Had there been a warning, a forecast? She went to the front door, crossed the walled-in porch, turned on the outside light, opened the door. Oh! she cried out loud. It was already piled up on the bottom step. The Pinestead she had known was gone. She was in a new place, entirely. Crystals of snow sparkled back at the yellow porch light. Oh, the kids were going to be enchanted. And the silence! She went down the steps in her socks and dipped a hand into it. No wind; it was all coming straight down. The parade of crystals came straight down onto her hair, onto her raised face and closed eyes like a dispensation.

Chains, she thought, and plowing the driveway. Oh my God—but it's Sunday. There's nothing to worry about, except mass. How are we going to get to mass? There is no mystery to putting on chains. I can do it, she thought. Oh, the kids are going to be thrilled. She had something to give them.

After an hour and a half's struggle, with Sean hovering around eager to help, she did manage to get chains on the rear tires. It was a first. So there! she said softly, to no one in particular. Becky and Melina were collapsing on their backs all over the yard, moving their arms to make wings in the snow. The dogs barked repeatedly, rolled over and over, then sneezed five times in a row. Excitement sneezes. Alex began a snowman. They headed out for mass with time to spare.

Turning onto the county road they drove up through fields and orchards they had never seen before, transformed.

"Look at the Christmas trees!" Becky called as they drove by Wilgosch's acre of baby trees, all capped and decorated. The sound of the chains, catching pebbles from the road, made Mary nervous; at first it sounded like the chains couldn't possibly hold. But they did. They even made it to mass on time, were greeted by a half-empty church parking lot. They were exceptional!

"By golly, kids, we did it! Nothing can stop us!" she said. "Now where's my hat?"

Sharon opened the glove compartment where Mary usually stashed her black velveteen bucket, ten years old and highly crushable. She giggled at the sight of her mother in a black velvet hat and Jim's old plaid jacket and wool pants, but no matter. That wasn't the point. How proud she was of her family this morning, as they scuffed across the parking lot in their boots, kicking at the snow. People straggled in late, the church wasn't half full. But the Leaders were here. We do what has to be done, she thought. What the heck is the problem? Weren't the locals expecting this? We were!

"It's still snowing!" the kids cried with ecstasy and relief, as they spilled out after the Ita Missa Est. The rumble and sputter of the chains now seemed to her a pleasant sound of security and self-reliance. She detoured on the way home to a bluff above the farms, the woods and lake. No cars before or behind her; she parked in the road. There was no panoramic view through the falling snow today, but that was the wonderful part: you knew it was there, only the landscape and nothing else at all, filling up with snow.

"Mom, what are you doing?"

She stepped out of the car. "Listen," she said. "Get out, kids. Listen."

"We want pancakes!"

"Yes, but listen to the silence!"

They groaned. "Pancakes!"

She walked a few feet away from the car. She wanted to pull the whole scene, the whole landscape, inside her as she pulled the lake inside her on Saturday mornings. The world was making her a big huge promise that it would keep this time: she could rely on this place.

"Maw-awm, we're HUNGRY."

"Come ON, Mom!"

"Damn it," she said, "would you kids get out of that damn car and listen to the silence?"

They stared at her and then began to snort with laughter.

"All right all right all right," she said, laughing at herself.

It didn't stop snowing after buttermilk pancakes, it didn't stop all day. They took turns in the driveway with a snow shovel, but what was the point? It didn't stop after dinner, when the wind began to blow and they could see the flakes swirling against the dining room windows in the darkness. It hadn't stopped after *Gunsmoke*, *Johnny Dollar*, and *Suspense*. They built a fire, and Alex made popcorn, shaking it vigorously over the gas ring, and Sharon melted butter. The snow didn't stop after Melina's and Becky's baths.

At six-thirty in the morning, it was still snowing through gusts of wind, and the radio told her that the schools were closed on account of the blizzard.

6

The electricity went out Monday afternoon when the wind picked up. The telephone held for another day. Chris Olivet and Mr. Wilgosch called to check on her, urged her to sit tight, and Chris promised that he would be over to the house with his blade to clear her long driveway as soon as the snow stopped falling. Mary felt a wonderful calm over a mild steady buzz of sheer joy in being alive and having such a clear, elemental task in front of her: stay warm, feed the kids, enjoy each other, and watch the transformation of the woods and the lake, between the gusts of wind. When the wind blew she couldn't see a thing. You could get lost out there, even in a place you knew well.

Then the phone went out, and the wind blew the snow in tight drifts against the front door. How would they get out, if they needed to, where could they go . . . but we have everything we need, she reminded them. Food, candles, plenty of water, each other.

The kids grew bored in the late afternoons with peanut butter sandwiches and the no-longer-fresh apples stored in the crawl space, but they were otherwise thrilled with the novelty of the storm, and endlessly inventive. They did not tire of puzzles, checkers, books, or shoebox villages. Every so often one or two of them ventured outside to fill buckets with snow to melt. Sean worked on his Cub Scout carving, the wolf head from a kit. Chris Olivet, who rarely spared more than a soft hello for the kids, had shown him how to use a knife, back in the fall.

"Don't wanna pull a sharp blade right toward your own leg," he said gently. Mary would have told Sean, but Chris saw it first. He put down his paintbrush and went over to Sean, who sat at the picnic table. "If it slips—or when it slips, 'cause they almost always do—it could fly right inta the inside of your leg, cut a big artery. Show you how I do it."

"Sure," said Sean, and gave him the wolf head. It was all blocked out for him, in the kit. The Scouts were just supposed to carve away certain chunks of wood, gouge nostrils, hollow the ears, score the surface to indicate hair, and then paint it.

Sean hadn't forgotten Chris's instruction. Mary watched him carve carefully away from his femoral artery. Alex snapped at him about getting shavings on the floor, and they quarreled briefly, but Mary brought over some newspapers. That was the only ruckus of the afternoon, except for the terrier Klondy nipping at Becky when she tried to dress him in doll clothes. He ran upstairs, his toenails clicking, and Becky hurled the doll jacket across the room, embarrassed. But Klondy was back when evening fell and it got to be the time to light candles, cuddle under blankets, build a fire, boil cocoa on the gas stove, melt cheese sandwiches, and reminisce. Reminiscing consisted of the kids begging her to tell stories about what they called the Old Days when she was growing up in North Carolina.

They seemed to think it was easy, telling stories.

They gathered around her like pups. The wind, driving snow against the house, sounded like an owl hunting, a lonely sound and yet comforting—the cold outside, the warmth within.

She remembered doing the same thing as a child, begging her mother and father for stories, as if they merely needed to open a trunk and select one of the many long strands heaped inside. Now, she was amazed at the difference between the stories in her head, the memories she wanted to share—and the words that came out of her mouth. The stories that came out of her mouth were different. She'd simplify things. She had to leave unspoken much of the color, the pleasure, the circumstance. But the kids didn't care. They supplied their own color.

Mary wanted to tell stories about how hard her mother worked to keep the family together after Hi Ashton went bankrupt and started drinking so much—if that's exactly what happened—she never knew if the Depression caused his drinking or coincided with it, more bad luck. Mary wanted to tell them about how her mother saved every penny, sold cakes to hotels, made cream for beauty masks out of Georgia clay. Clay that some people ate. She remembered the people they met in a pea field one time. They ate it for health reasons, they said.

"It's whut yuh need sometimes, settle yer spirit down," a woman said.

Looking back on 1931, Mary knew it was hunger. They wanted to stop their bellies from hurting so much. She wanted to tell that story.

But what came out of her mouth were loving memories of Hi, his warmth and humor, his gentle shrug and smile at all of his wife's correctives.

"You can make these eggs go further," Mary's mother scolded her one day. "For heaven's sake, Mary, stretch those eggs! Add water to them!" But Hi stopped her with a wink. "Best way to stretch eggs is add more eggs," he whispered.

"What story shall I tell?"

"Tell about when you were sick."

"Tell about the dime and the movie! The dime and the movie!"

That was a mistake; she'd never live that down. She and her cousin had the price of one movie ticket between them. She loved the story, but you can't tell that kind of thing to your own kids, how you broke the law when you were their age! She had stopped telling that story two seconds after she started it, that one time, but the kids never let her forget that promising beginning: "Once my cousin Betty Lou and I had only one dime, and we wanted to go to the movies . . ."

"There's no story there, there was no dime and no movie," she lied now, emphatically, as she always did whenever it came up. Sometimes they knew when to quit.

"Tell about when you and Daddy first met!"

"I'll tell about when I got sick," she said. "I got osteomyelitis, a terrible bone infection, in my pelvis. The doctor said there was no hope. Oh, it hurt so much! This was before penicillin, and people used to die from infections like this. When I pulled my hair as hard as I could, I couldn't feel the pain so much, so I pulled out my own hair by the handful. They bandaged my hands so I couldn't do that. But then my daddy said, we're not giving up. I don't care what the doctors say, we are not giving up. We lived up in Asheville then, but he bought train tickets to the brand-new Children's Orthopedic Hospital in Gastonia, and he held me on his lap the whole way. He cradled me in his hands because the train rattled and bumped, and that hurt terribly. They all said, it's God's will, but my daddy wouldn't listen . . . He said no, it isn't, it's never God's will that my child hurts.

"And when we got there, the doctors and nurses took care of me, and the pain went away. They put me in a cast from here to here . . ." Mary touched the side of her hand to Melina at the armpits and thighs. "They put me on a terrace in the sun. There were no antibiotics in those days, but the sun can heal you too. I thought to myself, this is what I'm going to do when I grow up. I'm going to work in a hospital. I'm going to take away people's pain.

"I was six years old, and I made up my mind then and there, to be a nurse. Or a doctor."

The kids were quiet, listening, spellbound. She listened too, as she finished and the story hung in the air. Was she bragging about her wonderful daddy? Her own children didn't have a daddy to save them, if anything went wrong, if other grown-ups made all the wrong decisions. What if they asked her, what about your mother?

But the kids didn't want to analyze the story, they wanted to be spellbound. Except for Alex. Soon Alex was going to ask questions, she could see that. Alex lay on her back, her head resting on top of her pale blond ponytail, gazing up at the dark ceiling through thick, black-rimmed glasses. "She looks like a young woman who reads books," said her history teacher at the junior high school open house. He meant it kindly, he meant that's where she gets her background knowledge to make those straight As, one after another, year after year.

"Alex, read a story," someone begged later in the evening, and Alex went to the bookshelves that lined the staircase and rummaged with the light of a candle. She brought back *A Child's Christmas in Wales*, a present last year from Aunt Tony. Alex read it like she herself had written it, like she was behind the words, driving them forward with the power and melody of her shaping voice. Mary was spellbound, a little child herself, letting Alex be the grown-up and carry them all to the Welsh seaside town and the little boy in the bosom of his aunts' and uncles' home. No mention of a mother and father; had he lost his parents, too?

Even if he had no parents, the world still took care of him, good care.

"I kinda like a storm like this one," Chris Olivet said with a rare grin. They stood at the end of her quarter-mile driveway, looking back at the plowed gully of the driveway, the faceted snow berms on either side. Chris's black hair emerged in sharp, greasy points from under the flaps of his cap. She handed him a ten-dollar bill toward the plowing and wondered if her wool jacket, once Jim's, looked as worn and frayed as the similar one Chris wore.

"When you're snowbound, it's fun to get some things done inside," she said.

"I can just paint all day," he said.

"Oh, the country is so beautiful with this new snow," she said, concurring.

"No, I don't paint this. I paint ideas from my head. I like to use color." He lingered on the last word. He must have finished something, really made some progress, she thought, to be so energetic in his speech today, to flash a smile at Alex, Sean, and Becky, hauling Melina on a sled toward them, heading toward Wilgosch's hill.

"When am I going to see one of those paintings?"

"Finished a nice one this week." She was right; it was success in painting that made him happy like this. "I'll bring it by sometime," he added, suddenly shy again, looking down. He put the ten in his wallet. "I'll give those kids a ride to the hill."

"They'll like that."

He stopped the truck up ahead where they trudged, and they looked back at her, as if to check before they climbed in. She waved and nodded. The adventurers. Sharon stayed home, reading a novel. She'd always rather stay indoors than knock about with her siblings. Sharon was a romantic, Mary had noticed. She liked to bake brownies, dredge them in powdered sugar, and eat them herself while she read novels packed home from the public library. Supplying her dreams with images, of adventure, of treasure, of heroes. And men.

She was glad to see the older kids including Melina this afternoon. Melina, unlike Sean and Becky at this age, dived into imaginative play even without toys; she leaped around on the furniture talking to herself in a soft voice as though the armchair had become a fort, a castle, a rock above the rapids. Despite her explosive energy, she showed every sign of preferring secure boundaries off which to bounce or crash. Just like, as a toddler, she would hang onto Jim's hands and walk up his legs, walk up his body, letting him flip her over. Did she remember him at all? They were such good friends.

The other kids knew a hole in their family, but maybe they were getting over it. There wasn't going to be a stepfather. A year and a half after Jim's death, Mary looked at other men and felt nothing. Maybe for a few men, like Chris, gratitude. For Jonas Salk, wonder and awe! But nothing inside, nothing in her body changed. At forty that part of her life was over. She couldn't imagine going through all that again with another man.

All that getting to know each other. All that accommodation. With Jim it was worth it. But another man? My God!

She started back toward the house. Yesterday the wind had finally stopped, while the snow continued to fall, so that now, around her, a couple of inches lay just as it had fallen. The beeches and maples held out graceful, gray limbs newly topped with a thick white outline. She thought, smiling, of Sean squeezing way too much toothpaste onto his brush, trying to get it from end to end of the brush with curlicues thrown in, just like the picture on the box.

"Sean, don't waste that! You don't need that much, just a spot is all!" she had shrieked at him, instead of letting it go. Why did she do that? Just like her own mother—stretch those eggs! She'd better take a few more things in stride if she was going to be the only parent, the only sun in their sky, the major weather system inside this house.

This frosting of snow was so beautiful above the dark limbs. Negative to positive. She kicked at the small, neat, castellated tread marks that Chris's tires had left in the snow. She had good memories, better than other people have. A better time in memory than most people had with their live husbands. Of that she was sure, from the stories she heard at work. What women put up with! Some of the stories almost made her ill. Women checking with their husbands about everything. Coping mightily, keeping all the painful secrets, but checking with them before they spent five dollars on a new dress. Who needs that? And once in a while, you saw an ugly bruise, on a woman's arm or a child's hip. Or a woman fell silent at an odd time. That risk, always there. What did you do then?

Did her kids need a stepfather, with that risk out there, an unknown man alone with kids he hadn't raised, obstreperous kids he couldn't even call his own?

She kicked hard at a snow berm, digging out a small cave with her unbuckled rubber boot. Some stranger, moving in with assumptions and expectations?

Supposing it were possible, that a forty-year-old woman with five kids actually appealed to someone. Maybe someone would salivate at the prospect of getting his hands on her half mile of lakeshore. What about that?

"No," she said out loud. "No. Not me."

One way or another, her kids were going to have their own daddy, Jim Leader, none other, at least through her memories, her stories about him. One way or another, she'd make him real to them. No one else was going to come along and take his place, not ever. They knew this was his old jacket hanging on her now over a bulky sweater, and his 1942 quarter turning black deep inside the jacket. It had fallen from the ripped lining of the pocket, right into the hem. She fished it out once and looked at it, then put it back. They knew that: Daddy wore this jacket.

Sentiment? No, she wanted no sentiment. She wanted them to have something of the physical reality of their father. There was only one way to let that happen: tell them stories—true ones—even some of the quarrels. Wear his jacket, show them pictures from the last few years, even ones that troubled her, the ones where he was gaining weight, even smoking a Lucky Strike. That time he chugged a mug of rum just to show off and got so sick. How stupid could you be! That time at a stoplight when the man behind us honked impatiently, and Jim got out of the car, walked slowly back to the stranger, and said calmly, "Was there something you wanted?" She was so mad! How dare he take those chances!

He was a big, complicated man forcing you to accommodate to him; that's one thing a father is. They could have a taste of that, anyway. And they could come to know him by his absence, that's what they could do. Know him by the hole he had left behind, left empty as time went by. The thought of another man made her ill right now, but she knew she was young for this fate, young to go celibate like a priest, just the same. She knew that much with her head.

But that was how it was going to be. Because she wouldn't stomach another man. Not ever. A stranger with all a man's wants and habits and assumptions, moving in on her, into the space reserved for Jim Leader—no. That would never happen. Together forever: Jim and Mary. It's no one's business but mine, and the kids.

Anything a man could do, she could do for them too, well enough, anyway. She'd find a way.

Of that, Mary Ashton Leader, crunching down the snow toward her own house and her view of the frozen frosted lake, was certain. For a few moments all the pain in her heart for Jim moved aside, replaced by a solidity of conviction that, if not as strong as steel, was at least as tangible and as cold. Alone. She would remain alone, if that's what it took. And, she thought, it sure does look like it's going to turn out that way.

7

At age five, pneumonia landed Melina in Miltonia Hospital, and when she woke up in a hospital bed she stared for a long time at the IV needle taped to her arm, wondering why it didn't hurt. Next to her bed was a tray with Jell-O and apple juice and, best of all, a pink, patent-leather box with a handle. A purse from their neighbors, Mr. and Mrs. Wilgosch. It was the most wonderful thing in the world. Even in memory, it pleased her. She didn't remember ever using it, only the great pleasure of discovering it next to her in the hospital. It snapped shut with a lovely soft click like the period at the end of a sentence. It was empty except for delicious rustling balls of tissue paper . . . but what would be good enough to go inside this amazing thing, a purse shaped like a box? They brought this present because she had been so sick. So sick that Mom was really scared. The purse and the blue plastic bracelet on her wrist with her name barely readable under the filmy blue and the three days at the hospital set her apart from the other kids. Melina was the only one with the bracelet and the purse, the hospital stay, and another week home from school besides.

But when she was well enough to play Bomba the Jungle Boy again, bare-chested, jumping off the couch in her footed pajama bottoms and sliding across the living room floor, she suddenly sensed that she might be ruining it for herself. The good times were over. Her family was not watching her with joy that she was well, but instead with skepticism. You're fine now, and it's the school bus tomorrow morning for you.

Too soon. School mornings came too soon. Mom gave shots all day long, all through northwestern Michigan. The bus from the private school came for Melina at seven in the morning. The others, old enough for public school, were picked up at eight. Mom, or sometimes Alex, carried a screaming Melina out to the bus stop against her will. Once, when they weren't out there at seven sharp, the bus driver came right into the house where Mom was still in her slip, trying to get a screaming Melina ready for school, and he just picked Melina right up and carried her out. He was mad. Everyone was mad at her, and she was mad, too, because she could never stop crying, once she started. She could never stop anything, once she started. Unless Alex threatened to mummify her; then Melina would stop.

When Alex looked after them, when Mom was away, if Melina got upset she could be in extra-big trouble. Melina enraged and roaring was no match for Alex's greater strength and savvy. "I'll mummify you," Alex would threaten, and if the threat didn't shut the baby sister up fast enough, she would come after Melina with a Hudson's Bay blanket, throw her on the couch or Mom's bed, and cover her completely with the blanket. Sit on her, threaten her with nothing to breathe but her own exhalations in a tiny black pocket of space.

Melina would scream, "I'll stop! I'll stop!" And mean it this time. What would have happened if she didn't swallow her rage and behave? She'd die, buried alive, it could happen so fast. Faster than even Alex knew.

Like the tomb robbers on *Suspense* one Sunday night.

Suspense came on the radio after *Gunsmoke* and *Johnny Dollar*; three shows in a row Sunday nights that the older kids made sure they never missed. They'd all lie on the big braided oval in the living room, in front of a fire on cool nights, with dogs and blankets, and let these scratchy dramas issuing out of the leather-covered hi-fi transport them. Melina loved these nights, because for one thing, she could never remember they were going to happen. Alex or Sharon or Sean would remember, turn on the radio, grab the blankets; it was always a surprise for Melina, like an extra dessert, like brownies or popcorn after dinner.

Gunsmoke was always safe and sometimes endearingly silly; they could all sense that. *Johnny Dollar* could be predictable. Johnny investigated insurance frauds. You could guess the plot, every time. Every fire was sure to be arson, every tragic accident a carefully planned murder, every jewelry theft masterminded by the owner. But *Suspense* was always different—you never knew what would happen or where it would take place, except that Melina knew she would be frightened to the point of nausea. She always thought after *Johnny Dollar* maybe they should turn the radio off now, but the older kids wouldn't.

The scariest show ever featured tomb robbers in Egypt, who failed to heed so many warning signs that she was going crazy under her half of Sharon's blanket. When dog-headed guards rose from the dead and chased the robbers up the narrow passageway toward the exit that you knew by now was sealing itself off, Melina wrapped herself around Sharon and held on, gasping. The dog-headed guards, risen from the dead, were barking and howling; the tomb robbers—characters that you had come to know, in the half hour—were screaming and running for their lives.

"It's only a story," Sharon kept saying. "Mel, it's only a story. Stop that."

So what? Only a story—did that mean it could not have happened? "Only-a-stories" could always happen. That was the reason they were stories.

It was years before Melina could bear to be alone in the house after that one episode of *Suspense*, and she never again went into the basement furnace room alone. No matter what.

Melina did not want to remember that one, or the time when she was six and riding the school bus home through a terrible thunderstorm, and the bus stalled on the road underneath waving power lines and bending trees.

The driver ground the engine; the bus didn't move. Somebody mentioned the power lines overhead. "We're going to be electrocuted," announced one boy sitting across from her. He was seven and didn't seem scared. "Unless that tornado gets here first. See how yellow the sky is?"

Terror that Melina didn't even know she carried inside her surfaced like an animal. Were they all going to be killed? "We have to get off!" she screamed, over and over, so hard the new driver finally slapped her because he said she was scaring the other kids. He wasn't the same one who came in the house. He was a new one, a strange one.

Melina didn't want to remember that day, and she never told anyone at home, but she could never kill that memory. Another time that driver spanked her hard on the bottom because the boys dared her to keep asking, "When will we get home?" and she did, over and over, even after the driver warned her to be quiet. He stopped the bus right in front of Pinestead.

"Bend over," he said, right in front of her own home. And she did, and he whacked her.

That cost him. Next day Mom went to the school to withdraw Mel, and the principal promised to fire that driver. "I don't care if you do or if you don't fire him," Mom said. "Just don't let him have anything to do with my kids, ever again!" Mom wasn't having anyone hitting her kids, she said. Any hitting to be done, I do it.

They listened to Mom at the school when she got mad. Back home

Mom told the whole story over and over like she couldn't believe it herself. She liked the ending—that Melina got a new bus driver. You could see how satisfied Mom was about it all.

It didn't even matter that Melina had disobeyed the driver; Mom made that clear. Whatever Melina thought she did to cause the spanking, she did not cause it, and he shouldn't have done that.

Still, she didn't like that memory, and she wished it wouldn't come up anymore. Memories made a row of images like a filmstrip. You could show it to yourself when there was nothing to do, like in school. All the vivid pictures in your head that set you apart, the real keepers and the ones you despised, and those pleasingly neutral ones that helped you figure out your own life.

A day and place called "Daddy's funeral" hung at the very start. A day bright as a flag with green grass straight from a paintbox. It was a festive day, sunlit, filled with loving faces. There were flags, everywhere, like at the gas station. When Melina wanted to begin at the beginning, she went to that memory, took satisfaction in the certainty of knowing the contents of her own mind. Daddy's funeral, and I'm two years old. That signal clarity snapped down for her whenever she wanted it. Like the teacher snapping down the vinyl-coated world map at school. I can remember back that far, and no one can say I can't. Daddy's funeral, because he died on my second birthday. That's where it begins.

She remembered, too, sitting on the back porch at Little Lambs Preschool, crying and crumple-faced. Her first day there she was worn out from screaming. Someone must have put her on the porch to scream alone, but what she remembered best was being allowed to scream out her rage. She didn't belong here! But they left her to bellow to her heart's content, until she must have started to accept that here she was staying, for the day at least.

Sometime later, Mrs. Fleming showed her how to make a small *a*. Melina had paper and a pencil, but Mrs. Fleming was walking around the room with a piece of chalk, and she bent down and used the chalk to make a couple of big small *a*'s, right on Melina's paper. Melina stared at the surprise of chalk on newsprint, dusty white specks of a perfect *a:* basketball with straight line attached, holding it up, a backbone.

Sometime during the year she was six, Melina was transferred to public school, and they put her into second grade. They skipped her ahead because she could read like a house on fire, someone said. But second grade was phonics, and it was the worst ever. They would take a story—any story was better than no story, even the duller ones in the reader—and slow it way, way down, chop it up into syllables like "chŭ" and "shŭ" and "phŭ," with a tiny dip like a clipped fingernail over the *u* to show you these were short vowels. The kids were supposed to say "chŭ" instead of the whole word, supposed to bark out "chŭ" instead of "woodchuck," instead of rattling off "Barney the woodchuck crossed the road. It was an asphalt road."

When Melina saw "asphalt" coming up in that next sentence, she knew the class would come to a halt for another fifteen minutes. Sure enough. At least it was more interesting, though, than the slow progression from "chŭ" to "woodchuck." "Asphalt" was a far better word. Asss-phhh, she said silently to herself, letting teeth caress her lower lip. Then faster, though still silent: asph! It even felt good.

Melina ached to bellow out the whole paragraph. Her best friends, Cameron and Leo, were stupid in class; they hunched over the reader struggling with "chŭ" while Melina waited for the class to reach "asphalt" and then for phonics to be over. The teachers never discerned any impatience, never scolded her. Maybe she didn't show any. Maybe, she would come to believe in later years, she did behave herself. Maybe at six she was learning to put on an incredible display of obedience and patient submission to the slow pace that Cameron and Leo set in phonics class, maybe that was what people meant when they talked about what a good girl she was. Because otherwise, Melina didn't think of herself as good at all, anymore than Alex did.

She played tetherball and pretend-fought with Cameron and Leo on the playground until Cameron hit her so hard in the back one day she could not breathe. She crouched on the sand in greater astonishment than pain. It was like falling out of the hammock. But she didn't tell on him. She must have gone too far, it was her fault. And if she told on the boys they wouldn't let her play Prisoner of War with them anymore in the gully at the end of the playground or on the piney slope. They had more fun than anyone else. They would do anything. They ran from the prison-camp guards, threw themselves to the ground, and flattened themselves behind a fallen pine log to avoid alerting the passing Redcoats or Nazis. All this time the second- and third-grade girls jumped rope or played four-square, taking turns. Everything one at a time. But Melina and the two boys mixed it up.

They collided, they exploded, they tortured one another until it went too far, which it did once a week or so. Like when Cameron slugged her after she accidentally beat him at tetherball.

Even so, fighting with him was more fun than complicated jump-rope games or four-square or acting out scenes from *The Wizard of Oz* the week after it was shown on television. Melina felt like the only kid in the whole school, along with Sean and Becky, who had not seen *The Wizard of Oz*, but you couldn't admit that, or say we don't have a TV. You had to listen to the chatter around you, so that if someone asked you, you could say oh yes, yes, and it was so neat when the witch melted!

The family from Kalamazoo checked out of Cabin Two the morning after they moved in. They took one look at the Duquesnes in Cabin One and started packing up. Melina and Becky watched from the porch as they loaded their suitcases and swim toys into the car.

"Don't stare," Becky hissed.

Mom had two kinds of anger: the hopeless kind, like when Sean ran the washing machine through its whole cycle just to clean his tennis shoes after he stepped in Klondy's mess, or when she found the new can opener in the dishwasher with its plastic handles melted, or when Becky couldn't eat a whole eighteen-cent chicken potpie herself and threw half of it away, still in its foil pan, and Mom found it in the trash can. There was a high-pitched whine in her anger those times, and it went right through Melina like a hot wire. But her other kind of anger made Melina feel good, feel secure.

"I don't need to ask how you'll vote on the Open Housing Initiative," the woman from Kalamazoo said.

"I'll vote the way I choose," said Mom. "I vote my conscience. And it is a mighty good feeling to know that. Here you are, sixteen dollars and fifty cents."

"We know this is costing you. We'll pay for tonight."

"No, you won't," said Mom. "I won't have your money for a night that you aren't here or a night that you're not comfortable. Nor do I need your custom if there is a problem. That's not how we do things at Pinestead."

"Really. Well, you shouldn't surprise people this way. We're on vacation, not interested in your politics. We drove five hours to get here. We were led to believe it was a family place, a decent place."

"It is, for most of us."

"I won't be sending my friends up here."

"Frankly, I'm relieved to hear that. We'll manage."

"I expect those people will be sending theirs!"

"They been coming here for years to fish and enjoy some peace and quiet, just like you're looking for, and I hope they'll come back long as they care to," said Mom.

"They ought to go to Nigger Heaven like others do."

"Goodbye," said Mom, coming out after them, as if to end the conversation, as if she was herding them to the car. They drove away, and she pressed a hand to her heart.

"Oh," she cried. "That kinda thing! Those people gave me the heebie-jeebies."

"Mom," said Becky softly, "what is Nigger Heaven?"

Mom looked at Becky and Melina for a minute. "It's a way of talking about a place north of Detroit, where a lot of the Negro people go on vacation. Some people are more comfortable sticking with people just like them, with the familiar. Like that woman who just left. How in the hell Mr. Duquesne's sitting in a bass boat at dawn is going to interfere with her vacation, I can't imagine. I would never use those words, myself."

That night at dinner she said, "Dean Holbus wants me to vote against open housing, too. Can you imagine that?"

"Why, Mom? He's a nice man."

"It's real estate values he's concerned with. Some men always watch out for real estate values. Think it's the right thing to do for their family. They are just being ridiculous." She laughed, as though anyone in their right mind would vote her way.

Melina felt proud. When she saw Mrs. Duquesne in the lake the next day, walking through waist-deep water while her daughter Armonica fluttered and bobbled next to her in an inner tube, riding up and down the small waves, she felt proud again. Mr. Duquesne left his tall, skinny wife alone most days while he fished somewhere. One night they hired Alex and Sharon to babysit when they went out for a whitefish dinner. That night he wore a shirt of some shiny thin white cotton so you could see the darkness of his arms through the material. In the heat he just slung his jacket over his arm. Mrs. Duquesne wore high heels that made her as tall as her husband, and she held his arm as they walked up the slope to their Oldsmobile. Mr. Duquesne broke off a cone of lilac at the top of the driveway, and rubbed his fingers with it. Like he was perfuming his hands. And smiled at his wife.

After dinner, Sean said, "When we got ice cream at Howie's yesterday, a guy there called us . . ." he looked over at Melina. "Well, something bad."

"Stupid people say stupid things. Don't rise to their bait," said Mom.

"Sean," said Alex, "what are you doing?"

Sean was mixing Nestle Quik in a quart-size Ball jar. "Making something to drink."

"We just had supper!" It was Alex's own spaghetti.

Sean shook the milk vigorously, unscrewed the lid, and drank half of it down at one go, gulping noisily and working his Adam's apple. His sisters watched, revolted. He took a bite of a folded peanut butter sandwich, then poured the rest of the milk down after it.

"That's disgusting," said Sharon.

"Sean, you're a pig," said Alex. "We just finished the dishes. Clean up after yourself."

"Oh, we just finished the dishes," Sean squeaked in a high voice.

"Quibble!" said Mom, trying to get them to stop.

"Didn't you like the spaghetti?" said Alex.

"I ate as much as there was," Sean said. "I'm hungry. Whyn't you guys leave me alone?"

Melina thought, what's going on? Why can't we go back to talking about the Duquesnes?

"What did someone say at Howie's?" she said.

"A very unkind thing," said Sharon.

"What?"

"Don't tell her," said Sharon.

"Melina's no dummy," said Alex. "They said," and she leaned toward Melina, "they said we're too friendly with the Negro people."

"That's not how they said it," said Sean.

"Enough," said Mom. "Look outside. Sunset!"

"Not quite, Mom."

"Almost. Where's my camera? Everyone line up on the dock, I want a picture."

8

Sunny days in October or November, Alex and Sharon liked to get off the school bus a few miles from home and walk the rest of the way. They found relief in swinging out their legs along the road. High school was an experience unlike anything Alex had ever imagined. How she survived it she didn't know. It wasn't only that she was a plump, plain bookworm in thick glasses, who actually liked an intellectual argument. It made her face hot with pleasure to think about the differences between the American Revolution and the French Revolution, just ten years later. Something else embarrassed her at high school, despite her efforts to ignore it. Something to do with her family.

She told herself that everyone at this ridiculous school came from a difficult background. It didn't help. Alexandra Leader still felt like a sideshow. Her fatherless family was odd, living all winter in an empty resort, and they needed so much taking care of. And it seemed to fall to her to take the care, to mind the details. Meanwhile, her interest in school went beyond a desire to get good grades. She wanted to know things, and it made her a freak. She could be excited by classroom discussions long after other students in the room had fallen asleep. They resented her for it, or put her in a category off by herself. Sometimes it was just her and the teacher, like Mr. Berry in world history today, going on about the eighteenth century—while other kids watched or napped. Mr. Berry liked speculating as much as she did. When the bell rang and the other kids scooped up their books and were out the door, Alex was startled for an instant. Oh, we have to stop now, she realized.

Now Sharon had joined her at Miltonia High School as a freshman, and Alex could see that Sharon fit in better. Sharon was calm and pretty, redemptive somehow. She sewed her own clothes and managed to use a six-dollar clothing allowance from Mom to build an acceptable collection of skirts, petticoats, and clean socks. She washed her sweaters and her new bra in Woolite every weekend, and she put her hair up in curlers every night. Alex did not know that Sharon carried the same sense of freakishness, the same longing to blend in. The two of them together did not go over their heartaches; they escaped them by talking about other things.

Alex and Sharon would get off the bus at the top of Hebron Road, two miles from home, and walk the unpaved county road up the hill toward Wilgosch's farm, then leave the road for the winding sandy track across his farm down to the lake.

Crossing Wilgosch's land, you could stay in the shade of the ravine among the blazing maples and white ash, wading through leaves, and maybe startle a deer or some pheasants. Or you could leave the ravine for the high ground, walk over the tops of the small, rugged hills, almost as sharp as breaking waves, that Alex knew were glacial moraines and Sharon knew were good places to stop talking and just walk while reliving scenes from the movies she had seen at the Luna this year and couldn't forget: *Carousel*, *Picnic*, and the reprise of *Gone with the Wind.* Such loneliness, such love. Someday she would have love in her life, just like that. Except that she'd do it right. He wouldn't leave her, whoever he was, because she'd do it right. She'd be irresistible. She'd be so kind, so understanding, so unselfish.

Sharon couldn't wait to stand up to a man's insecurity and ill treatment. To conquer his doubts. Almost against his will he would take her in his arms, against his dusty, sweaty, ragged shirt (missing some buttons?), he would hold her against him . . . sometimes the two of them were in Alaska, and he would hold her against his dense fur parka. Until they got to the cabin. And then he would start a fire in the little barrel stove, take off his parka, give her a hard, cruel, desirous look. In this story he would be wolflike and selfish . . . something like the Sheik in that book that mom brought home from the St. Vincent de Paul in Miltonia, laughing because she liked it so much when she was young and was forbidden to read it, had to hide it from her own mother . . . The man in the fur parka in Sharon's imagination would be like that, you had to be that way in Alaska. But again, Sharon's kindness and patience would prove strong. That is, she would have no choice but to give in, and yet . . .

"What do you think, Sharon?" Alex might say after a while, and Sharon would realize she had no idea what Alex was talking about. Civil rights marches? What to send Grandma for her birthday?

"I'm not sure what to think," Sharon would begin. Sometimes she would venture, "You decide." Alex always accepted that.

Near the top of Wilgosch's highest ridge they would quicken their pace in eagerness, without talking about it. One last step, and below them would appear a great spill of turquoise, gemlike in the sun, with shades of lighter blue near the shore. Their lake, Achill. And to the north, beneath a sea of orange, yellow, and deep green treetops, their house.

They said nothing to each other about the view, but they did not tire of it or of the proprietary thrill of the first glimpse. Behind them a day of unparalleled stress, but this view at the end of the day offered a compensation. Inside, unacknowledged between the two of them, was a flicker of satisfaction as they looked down on their own property and what all the Leaders described to each other, in private, as Our Neighbor the Lake.

Also unspoken between them was a shared sense that they liked getting home late, when they could. The afternoon, before Mom got home, was too long in the empty house. They would have preferred it shorter. It was Alex's private opinion that their mom did the same thing, in her way—she drove the long way home, even stopped at some secluded view spot or other. Mom liked listening to the car radio. Sometimes she'd sit in the car in the driveway and listen to the radio before she came inside. She liked getting home after dinner sometimes, knowing the kids would dutifully have eaten whatever she set out that morning, whatever she told Alex or Sharon to prepare.

"The sound of that dishwasher goin' is music to my ears!" she exclaimed one night last week, coming into the house, and Alex felt strange. You missed having dinner with us, she wanted to say. How can that be all right? But she knew it was all right, and she knew why. It was just all too much. All of it. Nice to have some time alone. That had to be it. And yet it still prickled.

This day in early October 1959 had started off cold but sunny, but by the time they were crossing Wilgosch's farm, waving to him where he walked the field with his hired hand, Clint Geoghan, the sun had long since vanished behind thin clouds, and the two girls were shivering. Breezes from the northwest, from off Lake Michigan, carried the knife edge of winter. This wind sure enough had teeth in it, as Mom said. At the top of the hill, looking down at their lake, they unconsciously moved against each other, fit their bodies into each other's for a moment, for the warmth, and then they headed for home. Their hands had turned into stiff, red claws around their books.

At the end of their long, curving driveway, near the house, they saw a familiar truck—Chris Olivet's old dark green Studebaker. Mom's handyman. Was he doing some work around the place this afternoon?

They were pleased; working away on something for Mom in the yard or the storage shed, he made the place seem a little less lonely.

And yet they were surprised. They always knew when he'd be by to do something; Mom reminded them and left notes. There were never unplanned visits. As they got closer they could see the truck was running, so maybe he was about to leave or had just arrived. And it seemed to have something in it.

They walked up to the truck and stared. "Oh my God," said Sharon. A deer lay in the truck bed, partly covered by a tarp. Its head was propped up against the wheel well, and its antlers rose above the sides of the bed. An arrow stuck out from an ugly red circle in its neck. The circle was only the size of a quarter, maybe. But the sight of it horrified them. The large, glassy brown eyes, the black nostrils, reminded Sharon of the neighbor's dog, a beautiful pointer. The deer's neck was propped in an agonizing position. But of course it didn't matter anymore.

She stepped away from the truck.

Alex stared at the red circle where the arrow broke the deer's golden brown fur. How close it was, death—not much had to happen. A warm, insulated body is claimed by a hunter, an arrow is fired, and life would leave. Like that. A smell rose from the animal, reminding her of a menstrual pad.

"Chris is in there," Sharon said, pointing at the driver's seat. Alex looked through the passenger window. Chris sat with his arms folded across his chest behind the wheel, his knees together, his head drooped, and his eyes closed. How could he be asleep in that position? She opened the truck door.

"Chris?"

He startled awake.

"Alex," he said thickly. "Hey."

He unfolded himself and got out of his side of the truck and came around the hood. She saw with astonishment that his jeans and corduroy jacket were sopping wet and clinging to him. He looked like he'd been drowned. Every few seconds he would shiver.

"Alex, hey. Can you do me a favor for a minute? Wonder if I could go inside and warm up in front of your space heater? I had to chase this fella into Lake Michigan, and my truck heater's bust, and I'se startin' to wonder if I'd make it home. Got pretty chilled so I pulled in here. No one home yet. I was just thinkin' what to do next."

"Sure," said Alex.

"People can get so chilled they stop thinkin' straight." He looked terrible: his eyes were very dark and staring right at her, and there was blood on his chin, on his hands, on his jacket and blue jeans.

"You'd better come in," said Alex.

Inside they stared at him while he stood hugging himself in the stairwell behind the kitchen. The house wasn't very warm. What should she do? People need a hot drink at times like this, she thought. In books they drink whiskey, but she didn't know if they had any.

"I'll make you some cocoa," she ventured.

"Alex, I hate to ask you, but do you suppose I could just take a quick shower, stand under some hot water?"

"Yeah. You can do that. That's a good idea. I'll show you the way."

Had he ever been inside the house before? Alex led him upstairs.

"I'll make you some cocoa while you're doing that," she said. "And I could put your clothes in the dryer if you want."

"I'm gonna be fine in two shakes," he said. He shut the door behind him, and she heard the water going. A minute later he opened the door and dropped his jeans and shirt in the hall.

She stared at that small heap of dirty, wet men's clothes and looked down at Sharon, who stood on the landing, halfway up the stairs, staring up at her. It would be nice to find some guidance in Sharon's face, some clue as to what to do next, how to feel about all this. But she could tell by the expression on her face that Sharon was in retreat posture. Sharon wanted this not to be happening; it was too strange and unexpected.

Alex did not want to pick up the clothes. She couldn't help but catch a glimpse of white underwear bunched inside the jeans. There was deer blood on the jeans and shirt, and maybe deer parasites and who knows what else. She went down to the kitchen and got a dishtowel and, wrapping her hands in the towel, picked up the clothes without actually touching them and carried them to the utility room.

"Come on," she hissed at her sister. "Open the dryer."

Mom would kill her. Maybe these clothes would ruin the dryer. Maybe get blood or deer guts in it, who knows. Weird deer stuff. What if there were parasites on these clothes? She should wash them, but that would take too long, and listen, the water was going in the shower. You couldn't wash clothes at the same time.

But a guy who was shivering and shaking like that couldn't put cold wet clothes back on himself. Hypothermic. That was the word. Hypo or hyper?

Hypo means lower. His temperature was too low.

She shoved the clothes into the dryer and dropped the dishtowel on the floor and slammed the dryer door. She turned it on hot.

"What are we going to do with him?" said Sharon.

"Let's make him some cocoa. I don't get it. Why did he shoot a deer in Lake Michigan?"

"And with an arrow?"

"I guess he's a bowhunter. I guess that's kind of nice, in a way. Or is it?"

"I don't know. Is it?"

"Well, it's nicer not to fire a gun, isn't it?"

"I'm calling Mom."

"Good idea," said Alex with relief. She was momentarily surprised that she hadn't thought of that herself. But it had just never occurred to her. She measured Nestle's cocoa and sugar into a saucepan, enough for all three of them, a pinch of salt and enough milk to make a smooth, thick syrup. She stirred and stirred, set it on the gas, and added a thin stream of milk until the saucepan was almost full. Stirring vigorously. She wanted him to like the cocoa, for some reason. She got out the vanilla extract.

"Mom wants to talk to you," said Sharon.

"Stir this," said Alex and went out to the telephone.

"Is he out of the shower yet?" said Mom.

"No."

"I'm on my way home. Where are the dogs?"

"Well, I haven't let them off the leash yet. They're still outside. Why are you coming home?"

"I think I would like to."

"Okay."

"Alex, listen. Are you comfortable? If you are the slightest bit uncomfortable, tell me now."

"No, I'm fine. It's all right, Mom, he's really cold. Oh, here comes Becky. And Sean."

"Unh," said Mary in frustration.

"I think he's done with his shower. I better go get his clothes."

"His clothes?"

"I put them in the dryer."

"Alex."

"Mom, I can take care of this."

"I know that, honey. I have complete confidence in you."

"This cocoa's done!" Sharon called. "I added the vanilla!"

Alex put the receiver down in confusion. What were we talking about, exactly? she wondered. The feeling of nausea came back into her throat for some reason.

The water stopped in the bathroom. In a few seconds the bathroom door opened, and Chris said, not raising his voice, "Alex?"

She climbed partway up the stairs, not as far as the landing, and called, "Yeah?"

"I guess I'll just take the jeans as they are."

She retrieved the hot, damp clothes, reminding herself that she used to change Mel's diaper, carried them up, and held them out to the open door. His arms reached for them. She saw his bare shoulder, the line of his bare back down to where a towel was knotted around his waist.

The cocoa was sitting in three mugs on the dining table until Becky and Sean came in, and they each grabbed one, so that was that. None for Alex and Sharon after all.

"Here you go, Chris. Why don't you have this," Alex said, giving him the last mug.

"You guys saved my bacon," he said. "Man. That lake water's cold. I shot the deer near the beach and had to track him, and he just plunged right in that lake. Just went in, and I could see he was wounded. I had to get him. A hunter can't just say oh, it's too much trouble. Can't let a wounded critter wander off. You gotta track 'em. Isn't that right, Sean?"

"Guess so."

"Gettin' your archery badge in Scouts?"

"Well, uh, yeah," said Sean. This was news to Alex.

"That's good. Maybe I didn't plan for everything that might happen today. Who'd have expected it?" He drank the cocoa and looked around at the four children, staring at him. Alex and Sharon wanted him to say, "This cocoa's good!" but he didn't until he finished it. Then he said, "Back among the living. Best cup of cocoa I ever had." He did look better. His skin was normal. Alex had never seen him so talkative. Maybe they did save his bacon. Did they do something wrong, too? Was it wrong to ask him inside?

Was there something wrong about him asking for help?

"Guess you saw that deer, Sean," he said. "Going to bring you all some venison. You like venison sausage?"

"You don't have to do that," said Alex. "We're glad to help."

"Better get going," he said. He started out, and they followed him to the truck, staring once more at the carcass with the arrow in its neck. They watched the truck moving up the driveway. At the top, it pulled to one side and stopped, and there, coming down, they could see the familiar hood of Mom's station wagon. The two cars remained next to each other for a while. They were talking. Good, thought Alex. She'll get the whole story from him. A tremendous relief filled her; there, it was back in grown-up land where it belonged, this whole afternoon. All of it.

Mom was chipper when she came in. Unusually high spirits for this time of day.

"Let's get in the car and wait at the top of the driveway for Melina's bus," she said. "And go to Burger Town for dinner. What do you say? Since I'm home early?"

"Burger Town!" Sean and Becky yelped for joy.

"First I gotta get this girdle off. Oh my land." She disappeared into her room. She didn't even want to talk about Chris being here or the deer in the truck.

Sean brought along his Scouting handbook. As they waited for Mel's bus, he turned the pages carefully.

"Mom can we stop at Tighe's Hardware?"

"Why, honey?"

"They have the merit badge books. Can I get one?"

"It's not on our way tonight, but I can get it for you tomorrow. Which one?"

"Archery."

There was a silence. She turned and looked at him, frowning.

"Archery?"

"Yeah, can I, Mom?"

"Oh God, Sean, the last thing I need is to be at work all day and you doing archery practice here with four little girls running around! People can't believe I leave you all alone at the edge of a lake, but I know you're smart and you follow the rules. But archery? I'd be away from home all day and someone's shooting a bow and arrow around here?"

"I'll be careful, Mom. I'll follow all the rules."

"Oh, don't you see? Oh, for Christ's sake!" She suddenly sobbed and hit the steering wheel. "For Christ's sake! That is the last thing I need!"

They waited, all of them, quiet and rigid, for her storm to pass. The storms came out of nowhere, and just as quickly they vanished. There was so much pain inside her voice at these times, no one could help her. Her voice sounded like a tree breaking. The pain she seemed to be in was like Alex felt when Sean gave her an Indian burn on her arm, that time they fought because he wouldn't help wash down walls and floors inside the rental cabins. He wouldn't do inside chores, he said. She tried to make him, and he grabbed and twisted her arm until Alex's skin felt like it was being pulled apart. That was how Mom sounded now. They didn't know what she wanted. It isn't fair, Alex thought, but she didn't know what wasn't fair, or to whom.

"Four little girls running around . . ." Alex didn't like hearing that, but she didn't like Sean getting everything he wanted either, just because he was the only boy and Mom didn't know how to tell him no. He had a bicycle when Alex didn't; he had a whole workbench in the garage just to himself; he had a fancy fishing reel, fancier than anything that she owned.

Why did Mom always act like this, like every bad thing that happened only happened to her?

"A bow and arrow," Mom said again, making the words into a grief-stricken prayer, and put her forehead on the steering wheel. "Why is this happening to me?"

"It's not happening to you," muttered Sharon in a delicate but firm voice. "It's happening to us." Alex turned and stared at Sharon. When Sharon got her mind off of romance in Alaska, she could see as clearly as anyone else. And she could put words to it, too. A bold, direct remark once or twice a year, that was Sharon.

Now Mom was looking at Sharon too, and Melina's school bus had arrived.

Melina leaped into the car ecstatic, crushed herself against Alex in the front seat. "Burger Town!" she yelled in delight, hugging Alex, hugging her mother. Alex wrapped her arms around Melina in a confusion of feelings, delight and resentment and shock, still, that Sharon had broken the code. What code was it? She wasn't quite sure, but Sharon had ignored it. Pretended to be blind to it. Good for her.

Melina wore old jeans, too loose for her, handed down from Sean maybe, that were lined with plaid flannel, and scuffed saddle shoes that sucked her thin socks right down into the shoe. Her ankles were bare. Her long, honey-colored braids were mussed, two or three days old by now. She pulled her feet up on the car seat and made herself into a ball under Alex's arm.

"I am going to have a burger with everything, okay? And french fries and a chocolate shake," she announced, oblivious to past experiences with that very meal. She could never finish it. It was too much for her, but Mom didn't hold back when they went to Burger Town. Melina had no idea that an hour from now she'd be groaning, pushing her foil-wrapped hamburger away.

Imagine, Alex thought, imagine such a feeling, that anything goes. You can do anything. You can eat a full Burger Town dinner with ease or learn to kill and butcher a deer or find love in Alaska. Never mind how likely it all is, never mind the likelihood. Or win a scholarship to Marquette or even to Interlochen High School, the new arts high school two hours south. That's what she would like, if she was going to imagine that anything could happen, anything at all, so long as you worked hard enough at it and showed up to claim your prize. Because she knew how to do that. She knew how to meet a deadline.

9

If only it hadn't happened. Chris Olivet coming to the house when she wasn't home, in such a state—and his strange story of chasing a deer into the lake—she didn't know what to make of it. Maybe this was a time when she should have let the children handle it, let them take over—and Mary wasn't ready for that. She just was not ready. And they weren't ready. Coming into her house alone with two teenage girls, giving them his clothes. No!

There were things they didn't know about Chris. Things she didn't know—why was he always alone? How did he spend his time? Painting, hunting—but he's a man, she thought. A young man, young enough. A man in his prime.

When she pulled off the main road, he was coming down the

driveway from the house. They stopped next to each other. His clothes and head were wet, his clothes dark and tight as a second skin.

"What on earth," she began.

"I went into the big lake after this buck," he said to her, grinning. Like Mary herself, Chris had bad teeth; one of his incisors was rotated and nearly black, and that was the least of it. "Had to go in so far after him, I was swimming. We was both swimming. Nearly thought I'd die. Your kids give me a second lease on life."

His eyes held a strange look, as though he'd seen things in Lake Michigan, as though he'd enjoyed his dunking. Freshly emerged from that unholy, cold water.

"That's quite a story," she said.

"I got the strangest feeling," he said. "I didn't know if I ought to get out of the lake, even. I didn't know for a minute if it might be all right to stay right there. The water was beautiful."

His eyes glittered. Small, dark eyes the color of a pond in the forest. She had once thought his eyes were pretty.

Now she thought to herself, I don't know this man. Where there had been trust and even a maternal feeling, and a sense that he liked her—admired her, in an old-fashioned way—there was now confusion. Now that he'd made himself welcome in her own home. She was at a loss—bewildered at her own feelings, angry with Chris. Must be she hadn't made the rules clear. Maybe she didn't have rules.

Her habit, her inclination, was to set things straight immediately. Wrestle the situation back to something she knew. She opened her mouth, and the words just came out, like she was at a fork in the road and she was choosing to go down a certain path and there was no turning back.

"Chris, I'm not sure about this. I need to know that when my kids are home alone, things are exactly as I planned them. Things are as I expect them to be. It's too much for them, otherwise."

It was as if she had slapped him. He started, and the light faded from his eyes.

"Oh, I reckon," he said.

"It's confusing for me and for them, people coming by when I'm not home," she said.

"Mrs. Leader, I am sorry."

"It's really better if you don't come by when I'm not home."

"Of course. Of course."

"They know better than to let strangers in, but you're not a stranger. You're a friend who needed help. But it makes me uncomfortable, just the same, because I'm not there, do you see?"

"I was stupid to let this happen."

"No."

"Yes, and I apologize."

"It's fine."

What the children didn't know, what no one knew, was how much Mary owed to Chris Olivet. Not only appreciation of his quiet handiness about the place, the quiet, polite way that he brought things to her attention that had to be taken care of, things she never would have known about. Getting the furnace and chimney cleaned every year, cleaning out the cistern, the need for gravel on the driveway, discouraging guests from feeding the mergansers so as to keep the beach clean, tuning up the outboards.

Chris Olivet, and Dean Holbus at the insurance company, who helped her understand all the paperwork of running a household—the two of them kept her panic and confusion at bay the first two years. They were respectful. So many other men around here had this way of pausing before answering a question she might have about the car or the heating system or trimming the maple limbs that were close to the cottages. Just a slight pause, just enough to let her know they'd never heard anything so dumb, and they'd have to pull themselves together to come up with an answer to something so obvious.

When the water stopped flowing from the taps that first winter, the plumber suggested over the phone that she lower a lightbulb into the well.

"What would I be looking for?" she asked.

That pause. "Well, ma'am. It's not so much that you'd be looking for anything, but the heat of the bulb would be enough to thaw the line," he said. "What would I be lookin' for," he repeated then, with a slight chuckle.

Chris Olivet had never done such a thing, never insulted her. She thought it was respect. Maybe it was just his own strangeness. Maybe he was so strange himself, nothing else struck him as out of place.

But the amazing thing she owed to him was a secret. One she wished she could forget. A secret she kept locked away so tightly that she could pretend it had happened to someone else, it belonged in someone else's life.

He found her drinking in her car at the top of the bluff over Lake Michigan, just west of the south end of Achill. A favorite spot. Probably where he'd killed his deer.

The very first year they lived up here, 1956. She had spent a day at the high school and decided to stop on the way home at that turnout, above the cliff, with Lake Michigan gray-blue and indifferent spread out before her. She had discovered how a pint of gin fit so well in her purse, and she didn't mean to, but she found she could sip it a bit while she stared at the lake and listened to the evening news and get a head start on winding down before she even got home. One or two sips took away all the edges inside her and outside.

Chris must have seen her in the liquor store and followed her.

He pulled up behind her on the gravel road, and while she fumbled in panic and confusion to hide the bottle, he opened the passenger door and said, "Mind if I sit for just a second, Mrs.?"

"I'm just leaving," she said. "I have to get home."

"I'll be one second," he said and slid onto the seat, leaving the passenger door open. He even left one leg outside the car. She pursed her lips and stared away.

"Forgive me," he said into the brittle silence that was between them. "Mrs. Leader, I know that you have no one to help you. But for the sake of you and Dr. Leader's kids, you got to be the one to hold it together."

In her entire life she had never been so caught out.

"My heart goes out to you," he said, like he was somebody else. She could not believe that her usually semimute caretaker was talking to her like this.

"Whatever it takes, for those kids, you are all that they have," he said. He wouldn't stop till he'd made his point. "I'm saying you, of all people, you can't wait till it stops hurting. You have to take charge now, for the sake of the kids, and pull yourself together."

"How do you know all this about me, Chris?"

"I don't know anything, except that you lost Dr. Leader. He was a fine person. He fixed birth defects in everybody. Sometimes even some hidden ones. He made people feel better about themselves. In my life I've had some hard times too."

She stared in silent fury out at the lake which suddenly seemed to her an ugly maw, a crazy place to look for comfort, an empty deep freeze.

Chris went on. "So I know about what it can make you do. I seen you here once before. It's for your and his kids I'm telling you."

"I have to go now."

"You deserve to grieve like this, Mrs., but you can't. You're the one person in this world who can't."

"Thanks for the talk, Chris."

He looked down, out at the lake, everywhere but at her. "I said what I had to say, Mrs. Leader. Don't know what gives me the right to talk to you this way, but something does. Something told me to do it."

"You going to keep working for me?"

"I hope so. I hope you're going to keep calling me. Please. I'm sorry, Mrs., but I'm thinking of those kids right now. And you have to do that too."

The humiliation was so severe she could hardly speak to the kids that night; she could hardly exist inside her own skin. She thought she'd never get to sleep. But then it got easier, she locked that memory in a closet. Chris never mentioned it again, and neither did she. Sometimes she thought maybe he hadn't even been talking about drinking, rather about the tears that were on her face and the self-pity. The thing that she decided to call despair. The way the past clutched at her.

A few Sundays later, leaning on her elbows at mass, it came to her as clearly as a line of music, as a prescription in Jim's handwriting on a pad: Despair is a sin. Take confession and repentance, and call me in the morning.

Father wailed away, his chanting dreadfully off-key, sounding like barbed wire, and beside her in the pew Melina shifted restlessly from her knees to the seat of the pew and back again, sated with her picture book of the lives of the saints. She had read the life of St. Rose a hundred times. Rose, Rose, the saint's brother chastised her, your beautiful hair is the devil's snare. In a minute she'd pull at Mary's sleeve and whisper, "When can we go?"

The other kids were leaning on their elbows, staring at the face of the dead ermine in the lady's stole in front of them.

It never bothered Mary that Father whined like a chainsaw or that the kids were restless and hungry. This was an hour a week for meditation in a safe place. And suddenly she saw it, she understood. The words sailed toward her in a complete sentence. Here's your recipe: Despair is giving up. Despair is a sin.

Christ said, "Take up thy pallet and walk," and despair was saying, "No, I won't, I don't believe you, go away, I'm staying in this bed on the ground." Rejecting God. Well, what could be more obvious? If that wasn't a sin, what was? Jesus said let's go, we've tarried here long enough, and the sinner refused him.

And if it was a sin, then Mary Leader could see it coming. She knew about sin. Why, she'd been dealing with sin all of her life, from sneaking into the movies to letting Sam McGilvray teach her to drive, twenty-five years ago, in exchange for a little fooling around, even though he was married. Took her forever to summon up the courage to confess that one, but she finally did. She took the bus to Charlotte to find a priest she didn't know. "How many times?" the strange priest said. She was lucky; he was a kind person. He wanted her to know that sins were things that you could put a number on, give a name and number and then repudiate the whole shootin' match. Get thee behind me, Satan. Same with despair. She could refuse it. If it was a sin, then it wasn't an inevitable state of being, because Christ would never leave us in sin. She didn't have to live in it. She did not have to stay there.

That was where she could find the urgency. The motive to hold together. That was where it was located. A star on a map, a winking, glittering star, the capital of North Dakota, the mark to live by: Sin. Despair is a sin. The urgency was located right there and nowhere else. If you commit this sin, you betray everything, everybody.

So, don't.

If you drink a bit, drink at home like everyone else. Saturdays at home. Don't you dare collapse.

At the hospital, she could see that sometimes despair and disease got all mingled in the wasted bodies of patients as if one invited the other. There were times it was hard to believe that anyone ever in this world stood up again, took up their pallet and walked. So many of them, they got sick and just laid themselves open to despair. Except for children. Children had done nothing wrong, did not deserve polio or meningitis or broken legs, or those many ugly bruises in secret places where a parent had whacked them with a belt or a strap. When children gave up . . . well, that was a tragedy, that was the parents' sin. Never the children's.

But except for the children, despair seemed to be a threat and temptation with every disease. Some more than others.

She kept thinking a day would come when she'd feel strong again, strong as an animal, unthinkingly at home in the world like she used to be. As unthinking and strong as she was years ago in North Carolina, as she was when she and Jim first bought the resort and worked all day, every day, to keep it going. Someday her strength would return full-bore, every cylinder.

That day just kept on postponing itself. It was true that as the months went by she began to take a little pride, now and then, in managing. She didn't mind those first fall storms one bit; she found out that she loved getting ready for a storm. She warmed to a prediction of foul weather. She loved the blizzards, and she learned to take care of the car in the winter. The darkness of winter was difficult, but once a good snowfall arrived, Pinestead became a whole new world to explore.

And after that afternoon, after that incredible, humiliating feeling of exposure when Chris trespassed into her car that way, she only sipped from the gin bottle when she reached her own driveway. Despite herself, the words he spoke that afternoon often sounded in her head. Friday or Saturday evenings, when everybody in her family was accounted for, that was the only time she let herself sip to the point of nodding off, the delicious oblivion of a nap. That's what she called it—a nap, when she emptied the bottle and her eyelids felt so heavy and the floor rose up to meet her in her back bedroom.

That afternoon in her car above Lake Michigan would never be mentioned between them, might as well never even have happened. Put it in a box, and never open it again. Think of it as if he just happened by and changed a flat tire for her. Something that he just did, because of knowledge that he had. Something a man would do for a woman, that's all. Just exactly like changing a tire or saying, "Lady, your car has vaporlock, gotta let the engine rest." That's what it was. Now forget it.

God forgets things, that priest in Charlotte told her after she confessed about Sam McGilvray.

"Did you know his wife?" he asked.

She waited a while before she whispered, "Yes."

At our best, he told her, we forgive each other, but God, he said, does even better. God forgets it for us. Like it never happened. Absolution is that powerful. That's the only way we can understand it—it's as if God forgets it.

Maybe she and Chris could forget some things. She could forget him climbing into her car.

But she couldn't forget this, him coming into her house when she wasn't home, try as she might. Alex and Sharon needed to get a little closer to adulthood before they—before they faced that kind of thing. She didn't know Chris well enough. And she was so far away, every day, sometimes she didn't even know what village she'd be sent to. She had to have rules.

But the look in Chris's eyes when she told him not to come over when she wasn't home, it was like she'd slapped him, like she'd betrayed him. For crying out loud.

Taking care of five kids by telephone, by making sure that there were carefully prearranged activities for everybody. Making sure that they always, always knew how to reach her. Everywhere she went—and an itinerant nurse in these parts traveled everywhere—she told people: "These are my children's names. If one of them calls me, get me. I'll stop whatever I'm doing to talk to them." She never asked permission anymore, "May I give my children this phone number?" She just did it, every morning. On a sheet by the telephone in the living room. This is where I am today.

Everything depended on control from afar. Knowing what we expect of each other.

And he just shot that down. All by himself, someone she'd been relying on. Too much, apparently, if he thought he could just come in the house, strip naked, hand Alex his filthy clothes, and take a shower!

That remark about the birth defects, his friendship with Jim. What did Jim know that he never told her? What did Jim see in Chris and try to heal?

I have to look out for these kids.

I'm keeping some things out there at bay, and I can't let up. It's like this damn girdle I'm wearing. You have to have standards. I've tried to keep the list short, but we have to have these rules in place. They don't go down to the water when there aren't grown-ups home. They don't let strangers in. They know where I am. They don't go anywhere that's not prearranged.

They don't drink whole milk because, one, it's too fatty and, two, it's too expensive, so I mix up nonfat powder a couple times a week in my mix-a-blend. I have noticed that they don't drink that either, unless it's mixed with Ovaltine or Nestle's. Never mind, we have it in the Frigidaire. And this is how we do it, and no one expects any variation.

Standards. It works. Having standards works. This is how the Leaders do things. Take pride in it.

We have a brand-new dishwasher because it's easier and cleaner. We don't have a TV because they need to do their schoolwork, and I see nothing valuable in those TV shows. Yes, I'm doing my best to keep the world out. Parts of the world. I'm doing my best to show them that you can be selective.

Would someone please, please tell me how I'm doing?

And now this.

I never did know him very well. Maybe it's nothing. Maybe it's just what he said . . . the excitement of following a buck into frigid Lake Michigan. And I'm getting back at Chris now, because he caught me out once. Is that it?

No, that's not it.

Sharon and Alex, thirteen and fourteen, alone in the house with him. Pretty young women who had never in their lives been made uncomfortable by a man, and now this? First time he's come in the house in years. Why hasn't he come in the house before? What are his birth defects? "Leave him be, some men are like that," Jim said. "Some men up here are like that."

Like what?

Did it ever occur to you, Jim, that I could have used a little more information about a few things? Men. And their codes. One word standing in for twenty. Wouldn't it be better to use all twenty words and explain the situation?

Two days later the last and best chicken dinner of the season was held up at Glacier Point Resort. It was now October, and the vacationers had gone. This one was really for the owners and the workers.

Glacier Point had been a luxury full-service resort in the old days. It was three road miles from Pinestead or a one-hour paddle by canoe across two coves. Since moving north, the Leaders had never missed the last chicken dinner of the season. The kids loved the meal: fried chicken as good as Mary's family ever made, home-canned corn and canned green beans with bacon and red pepper, pickles, slaw, mashed potatoes and biscuits and fresh blackberry pies. Just thinking about those pies made Mary's palate tingle.

She had always invited Chris before.

He did odd jobs at two other resorts that she knew of. Maybe they'd ask him.

If she didn't call and invite him, he'd get the message. What message? If she did invite him, was she asking for trouble? Damn you, Jim Leader, what do I do? I liked Chris well enough, and that's my problem, MY problem. I liked him because I was lonely, and his being around here flattered me. I was buying his company and buying only so much of it.

But he didn't stay in his place, damn it. Oh, that sounds terrible. I'm sorry. But my children come first. Sentiment won't save my girls if someone touches them, if they see something they aren't ready for.

She put off the decision. Resentful, she kicked into the next day and the next, and finally it was too late. It was time to paddle up the shore to Glacier Point, and she hadn't asked him.

The weather was balmy this afternoon and the water still, so they paddled across the cove, Mary in the stern and Sean in the bow, and all five of Mary's ducklings before her paddled without stopping. Even Melina with her stubby child's paddle was diligent. A long-overdue, unexpected sense of pride settled about Mary's shoulders as she eased the canoe up onto the sand at Glacier Point, and the kids spilled in several directions.

Mary always liked the atmosphere at this one dinner. When people told stories about crazy renters, she retreated to the edge of the crowd; she didn't like the shrill voices or the laughter, but she did like being with all these people at least once a year, just the same. She was here tonight as a fellow property owner, not a widow, not a woman in a man's world, not someone to look out for, but one of those people whose hard work inspired city folk to come up to Achill and spend money every summer. She bought a family dinner ticket so the food was a bargain, the best you could get outside of a fish fry, and the kids always found friends to play with while she sat on one of the big Adirondack chairs and watched the lake change. And she tried, after the big chicken dinner, to finish at least one piece of pie.

"I'm selling tickets to the Lions Minstrel Show," Asa Tighe from the hardware store said, moving through the line of chairs. Mary shook her head, smiled at him.

"Our big fund-raiser, Mrs. Leader," he persisted.

"Not tonight. I'll get mine later on," she said. Grotesque thing, the Lions Club Minstrel Show, businessmen in blackface acting like country bumpkins. These Northerners didn't know how bad it could be, didn't know what they were playing at. Her own mother never let her go to minstrel shows back home, but when they did catch glimpses, Mary and her sister understood why. The music was fun, but once you start mocking each other that way, anything goes. Anything could happen.

On the other hand, it felt good to be among the Chamber of Commerce types tonight. It felt safer.

"You do good things," she said, "all you Lions. I thank you for that. Get my ticket another time, though."

In the rapidly cooling twilight, she rounded up the kids for the canoe ride home.

"Get you launched?" someone said, rushing down to the shore.

"No, no, we're fine," she insisted, "we're fine," and she pushed out the canoe, stepped in the water and over the stern to her seat. She picked up the paddle and gave it a few strong strokes to get them well clear of the other boats moored there. Then they were out on the still water, Mary and her five well-fed paddlers, and behind her the whole community could see how well they were doing. They were doing okay, they could make this boat move in a straight, powerful line toward home. They were six strong easy paddlers who didn't splash each other or rock the canoe or have to switch sides. They fit the canoe like they were born to it.

About two hundred feet from shore they crossed over the inky stain of the dropoff, where the bottom of the lake had a cliff in it. Dropped straight down. A good lake, this one, for families. You could walk out farther than you'd want to swim, even, before the lake bottom disappeared. With all six of them in the canoe, the freeboard diminished considerably, and they usually hugged the shore, but sometimes on calm evenings Mary sent the canoe back and forth over that line in the water, just for the strange thrill of being above that depth.

Although she couldn't figure out what to do about a number of things, tonight Achill Lake, at least, could tolerate her indecision. Evening would come, and the air would change, the sun would set and the loons call out and the geese pass by overhead on their way from Alaska, and the orange maple leaves would blow into the water, and she'd get another chance to do the right thing. There was time to make decisions.

Each stroke of the paddle tonight was precious and perfect, and her soul yearned for this exercise. This evening at least, they all fit here, this family of hers, the Leaders fit this country. The lake didn't take part in the confusion that people created, she realized. She stopped paddling with that realization, laid the paddle dripping across her knees, and tried to find that truth again: The land is here, waiting for us. It's here waiting.

"What's wrong, Mom?"

Without her J-stroke the canoe had nosed out into the ink. They were yards and yards from the lighter color. She had been watching the canoe drift without even thinking about it.

"Just loving the pretty evening," she said, and dipped the blade into the water, turned her wrist to bring the bow around.

10

Alex smacked the tiled counter with a hot, soapy rag and thought, today I could use an invisibility cloak. Home from Interlochen for the long Columbus Day weekend, she'd see kids from the public high school where she'd suffered two years before Mr. Berry, her history teacher, helped her get the scholarship. How can I see without being seen? she asked herself, going after black lines of mildew with what President Kennedy called vigah. We sure as hell need more vigah around Pinestead. How could Mom stand to let things get this way! Everywhere you looked, signs of neglect.

As always Alex tried to make things nicer around the house. She made Becky clean the upstairs bathroom with diluted ammonia and then vacuum. Alex herself did the downstairs bathroom. Then she set a roast into a marinade of vinegar and used the rolling pin to crush twenty-two gingersnaps for the gravy, following a recipe from a library cookbook. While doing this, she nibbled the edges of about ten more and threw their soggy middles into the trash can, burying them deep in the trash so Mom wouldn't notice and start wailing about the waste of food. Then Alex scrubbed the greasy kitchen till it sparkled. This all took up most of the morning. Sharon was off babysitting. Apparently there was a three-year-old named Heather who thought

Sharon was the greatest person in the world, and the feeling was mutual. Fine.

When it was time to go retrieve Melina and Sean from Saturday-morning catechism class, Mom was deep into her nap, nearly comatose under her bedroom window. Becky had tried to wake her. She shook her mother by the shoulder, lifted and dropped her arms, took off the unzipped sleeping bag that Mom liked to sleep under. She even pried up Mom's eyelids, but got no response. She fetched Alex, and the two girls studied their mother.

"She's faking, she's pulling our leg," Alex said.

"You sure?" said Becky.

Alex thought, is Becky really scared? If this was a game, it had to stop now. Something had to be done immediately. Alex reached down and lifted her mother's skirt. At this assault on her modesty Mary laughed and sat up, grabbed at her skirt, and tucked it underneath her legs. She muttered, "Oh ptssh! Good grief! Can't I take five minutes?"

"It's time to get Mel and Sean," said Alex. "Want me to go?"

"If you like, honey. The car keys are on my desk," Mary said, pulling the sleeping bag back over herself.

A vine from the untrimmed rose bush on the damp side of the house, where shade trees kept the moisture from burning off each day, had snaked under the window frame. A long tendril with thorns on it circled above Mary's pallet. It was amazing, the force of that thing, and kind of hilarious, Alex thought. Everything around here is so uncared for. It would not be difficult to improve things a little.

"Improve!" she said to Becky. "Entropy is setting in!"

"What's that?"

"It's what happens when you don't improve. It's loss of energy."

"You're not cutting my bangs."

"Who said anything about that?"

"You're just not. Can I go now?"

Alex gave her younger sister more careful scrutiny. So Becky was growing out her hair, that's why it looked so much like a folksinger's. Thick and straight, falling just past her shoulder blades. Unstyled, except of course for all of that shampooing, crème-rinsing, and vigorous brushing every day.

Becky was thirteen but looked and acted sixteen. Alex figured that Becky could outrun and outfight her older sister, if it came to that, if she tired of household chores. She just didn't know it yet. Becky wore cut-off jeans that were too tight and a Mexican-style blouse with puffy sleeves. There was a roundness to her that was definitely not childhood plumpness. What was Mom doing about all this, Mom who had never once talked about bras and sanitary napkins with her two oldest daughters?

You'd think a nurse, especially one who'd been married to a doctor, would volunteer some information about these intimate things. Mary would answer any question put to her, but she never volunteered difficult or personal information. Not in the detail you needed.

She once told the oldest girls what happened when she asked her own mother about sex. At twelve years old, having found a copy of *The Sheik*—and keenly aware of Rudolf Valentino, who had appeared in the movie version—she asked her mother, "What is sex?" and their faintly remembered, sugar-loving grandma from North Carolina had whirled on her with a furious response: "Don't ever say that word again!" And at that story, Mary would laugh. The implication was, she wouldn't be that way. Go ahead, kids, ask away.

As if anyone would ask! Ask what, exactly? Mom, why do I feel so uncomfortable, does life ever get easier than this?

There was that one story Mom had hinted at, last year during a driving lesson, but then she changed the subject. Never another word about it.

"I don't want to learn to drive," Alex had complained, hot and frightened after negotiating a left turn in Traverse City.

"I'm teaching you to drive so that someone else doesn't," said Mom. "You don't need some fella saying here, honey, sit behind the wheel, and I'll show you everything there is to do."

"What?" Alex looked at her mother in surprise. Mary didn't meet her eyes.

"Just remember when you make a left turn across traffic, look every which way, but then you can still go after the light starts to turn if you've moved out. So long as you signal your intentions, and the way is clear, it's legal. And safer than backing up."

Mary would rouse herself now to run this errand, in an instant, if Alex insisted. Maybe she'd had a little something to drink, but it didn't seem that way. It was quite possible that she really was deeply fatigued.

Two years ago she'd retrained for half a summer in Ann Arbor to become an emergency room nurse. The past two years, since she'd found fairly regular hours in the Miltonia Hospital emergency room, one place to be all day every day, had been easier on the family. They'd settled into an easier routine, now that Mom was no longer an itinerant public health nurse but could be found up at the hospital, guaranteed, between ten and four every day. But from her occasional horror stories, you knew the work was severe. A boy on a motorcycle got thrown into a tree and actually had a branch go right through him. Amazingly, he lived. It missed his heart and lungs. Mary was a few hours late getting home that night. I guess that's it, Alex sighed, feeling the pleasurable uprush of one more way to be useful, it just wears her out.

"I'm going up to the church to pick up Mel and Sean," she said to Becky and crossed the room to Mom's desk. "Want to come?"

The keys sat on top of a bath towel, spread out over the papers on Mom's desk. The towel covered the wrack and ruin of unsorted paperwork and provided a fresh surface for a new set of letters and bills. Alex picked up the keys and then lifted the edge of the bath towel. Sure enough, a mess of letters, like cake filling, lay underneath, but to her surprise another bath towel lay under those, with more papers and envelopes. And could this be true? There was one more bath towel, atop the paper clutter that lay on the desktop. A layer cake, three towels deep.

"Good God, Mom!" she said aloud, almost tempted to laugh. She thought, I can't help you here! "How can you let this happen?"

"What?" said Becky.

"I'm getting to it," from Mary, her eyes closed again. Returning to her nap but watching her daughters through her shut eyelids.

This was no better than Sean's or Mel's bedrooms which you practically waded across, ankle deep in clothes and parts for things, toys and books and saucers off of which they ate towers of Saltines and peanut butter. Ugh. Sean's room smelled. Sean got away with everything.

"Come on, Becky. Let's go to town, want to?"

"Well. . . ." Becky appeared to be somewhat tempted. She probably longed to be more visible rather than less, but she was not used to Alex as a driver.

"Fun and doom for all!" Alex teased. "We'll get an ice cream. C'mon."

The ice cream may have cinched it, with the promise of increased visibility while waiting in line. A chance for Becky to pose for any eighth-grade boys who might be sauntering down the streets of Miltonia.

They crossed Achill Lake Drive and headed up Hebron, and suddenly, shockingly, this afternoon drive became a delight, more fun than the two girls could have guessed. It was like being hot and sweaty, and then a cool wind blew at you and everything you were made for became clear. You were made for this, Alex thought, to make this big old Mercury station wagon mount the hill, swing left along the ridge over the lake, ride the crest of the landscape.

Even Becky was smiling, and Becky didn't smile much these days, not because she was sad or serious, but because it was uncool to smile. Flat lips were the in thing. Kids and parents betrayed emotion, but not teenagers. For the trip to town Becky had pulled a loose gray sweatshirt, like beatniks wore, over the pretty Mexican blouse. To Alex's mind, she looked kind of awful and yet kind of appealing. When you wear the right thing, you let the world know you're available.

Alex wanted to have fun, too. Are we a team, she wondered—are we in this together? As if testing the atmosphere, she hollered out, "We know how to have fun!"

"Mnh," Becky grunted.

The county road ran along a ridge, and they fell silent, watching the flaming hills, the outcroppings of granite above the lake and the blue water. The view was always changing yet always restoring itself, hitting a familiar note. Light and color moved across the pattern that over the years had inscribed itself in their imaginations: this is beauty, this is our home. Then they turned east and descended into farmland, uneven fields of potatoes, berries, Christmas trees, and scrappy little orchards. They drove through the scrub pine and the woody ravines and past the trailer park toward Miltonia.

On the main street Alex slowed behind a hay truck and stalled the car. Becky winced in embarrassment and slouched down onto her spine. Then they crawled along, as though there was an accident up ahead.

"What's all this traffic, do you suppose?" asked Alex.

"Oh, it's the Lions Club Saturday. I see a banner. You know, they have some booths and games and a minstrel show at the fairground. It's supposed to be a lot of fun."

"Do you know what a minstrel show is?"

"Well, everyone says it's fun. Some kind of music and skits with a musician from Detroit maybe. Can we go to it, Alex?"

For a moment, Becky seemed to show eagerness and emotion. The excitement of driving with her sister instead of her mother had coaxed her to a new place, as it had for Alex.

"I think we're in a traffic jam," said Alex. "Wow. My first ever traffic jam. See, people are pulling into that field to park. It'll be okay up ahead."

"Oh, there's Bernie."

"Who?"

"A boy I know." Becky rolled down the window and pushed out her elbow, increasing the likelihood that she would catch the eye of this Bernie, but she looked straight ahead, so that if he saw her, their eyes would not meet. This action was not lost on Alex, who had never done such a thing herself. Where boys were concerned, Alex never calculated. What would be the point? There was little interest in a plump, serious A student with thick glasses, plain straight skirts, and plaid blouses from the Nifty Thrifty, her thin hair pulled back inside a rubber band. Her favorite teacher, Mr. Berry, had taken an interest in her ideas. But there was never anything between them that was not completely cerebral.

She was friends with Wylie Hoke at Interlochen, but Wylie was different. Almost like a girlfriend. He told Alex that he was applying to New York University so that he could hang out in Greenwich Village. Alex supposed that he would be very peculiar when he grew up. He was very small and liked poetry, though his parents, both of them, were engineers.

She saw Sean and Melina walking up the sidewalk from St. Mary's. Where the heck did they think they were going? Melina kept hiking up her hand-me-down jeans which were too big for her. She'd step on the hems every few feet. Sean was taking potshots at targets in the maple trees with an imaginary gun, walking three feet ahead of Melina and ignoring her. Alex honked and pulled over at the hardware store. They broke into a run toward the car.

"Can we go to the fairgrounds, can we? To see the show?" Melina begged. Her braids, unkempt, frayed, must have been three or four days old. Alex recognized her striped t-shirt as one that Sean was wearing last year.

"That where you guys were going? You were supposed to wait at the church."

"Looking for the car is all," said Sean. "We weren't going anywhere. But let's go to the fairgrounds. Everyone says it's fun, and it's a good cause. The Lions take care of poor people's eyes. Everybody else is going."

Alex looked them over, her brother and sisters, and thought, why not? What is so urgent to get home for? It's now or never. Never back down from a challenge.

After their busy morning she couldn't claim there was urgent work at home. Things were in place for the weekend. A place for everything and everything in its place. Mom claimed that was her motto, which wasn't exactly true for most of the clutter back home, or maybe it was true in a rough-sort kind of way—clothes in laundry baskets, paper clutter on the desk between the bath towels, kids retrieved from catechism class, beef round sitting in its marinade in the Frigidaire. Alex home from Interlochen, Sharon playing with Heather Somebody, and Mom at her nap.

"I guess so, guys." With her words a little excitement hit them all. Maybe we are a team, she thought happily. "Why shouldn't we have a little fun, like country kids come to town for the day?"

"Huh?"

"Well, look at us. We're a bunch of ragamuffins. We look like kids from the boondocks. But we do have a station wagon. We can go anywhere. So let's go to the fairgrounds. Anyone have any money?"

They dug in their pockets, through Alex's purse and the glove compartment, and Sean ran his hand under the car seats. They came up with $2.27, plenty for ice cream.

"Oh, yay," sang Melina, "we're going to the fairgrounds, the fairgrounds!" Becky combed her bangs with the five-cent comb she kept in a back pocket.

The afternoon sun, unshaded over Achill Lake, warmed Mary Leader's skin through her bedroom window. She came half awake from her nap to the sensation of her limbs relaxing into the mattress, and she stared happily at the backs of her sunlit eyelids. A pillow beneath her knees stretched her spine just enough to ease the hot pain in her sacroiliac joint that came and went these days. The kids were accounted for; things were working right. Alex and Sharon were enjoying their independence today, no matter what they called it, she thought. Alex calls it taking care of things, and Sharon calls it getting out of this house, but it's independence. My kids are right on schedule, after all.

She lifted her eyelids and focused on the nearest thing, a dust mote, drifting across her eyeball. She followed it off-screen, and then she found another to follow. The hospital emergency room seemed a million miles away.

This job was better than driving all over creation with the Public Health Department and feeling out of touch with her own kids during the day. Last summer and the summer before she'd spent weeks in Ann Arbor for continuing education, thanks to Grandma and Aunt Tony again, who helped Alex look after things here, and it had all paid off. No question. How could you leave those kids? the other nurses in Ann Arbor would think, staring at her. Her answer, unspoken, was ready: Because my kids can handle it. They're fine. They're smart. They can help look after themselves for a short time.

She remembered that she had promised to do potatoes for Alex's sauerbraten supper. The kids loved mashed potatoes. Melina especially, a mountain of them, with a pool of oleomargarine melting on top.

Mary raised her arm and looked at her watch, let it fall again. It was still early. I'm going to lie here one more hour, she promised herself. One more hour, and then I'll get up. For some reason the things I have to do are all at bay. I can't think of anything nicer, right now, than to have nothing pressing.

And tomorrow we'll go canoeing. Up around Glacier Point to those woods on the north side. Maybe find some morel mushrooms hidden in the duff and twinflowers on the forest floor. The mushrooms were pure flavor. All hers to eat, because no one else but Alex and Melina would even sample them. You never knew what you'd find, down low to the ground. Even the twinflowers surprised her, pink and crisp, tiny as barnacles, each stem with twin bells like a little fairy necklace. She put her face into them and inhaled an astonishing sweet fragrance.

I love my home, she thought. Especially right now, with everyone accounted for and leaving me in peace.

She heard the click of Klondy's toenails on the floor. She opened her hand and held it out in the air, without looking around, and the dog inserted its angular head into her hand for a scratch. The dogs were a lot of trouble, but they kind of filled in the spaces, the empty parts in the family. She was particularly fond of Klondike, since she'd tended him so many times—pulled out nineteen porcupine quills with the pliers once, and stitched his head up after a dogfight. Her finger caressed the scar now. She hadn't done a bad job at all and had saved a bundle on vet bills.

He ventured down to her feet, where he circled a patch of mattress and curled up with a soft groan. She listened to him swipe his muzzle with a big sloppy tongue, and then she drifted back to sleep.

Melina loved shows, and when Sean told her the Lions did a talent show, she took that as a promise for the afternoon. The thought thrilled her. And she even loved the smell of the fairgrounds—tramped grass and dust mixed with a scent like vanilla extract and the smell of horses from a corral where high school girls with expressionless faces rode them in figure eights, then kicked the horses' sides and galloped to the gate.

She followed her sisters and brother to the ice cream. They stopped on the way to peer over a crowd of kids at something called a Duckling Ring Toss. In a large pool, terrified yellow ducklings zigged and zagged to avoid the soft cloth rings coming at them from screaming little boys. All the little kids around the pool stared in amazement. It wasn't often they were encouraged to throw things at ducklings, but you could see those rings didn't hurt. Abruptly Alex yanked Melina away, pulling on her arm.

Melina was eight years old and had written a novel. She called it "An Old Time Girl." It was about a girl named Eliza with long braids, who usually went barefoot but sometimes wore high-button boots, a skirt, and a pinafore and grew up in a small town but then went away to the city in a stagecoach. Melina had even illustrated the book—drawn a picture of Eliza, her heroine, at the bottom of every page. So Melina was a writer. She knew what she was going to be when she grew up. That was settled. Right now she had to choose between cotton candy and ice cream, but Alex insisted that she choose ice cream. Cotton candy cost more, and it wouldn't be fair if Melina got something more expensive, even though she really wanted one of those huge colorful puffs the size of a loaf of bread, inside a paper cone. Her tongue would make wads of it disappear against the roof of her mouth, bathing her whole mouth in sugar. To want something that much was to deserve it, too. But the older kids ignored her. She took her scoop of chocolate ice cream, wanting to cry with disappointment.

The four of them broke up after getting their ice cream. Melina was supposed to follow Alex, but Alex walked right by the canvas hut with a yellow banner over the door that said "Talent Show." Melina went inside, licking the chocolate slowly. Maybe if she hadn't been a little mad at Alex about the cotton candy, and the big kids making her feel ashamed of wanting it so bad, she wouldn't have slipped away.

There were lots of folding chairs, but no one sitting in them. The show was over. The air inside was cooler than outside and seemed to be humming, as if with an activity that had just now stopped. On the stage were six chairs in a semicircle, and a banjo leaned against one of them. As she watched a long, brown hand closed around its neck and a man swung it up. A very tall Negro man, tall and skinny like Mr. Duquesne, who stayed at Pinestead Resort in August. He had on a straw hat and a striped vest.

Some other people in fancy outfits and with faces painted black, with red lips like clowns, were talking and drinking from pop bottles with straws sticking out. One woman with pigtails sticking out all over her head hit a tambourine against her own behind. The banjo player was ducking to go through a curtain at the back of the stage, but he turned back at the sound, said something in a low voice, and hit his banjo. At least it looked like he just hit it, his curved hand went against it, but what Melina heard was a rattle of sounds like a whole bunch of dice or candy rolling out along a floor. She walked up the aisle.

The banjo player went through the curtain and down the steps and out the back door. She followed him. It was exciting to be next to performers, dressed up and kind of sweaty even through the ugly paint, although Melina had never liked clowns. They always seemed to be too pushy, wanted you to share their mood or you'd be called a bad sport.

Outside, behind the building, they all kind of fanned out and wandered in separate ways. The banjo player hiked the banjo around his shoulder so it rode on his back like a backpack and headed toward a nearby water fountain and a spigot. He bent over the spigot and splashed water on his face.

Melina stopped walking, stunned by the pleasure of watching his long, angular hands so neatly and perfectly cup his face. She liked to draw things that struck her fancy like that—pick up a pencil and copy what she saw, and she wanted to draw his hands, right then, holding his face that way.

He filled his hands again. This time his straw hat slid off. It hit the ground on an edge and skittered a little with a gust of wind. The banjo player finished washing his face, shook his hands, and studied the runaway hat like it was a bad dog. Melina went after it and picked it up. It was made of straw coated with something, and it was surprisingly dirty inside. She handed it to him.

He smiled and nodded. Gray hair hugged his head like grains of sand.

"Kind of you," he said. "Got a little chocolate round here," and he circled his own mouth with a long finger.

Melina took his place at the spigot and rinsed her face.

"Ice cream is sure a temptation," he said. He held the hat out and looked at it, then crammed it back on his head. He headed off toward the edge of the fairground.

"The ice cream's this way," Melina called.

He turned.

"Have to pass for now," he said. "I ain't been paid yet. You like the show?"

"I didn't see it. I came too late."

He studied her. "That right?"

"We always come too late."

He smiled, a big smile, like he was laughing at something, but not at her. Then he slipped the banjo on its strap around to his chest and hit it again. The music rolled out from his clenched hand. "Late she came, my little girl," he sang. "She always came too late." He made a song out of something she said, just like that. Melina put her hands to her mouth.

"Look how you staring at me," he said. "Like you can't believe I exist. You never see a banjo before?"

"No."

"Well, I'll work up that song in your honor. That's gonna be a good little song." He looked around, at people milling beyond the Quonset hut. "Here's another one that we do." He turned a couple of the pegs that stuck out from the neck and started to play.

"The fox went out on a chilly night, prayed to the moon to give him light . . ."

The twanging notes, like ringing bells, were metallic and pretty but soft enough so that Melina could hear the words to his song, and it was not a hard song to understand. A brave fox stole a gray goose from a farmer and took it home to his family. She watched his left hand go up and down the neck of the banjo. She had never seen fingers move like that, cover such a distance so fast.

"Daddy, Daddy better go back agin, 'cause it must be a mighty fine town-oh, " he sang. "Like that one?"

"Oh yes," she said.

"Your daddy here today?"

"My daddy died, but my mom's a 'mergency-room nurse." That was her standard answer. Kids always asked each other, what does your dad do? If your dad was dead, you still had to answer the question.

He stopped smiling.

"I'm sorry to hear that."

"Oh, it's all right. I never knew him, I was only two."

"Ah." He nodded. "So you'd sing it this way, maybe. 'Momma, Momma better go back agin, 'cause it must be a mighty fine town-oh.'"

"I like it the first way."

"Yeah. Why not? It's a good song. The thief gets away, and the town people, well, they jus' get stuck! Too bad, the gray goose is gone." He chuckled. His lips were very dark, almost bluish. "Here's a last verse." He started playing again: "The fox and his wife, without any strife, cut up the goose with a fork and a knife. They never had such a supper in their life and the little ones chewed on the bones-o, bones-o, bones-o . . ."

Melina walked closer to stare at his hands. His brown thumb, hanging on the top string, was as long as a finger, and it moved like it had a life of its own. It waved and wagged around the top string.

He watched her watching his fingers and chuckled. "You can't get enough of this banjo, looks like. Man I could chew on some bones-o right now," he said. "Young lady, I need to go and get me my supper out of my truck." He was taking a few steps back, even as she walked closer. "Get hooked on banjo tunes, and you'll be sorry," he said and chuckled again. Then he looked up, and his face changed. He stopped smiling and reached up a hand to his hat and smashed it down further on his head.

"Melina!" A hand came down on Melina's shoulder. It was Alex's.

"Find our missing girl?" That voice came from a heavy old man who was with Alex. He wore a bright yellow Lions vest with a Lions hat on his head. The Lions were grown men, but they wore hats like paper boats, covered with trinkets. The banjo player was stepping back, nodding, and he hiked his banjo over his shoulder again.

"How you all doing," he said.

"Hello," Alex said. "Mel, why'd you wander off?"

The banjo player bowed to them, as if he had been playing a concert, still stepping backward. "Gonna make myself invisible. Lunchtime for me," he said.

"Goodbye," Melina called.

He didn't answer, but turned and walked toward the edge of the field and the row of dusty cars and trucks parked there.

"Guess we missed the music," said Alex. She turned to the Lion. "Thank you, everything's okay. This girl wanders."

"He played me a song," said Melina.

"They play again tonight," said the Lion. "Best place to watch 'em is in the auditorium. Don't ever chase after these buck niggers, they're used to a rough kind of life. See a buck nigger, you go the other way fast."

Alex reached down and took Melina's hand and held it tight. "Everything's okay."

The Lion's words shocked Melina. She thought about the banjo player's huge hands. They were like shovels, brown, rusty, strong shovels. But they skittered over the banjo strings in a way you couldn't even see. How did he do that?

"We'll go now," said Alex. The Lion was looking in the direction of the banjo player. "Really," said Alex. "She loves music. We're okay now. There was never a problem."

The Lion's gut was huge and hard-looking, almost square. Alex was frowning and tense. Melina could tell she wanted to leave.

"I really want to go to that show," Melina said to Alex, pulling at her hand.

"You wouldn't like it. It's dumb. We can hear some real folk music at Interlochen sometime."

"Why is it dumb?" They were walking fast, away from the canvas building and the banner.

"It's old-fashioned. They make fun of people, they try to get people to laugh at each other. Like what he said. We don't ever talk like that."

Melina trusted Alex, Alex knew what she was talking about. But she hadn't heard the banjo player.

All the way home Alex's heart pounded. The annoyance of losing Melina had turned into something scary, unpleasant, when that Lion got involved. The second she said, "I can't find my little sister," he swung into action, came racing out from the booth to help her. She wouldn't even have asked for help, Melina wasn't gone that long, but when Alex walked by a booth and saw the words "Lost and Found," she jumped at the chance to get help. It was silly. Why had she given up so fast?

You could invite trouble by asking for help too soon, from someone like this. It made her feel uneasy. And it was impossible to explain, especially to someone as little as Melina. There really was something out there that Mom tried to protect them from, something ugly and hurtful, that was just as likely to come from a Lion as from a traveling banjo player.

She remembered the deer that Chris Olivet had shot and left in his truck. To think that had shocked her once—she was fine with it now. What's a dead deer? They're everywhere, during hunting season. You get used to things. She'd get used to this. Even Melina, sadly, would get used to this, to ugly speech like she'd heard just now. Oh, this town. To think they could have grown up in Chicago.

Into Alex's confusion came a triumph. The sauerbraten was a success. Gingery gravy and vinegar and the tender meat, falling apart with a fork, were impossible to stop eating. To Alex's surprise, and possibly her horror, the six of them ate every bite. They couldn't stop dredging the tender shreds in the pungent sauce. They hardly talked, just oohed and aahed and crammed it in, until the platter was empty. Usually mashed potatoes were the big hit, and the roasts were on the dry side, but this one was like candy.

"Wow," said Sean.

"Geez, this is good," said Sharon.

"Oh, Alex, you have to make this one again," said Mom.

Alex wasn't sure. She was pleased, but it surprised her to see everyone—herself included, to be fair—acting like hogs at a pie-eating contest. Why couldn't they all eat with a little more restraint? She almost felt more comfortable when things weren't going well, when they all bickered, but the only thing wrong with this meal was that it ran out—they ate every bite and sat around groaning with pleasure like after Thanksgiving dinner. There were supposed to be leftovers for Sunday. Looks like we have to start all over again tomorrow. Why can't this family make any progress? she wondered.

When it was time to do the dishes, Melina's turn tonight, she'd disappeared again. Of course. Ran off on purpose, upstairs drawing or reading, inside her daydreams again, as though dirty dishes didn't exist if you just turned your back on them. And it really was for sure her turn, because everyone else had already done their part today. Someone would have to go find her. Drag her downstairs. Alex looked across the table at her mother, who cocked her head and smiled.

"How was your day?" Mom asked.

"Oh, good enough," Alex responded automatically. Immediately after she spoke she thought, or should I tell Mom everything that happened? How I lost Mel, that banjo player with the lonely-looking eyes, that creep in the Lions vest? Who would ruin someone's nice day by bringing up any of this? It's not like she could do anything about it. Hard enough to get a peaceful moment. "How was your day, Mom?"

"Just grand. Lordy, what a meal. Thank you, honey." Mary picked herself up and looked in the kitchen, where someone had stacked the plates. "Whose turn is it tonight? Time to get this organized."

Alex swiveled in her chair and looked out at the lake, turning dark under a cloudy sky. After all her own hard work she deserved a few minutes between activities, for what it was worth. She looked at the water and the changing leaves, some already gold and red and butterscotch. She dared the lake to cast its spell, to change her mood, to make it all worthwhile, as Mom sometimes said.

11

Mary gently supported the girl's shoulders as heaves convulsed her again, and this time, after five hideous deep spasms, a spoonful of green bile came up. The seventeen-year-old had survived half a bottle of sleeping pills but almost succumbed to dehydration and exhaustion. The IV would restore her and give her some rest. Mary helped her lie back down and washed the stains from her face. Why didn't someone see this coming? What was her mom doing with those pills in the cupboard anyway?

"I didn't think she was serious," the mother, her face battered with terror, repeated to Mary and Dr. Bodamer. "Kids say these things."

Then pay attention, Mary thought. If she says something, don't ignore her! Dr. Bodamer nodded and grunted. Mary wanted him to say a few more words; never dismiss a suicide threat, she'd been taught. Was he going to say nothing more?

The suicide attempt was followed shortly by a motorcycle crash. The teenage driver's girlfriend, wearing their one helmet, had broken her collarbone and lost skin along one arm, but her whimpers and moans had a healthy, petulant sound. The boy, just sixteen, was in a coma. The fathers of these two victims came to blows in the parking lot, each blaming the other's child, and state troopers arrived to break up the fight. Before they moved him up to ICU, Mary brought a cup of coffee to the boy's mother, who sat rigid and silent at his bed, hunched like a small dark bird, her eyes not leaving his face. You could hear the girlfriend's mother out in the hall for a cigarette, mumbling, "Oh my God, oh my God." Her noises angered Mary. The smoking and fussing made this accident seem all drama and inconvenience, not the life-changing blow it could well be for the other set of parents. Who knew when this young man would wake up, if ever?

Mary came out of the boy's cubicle and stopped the girl's mother where she paraded up and down the hall, hacking and wailing. "Come, let's stay with your daughter, just stay with your daughter," Mary said, directing her back to the girl's bedside with a firm arm. "You need to hold her hand for a bit." What she didn't say was what she thought: let this change your life.

An hour later, it was peaceful again. No gunshots this week. The month of May was light for gunshot wounds. But come summer, and then hunting season . . . That was one interesting thing about Chris Olivet, his bowhunting. He didn't even own a gun. Why not? she had asked him once, after that time with the deer. He'd come to Pinestead to clean the cistern and replace rotting boards above the foundation. He said he was going bowhunting again. That's when she asked him, just to talk a little more and move past the recent tension and distance between the two of them. Since that afternoon with the deer. He did odd jobs, but they weren't so close anymore.

"Why not a gun?" she asked.

He was silent for a long time. Maybe she'd overstepped, and he was not going to answer. But finally he said, "I tried to figure out why. Sometimes I . . ."

"What?"

"I can't see hurting myself with a bow and arrow. It'd be almost impossible."

She stared. "Hurting yourself?"

"You're out hunting, it doesn't take much of a mistake."

"I can't imagine you being careless," she said. "One thing I can't imagine anyone saying about you—careless."

"Oh," he shook his head and chuckled. "I reckon not, no, they don't say that. I used to have guns, but then I found bowhunting suits me. Not for any clean or spiritual reason, not to be closer to the ancestors or that. It just suits me."

What did that mean? Whose ancestors?

"MARY LEADER TO ER, PLEASE."

The first resorter's accident of the summer of 1963 greeted her: a little boy's bleeding hand and vigorous, outraged screams because a squirrel had bitten him. He had trapped it and caged it the night his family arrived at the lake from Chicago. This afternoon he had tried to put a leash on it, to walk it like a dog.

No need to lecture him. He had found out on his own: wild animals are not pets. Whether he'd respect them or hate them from now on, who could say, but he sure wouldn't try this again. What a relief to have a bloody hand and embarrassed child to deal with, rather than a teenager's suicide attempt or near-fatal crash. I love it when they aren't going to die, Mary thought.

Melina liked it when Mom's friend Miriam Huley came up for a week in July. The bigger kids liked it too, she could tell. Having two grown-ups in the house instead of one made them all behave better. Sean and Alex didn't quarrel, and Sharon didn't find excuses to head to her room, where she could barricade the door and read in peace for hours. A grown-up world with two people in it made everyone nicer.

Every afternoon Miriam put on a black swimsuit with a skirt and a turquoise blue bathing cap, made of petals. She took ten minutes to get waist deep, and then she walked up and down between the raft and the house. Melina swam near her and reached over to pet the odd bathing cap. She wanted to feel those petals flat against her palm.

“Why do you need this?” she asked Miriam. “No one else wears one.”

“Believe you me, my hair don’t need to go swimmin’!” Miriam said.

But they never saw her swim. She just walked slowly through the water, and on the hottest day she bent her knees and dipped in as far as her neck, then stood up with a shrill “Whoooo, my!” She never even dunked her head.

Mom used to work with Miriam in Chicago, and this was her second visit to Pinestead. She stayed in the downstairs bedroom next to Mom’s, and Melina moved into Sharon’s room, Becky into Alex’s. Melina liked sleeping on a cot mattress next to Sharon. Sharon told her about her latest book, the story of a prospector’s daughter in Alaska. Sometimes Melina would reach up her hand, and Sharon agreed to hold it while she talked, and her long, calm, detailed story about chasing gold strikes across Alaska would put Melina to sleep.

They all went blueberry picking at a farm, and Miriam made pies, four to eat and eight for the freezer. She made cottage ham, greens and grits with red-eye gravy, and Mom’s favorite, bread pudding with a thick sauce that had whiskey in it. In the afternoon Mom and Miriam would walk up the length of the property to the north, in the shade of all the maples and beech trees, then go swimming, though Miriam just did her walking up and down while Mom put on flippers and swam the length of the property. Later Mom would say, “You need to keep your legs elevated, Miriam,” and fetch her one of the wicker hassocks to use on the porch and a beer-and-lemonade shandy. They sat together and made jokes about being in their forties.

“The season of mist and mellow fruitfulness,” Mom said.

“Is that what it is,” said Miriam, with a laugh.

Sometimes they talked about Chicago.

“You did the right thing leavin’, Mary,” Miriam said. “Who’d have thought things could get so much worse? I’ll be in Gran’ Rapids next year with my grandkids. One more year at the hospital, and I’ll have enough of a pension to start over.”

“How bad you think it will get?”

“Mary, the cat’s out of the bag. You can’t put this anger away. People say we need to take it slow? Who they talkin’ to? Not to me, and not fo’ me. Oh, I could weep. There ain’t gonna be any progress till we convince folks we mean it this time. Maybe the time has come around. I hope so anyway, and I'm glad of it. In my own way."

This was something urgent and exciting, and Melina liked sitting nearby with her own lemonade and listening.

She liked showing off for Miriam, too—showing off her drawings and her writing and her brand-new-this-summer somersault dive off the raft. Even though Becky was the best at diving and waterskiing, and Becky liked showing off too, there was still plenty of Miriam's attention to go around. What she gave to Becky and Sharon and Alex didn't mean less for Melina. Or Sean.

They were sorry when she left. Things felt kind of flat, but then Marty Fleck from next door—up the lake half a mile—came down in his Chris Craft to see if anyone wanted to waterski. He did this twice a summer, at least. Marty was eighteen, thin and bronze and handsome and nice to all of the Leaders. He was the youngest child in a big rich family and the only one to spend the whole summer at the lake anymore with his parents. Mom thought he was a little lonely, and she always made a fuss over him. And Sharon especially acted different around Marty. She turned all happy and kind of even-tempered, able to accept whatever was going on, even more than usual. She changed when Marty showed up at Pinestead—whatever she was doing, she calmed down and started smiling and getting playful.

But she wouldn't waterski, even to show off for him. Becky and Sean were the waterskiers. Alex tried, she liked the thrill of it, but Melina and Sharon had little interest. They were content with being able to stand up on skis, and once they'd achieved that milestone they were done. Sharon preferred riding in the front seat of the Chris Craft with Marty to waterskiing, sitting near him on the red leather seat while he turned the steering wheel at that amazing dashboard covered with silver-rimmed dials just like a car's. Melina sat up there with them, while Alex and Sean and Becky took turns spotting the skier from the rear seat. Riding in the Chris Craft was a lot like riding in a car on water.

Alex wasn't very athletic, but she said they should all get better at waterskiing, so she was often ready to use their own boat and the 18-horsepower Johnson Sea Horse on still days, days the lake was a mirror. Mom called them "glass-blue days." They were all very careful, for some reason, not to pester Marty to use the Chris Craft. It always had to come from him, the invitation. That was like an unspoken rule.

It was on a glass-blue day in August when Becky got hurt.

Mary took another sip of beer and set the glass on the little metal tray under her ironing board and turned back to the mangle. She had to laugh as she always did with this particular chore. Beautifully pressed sheets were so nice, she just loved a tall stack of them in the cupboard, but it was hard to find the time. How the mighty have fallen, she thought. I used to be at the front counter of the Bee Laundry, now I'm at the mangle. But thank God I'm on my own porch, looking through the screen at my own woods. The little metal tray under the ironing board next to the mangle was meant to hold a bottle of water with a salt shaker head, for damping the clothes. But she always kept a glass of beer there. Anyone mangling sheets on a hot still Saturday gets a beer. That's my rule, she thought.

She couldn't see the lake from this porch, but she could hear the Sea Horse rising to power then dying down when the waterskier couldn't get upright. Alex and Sharon were helping the others get a little practice, along with two boys from one of the guest cottages. Becky had just trotted past the porch, on her way to the water, carrying a towel and wearing an open blouse over her new two-piece bathing suit. She looked beautiful, but with her stomach bare, she was acting shy. Years of running around all summer in a bathing suit hadn't prepared her for turning fifteen and finding herself an object of a new and almost unbearable kind of attention. I'm going to check on all of them in a second, Mary told herself. All the sounds of the day seemed to be dropping into a still and beautiful place, like a sound mosaic: the cries of the kids out on the water, the birds, the meditative hum of this mangle, the outboard.

Becky tossed her shirt onto the grass and walked out on the dock. From the boat Alex watched her sister and thought she seemed a little less devil-may-care than usual. Not used to being in a two-piece. Sean was in the water on skis, Sharon and two boys from one of the cottages in the stern of the boat. Alex watched Becky, but her own thoughts left the scene and returned again to that choice she had to make. Three colleges wanted her, with scholarships: which one to select? Seattle University, Marquette, the University of Detroit? Somehow the latter didn't appeal, despite being closest to home. Maybe because of being close to home. She'd keep on helping out. She'd be home every holiday. She'd roast the Thanksgiving turkey. Almost a full ride, Detroit offered, but Mom said not to worry about that. Mom said, you choose. Wherever you want to go. And Uncle Nat said Seattle was beautiful. Mom said you go right ahead and make your own choice.

But she always talked like that. What did she really want? What was the right thing to do?

Becky dove in and started swimming out to the boat. She was eager to get submerged, Alex thought, to hide in the water. She was doing an underwater breast stroke out toward Sean.

Well, I've been at Interlochen for two years, I reckon everyone here can get along without me, Alex told herself. It's Sharon's turn to run things. Sharon gazed out at the water, waiting for Sean's signal to put the boat in gear and roar out to deeper water, a slightly vague expression on her face which probably meant she was hoping Marty Fleck would show up today. Or that they could zoom by his house and wave. Sharon had on a white swimsuit with a shirred front; she wouldn't wear a two-piece to save her life, nor would Alex, not in a million years. Becky had an athlete's body. She could get away with it.

The boys in the stern were eager to get going.

"Can I start the boat this time?" one of them begged.

"Hmm?" said Sharon.

Where was Becky? Alex leaned out over the water. Sean gave a thumbs-up; he was ready. Becky was still underwater. Alex and Sharon did not give the go-ahead. They would never have done that without knowing where Becky was, but Becky was swimming underwater and didn't know the strength of her own arms.

"Can I do it?" the boy who pressed against Sharon repeated, and without waiting for an answer, as the boat washed closer to shore in the wake of another passing motorboat, his arm shot out, and he pushed hard on the little red gearshift. The motor roared, and the boat leaped backward.

Becky had just turned her face away from danger in that second. The propeller blade sliced her upper back, and blood flooded the water. The girls in the boat screamed and cut the motor.

Becky kept going, back toward the dock. Moving her arms as though nothing had happened. Alex leaped out and splashed after her, crying out, "Oh, Beck, Beck, oh honey," and she swam through the redness in the water to her sister. Becky's mouth was wide in shock, her eyes bulging. Alex tried to push her forward. Then Mom was there, running out on the dock, jumping right into the water in her clothes. Mom and Alex helped Becky up the short wooden ladder, and she collapsed to her knees on the dock. The top of her sliced two-piece fell onto her knees. With her right arm, she covered her breasts.

Mary looked at pink stripes of muscle and Becky's ribs, before the wound pooled up again with blood.

"Alex, on the side porch are clean sheets in a stack, bring me a couple," she said. "Lie down, Becky, let me look at this."

It was almost star-shaped, the wound, clean from the water, but with the blood rapidly pooling and filling the wound again.

"Mom, am I going to die?" Becky gasped.

"No, you're only going to need stitches, sweetie."

"Am I bleeding to death?"

"No, the stitches are to help the skin heal, not to keep the blood in." Mary looked up at Alex who was running back down the dock with a stack of sheets. She wrapped Becky's chest in the sheet and called out to the kids behind her, "No more boating today. Get the boat up. Becky's going to be fine, we're going to the hospital. Sharon, you are in charge."

Alex heard her mother speaking as calmly as if Becky were someone else's child, and she thought that was a good sign. She tried to follow suit. And it turned out that Becky could actually walk, but halfway down the dock she suddenly cried, hoarsely, "It almost got my face! What if I hadn't turned my head!" and she threw up right there at her feet. The strain of vomiting made her scream with pain.

Mary looked at the mess, and her face stayed calm.

"No blood in the vomit and a good loud scream," she said. "Music to my ears. Can you keep walking, honey?"

Then they were in the car, and Alex held Becky in the backseat, while Melina, pointlessly, cried out, "Can I come?" and Mom said, "Yes, get in."

"Mom, I don't know how this happened," Alex cried with her arms around Becky as the car bounced up the driveway and Becky crouched in her lap.

"I should have been there," said Mary, and then they all fell silent as the car approached an unexpected barrier. In front of them, blocking access to Achill Drive, was a huge, brown heap of something, three or four feet high, across the driveway.

Mary stopped the car, and she and Melina got out and ran forward. It was strange, soft, oddly familiar stuff. Mary put her face close.

"What is it, Mom?"

"It's—it's, well, it's manure. Fertilizer."

There was no way they could get around it.

"Alex! Run back to the house and call the operator, have her send an ambulance." She took Alex's place in the backseat, holding Becky, who cried out in pain as Alex moved.

The sheets were only staining, they were not sodden. She touched her fingers to Becky's neck to take her pulse. Becky moaned. "Oh, Mom!"

"I know, honey."

Alex ran back with the other kids. Sean walked around the heap of manure and came to Mary with his fists clenched, his eyes wild.

"Mom," he said, in a strangled voice as if his own lungs were punctured.

"It's going to be all right," she said. "Go on out to the hard road and be there to wave to the ambulance, would you?"

All four of the kids were up on Achill Drive, looking for the ambulance, when a truck slowly came toward them with four teenage boys in the cab.

"What are they looking at!" cried Sean.

"Maybe they did it," Alex said, suddenly certain. No maybes about it. "Get their license plate, Sean!"

The truck speeded up as it came near, then kicked into a high speed and almost roared by.

They almost didn't hear what the boys in the truck shouted out at them, as they hurled something out the truck window, a brown bag that hit the swinging wooden sign with carved pine trees. The bag fell to the ground, split open. The boys in the truck shouted again: Nigger lovers! Leaders are nigger lovers!

"They don't come any dumber!" Alex roared, hopelessly, walking after the rapidly disappearing truck.

"1072DT," Sean cried. "That's the license. 1072DT."

The bag had been full of rotten black bananas, which now made a pulpy mess around their sign.

Dr. Bodamer put twenty-seven stitches in a star pattern over Becky's ribs and confirmed Mary's hopes: nicked ribs, yes, but no punctured lung.

"Accidents DO NOT just happen," Mary always told the kids. But this one—whose fault was it? Her own, surely, and that little brat who grabbed the gearshift. Not Alex's or Sharon's. Her own. She was supposed to have the big picture. The big picture was her job; instead she was mangling sheets on the back porch. Out of sight of the lake. With a glass of beer.

When Becky was stitched up and sleeping, she called Dean Holbus.

"Dean, Becky's okay, and there's manure across the driveway," she blurted, astonishing herself. A huge hot fist of emotion rammed up in her chest, and she nearly broke into tears.

"Mary, Mary, start at the beginning."

She told him the whole story.

"Oh sweet Jesus, haven't I—oh Mary," he began. Then he was silent.

"Haven't you what?"

"First thing, let's get your place cleaned up," he said.

"I think Mr. Wilgosch can actually use it, maybe he'd help me clear it out," she said. "I gave the license number to the troopers."

"Mary, these wild kids, they're not worth the anguish," he said.

What was he trying to say? Shrug it off?

"You weren't stuck behind a pile of manure with an injured child, Dean."

"Let's think about your business. Let's bring those boys in and talk to them. What do you say?"

"Just a minute, Dean." Mary swung the phone down to her side, pressed it into her leg, and took a deep breath. She blew it out with pursed lips like a woman in labor. Something strange was happening. She was about to cry over the phone to the wrong man entirely. Hell, any man would be the wrong man because she shouldn't be crying. If she cried she'd lose her anger, the only thing that was keeping her upright.

"I'm going to call Mr. Wilgosch," she told Dean.

"I'll call him, Mary. Then I'll come on over and get you. I'll bring you home. We'll get this cleared up and those youngsters hauled in. Mary, there's going to be some mighty sorry kids tonight, you'll see. Now you stay calm, and we'll get this figured out."

"Dean, I'm mad as hell. This is beyond a prank. Anyone who would subject my kids to this kind of low, disgusting—and dangerous—words fail me!"

"I'll be up there in one shake. Wait for me."

Anger wasn't much better than tears. There was so much anger back there, if she let it go there'd be no stopping it. The fury back there could ruin everything.

Dean Holbus drove a quiet, powerful Oldsmobile, just like Mr. Duquesne. When they got back to Pinestead, Mr. Wilgosch's truck was parked on the shoulder. Mr. Wilgosch, Sean, and that handsome Fleck boy were pitchforking manure into the bed. Marty Fleck had his shirt off in the boiling heat.

"What an ill wind," said Mr. Wilgosch, after he asked about Becky.

"I sure appreciate you doing this," she said. "I'm bringing you all some lemonade."

"Now Mary," said Mr. Wilgosch, "you don't need to bother about us."

"Well I do, and I certainly will." She walked toward the house, and Dean Holbus kept pace with her.

"There's no excuse for this juvenile vandalism," he said. "But now, let's be practical. About the state troopers. Mary, you need to know about the folks around here. When it comes to our kids, we got to think twice about how far to take things. Folks tend to be rough about kids but also to cut them slack, too, let them be kids. Let them be teenagers. Let the parents handle some things. Do you know what I am trying to say?"

"Dean, don't I know the people around here well as you do? Don't I take care of their cracked-up bodies in the ER at Miltonia Hospital? I know them plenty well. How could I not? I come from a place like this one. I didn't grow up in Chicago. But I need to show my own kids—there's something I need to do for them, show them we don't take this lying down."

"What do you mean, Mary?"

"I mean my kids are going to have to get out in the world and cope with it when they're older, so they need to know what's acceptable and what's not; they need—they need to see a line drawn, that no one can rightly treat them so bad. That's what I mean. They need to know the law is on their side."

"Mary . . . I feel a certain responsibility here. We been friends for a long time. Since when was it, late 40s, you first come here? There is nothing to be gained by letting something like this beat you. Take over your life. Don't let this poison things."

She stared at him.

"What exactly do you mean?"

"Act in calm."

"Anger's all I have going for me right now."

"Mary, that's not true."

If Jim was here, is this what he would advise? Take this ugly thing in stride? Do men really know something about the world I don't?

"Act in calm is good advice, Dean. Sure I'll do that. We need to talk to those kids. Then we'll see."

"If, when, the troopers call you back, you call me, okay? You aren't alone, Mary."

"All right, I'm not alone. No, that's not true, I am so alone."

"This time you're not."

"There's no manure in *your* driveway."

Dean Holbus sighed and nodded. He'd said his piece. Any sensible person would listen. Cut the kids some slack. It wasn't their fault that Becky needed twenty-seven stitches and a night in the hospital. Whose fault was that?

It's my fault, Alex thought. She would never forgive herself for this. It was the worst day of her life. Something like out of a Faulkner story, those kids with the manure and the bananas. That story where a man named Snopes smears manure on a rich lady's rug. That kind of thing. On top of what she herself had caused, taking her eyes off the kids in the water and the kids at the outboard, letting that happen to Becky. What if the blade had sliced her face?

"It's not your fault," Mom had said. "It is absolutely not." But I was daydreaming. Wondering what Seattle might be like. Theodore Roethke taught in Seattle, but he had just died. He read his poems at Interlochen once. She thought it would be wonderful to be his student in Seattle or at least to hear him read again. But he died.

Sharon kept crying, she couldn't stop. She said it was her fault. Alex said no, no, no. They both felt better when Mom drove them to the hospital after supper and Becky was wide awake and looking perfectly healthy, except for the massive bandage on her back and the IV drip in her arm. Becky wanted to hear everyone's version of the story, because she couldn't remember too much herself.

"Oh God, did my bathing suit come off?" she whispered and rolled her blue eyes.

Later that night a trooper brought the boy who drove the truck and his father to Pinestead. Mary stood in the open door. She did not invite them in. Dean Holbus had come over a few minutes earlier. He stood behind her shoulder and wanted to talk to the police, but she wouldn't move out of his way. The trooper and the boy, Douglas Hatch Jr., and his wooden-faced father, Douglas Sr., small and round in painter's overalls, stood on the step under the pale yellow lightbulb which called insects out of the darkness. They all kept brushing moths and flying spiders from their bare arms. The men did it with calm and resignation. The boy kept staring at the insects and staring at Mary as though she was crazy.

Her own kids were massed right behind her with Dean Holbus.

"Your prank endangered the health of an injured girl who needed to get to the hospital," the trooper was saying.

"Now, that's hardly my fault," the boy said.

"Say what, boy?"

"I didn't know someone was gonna swim into a prop. I wouldn'ta wanted that. How can you blame me for that?"

"Hey," the trooper said, and "Damn it," the father added, but Mary interrupted them. She spoke loudly; she wanted her kids to hear.

"I do not have time for a discussion," said Mary. "I do not have to tell you about the stupid, cruel thing you did today. But one thing you need to take away tonight, and that is to keep your foul mouth and cow manure and your truck and your friends away from this property. Turns out that we don't mind being able to share a little extra fertilizer with our neighbors. But if you want to make a delivery again, you call first and make an appointment with the farmer next door and make sure he actually has some use for the stuff."

She heard a snicker behind her. The boy shifted and scratched his sleeve.

"Douglas," said his father.

"Wan't my idea, in the first place," said Douglas Hatch Jr.

"Boy, this is your last chance with me," said the trooper. "I hear a proper apology, or you're heading to court."

"What the hell you talking like that for?" Douglas Hatch Sr. said to his son, speaking over the trooper. "Miz Leader, we'll pay for what damages there is."

"I do think you should make amends," Mary said. "But not to me. We don't need anything from you. No damages here. Your prank didn't damage one thing around here." Wade into a pit with these characters, how do you keep yourself clean and sane? Pull out, pull up, she told herself. Take this conversation somewhere else.

"You see these boys drivin' by, even drivin' down Achill Drive, you call me anytime," said the trooper. "They ain't usin' that road again for a long time."

"I won't bother ya," said the boy.

"Get your mouth in proper gear," said the trooper, "this minute."

The three adults stared at him and waited.

After a few seconds the boy said, sounding strangled, "I regret what we did, Mrs. Leader, and I want to do that, to make amends."

"Then keep your distance. And for the love of God, read something about the people you insulted today. Because it's not just me you owe amends to."

"Maybe yer daughter that got hurt? Yer guests here?"

"For the love of God. You really need me to spell it out? Black and white, we all live in the state of Michigan together. You do not own the place."

"Now listen, ma'am," said Douglas Hatch Sr. "We ain't prejudiced, but we each have a right to our opinions. What my son did was vandalism of private property, and for that we apologize."

"And he wants to make amends," Mary said.

Dean tapped her shoulder. She ignored him.

"Mary, your business," he murmured. "Life goes on."

"So my suggestion for amends is this," she said. "Figure out another way of looking at things. Learn to walk in another person's shoes. Read a damned book once in a while! You can read as well as anyone else. You don't need permission to educate yourself. Read a book about your country, Douglas Hatch Jr. And don't come around here again. Not ever."

No one spoke.

"Douglas?" said his father finally.

"Yes ma'am." Rehearsed words. "Thank you for yer, for yer—thanks for talkin' to us."

"Good night," said Mary.

When she turned back to her family, the first thing she saw was that knot between Sean's eyebrows, that tortured look. He was gripping his own upper arms. Hugging himself.

"Well now, how did we do?" she said, feeling oddly relieved, even spirited, but for that look on Sean's face. She had found something to believe in again. She had found a sense of purpose. Something bigger than what had happened. She could explain to them. Even to Sean, in time.

"But Mom," said Sean. "You have nothing to back it up with."

Dean Holbus put a hand on Sean's shoulder.

"But Sean, I do. We do. We are right about this. And it's a good feeling to know that you are right." She needed to hold someone. She wrapped her arms around Melina and lifted her off her feet. Ten years old, not a baby anymore, though Melina hugged her back, tightly.

What did Sean mean? she wondered. Does he think courage needs a gun? Or something else I don't have?

Or was that just reflective of his own feelings of not being up to this job, being man of the house. Well, he doesn't have to, he isn't. He's only fourteen. But maybe in his psyche he needs to take responsibility for us. Oh my God, I need to read some books myself. Adolescent male psychology. What goes on inside the head of a teenage boy who doesn't have a father. This is just out of my ken.

12

Two weeks after the manure in the driveway, school started. And Alex had made her decision: in one week, she'd be leaving for Seattle.

When she looked up at Sean leaning in the open doorway of her bedroom, the night before the first day of school, she thought, he knows we'll miss each other, and she warmed with an odd feeling of tenderness and vulnerability. She smiled at him.

"I'm not riding the school bus tomorrow," he said.

"Oh." She turned her book face down on the bed and wondered what he wanted. It wasn't a tender goodbye, after all. It wasn't a moment of team spirit. "How you going to get there?"

"Ride my bike."

"Yeah. So, what's the problem with the bus?"

"Just ain't going to ride it. You know how they do." He folded his arms and scowled at the floor. "They all know what happened. They'll say, you still got some on your shoes."

"Aw, Sean."

He was embarrassed. "Fine, it don't matter to you. Ten miles? I can do that in forty-five minutes, I guess." He peeled himself off the door-jamb and looked at her. "Or you're not doing anything, you could drive us."

Of course he was telling the truth. Kids getting on the junior high school bus at rural stops were often teased. "What's at smell? Eww God man, whyn't ya clean off your shoes," a boy would erupt in a pretense of spontaneous insult, as the farm kid came down the aisle; and then a few others would make a show of moving to different seats. The last kids on the bus had to sit next to the unlucky kid tainted by manure or stand. The bus driver would pull over and yell at all of them until the perpetrators abandoned their act and everyone took a seat.

She saw the dread in his tight face. Kids would know that Sean Leader had shoveled a truckload of manure from his mother's driveway, wouldn't they? They'd pretend to smell it on him, even two weeks later.

"Mom needs the car for work," she said.

"Yeah, but not till later. You can take us in if you want. I don't care."

"You think that will help?"

"Like I said, I don't care. I'm just not riding the bus."

"Well," she said at last, "why not? I'll see if it's okay with Mom."

His face relaxed. Would an actual thank you be too much?

"Nnnh," he said and turned away, but she heard the grudging "thanks" anyway. He spoke to the wall, but she heard it.

How much would they all miss each other? It felt strange that you could break up a family, just like this. But in two years at Interlochen she'd gotten used to goodbyes, and used to her own freedom. This time, though, she couldn't come back, not until Christmas.

When Melina threw her usual tantrum after being told to wipe down windows or help fold sheets and mop floors, and screamed, "I hate you! I can't wait till you leave!"—when that happened, Alex would say, "Really?" and they'd stop fighting and gaze at each other, and Melina's eyes would widen with a sudden perception of what it really meant, that Alex was really leaving them now. And she'd rush forward and say, "No, don't go," and hug her sister in a confused mix of dread and sentiment.

Dread and sentiment, that's how it felt, tons of that. And a little bit of excitement like a mustard seed sprouting.

She drove her brother and sisters to their three different schools all week, the high school last, and then she turned off the car radio with relief; Sharon and Becky insisted on shrilling along to half the dreadful tinny songs that assaulted her ears. "It's my party and I'll cry if I want to, cry-yi if I want to." She drove her mom to work and then picked everyone up, late in the afternoon.

Friday morning in Miltonia she saw Mr. Berry walking down the main street right outside the hardware store. She hadn't talked to him since last year, when they reviewed her college essay. Why wasn't he at the high school, bringing history home room to attention? She pulled over.

"Hi," she said.

"Alexandra," he said. He had often called her that—not always, but once in a while, and she had liked it.

"Why aren't you teaching?" she asked. They had been good friends; he was not old enough to be her father, more like an older brother.

"Fact is I'm heading off myself. Graduate school."

"No kidding. Wow."

"When are you off to Seattle?" He had written a letter of recommendation.

"Next week." A short silence. "I'm a little scared," she added.

Mr. Berry's incredibly fair face made her think of orange slice candy—he had the fairest skin, light blue eyes with pale lashes, and a thick reddish-blond crewcut. He cocked his head and smiled.

"People at Seattle U ought to be scared you're on your way. You're going to see right through a lot of things, Alexandra. You're gonna make the teachers shift into a higher gear. How would you like to scandalize the town by getting something at the Dairy Twist?"

"At nine-thirty in the morning?"

"That's what I mean, it'd be a scandal. Or do you drink coffee?"

"Sure."

She parked in the hardware store lot and saw Chris Olivet coming out of Tighe's Hardware with two paint buckets. He set one down to wave back. Chris was always pretty nice, although strange and solitary. Mom said once he was as tight as a pinecone and just as prickly, an expression which surprised Alex. Her mom had a fair amount of those sayings, but it was always a surprise, just the same, the way a colorful phrase might slip out so unexpectedly and effortlessly. Because Mom's reading habits were mixed. She read mostly natural history and local history, like *Holy Old Mackinaw;* she didn't read literature at all. Except for the occasional blockbuster, *Anatomy of a Murder* and *Gone with the Wind* and James Michener's *Hawaii*, which Mary liked a lot even though Alex told her it was flawed.

To Alex's surprise it was fun seeing people she knew this morning, out and about in Miltonia. It was a new experience—not to be in school, not picking up Sean from baseball or football or Scouts, not rushing to return books at the public library. As she and Neal Berry walked across the parking lot she looked back and saw Chris looking after her. Wondering what she was up to. Let him wonder.

"What are you going to graduate school for?" she asked as they sat over coffee.

"History," Mr. Berry said. "I'm interested in what they call popular culture. The lowbrow, that's what I like," he added and leaned toward her conspiratorially. He always did that, made her a coconspirator in his ideas. She giggled.

"Like what?" she said. "What is lowbrow history?"

"Well, for instance," he began. "Minstrel shows. Like the one the Miltonia Lions Club does. Unbelievable. Don't you think?"

"I've never been."

"Never been! Good thing not to make a habit of such junk, especially if it interferes with your reading, but I think it's a remnant—the last in the whole country, maybe—of something that was once as big an entertainment as TV. Imagine that."

"We don't have a TV."

"Still? Good for you. Radio, then. As big as radio. Imagine that."

She knew he was exaggerating for effect. "Come on," she said.

"No, really. What draws people into a crowd, for good or ill? Entertainment, politics, having fun with the social order, all these things. But something else too. They want it. Americans want this kind of entertainment. They need it. It's a way of expressing anger at things that are happening and that they are powerless to affect. Like, oh, the stocks. So, if you pay attention, you can learn something about what

Americans think of each other. Plus you have the odd bit of good music, to boot."

"The Miltonia Lions do all that?"

He laughed, happy to be caught out. "No, of course not. They're a remnant, if even that. But what they're playing at, well, it used to be a big deal in America, and I'm not sure there'll be a chance to see anything like it, ever again, in a year or so. It's pretty awful stuff in most ways. It really is. They're doing it this weekend. Let's go see it."

She stared at him, briefly puzzled as to what he was asking; then he added, "Bring your sisters, maybe, anyone who wants to come along."

"Mom doesn't approve of it."

"Well no, of course not. Your mother can't afford foolishness like this. But you know, it fascinates me, this remnant of an older culture in our midst. This scrap. This fossil. Time you graduate from college, no one will admit to ever seeing a minstrel show, let alone acting or singing in one."

"Aw, come on," she said again.

"Yup. That's what I think."

"I thought it was just a talent show."

"It's a talent show with a few peculiar, traditional set bits. A talent show where people black up. Masks are very dangerous."

"Dangerous!"

"Yes. Very, very dangerous." He was speaking low again, and his pale blue eyes seemed filled with amusement. Mr. Berry had always been inclined to seek out what amused him. She remembered days when he abandoned the curriculum, abandoned wars and the succession of presidents and the Era of Good Feeling, to talk about quack medicine schemes in the nineteenth century. When he taught the Boston Tea Party, he told them about how the colonists used to tar and feather people, dress up so they couldn't be recognized, and ride people out of town on a rail. He changed the Boston Tea Party from a patriotic act to something wild and half criminal. He loved a book called *The Confidence Man* by Herman Melville, she suddenly remembered. She had forgotten to read it this summer; she meant to.

"How is it dangerous?"

"It takes you places most people do not want to go. The very edge of racism, or classism. Is that a word? Now I'm going to bore us both if I keep talking. Here's the advantage of graduate school: you get cheap loans to spend your time going down deep in stuff you want to read about anyway. But every time you come up for air you got to say something academic, or pontifical, so people will know you're serious. Gotta play along. And you, Alexandra, what are you going to study?"

"Theology. Or literature. Or both. Maybe I want to be a teacher or even a minister—though I'd have to change religions. Mom says to get a degree in something I love, and then whatever I decide to do, I'll be better at it—more well-rounded."

"She is right. And how's that little sister of yours who wrote the novel?"

"Melina's in sixth grade, and she's a terror."

"A brilliant student, I guess, like her big sister?"

"Not at all. She barely manages. I'm worried. She's always writing and drawing, though."

Mr. Berry laughed. He liked hearing that. He really respected her family; he had encouraged and praised her and written glowing letters and talked to the people at Interlochen Arts High School, helped her get scholarships. Thanks to his efforts, in part, she was getting out of Achill County, she was going to meet people who cared about intellectual pursuits. She couldn't believe it sometimes.

She refused a refill on her coffee. Mom was probably expecting her home.

"And the minstrel show?"

"Well, maybe."

"Okay, if we still want to this weekend, let's get in touch. You never know, enthusiasms come and go, sometimes they vanish overnight. I might completely lose interest in twenty-four hours, though I don't think so."

It seemed to Alex that he'd left himself an out. So it probably wouldn't happen. She wouldn't mind going, though. She felt safe with Mr. Berry, and he probably felt safe with her, even though she knew their friendship was unusual.

Driving home she came down the steep part of Hebron toward Achill Lake. Hebron dead-ended at the lake itself, at a public-access boat ramp for local fishermen. The little bit of public beach access cut into the woods was no more than a place to park. A familiar pickup truck filled the space. Chris Olivet's green truck.

She still felt excited and happy from her visit with Mr. Berry. Maybe she should say a hi and goodbye to Chris, though he wasn't a very social fellow, and what was he doing here, anyway? Unable to decide whether to stop or to turn south toward home, she slowed and hesitated on the far side of Achill Drive. It was a lovely day; maybe he'd stopped to enjoy a few moments of the forest and the water, the way Mom did. He and Mom were alike that way.

Something, someone, the dark head of an animal, maybe, was in the water.

She remembered that time Chris came by the house wet and freezing and slightly crazy from a dip in Lake Michigan, with a bloody deer in his truck. She remembered the arrow that went through the deer's neck. She remembered handing Chris his clothes, his thin wet torso above the towel knotted at his waist.

Whatever was swimming in the lake, an otter or a beaver, was moving toward the beach. Then, to her amazement, as it drew closer, she recognized a human being. He rose, dripping wet, waist deep, and walked toward the shore. Fully clothed. Chris himself, water streaming off him.

Alex's mouth dropped open.

He'd see her in a minute.

It seemed like there was a second of indecision, but that was all. She crossed the road and drove in behind his car. In the second or two that it took to drive across Achill Drive and park behind Chris Olivet's truck, she shed one stage of her life and accepted another. And she could feel it. She had no idea what was going on, only that you didn't, you mustn't, turn your back. Don't pretend it's not happening. Whatever it is. Don't drive away.

"Good morning, Chris," she said, walking toward him.

"Hey there," he said. He sounded normal, but he shivered.

She waited a few seconds for an explanation, then rushed ahead. "Come down and swim at our place sometime. Sean and Becky are still swimming, though the rest of us think it's getting too cold."

"Thanks. I'll do that, Alex."

"I'm going to college next week. Can't believe I'm leaving."

"Is that right? Where you going?"

"Seattle."

"Oh my. Out west. Hear it's nice out there, real nice country."

"You got a towel in the truck? You better get it."

"I will." He looked suddenly sheepish. "I must look a little silly. Sometimes, you ah, you just got to get that paint smell off. I been painting all week, and I just get so sick of it. Sometimes I take in a bar of Fels-Naptha and wash my clothes right on me. We all used to do that."

Alex smiled then, a big, relieved smile, so he would think she believed him. Which she almost did.

"I guess you'll keep looking after things here. I'll worry about Mom and everybody," she said.

"You don't want to worry," he said. He opened the door of the truck and took out a jacket, put it on over his wet shirt. "You're going to the University of Washington?"

"Seattle University. For starters. Maybe I'll transfer. It's a Catholic college. Something familiar."

"Oh yeah? I used to be Catholic. Well, Alex, you sure doing everybody proud."

It seemed like he wanted to escape the conversation.

"See you Christmas or next summer," she said. "And come down to Pinestead." He probably didn't have a towel or dry clothes with him in the truck. It was something impulsive that made him go swimming.

"I'll do that. Good luck in school."

They said goodbye and got back in their cars like it had been a perfectly normal meeting, like he hadn't just emerged fully dressed from Achill Lake, like it was a day in the middle of summer. But it wasn't. The lake water was plenty cold. Way too cold.

But she had acknowledged him. That was her impulse, and she had followed it. There could have been something wrong, some way she could have helped, and if needed, she'd have been there. That's what a priest would do. Be standing by. Is there a priest in the house? Medical things didn't tempt her, injuries like Becky's when she got cut by the propeller, not at all, or that time a tree branch went right through a boy driving a motorcycle. Alex cared about trouble in mind. That's what she was interested in.

Chris had some, he sure had some trouble in mind. Washing paint off? Come on! "Used to be Catholic," he said. What happened?

Mom had the day off, and she was making pot roast sandwiches. She looked over her shoulder with a grin as Alex walked into the house. Alex smelled horseradish.

"Hello, honey," Mary called. "We can do whatever you want today. The canoe is waiting, if you want to go up to the point. The lake is so still this morning! Or do you want to go shopping?" Mary turned from the counter and faced her daughter. A day together before she left for college: Alex could see it, suddenly, how her mom's heart exulted. There weren't many days like this, ever, the two of them with time on their hands, not doing some task together but being with each other, no other kids coming between.

It was almost scary. The look in Mary's eyes right now was almost that of a child—filled with anticipation, as if looking forward to Christmas.

Alex had been all set to blurt out the news that Chris Olivet was swimming with all his clothes on, up at the public-access boat ramp. Or she could keep that information to herself. She could keep the trouble of it from changing her mom's face back to that painful set expression where life was one difficult problem after another for her to solve alone.

Mary Leader didn't have days like this one as a matter of course. Almost never. Alex could keep her mom carefree like this, just a little longer.

Alex moved over to the counter and picked up a scrap of pot roast from the cutting board. "Mmm. Maybe we could put the canoe on top of the car," she said, "and drive up to the landing in Spawn and paddle down the Florida River a ways? We'd loop back to the car in time to get the kids."

"Wow, you're ambitious! I don't see why not."

Mary turned back to the sandwiches. She drew out what looked to Alex almost like a yard of waxed paper to wrap each one; she loved wrapping sandwiches, folding the paper in an accordion pleat over the top. She loved packing a box of food for a boat trip. Something was going right.

The eighteen-foot Grumman was painfully heavy, but they could manage with effort and coordination. "Bend your legs, don't strain your back," Mary would call out half a dozen times. And they'd drive by the boat ramp, and if Chris's truck was still there, they'd stop, and if it wasn't—then what could they do? What would be the point of worrying? What would a priest do? Or a friend, because Chris was a friend of theirs.

"Maybe we could check on Chris Olivet then, too," Alex ventured, slowly, reluctantly, her back to Mary.

"Oh?"

"He was swimming with his clothes on as I came by the public ramp just now. It seemed strange to me. He got out of the water and said that he was sick of the smell of paint on his clothes. Pretty soon he started shivering, and he put on his jacket."

Mary packed the sandwiches into an empty potato-chip box.

"You think he's all right?" Alex said.

"Well . . . that is a strange thing to do. Tight fellow. Sometimes I wonder what's going on with him. Let's get ready."

Alex went upstairs, and Mary went into her office-bedroom and sat down heavily, resting her elbows on her knees and her head in her hands. Surprisingly, out of nowhere, she suddenly thought about the pint of gin for later on in the weekend, tucked way in the back of her file drawer of bills, a drawer she knew had no interest for her snooping children—they were always coming in here to look at things, to dress up in her ancient costume jewelry, the kimonos Jim brought back from Korea, to rifle through their own saved report cards and schoolwork in the bottom drawer of the big file cabinet. They left the one marked "bills" alone. The gin was for nighttime, after everything was taken care of. To help her sleep. Odd that she'd think of it right now. Even a sip would alter this day, ruin it.

There was another filing cabinet with two drawers that she almost never opened; it was Jim's patients' records, notes for journal articles, letters to and from other docs. Some of these records described patients he'd seen outside of the office. He used to call these files his "medical diary"—a record of what he'd observed, diagnosed, prescribed, outside of the hospital. He never encouraged her to look at any of it. It was confidential, he said, and after he died she didn't care too much to explore the files, to fill her head with how much time and care he'd lavished on other people.

Then, later, she realized that here was a drawer filled with his handwriting and his thoughts. She had pulled out the drawer many times just to look at his handwriting, but the severely economical language he used as a doctor always surprised her. She didn't care a whole lot for it. And she knew that this private information about people she might know had never been intended for her eyes.

Had he ever treated Chris? It seemed like they shared things apart from her. Not just their fishing trips. "Leave him be," Jim always said. "Some folks up here are like that," as though Chris was understandable, in his own way.

She pulled open the drawer and looked at the files, and the old, dreaded heaviness hit her again. An angry feeling. This was the part of his life that Jim stopped sharing with her, and he didn't even mind. He didn't mind keeping things from her. Probably he felt that blood clot in his leg, moving up to his lung; all he had to do was say, "Hey I feel funny, I feel terrible, what do you think's going on, Mary?" But oh, admit to it, never.

"Mom, you all right?"

Alex poked her head in, checking on her. Mary slid the file drawer shut.

"Yes, I'm just getting Chris's phone number. I'll give him a call later on."

She didn't know where he lived—with an uncle, maybe. Or next door to an uncle on some family property, way north of the lake. Funny that she didn't know where he lived, exactly. You'd think different. All these years the Leaders living here, calling him at every crisis.

But she'd been so busy. It was all she could do. Keeping everything going, with some time for the extras that make life worth it. To Mary's astonishment, she felt her eyes filling up with tears. My God, what's this? Am I feeling sorry for myself again? Dear God, am I not tired of this self-pity yet? You bet I am.

"Mom?"

"Let's go, I'm ready."

Alex stood back and smiled at her mother when the canoe was successfully tied down on top of the wooden car rack. They were proud of themselves. After Mary took a picture of her, Alex took the old Argus from her and snapped one of her mother. It was one she would save, later, for years—Mary in Jim's rolled-up woolen pants and that ancient corduroy jacket faded from a hunter's orange plaid to a pinkish brown, the ever-present bandanna holding her thick brown hair off her forehead, and a deep, unselfconscious smile, the smile that accompanies the end of exertion, the end of the worst part. The canoe's on the car; it's easy from now on. But in addition to the smile, there was something else—a slight exasperation and surrender in her face. She had to give up the camera to her daughter. She was caught. It was a photo of a woman inside the give-and-take of raising children to adulthood. In this snapshot—Alex was to decide later as she studied her mother's expression—Mary was looking at an adult. Not a peer, but at least a grown companion. An equal of sorts. She wore that expression a lot, in fact, and Alex just had not recognized it before.

13

At a village with the ludicrous name of Spawn, a dock and gas pump served boaters on the Florida River, which flowed from a small lake through Spawn and then through a marsh into Achill Lake. This marshy stretch was still wild and beautiful when the summer tourists left. Some of the wealthier property owners considered it a bird sanctuary and had nailed up signs that begged boaters to leave no wake. The Florida was shallow and filled with reeds, cattails, and lilies. When you stopped paddling, a definite current ferried you ever so slowly downriver, but when it was time to turn around and paddle upstream, it wasn't a major effort.

Mary knew they'd find the marsh absolutely deserted on a weekday with school back in session. Deserted except for loons and ducks, swans, painted turtles piled on the snags, otters and muskrats. Red-tailed hawks in the treetops, watching, and yellow warblers flitting over the leatherleaf bushes. Pleasure at being alone on the water with Alexandra flooded through her as the Grumman hit the water. Because it was fed with warmish springs, the Florida never froze over. You could come here all year round, paddle this river in January with mittens on, if you wanted to, between cattails sticking above the snow. Oh God, it was beautiful then, the water slate gray under the winter sky. She had described the Florida River marshes in her journals in every season of the year. But the younger kids were increasingly reluctant to leave their own activities on a weekend. And she had so much paperwork all the time, and housework, it seemed, that she'd give in to inertia herself, stay home all day on a Saturday.

Mary sat in the front and took several long, deep strokes away from the dock, then rested her paddle across the bow to gaze at the marsh, while Alex pointed them downriver. What a wonderful idea, to come over to the Florida this morning. Alex always liked to push things a little further, try something new. That sense of adventure would see her through, out there in Seattle. But how Mary would miss her!

A neon-blue damselfly took a rest on the green-painted handle of her paddle. Mary thought she saw a muskrat's head. She turned back to Alex, finger to her lips, and pointed. Alex nodded and smiled. If it weren't for this nagging sore spot about Chris, Mary's elation would be complete.

What was wrong with him, to do that—and so close to her own house? To unsettle her like this. He was working in the area and covered with paint and sick of the paint. We all know he likes a cold swim. Somehow she didn't believe it.

And where in the hell was Mary's own empathy this morning? But she wanted to enjoy her favorite activity in the world with one of her favorite people, damn it; she did not want to worry about Chris Olivet.

Alex was talking about living in the big city during the next few years, wondering how that would be for her. Mary had missed a few words.

". . . trying to find my way around, stay out of unsafe neighborhoods like Grandma said to do," she called to Mary from the stern of the canoe.

"Seattle's not like Chicago," Mary said, twisting around again. "It's smaller, and Nat says it's beautiful, and out there in the West things are . . ." How were things in the West? She didn't really know. "There's the mountains. And Puget Sound."

"I hope I can learn the ropes," said Alex.

"Indeed, you can," said Mary. Did Alex need a pep talk? If so, it had been years since she needed one. Years.

Mary set her paddle down again.

"I tried to make sure you kids knew about the wider world," she said, "even living up here. This is my church, this wilderness—don't tell Grandma I said that. But there are huge advantages in a city, like Chicago or Seattle. I tried to make sure you kids knew about things—art, and music, and the news of the world. I never intended to build a wall against the world, not live in isolation. Think about this . . ." She took a small notebook out of her breast pocket and opened it. Doing two things at once, but she had to make a note of the muskrat, the date, the damselfly, and that goldfinch above the bushes just ahead.

"Think about this, Alex. I would have liked you kids to know a wider variety of people. That's why I think that integrated schools and open housing are good ideas. Even in Northern Michigan, a person can meet a variety of people. If you kids could have gone to school with other races, with Negro people, I would have supported that. I would have been all for it."

She knew that Alex lived in a different world, a world of exploding possibility. It was different from Mary's world, where you wanted to hold things at bay. Change, for people Mary's age, usually meant a loss.

"I'm so glad you'll be meeting people from other places, from all over. Those kids who dumped the manure pile in the driveway . . . they were ignorant. In a way they were experimenting. They just needed to be stopped, to be told, read a book instead! They were not like this man Wallace down in Alabama."

"I'm not asking about Alabama. I know what it's like down there."

"You do?"

"Well sure."

Mary did not want to put any kind of damper on Alex's spirit. She never wanted to do that to any of her kids. She wanted to share her optimism with her kids, not her trouble. Some things you tell kids and some things you don't tell 'em.

"One time when I was working at this laundry in Gastonia . . . I came back to the house for lunch. Mom had a woman helping her at that time, a Negro woman, helping her with all the things she was doing, and this maid—I can't remember her name now—she was sitting at the kitchen table eating her lunch. So I got my lunch and sat down too." Did she want to tell Alex this story about their sweet, white-haired, rosary-saying, sugar-dispensing grandmother? No, she didn't. But she went on. "The only two people in the house, both eating our lunches, why not sit at the same table? Then my mother came home and didn't say a word, but later on she said to me, 'Mary, don't you ever do that again.'"

That got Alex's attention. She stopped paddling. "Why?"

"I was grown up. I wasn't a little girl anymore. Negro people and white people didn't do things together. We did not do things together. Not even accidentally, most of the time. Customers might have come for a cake or something, and there we'd have been, eating together. Mom didn't want that to happen."

"That's awful!"

"Well, I think so now. Back then, I did what she asked."

"You had a maid?"

"Oh my gosh, don't think of it like that. I don't know how much that woman was paid. Very little, I'm sure. This was the Depression, Alex. People did things for very little. We made beauty products in the kitchen and sold them, we baked cakes for the hotels, that kitchen was a factory . . . But once I got up here, I came to see it wasn't necessary to live like that, segregated. I do wish you kids had been able to go to school with Negro kids. I wouldn't have kept you from that experience."

"Grandma said to keep safe in Seattle. She says around the college, it'll be safe."

"That's Grandma to a tee. But I'm not worried about your being safe. I mean, you have good sense. And you are made for this." Mary rotated on her seat and looked back at Alex. "You were made to set out for a new adventure. Just like the birds here, they were raised so they could fly away from this marsh every winter, to see the world."

Alex smiled; such talk was familiar. This was not the first time Mary had sounded this note.

Mary was stimulated by her own idea. She wrote in her notebook: "Alex like these songbirds and waterfowl, compelled to leave this place."

Compelled, that was a good choice of word. An imperative inside her!

After school, the canoe upended on the top of the station wagon gave it away. Mary and Alex had spent the day having fun, and now they had to make it up to the others. It was off to Itara for fish-and-chips and a stroll down the peaceful Main Street recently vacated by summer visitors. You could buy tourist knickknacks, honey and peanut brittle, polished Petoskey stones and arrowheads, and cherry butter for half price. Melina insisted on the most expensive item, a little wooden lighthouse.

Mary telephoned Chris that night, and he sounded fine, normal even. She asked when he could help her winterize the plumbing in the cabins. She mentioned Alex's story, and he laughed and repeated that he had been rinsing off a paint smell. "When you're just looking out for your own self, you do what strikes you. Sometimes I forget how it looks to other people," he said, and she decided to take him at his word.

On Saturday Alex and Sean decided to go into Miltonia after supper for the movie or maybe just ice cream. They agreed that Melina could come along, and Mom said okay. They almost never did this, went into town in the evening, and Melina sensed that the thing to do was to act calm, act like they did it all the time. Calm was essential. Hopping around in excitement would probably cause Mom to change her mind.

Mom came out and said, "Check the tires and the gas tank," and Sean even checked the oil. She stood and waved while the three of them headed down the driveway.

"This is a treat for her, she's almost never alone," Alex said, looking back at Mom in the rearview mirror. With Becky at a sock hop with a boy, and Sharon babysitting, Mom had the place to herself.

"What do you mean? She's always alone," said Sean.

And then the two of them started arguing about the meaning of the word alone, while Melina began to feel uneasy. When the big kids got to arguing they couldn't stop. And it was always about the meanings of words. "Quibbling," Mom called it. Maybe she wanted to go back and be with Mom. Alone was not good—Melina hated to be alone in the house. She twisted in the seat and looked back, but Mom had gone inside.

When they got to town, Sean said, "I'll meet you back here in an hour," and Alex said, "Now look."

But it was no use. The party had broken up.

"Personally I happen to think that he's embarrassed to be seen with me," she said to Melina. "Picked a fight on purpose. He just wanted to get into town."

They stared at each other. What now?

"Well, come on, let's look around," said Alex. "Look, the five-and-dime's still open. You want to go there?"

The five-and-dime was next door to the Dairy Twist. This was promising.

Alex said she wanted two toggle buttons for her good wool car coat. She led them to the notions counter, and Melina wandered off down a nearby aisle. She found it odd that lots of things cost more than a nickel or a dime. She admired a plaid wide-mouth thermos bottle, imagining briefly a life in which someone would pack her a lunch every day that included this thermos, filled with chicken noodle soup. She fondled a stack of small, heavily varnished wooden plaques in the shape of lower Michigan. In the middle of one plaque was a photograph of a man catching a fish, his pole nearly bent double. Another held a photograph of a lighthouse, which she liked much better, though not as much as her new wooden lighthouse from Itara. She dipped her hand in a tray of polished rocks and let them cascade over her fingers.

Alex found some buttons, three to a card, but they didn't match the old ones exactly. She wondered aloud to Melina if she should buy two cards and replace all the buttons, or one, and just have an imperfect coat.

"You think people in Seattle would notice?"

As she and Melina walked past the magazines, a girl reading a *Mademoiselle* looked up at them.

"Oh hi, Alex," she said. "Is this your little sister?"

"Hi, Livvie," said Alex.

The girl had already caught Melina's attention because she seemed to be doing such a fun thing, reading a magazine with a big bottle of Tame crème rinse under her arm and a six-pack of Coca-Cola at her feet, and because she was dressed so prettily. Alex was wearing an old skirt, but this girl was wearing crisp, tight blue jeans rolled up above white socks and snowy white sneakers. She wore a University of Michigan sweatshirt, and her blond hair was beautifully cared for; behind a plastic headband it spilled down to her shoulders like it had just been taken out of curlers.

She joined them at the cash register and began to chat. Alex didn't have time to consider her purchase thoroughly; confused, she ended up buying both cards of buttons. Livvie bought the *Mademoiselle*, the crème rinse, the Cokes, and a package of candies called Chicken Bones.

"My boyfriend's just left for Ann Arbor," she announced out on the sidewalk. "I am in despair. Whatchall up to?"

"I'm meeting a friend," Alex said.

"That's nice," said the girl. She smiled down at Melina, who had decided she was looking at true beauty; Livvie had gray eyes, and she was slender as a ballerina, and her fingers holding a Chicken Bone had polished, pink nails.

"Want one?" She held out the bag to them.

Melina took two.

They were buttery and crunchy, broke right apart in your mouth. What a good idea!

"No thanks," said Alex.

"You're going off to college, aren't you?" said the girl.

"Seattle University, I leave next week."

"You are so smart. I'm going to go down to the junior college in Traverse, just for this year. I can't wait to transfer. But you know what? At least we're not in high school anymore. Oh man, I can't believe my luck getting out of there!"

"Luck didn't have much to do with it," said Alex.

"What?"

"Well, we were always going to graduate this year. Where does luck come in?"

Melina stared up at Alex. Why be like that?

The girl had another Chicken Bone and seemed to think it over.

"You're right. This was comin' at us for years. Well, it feels like luck is all I know. 'Course you were at Interlochen, I bet you had fun there. G'night, guys, and Alex, very very best out there in Seattle!"

"Goodbye, Livvie."

"Oh hi, Mr. Berry," Livvie said next.

"Hello there, Olivia. Hello, Alexandra. Hello, Melina," said Mr. Berry, suddenly appearing from the Dairy Twist. "What can I get you all?"

"Nothing for me," the girl said. Her voice was like singing.

"Are you sure?"

"Oh, I'm sure. I'm all set."

"Aw, come on, you need some ice cream," said Mr. Berry, rather slowly, still smiling. They were all smiling, though Alex's smile was stiff, as though merely holding her mouth open was an effort. Why was she acting funny? Melina wondered. "Come on, let me buy my top two students an ice cream. Between the two of you girls, I felt my time here wasn't completely wasted."

Alex didn't look happy, but Melina was thrilled. Her medium cone turned out to be huge. She was completely happy as she lowered her mouth to that top curlicue of ice cream. Livvie and Mr. Berry ordered cones too, and Alex had a cup of root beer, and they all four wandered toward the city hall and the Lions Barn behind it. There was a general milling of people, and Alex was saying she had to watch the time, and Mr. Berry announced that he was buying tickets.

"How many? Olivia, are you joining us?"

"Not for me. I'm expected home. Have a blast, you all." She waved her pink fingernails at them. She was a girl right out of a magazine—and yet, Melina could tell, her smile was genuine, her face intelligent. Why was Alex acting so. . . funny? It made Melina uneasy, to sense that her big sister was at a loss.

But then they joined a throng inside the Lions Barn, and wonderful music was coming from the stage—a banjo and ukulele and tambourine, a harmonica, a set of spoons and a set of animal teeth—a moose jaw, it turned out. The semicircle of musicians on the plywood platform all had painted black faces with big, clownlike mouths. One had long black ringlets, a Halloween wig, and he waved his tongue out of his mouth as he grinned and plucked. He was ugly, his clownish looks didn't match the music.

Melina's cone leaked. She went back and forth from the rim of the cone to the soggy bottom, trying to keep up with the dribbles. She lost track of the show when they stopped playing music and started telling jokes. The audience around her roared, but she didn't follow the jokes, and she didn't want to. She swallowed the last of the cone and put her head into Alex's shoulder. It was uncomfortable to be in the midst of a crowd of people when laughing was almost obligatory, but you didn't get the jokes, and you didn't think anything was funny.

"What is a vacuum?" one of them asked another.

"I can't—er—can't quite describe it. I have it in my head."

Melina always felt this way at cartoons, too—she couldn't laugh, and kids around her would be shouting with delight as the cartoon characters had one mishap after another. Right now one of the men was bragging about how he could wrestle lions, ten-foot muskies, and wolves from Isle Royale. Melina didn't like tall tales at school either; she thought Pecos Bill and Paul Bunyan were tiresome.

"You ain't no lion tamer!" the ukulele player shouted. "You jus lyin'!" Was that funny? The crowd thought so.

"When are we gonna go home?" Melina whispered to Alex. Alex put an arm around her.

"In a minute."

Now one of them was pretending to be a doctor and was treating another one for aches and pains with all kinds of huge carpentry tools. This led to a chase around the stage, and then three of the men were dancing in a line, one behind the other, leaning way back and flinging their legs out.

Another musician came out on the stage with a banjo. He was a tall, skinny Negro man, not painted but a real Negro, in a red and white striped vest. Melina took another look when he began to play. Then all the men stopped their awful joking and just played music, and the one man, the real Negro, began to sing. He sang a slow, beautiful song about floating down the river in a gum-tree canoe, and it changed the mood in the hall, just for the length of the song. When he finished people clapped and pounded their feet on the floor.

Just as the song ended a string on his banjo popped, and zinged as it flew off past his ear. He laughed and put his hand into his vest and pulled something out. He sat down on a stool and hitched his long legs into the rungs; then he started to fix the string, and when the applause died down he talked.

"Some people think the banjo's low-down but you people here in Northern Michigan—you all keep on askin' us to come back ever year. My opinion, it's true what dey say 'bout Northern Michigan. Up north, if you want to talk to the Lord, well, heaven's just a local call."

The audience knew this was coming. They pounded their feet and hollered approval.

"Did y'all know that banjo music's the original rock and roll music? Banjo's got steel strings you can play loud an' fas' and then even louder and faster. Comes to music that makes you wanna move aroun' you can't beat a banjo. Almos' any poor kid can get one. This ain't no Stradyvarius. That right, ain't it, Daddy?"

"That right," hollered one of the men in black paint.

"So like I sayin', it's what used to be rock and roll. Loud an' fas', loud an' fas'. Some people don't approve of it. It's raucous. Rings out too loud for some people. Sometimes, someone's momma won't allow no banjo playin'."

"We don't care what Momma don' allow," called the tambourine player.

"'At right? Gon' play that banjo anyhow?" called the tall Negro, and suddenly the string was fixed, and they were all playing. Everybody got a chance to play alone, hard and fast. Momma didn't allow no moose-jaw playing either, or spoons, tambourine, or washtub bass, but they all got back at her, especially the banjo. The audience roared with delight.

"Now I going to sing you a song called 'Run, Preacher, Run,'" the banjo player said. "And you tell me if it don't sound like someone running and jumping and running, like he's only one step ahead of the sheriff. Ain't very many things in this world so sad there ain't somethin' funny in it somewhere. Even runnin' from the sheriff. Here we go. Y'all ready?"

"That really what the song is about?" one of the men in black paint called out.

"Ain't this a family show? They's women and children here!" the banjo player said.

There were no words to this song, just music, and it sounded like someone running fast through mud, Melina thought, just about to lose his balance with every step, but not quite. Despite herself she laughed. The music was making her laugh. So she was almost sorry when the song ended and Alex said to Mr. Berry, "We've got to get back to the car, we're meeting my brother."

The banjo player was singing "Shady Grove" as they left. She knew that because the Kingston Trio played it too, on a record of Sharon's. She stopped to listen, and Alex had to pull her.

"I remember hearing him, that banjo player, once before," she said to Alex.

"We've never come to this show," said Alex.

"But one time, we did. Because I heard him before."

"Trippin' down the dusty road, toward the pearly gate," he sang, softly now. Alex pulled, hard, on Melina's hand. "My brother's waiting for us," she told Mr. Berry, who was staying at the show. He walked them to the back door and made a point of wishing Alex good luck in Seattle.

Sean was sitting on the hood of the car, no longer surly. He had found some friends and gone down to the river at the far end of town. He sat in the backseat and studied a new chisel that, he said, a friend had traded him.

Melina gazed out the window on the way home and tried to figure out how banjo players lived. Did they travel from town to town? Alex was quiet, as if something had gone out of her. Melina felt uneasy that her big sister had been thrown off course by something; it was even a little frightening to see Alex having a bad time.

But that music. There was something to that music. She wanted more of it. Maybe she could be a banjo player's daughter. She could tell there was more to it than what they saw and heard tonight. What they saw and heard tonight was just a fraction, just a tip, just one end of the rope. The rope stretched back out of her understanding, back to strange places, and you had to be willing to take risks if you wanted to go there, if you wanted to be the kind of person who could move around freely into dark places. You had to be really relaxed and easy. She could tell.

She concentrated on the tip of the rope. She wanted to follow it. That banjo player was handsome, but she couldn't be his daughter, because he was a Negro. They'd be something else to each other. What? Now there was a problem. A knot in the rope. She could pick it apart. Melina liked story problems.

Alex sat on the porch, where the darkness shielded her from her own embarrassment and anguish. She had wanted something from tonight, but the evening had betrayed her.

When they came home, Mom was sober and happy to see them. But Alex could barely speak, she was so disappointed in the evening. She had imagined . . . what? That she and Sean and Melina would be a merry threesome, able to sample the town and not be one bit affected by any of it, on almost her last night here in Michigan? Or that Mr. Berry really held out hope of spending a few minutes with her?

Things you don't even know you want—your secret heart starts building castles without your even knowing it. That girl Livvie was a reminder that Alex was not and never would be pretty and confident. Mr. Berry had seemed to enjoy Alex's company so much, and then it turned out that he liked Livvie just as much—how could he? And that gross and ugly and outdated show, to which she'd exposed her little sister. So vulgar! Mr. Berry! What was wrong with him? What was wrong with Alexandra Leader?

She felt her eyes filling with tears of self-pity. She would never make this mistake again.

Mom came out and sat near her.

"Is anything wrong, Alex?"

Alex would have liked to tell her. Now Mom was going to be disappointed too, one more victim of Alex's letting her imagination run away with her. Thinking she was going to have a good time in Miltonia. You never had a good time in Miltonia!

Alex reached out a hand to her mom's arm and lied.

"I'm sorry to be leaving. A little scared."

"Oh my. Well." And Mary quoted a favorite children's book: "'A little bit sad about the place they were leaving, a little bit glad about the place they were going.' Like that, honey?"

"Yeah."

"Shall I turn on a light?"

"Oh no, don't. It's so pretty."

They could hear the lake water lapping on the rocks, and sometimes the dim groan of the hoist and a very faint and occasional boom as one of the drums of the raft lifted up above the water then settled back down. It's unusual to grow up on a lake like this, Alex thought. I wonder if it's done me any good.

"When you look at the lake, when half of the world every day is so beautiful and so . . . placid, it's a shock to go into a place like Miltonia, or anywhere away from the lake, and find out that . . . that most people . . . are surrounded by other things, by clutter and . . . struggle," she said at last.

Mary didn't speak for a moment.

"Did something happen in town?" She said at last.

"It wasn't as much fun as I'd hoped."

"Seattle is on Puget Sound and Lake Washington, both. You can't go wrong, near a body of water. I've always hoped that the life here would stand you kids in good stead. Even though some things we didn't have exposure to. Like you were talking about in the canoe yesterday. But I've always hoped . . . this beautiful place would be worth the exchange. We don't have the city, but we have the lake, the Northern woods, the North itself. I'm sure it'll turn out to be useful to you. Promise. It will."

"Really?"

Mary laughed and said, "Here on the water is a good place to be for a spell, and learn some things, but now it's your turn in life to explore. Oh, I'm so excited for you, Alex. All the hard work you did growing up . . . it's made you independent."

"Oh, I know it, Mom."

"Things you've learned here will see you through. They really will."

Alex could not stop the discomfort inside. Over that ridge on the other side of the lake, that forested ridge where only three house lights shone among the trees right now—over that ridge, across Lake

Michigan, west to Seattle, the trip waited for her. It felt good to sit with her mom like this. Why couldn't she have had the going-away night she wanted? Why couldn't she? Never mind. Enough fussing and packing. I'm going.

"Ready or not," she said.

"Sure, you're ready," Mary said, and reached across to Alex's hand. "Fact is, we don't know what we're capable of, until some new completely incredible challenge calls us to meet it. Like when your father died." Her hand tightened on Alex's. So tight, it hurt. Alex looked at her mother but didn't pull back her hand. "That's the definition of adventure, I think," Mary said, looking out at the black water. She never turned on the floodlight anymore. When had she stopped doing that? And why—to save money or to avoid calling attention to Pinestead?

Or maybe to see the stars better, sometimes even the northern lights. Guests always said the stars were thick here, like nothing they'd ever seen before.

14

Sunday mornings after mass, the girls sprawled on the living room floor with the funny pages from the *Detroit Free Press* while Sean made buttermilk pancakes. He had taken pride in making the pancakes for the past year. They were better than Mary's. His batter was bubbling and lumpy, he didn't beat it tough and smooth, so that tender lumps of baking soda and flour opened right under your fork. He warmed the maple syrup on low heat in a glass jar set in a saucepan of water. Sean made the pancakes because he liked to eat them, at least twelve at a time, and also because he liked the chemistry of it. Out of ordinary things, a miracle, and different every time.

And while he made the pancakes, Mary strolled happily through the house and garage, putting things away, and that's when she found the brand-new Stanley plane. The new chisels she had seen Sean with didn't bother her so much, but that gleaming plane on the workbench astounded her. Those were mighty expensive. She knew that much. Jim had wanted one. Whatever had inspired Sean to spend his small allowance on that? Or did he?

The pancakes were delicious, but she could hardly eat. Melina wanted to talk about the Phantom, the Ghost-Who-Walks, from the funny pages because she had dreamed he was coming across the yard to get her, she said, and she couldn't scream. She was paralyzed with fright; she could not take a breath. "Like I had polio," she insisted. "Tell us about iron lungs, Mom. Tell us about all the kids in the hospital when the power went off, and you had to pump the iron lungs by hand."

"Oh, I've told you all that plenty of times," said Mary. She watched Sean carve a forkful out of his stack of five pancakes. "These are delicious," she said, though they filled her own mouth like bedsheets. She wanted to cry. She knew what Sean was going to tell her, when he finally told her the truth.

After breakfast she asked him to come out to the garage with her. He worked his way through several fibs before he dug himself so deep that he gave up and confessed. He had stolen the chisels and the plane from Tighe's, one at a time, over the summer. That time he went into town with Alex and Mel, before Alex left, that's when he took the third chisel.

They were both so stunned by the reality of this, they could hardly talk. She did not know what to do; Sean was too humiliated to speak. As they left the garage Klondy raced up with a muzzleful of tennis ball. Sean wrenched it savagely from his teeth and hurled it into the lake. He threw beyond the raft. The dog ran to the water, bewildered. Klondy was no swimmer.

Mary knew that she should take Sean to Tighe's to return the tools and ask to pay for them. Isn't that what a father would do? What if Asa Tighe wanted to call the sheriff, what if he . . . what if he pressed charges? What if Sean had to go to court? How far did you push this? Sweet, sweet Mother of God. There was just simply nothing to go on, beyond thou shalt not steal, and you're my son and I won't let any harm come to you. Never.

Together they went to Tighe's after school on Monday, Mary with her checkbook open and her pen out. Sean set the chisels and plane on Asa Tighe's desk.

"My son is very sorry he neglected to pay for these," Mary said. "We'd really like you to accept a check and our apologies."

Asa Tighe stared at the tools and at them. "Well," he said. "I wouldn't ever a thought, Sean." I have spent lots of money here over the years, Mary thought. Let that count for something.

"Young men do like to be around tools," said Asa. He waited. As if the excruciating silence were part of the treatment. Then, with a sigh, "Sean, you need to find another way. Don't torture your mother like this. You need to be a help to her. She's a good mom."

"Yes sir," Sean whispered. He was digging his nails into his palm. He couldn't even look up. Mary knew they'd never go through Tighe's door again.

Sean began making amends around the house, with extra chores and forsaken allowances. Then one day he handed her a ten-dollar bill. "I cut half a cord of wood for Mr. Wilgosch," he said. "Just ask him. He's got other chores for me too." For the first time in a week he looked directly at her, and his eyes shone.

Mary spoke to someone in Traverse City at an agency called Big Brothers. It sounded like such a good idea, to get your fatherless boy hooked up with a grown man. But a stranger? She couldn't get comfortable with that idea. She never called back.

The two of them never spoke of it again. There was never a chance to convince him, now listen, in the big picture that was nothing! Almost every boy does something like this, it was just a mistake! She would have liked to take it all away from him, but that's not what a father would do. Fathers let their sons know what consequences are, didn't they? Fathers trusted them to take the fall and get strong. She wanted to know how Sean was coping with all this, but you couldn't do that if the topic was off-limits, way off there where everyone was trying to believe it never even happened, so long as no one ever mentioned it again. Keep that door locked tight.

The sixth-graders went five at a time down to the library to write about South America. You looked stuff up in *World Book* and transferred it to a piece of paper, and if you didn't die of boredom, you'd probably get an A. Melina was doing Bolivia, and after she drew a box for the flag and put a wreath in the middle of it, she borrowed crayons from the second-grader across the table to color it in. The second-graders were supposed to be rubbing crayons over huge red maple leaves to bring out the veins.

These crayons were unwrapped, flat on one side. When she picked them out of the cardboard tray and caught the smell, Melina froze, assailed for perhaps the first time in her life by an overwhelming nostalgia. She turned one on edge and moved it down the paper. She drew a large red face. Well, it wasn't so much fun to use, after all. What was it about them that she craved? How could you want to get back to something you'd never really owned?

She drew and colored another Bolivian flag, gave the boy back his crayons, and looked again at the encyclopedia, but the mining of zinc and antimony could not hold her attention. Her pencil and the blank white paper called to her. She began to draw, figure after figure. A girl with a pistol in her belt. Then a girl with a banjo slung on her back: running for her life, climbing rugged dry boulder-strewn mountains, a gypsy girl, a robber girl, free and bold, loose in the wilderness. She thought about Sharon's Kingston Trio records: "When the lion still ruled the barranca . . ." This fearless banjo-playing girl is at home on the barranca, she decided. When her paper was filled with drawings, she slid it underneath a clean sheet and returned to Bolivia, but she couldn't help herself. Soon she started drawing again. After half an hour her report on Bolivia consisted of the tricolor and below it the words "Capital: La Paz. Minerals: Antimony, Tungsten, Zinc, Silver" and nothing else.

But shouldn't they be going back to the classroom soon? What was going on? There had been no fire alarm, but people were moving around. Teachers had come into the library and were talking to each other. There were kids out in the hall even though it wasn't recess time or lunch. Then the librarian said they were all to go outside for a while, like it was a holiday. No one formed a line. Melina picked up her drawings and folded them into the sleeve of her sweater but left her report on Bolivia behind. They shuffled in clumps, confused, toward the dodgeball court and then the playground. And then someone was saying, and others were repeating it: "President Kennedy was shot. The president was shot." As if by saying it over and over they would find out what it meant.

The teacher on recess duty walked the perimeter of the playground with a transistor radio to his ear. No one felt like playing. Were you supposed to cry or feel scared? Melina stood with five other girls, and they stared at each other. Were you supposed to feel sad, like you would for a relative? Boys huddled in their circles, girls in theirs. You would think there'd be some excitement to this, with school dismissed, teachers leaving them alone, the president shot. But there was no excitement, instead a kind of awe that was actually uncomfortable.

It was too big. They looked at each other and could not find help in each other's faces.

Mr. Flint's belly made the LPN gasp; it was rounded and taut like bread dough in a bowl that had been rising for an hour. Mary Leader sent Adelaide away and took over. She watched Dr. Bodamer's fingers press gently into the white skin and thought: peritonitis. The old man flinched and jerked in pain.

She was right. Dr. Bodamer drew the drapery up over Mr. Flint's belly and gave him a quick smile, then looked at Mary and walked out of the curtained area. "We need to get him upstairs for surgery. Something perforated. From his history could be the bowel. There's no doubt he has peritonitis. I'll call a surgeon before I talk to his people. Would you send him upstairs stat, dear?"

I'm not your dear, Mary thought automatically, but she liked Dr. Bodamer. He couldn't help all these absurd conventions. Sometimes, when she was especially tired, she even thought she'd like to just lean against his bulk for a minute. Maybe that was all she needed, a man like a tree to lean against, take the weight off her own feet, say for ten minutes a week.

Two other beds in the ER were occupied this morning. A mechanic had come in with first-degree burns on his palms from a hot engine, and the mother of a thirteen-year-old boy with black tonsils waited for a throat culture. Adelaide, the baby LPN—that's what Mary called girls fresh out of the program, especially those who were as tender as Adelaide—was looking after them. When Harry Flint was wheeled upstairs, Mary could get a cup of coffee and maybe take a short turn outside, walk around the building. Across the parking lot was a meadow and a bit of red maple forest. It was a beautiful day. Something about fall made you so hopeful in a strange way. When the leaves fell, when the stalks died and turned yellow in the meadows, when all you saw was the skeleton of the plants . . . you had a different feeling for them.

You could see how hard it was for the plants, too.

Was that it? Am I right about that, is that what I mean to say?

Mary found her pocket notebook, half full of scratchings, and wrote it down: "In the fall when they are stripped bare you can see how hard it is for the plants, too." Reading Anne Morrow Lindbergh was doing this to her. She loved that book, *Gift from the Sea*, which she was reading now for the third time. Why shouldn't Mary Leader collect her own thoughts in a book and call it "Gifts from the Forest"?

The orderly came to ferry Harry Flint and his panicky wife and son, and Mary reached for her sweater before she heard the ambulance. Aii-yii-yii, not so fast, my dear. Here comes another accident that may not have needed to happen.

Code CRT. Suicide.

It's not like one person says the word, suicide, it just gets transported from the ambulance into the hospital ear to ear, or hand to hand, like a bucket of water at an old-fashioned fire brigade. Male, likely to have succeeded. Cut himself. Did a job of it.

He was going fast, but not gone yet. Dr. Bodamer, at the sight of the bloodied figure, let loose a rare exclamation. "Oh Christ!" He never did that. Things didn't shock him.

Mary had not seen so much blood in a long time, if ever. Her fingers were instantly seeking a pulse on the man's arm, then his groin, lifting the shreds of blue jeans which had been slashed by the medics.

"No pulse," she cried. She laid the bloodied, torn wrist back down on the sheet and with scarcely a look at the patient's face raised his chin and put her mouth to his. She breathed in and out until Dr. Bodamer's hand on her shoulder stopped her. The man must have died on the way in. She took a good look at him for the first time. And then she raised her left hand and let it come down on Chris Olivet's blood-matted hair.

An orderly was shoving to the bedside with a pole and a bag of blood. Dr. Bodamer turned and shook his head.

"No," he said. He looked at Mary. "Mary?"

"I know him."

"Get Adelaide," he said to the orderly.

"Maybe I'm wrong," she cried. She wet a towel and touched Chris's bloody temple. What was in his eyes, staring up, as if he was trying to look behind him? As if he was looking for something just before he died, and he almost saw it. Almost. He was still looking for it, to make sure, and then he died.

Dr. Bodamer reached out and gently closed the eyelids.

"Who is it?" he asked.

"My handyman. Our caretaker." She washed Chris's forehead with the towel and began to smooth his hair back from his brow. His dark hair was filled with blood. She turned the rag and looked at it, dark now with blood. "A friend," she said. Under the blood his skin was pasty. Over his sharp cheekbones the skin seemed so thin it might even break. "I've known him ever since we've lived up here, back when we used to come for the summers. Way back. Oh, Chris. Oh no."

When Adelaide rushed in, Mary dropped her towel and retreated. She went into the nurse's bathroom, turned on the water, and splashed her face. A sound emerged through her fingers. She sounded like an owl hooting.

I dreamed it; it's not Chris. Go back and see.

You wouldn't make this up.

There's a world where this didn't happen. Yesterday, this didn't happen.

What do I do?

There's nothing I can do. He's gone.

Can't we pretend this didn't happen? Can't I believe this didn't happen?

Friend of yours? Then why didn't you know?

She sat at his bedside until his uncle arrived. A tiny Ojibwa, with a face as dark and shriveled as a walnut. Mr. Olivet sat down next to the sheeted body and touched Chris's arm. Tears glittered like beads of mercury in the deep creases of the old man's face. He was dressed like Chris—a dark green work shirt half buttoned over a t-shirt, worn and stained jeans. He wasn't that old, Mary thought, seventy?

She couldn't desert the ER. There was no one else to check in the next arrival, a sprained ankle. Dr. Bodamer taped it up and sent the man home with aspirin and codeine. A lab tech brought down some results; the boy with the necrotic tonsils had mononucleosis. She handed the results wordlessly to Dr. Bodamer.

"He could have picked this virus up any number of ways," Dr. Bodamer assured the boy's mother as he signed the hospital admission. "Sheer nonsense to call it the kissing disease. We're going to make sure the antibiotic will kick in for the sake of the tonsils; we'll watch those tonsils for a couple of days, and then he'll come home. He's going to be fine with bed rest. Lots of bed rest."

The mother's eyes were round and huge. Mary thought, looking at her, neither one of us will ever forget this day.

Chris had cut his wrists, but maybe that wasn't working fast enough. He had attacked his neck and his thigh. He fully meant to do this, put this life out, as if driven by hatred or revulsion. Someone out for a stroll with his dog walked by Chris's truck, parked on the bluff over Lake Michigan, and saw what was going on inside. The motor was still running.

He probably died in the ambulance or even as they carried him in.

Mary pulled up a stool next to his uncle and laid her hand over his. His hand was gnarled with arthritis, a dark, discolored claw.

"I'm so sorry," she whispered. There's nothing I wouldn't have done for him, if I'd known, she wanted to add.

But what more could she do? No matter what, life was worth living! What could he have been thinking? We work so hard to keep people out of the grave, on this side of the divide. Is that entire effort his just to throw away? As if his life and death mattered to no one else but himself? What am I thinking? My head's a mess. My heart is breaking again.

In a few minutes she went back to Dr. Bodamer. Would the old man benefit from a phenobarb or a sedative? she asked him.

"I don't know; we'll see. How about you, Mary? Would you like something to take home?"

"How could he do this?" she erupted, surprising herself, and her hands jerked at the air as though she could jerk comprehension right out of space.

Dr. Bodamer was a short and solid man in his forties, with a thick crewcut of whitish blond hair. Something about his hairline reminded Mary vaguely of Jim. The way it peaked in the middle of his broad, pink forehead.

"Mary," he said, and took her hand. "Have you ever had a suicide close to you before?"

"What do you mean?"

"A friend, a family member?"

"No."

"Well . . . it did happen once to me. I surprised myself by getting angry and feeling angry for a long time. It's our job in here to save lives. Here comes someone not doing what we want him to do, refuses to live. Waves off the whole effort. All this is set up to save lives, and he rejected it."

"Yes, that's right."

"But, that's not the only thing that happened. That's all I can say."

"What do you mean?"

"Well, you knew him, and I didn't, but people can hide pain. They do hide it." He shook his head and pressed Mary's hand. "Pain . . . can be such that, well, it can be so severe that action is taken, even though you can't see the pain from the outside."

"But not everybody in pain . . ." she protested.

"No. Not everybody." He turned to the desk and patted papers with his hands, looking for something. "There's something here. Look at this. I never thought this was true when I started out. Used to be more of an idealist. But after eighteen years—I do now." He turned the pages of a medical journal, to a big, slick ad for a prescription painkiller. "Look at this," he said. "I believe this is true, Mary. In my experience as a physician."

It was a quote from some ancient writer. She looked through a blur at the words.

"Of all the boons that we can gain," it said, "Man's greatest happiness is relief from pain."

"Any idealism I had in medical school, really, it comes down to this," he said, ripping out the page. "I know you like to write, Mary. I think this is well put. Maybe you want to take this."

Adelaide was suddenly between the two of them, panting. Mary's most recent hire, Adelaide Pellston was gifted with the energy of a whole herd of LPNs, and she coped mildly with initial shock and resistance from patients who had never been treated by a Negro. But after all, she was only twenty-one, and she sometimes seemed downright scatterbrained when she spewed out an extreme response to new information—or what was more difficult to take, when she tossed off an enthusiastic reception to one of her own ideas—"What if we did this!" When she was not busy, she could be all over the map, but Mary could not forget the tenderness on Adelaide's face one day as she wiped the vomit from an unconscious patient's mouth and called out to Mary, "Mouth to mouth?" without hesitation.

Now what?

Adelaide's face was twisted with distress.

"What is it, Adelaide?" said Mary.

"They're saying that President Kennedy's been shot," she said, and suddenly she burst into tears, hearing her own words. "In Dallas. Come listen."

15

Mr. Wilgosch invited them over to watch the president's funeral on his new color TV. She knew the kids should see it, should take part in the historic moment. It was a way to hang onto their handsome young president as long as possible. She joined them in the farmhouse's shabby, dark living room, around the small screen that really did pull them all together into a common experience. Her eyes hurt as she watched, but she couldn't cry.

She could barely speak about Chris to anyone. She hadn't told the children. All she could do was keep moving. "Man must endure his going hence, even as his coming hither," she shouted to herself in the car, driving home that awful evening. Chris couldn't endure, but Mary Leader had to. I have to. Despite grief barreling toward her one more time. Like a freight train.

She didn't plan to keep the news from the kids. She just couldn't be the one to speak the words. Soon they found out, but in the rush of news about the assassination, there weren't too many questions.

"Be getting your own television one of these days?" Mr. Wilgosch teased her, and she snorted. The kids recognized her sound of dismissal: "Ptssh!" It certainly was interesting to watch this public event, and it drew folks together in an interesting way, to all be watching the funeral cortege. But usually the sight of someone watching TV—slack jawed, eyes glazed—did not look healthy to her. She didn't want to see her and Jim's kids looking like that. Childhood was for play, and high school was for learning, and spending hours gaping at a little blue box didn't fit in one iota. Melina begged and Becky begged, but they knew it was no use.

"When? When would you consider buying one?" Melina pushed her.

"Eight," said Mary.

They groaned. "Eight what?" said Sean. "You can't just have eight. Days? Years? Minutes?"

"Eight."

They knew it was no use; they dropped it. She never retreated from "Eight," nor elaborated on it.

At night, blessed oblivion. She washed down a phenobarb from Dr. Bodamer with a gulp of room-temperature gin. Seagram's in the bottle with goosebumps on the shoulders was her favorite, sweet and spicy, not like swallowing knives. It tasted like juniper trees.

She didn't even go to Chris's funeral mass, though she knew she ought to go visit Chris's uncle. Take him some food. She drove by St. Mary's of the Lake the afternoon of the mass, but she couldn't bear to go in. Suicide was a mortal sin, she even believed that, and yet if Father dared to talk about sin—if he dared to mention sin, or hell, in connection with Chris Olivet—why, she'd have to walk out, or kill him.

"The Lamb of God who takes away the sins of the world," the missal said, and sometimes Mary thought to herself, "And you priests bring it right back." She remembered how it helped her to decide that despair was a sin. Yes, but it helped because I made the decision that I was in despair. I named the hour and date and flavor of my sin. I came to it myself. It was some kind of decision I made; it can't be made by someone else. Why doesn't the church trust us one bit to be capable of . . . dear God in heaven, what's the right word, growth? Discovering who we are?

What Chris had done enraged her, just as Dr. B. had predicted would happen. Man must endure his going hence, and Chris could not endure it. Why couldn't he ask for help? What was so terrible that someone, somewhere, couldn't help? How could she go on, if every important friendship in her life was going to be so unpredictable, so painful, the very floor upended on her like this, broken into a thousand pieces when she needed it most?

The day of his mass she drove to the church, then drove right on past. On impulse she went up to the bluff where Chris had destroyed himself. She looked at his last view. She parked and climbed down the cliff to the shore of Lake Michigan, and walked up the deserted beach. In the offshore wind, surf broke like a froth of dirty, frayed lace against the sand and pebbles. Bits of foam flew in the air.

"Some friend," she said aloud. "Some friend!" Who did she mean, herself or Chris? Did it matter? "I would have helped!" she cried. Her voice rose. "Chris, you should have tried me," she called louder. "Chris, you should have tried me! Even this is better!" She dug her fingers into the cold, hard sand. She kicked at the detritus, the lake trash. A bird skeleton, a beer bottle. Even this! All of it!

She shouted again and again. She shouted whatever came into her mind. For once she couldn't miss; her wild fluency, unstoppable, amazed her. "You should have tried me! I could have helped you! I'm not a magician! But I could have helped! Why didn't you try me! I did care! I did! I do care, I do, I do, I do!"

After a solid hour of shouting out loud, an hour of walking up and down the beach, she made her way back to the car. She was wrung out and yet extraordinarily relaxed. Almost used up. As she drove home she sensed that something awful had left her. The grief of Chris's death would ride inside her, a permanent passenger until her own dying day. But something had been released. Not everyone could leave the worst behind and go on. Was that it? But she could go on. She wouldn't keep looking back. Hit the ground running. Go forward, Mary.

She just had not thought about how much the possibility of friendship with Chris meant to her. No matter how she acted on it from day to day. And now he was gone, that possibility withdrawn.

When the kids did bring it up, Mary shook her head and said, "There's always another choice, there's always something better than suicide. If anyone you know ever mentions it, even jokingly . . . tell someone. Take them seriously." It seemed to her the most important thing, to tell them that—this was not the answer. It was the only thing she could say with certainty. They needed some interpretation from her, and once they got that much, they let it go.

Alex, home for Christmas, thought that Mary's sadness might come from reliving, in President Kennedy's death, the loss of her own husband.

"He was like Daddy, practically Daddy's age when he died," Alex told Sharon, as they looked at the magazines Mary brought home from the IGA: *Life* and *Time* and *Look* and souvenir booklets about the funeral. It was not like their mother to buy all this stuff, but they devoured them, page after page of the riderless horse, John-John's salute, Jackie and Robert Kennedy together in their new and tragic bond, the loss they shared together.

"For her it's like losing Daddy again," said Alex, as they pondered the pile of booklets. "Or maybe it reminds her of when Franklin Roosevelt died. That was a huge thing at the time, like this."

Alex came back for Christmas different. Slender, with a brilliant smile. Up-to-date glasses—rimless, octagonal lenses instead of those black cat's eyes. A few nights later the four sisters were in her and Sharon's bedroom, and Alex got up to turn off the light so they could look out at the stars and the moon on the water. Melina watched Alex cross the room to the light switch. She was wearing red long johns, and Melina suddenly realized that Alex's waist had shrunk. Alex was getting skinny!

And she'd grown her hair long, too, and sometimes even curled it, on jumbo rollers, so it bounced with air. Though she wouldn't sleep in curlers, like Sharon did.

When she wore a certain navy blue turtleneck sweater, she was beautiful. And she was slightly giddy too. And yet at the same time, she was still full of ideas, full of impatience, not at all content with Pinestead the way it had become in her absence, which is exactly what they had predicted, waiting for her in Traverse City.

When she got off the bus and they saw the new Alex, they all felt a little shy and uncertain. Despite the hugging and shrieking no one knew how to talk about the changes, so it was a relief, two days later, when she organized a housecleaning team after breakfast—that was Alex's true return to the family. But it didn't take away that she had changed greatly on the outside.

After Christmas, her eyes opened, Melina observed that all of her family was different. Sharon wore high heels now, making herself taller for no good reason. She was already tall. Sean and Becky went out almost every weekend night. Mom didn't seem to care too much if anyone did the chores around the house. When she was home she spent a lot of time in her room, reading or working at her desk or just dozing.

There was something else wrong, too. Something you couldn't even name. All Melina could say for certain was that they had been happier once. Things had been better at home, once. She couldn't describe how.

She went into Mom's room a lot, when Mom wasn't home, as if to find what was missing—or as if to verify that yes, something was indeed wrong, the way your fingers would keep touching a wound. She'd go in Mom's room and stand there, wondering what she wanted. Stand there in the midst of the very absence that hurt her.

"Chris was a friend of mine," Mary said.

Mr. Olivet nodded and blinked rapidly. The cabin behind him was dark; the glare off the fresh snow behind Mary must be blinding.

"You come in," he said.

She had finally found the Olivets' place in Paradise Valley, a hamlet tucked down in one of the valleys north of Achill. There was one of those shabby Pentecostal churches, two garages, an old orchard right in the center of the village, and the Olivets' land—several acres, to her surprise, of meadow and trees. Once a farm, now grown over. Chris had lived in a wide trailer with a built-up wannigan; his uncle lived across a field in a very old cabin of square-cut logs. They had a big, separate garage or workshop. Everything looked so pretty, dusted with fresh snow. Neat and clean.

She began to explain her reason for coming by. All she could think of to say was that he was a friend. But somehow she had to tell him that she understood now. Chris had his reasons. She had found it in Jim's private files.

Mr. Olivet's dark flannel shirt hung unbuttoned over his narrow shoulders like it was draped on a tiny wire coat hanger with the ends twisted in. He kept rubbing his stomach through his t-shirt. She was taller than he was by an inch or two, and Mary was a short woman herself.

"I'll make you some tea. Please, you come inside and sit down."

There were just two rooms to the cabin. In the main room, a red and black Hudson's Bay blanket covered a bed. On the floor, leaning against the bed, were a dozen or so paintings on unframed canvas.

"Chris's paintings, I keep lookin' 'em over," he said, waving a hand toward them. "Come into the kitchen now. You sit down here." He set a kettle onto an old cast-iron cookstove. The floor was covered with dark and warped linoleum. It almost had waves in it, like the lake surface in a chop. She knew, from what Chris had said once, that his uncle did a lot of preserving in this kitchen. Chris said he canned gooseberries and corn and tomatoes and even put up jars of smoked whitefish. She could not imagine it. She liked making jam and syrup, but when people gave her canned goods, she often tossed them out. Mary had seen botulism cases. It didn't take much. Anything from this big, dark, old-fashioned kitchen she'd probably toss, just to be on the safe side.

He made the tea of loose leaves from a tin box. He put a cup in front of her and poured from a brown, stoneware teapot. He moved a jar of honey toward her with his brown, scarred fingers. She recognized it as Arnie's, a local beekeeper.

"Chris was friends with my late husband," she began.

"Yes, Dr. Jim used to come by here."

"He did?"

"Oh yes. Years ago, Chris was having a real terrible time. Dr. Jim, he come right over. I remember that he told Chris, why don't you do what your uncle does, Chris, you follow your own uncle's footsteps! Walk in his footsteps when your own give out." At that Mary heard him chuckle. "Now let me see. I have some macaroons here."

"None for me, thanks," she said.

He ignored her protest. "I like macaroons because they are soft and a little easier to eat these days." He put a waxed-paper bag from the supermarket on the table. "Help yourself, they are nothing special. I knew you was coming, I'd a got something nicer. Yeah. That's what Dr. Jim told him. Chris had days . . ."

"Days?"

"He had days when he had to be out in the woods or on the lake, and that usually helped. Finally it wasn't enough. It wasn't enough. You don't see these things coming, only when you look back." They drank tea, and the knot of grief seemed to tighten. Funny how it caught you like this. "Now," he said. "Please. You have one of them cookies, tell me if they're any good. I have plenty of them." She took a macaroon to be polite, to be doing something. To her surprise, they were delicious; the taste of coconut reminded her of her own mother's cooking.

"Thank you, thank you," she said. She had another. It was as if her body had been waiting a long time for coconut macaroons.

Mary had not thought to go through Jim's files after that terrible day, not for weeks. But one night in her bedroom, she was surveying things the kids left out—her kids came in here all the time, she knew it. She didn't mind. They liked to put on her earrings or beads, or dress up in the kimonos from Korea. They liked to look through their own files of report cards, clippings, drawings, and letters, things they had created back in the forgotten years when they were three and four and five—their own history, from which sixth grade always delivered them, irrevocably, shooting them forward across a gap from childhood to adolescence. Between sixth and seventh grade they almost forgot who they used to be. Then they'd come in here to find out.

This time someone had been looking at Jim's obstetrics textbook.

She kept it because they might as well find out about sex from a medical textbook as anywhere else. Her daughters and her son had no doubts about where babies came from after looking at those pictures. Or the dermatology textbook. Same thing. Children had an appetite for deformities.

If she found the books out, she put them away without saying anything. They belonged on the top shelf of the shelves that rose behind her desk, almost to the ceiling. She had to stand on the desk to put them away. Just like the kids did, when they got the books down. No need to make it easy for them, after all. You'd want it to be entirely their own idea. How else would you know they were ready, if they didn't take action on their own?—then she turned and looked down at Jim's filing cabinet and thought, Now. Now I'll find out.

She pulled the drawer out and flipped back the tabs and studied the names. Chris Olivet.

Jim's handwriting broke her heart. Narrow, slanted, perfectly balanced. Heavy and even; he put his whole arm into his penmanship but still used a doctor's shorthand: *c* for with, *x* for times.

He had treated Chris for what he called a severe depressive episode in 1952. Brought on by the end of a friendship with someone named Lucy. No information about Lucy. Chris had thoughts of suicide, and Jim told him to get rid of the guns in the house and offered to help. Jim even went to Chris's trailer to get them.

"Sobbing, rocking. Said it had been going on for two weeks. Related childhood episode of abuse at Catholic boarding school in Wisconsin. One of several boys raped. Forced to be intimate with older men. Complained to his grandfather, who then brought him home. 12 yrs.

"Unable to complete intercourse without reliving the experience. Nor talk to Lucy about it. Severe reaction to her departure.

"Tried to bring out more memories of the mission school; certain kids there targeted for some reason. Race? Passivity? Refusal to fight back?

"Chris said, 'I'm like some ugly scar crawling around on the earth. That's what I am.'

"This is shaming children for what is done *to* them. Using shame on children. A kind of violence. Don't say shame on you to my children."

He had written prescriptions for Chris, over the years, up until 1955.

"Mom?"

Becky came into the room, seeking permission to go downhill skiing with Bernie.

"What's wrong, Mom?"

"Nothing."

"You look sad."

"I'm sorting papers. That's all."

"So what about skiing? Can I go?"

"I'll think about it."

"He's on the phone, Mom, I have to tell him now."

Mary had been sitting on the edge of her cot, staring up from the files, for several minutes and not moving before Becky poked her head in. This was a circle of hell she had not known existed. She had been kept ignorant. Neither man had thought she should know about things like this, even though it had to do with people she cared for. Doctor-patient confidentiality. Jim would never have told her anything, but meanwhile, Chris was hanging around her own children, watching them all day . . . you didn't know how these traumas affected people. She was supposed to just trust Jim. Just trust him. But he went and died.

"Mom."

"Becky, I'll think about it. You may tell him that. Or you may tell him no, and if you need me to find some housework for you. . . ."

"Ohh!" she withdrew in frustration.

But in her own life, Mary did know about things like this. Cruelty upon those who could not fight back. The endless appetite some people had to torture those who could not fight back.

Going into people's homes as a nurse she saw scars and bruises. She knew of homes where children were whipped and women were knocked back against the wall. A fourteen-year-old girl had a baby in the emergency room two years ago and didn't know which one of her father's hired hands was the father.

This—this story in Jim's handwriting—this was harm done to someone she herself depended on. And neither one of these men had ever thought she should know anything about it. They had protected her from it. This was more than doctor-patient confidence. This was that damn manhood thing, something to do with that, with keeping things secret.

How could grown men touch children this way? That, she could not understand. But shame, yes, and secrecy, and something else Jim had written down here—"severe self-loathing."

A scar crawling around on the face of the earth.

That time he shot the deer and came over, if she had known about this, what would she have done then? She knew there was something troubling Chris, or she wouldn't have been so nervous. She sensed something. She was right. Her intuition was right.

Never say shame on you to the children. Had Jim ever told her that? No, she couldn't remember such a conversation.

It turned out that Mr. Olivet knew most of this. She said, "I would have helped if he asked for help, but I didn't know how bad it was." She blurted that last out without thinking and wanted to take it back. It sounded like she was blaming Chris for something. But Mr. Olivet nodded.

"He got hurt bad as a kid. I was away in the army then. I didn't know all the details. But after that he done the best he could." He put his hands flat on the table and pushed himself up, went to the sink. He picked up a handleless mug that was sitting on the sill and turned it over. A folded piece of paper dropped in his hand. "Here, he left this here. Do you want to see it?"

He came back to the table and sat down and unfolded the paper. Mary thought that his eyes filled up as he looked at it, or they could have been just tired old man's eyes.

Chris's troubled handwriting, half printing, half cursive, lower case and capitals mixed, was familiar to her, from notes over the years. This was a suicide note, she realized. Like Jim, he had borne down hard on the pencil. It was unsigned.

"I will try and bring words to this. It's been coming a long time. I used to look forward to morning. But now there's nothing there, of use to me. It's not your fault. Please believe I'm truly happy with this decision for the first time. I know what is coming at me and I can't go through it. Thank you to those who tried to help, there were many. I'm sorry."

It was hard to stare at these letters on the scrap of paper—to think that he drew himself together, bore down on his emotions, brought it all together and picked up a pencil, and formed letters and sentences, and it came to this.

"I think that he would like you to have one of his paintings," Mr. Olivet said.

"Did you know Lucy?" she asked.

"Who was Lucy?"

"A woman—a girlfriend maybe, years ago. Chris came to my husband after she, after they—parted ways. I take it Chris did not want it to end, but she, Lucy, ended it." Clearly Mr. Olivet did not remember Lucy or never knew about her. He looked curious but unalarmed. Mary stumbled on, "That's what brought on a real episode of, of depression, in 1952."

"I didn't know. Maybe he never brought her to meet me. That might be. I remember your husband coming here, but never no gal named Lucy." He stirred his tea and took a few bites from a macaroon. "I wondered why he didn't bring a lady around. Sometimes I wondered that."

He shook his head and looked down at his cup. His mouth was drawn tight like a knothole in a plank, tight and dark. He squeezed his eyes shut for a minute.

"Never had a steady gal in my own life, either. Not much of a success in that. I guess the important thing is we go on," he said. "There's the living and the dead. The living carry on."

It sounded meaningless, what he said, and yet his words helped. Don't feel guilty about not looking back, he was saying; you're still alive, you keep trying, you go on.

She chose a small painting of a wolf in late autumn, not for the black, yellow-eyed wolf, but for the beech trees behind it. They were gray and straight and nearly bare, with bits of orange leaf scattered on a few twigs. Mary knew that set of colors and loved it: there was a week or two when you caught that combination in her woods. This could be her woods. The wolf was out of Chris's imagination, or a wildlife book, or both. So the wolf was a dream of his. A dream of power and solitude.

Driving home she looked at the painting in the passenger seat with a sudden rush of satisfaction. Chris as a wolf. She liked that.

"Myself, I'm a fox," she said aloud, as if talking to him. "Making my way through the snow to forage for my kits. And always alone. Tail fluffed out for warmth. I see a mouse, and I pounce!" She smiled at the memory of a fox she'd seen early one morning last month, leaping above the snow, landing in a spray of white.

The wolf was crude, but she recognized Chris in it, in the thick black paint and the great care taken to get it right, and she liked seeing his touch in the ease of those orange leaves, like kites flying against the gray trees. What had she given Mr. Olivet? Nothing. She had thought to bring him something to eat, but it didn't turn out that way. The giving flowed only one way.

Find some footprints and follow them, when you're really lost. If only someone who knew him better had been around to say that one more time to Chris.

Bread pudding—she would take Mr. Olivet some bread pudding, Miriam Huley's recipe. Soft food for an old man whose teeth were bad. She would take it next week. She would remember.

16

For his fifteenth birthday Sean wanted his driver's permit. He got behind the wheel that first day and did so well from the start she knew he'd been driving already—maybe up on Wilgosch's farm.

He drove her out to Mr. Olivet's place in Pleasant Valley one afternoon, with a gift of bread pudding. A rare moment together for the two of them. Maybe this would be a good time for a certain parent-child talk she had been puzzling over. It would have been Jim's role, not hers, but there you are, once again.

Sean's broad hands were brown and scarred from a summer's adventures and as relaxed on the wheel at ten o'clock and two o'clock as if he'd been driving for years. His hands, feet, and knees were outsized at the moment. His knees were sometimes inflamed from growing so fast. The man he would become was making an appearance, a glimpse at a time.

"Something I need to tell you," she said.

"Yeah?" Sean said after a silence, watching the road.

"With you driving and everything and in high school, life can get complicated."

"Sure, Mom," he said, as if she had suggested they stop for apples at the next roadside stand.

She soldiered on. "You see, it's important that I tell you this, what your dad would have told you—you can't go wrong when you respect other people. Ever. You can't ever go wrong when you respect people, male or female. Especially female."

He gave her a quick look. There's more, she thought, I'm not done yet. Don't touch that dial!

"Even when they don't seem to respect themselves, you have to respect them. That's your responsibility," she said. "So, I expect you to do that. God expects you to do that. Young women, they need that. Respect."

"Yeah, okay," he said, but with mildness, not dismissal. Trying to imply, I know this is real, with his tone.

"Do you have any questions?"

He smiled, looking ahead. "No, not really."

She couldn't think of anything else to lob into the silence between them. At that very moment a deer leaped out from the left, practically onto the hood of the car, and Sean did exactly the right thing, braked and wrenched the car onto the right shoulder. The station wagon skidded across the shoulder and tipped slightly into the pine trees.

It needed to be pushed from the front end, back up onto the shoulder. At his insistence she took the wheel, and he leaned against the hood, trying himself to shove it back while she gunned the engine in reverse. Within a few minutes a truck pulled over. Wordlessly the driver joined Sean, and this time Mary reversed the station wagon back onto the road.

They went on to other subjects, deer collisions and near misses they had known. Sean's left leg vibrated with adrenalin all the way to Paradise Valley.

Since the episode of the stolen tools he had never, so far as she knew, crossed the line again. Sean was helpful around the place, smart, strong, and sometimes funny. He was going to be good-looking, too. Some things would come easy to him. Good looks and mild humor were great favors in life. But he kept too much to himself. The books on adolescent psychology that she read frightened her; things could go wrong so quickly. Boys had a unique delicacy. He needed more patience than she could provide. Mary felt that she always reacted too soon and too strongly when something came up between them—and his sisters gave him no mercy!

At Pleasant Valley, Mr. Olivet insisted they sit down for some bread pudding together. Then, as they were leaving, he thrilled Sean by giving him an otter pelt that Chris had tanned decades earlier. The pelt took Mary's breath away: it was stiff as a board on the tanned side, but the fur was silky and dark and ran like a river with your hand. Sean took it from Mr. Olivet with awe in his face and laid it on the backseat of the car like it might break.

Otters were disappearing from Northern Michigan rivers, but Mary remembered watching them in the lagoon at the south end of Achill or sliding into the Manistee River like children at a park. Human in their playfulness. She and Jim had come around a curve on the Manistee once and seen them playing. Jim held the canoe in an eddy, and they watched for almost an hour, not daring to move.

Mr. Olivet always reciprocated too much. They couldn't let this go on, it was not fair to him.

With the girls, she was more confident. She could see what was going on in their heads. Sharon, for instance, carried a powerful certainty inside her, and it had to do with finding a man who was at home in Northern woods—a man to fill the exact absence left by Jim Leader.

At seventeen, she didn't see the likelihood of such a dream figure appearing to her on the home ground of Michigan, so she set her sights further. Bold as any seeker after treasure, she announced that she was going to the University of Alaska.

She didn't say she was going in search of a man, she didn't even realize it; that was Mary's own thought, and she kept it to herself. And when Mary saw the price of tuition at the University of Alaska, she cheered right up. Now that was one inexpensive college way up there, even for nonresidents, and Sharon would be a resident by her sophomore year. You had to applaud this adventurous spirit. You had to.

Sharon sent off her application the week before Easter, way early. A few days later, news of the terrible Good Friday earthquake in Anchorage and a tidal wave in Valdez didn't weaken her resolve one bit.

"She still gonna go up there?" Adelaide asked Mary at work.

"Of course," said Mary. She knew that it hadn't even occurred to Sharon to back away from her plan. Dangerous? Alaska? Danger didn't enter into it. In some ways, to Mary's wonder, Sharon was turning out to be a remarkably independent young woman, though she hated to call attention to herself, struggled with stage fright before every oral report, refused to ice skate until someone had chiseled a hole and shown her the depth of the ice, refused to hurl herself down ski slopes or canoe the mile and a half across the lake. She didn't even date; boys made her uncomfortable, except for that gentle Marty Fleck next door. She adored Marty but had no use for local boys; she was waiting for a man.

She had saved every penny of that babysitting money all these years. She was a frugal, resourceful, methodical girl with a treasure inside her, and that treasure was wild romance. Like in Kipling's poem—"and all unseen, Romance brought up the nine-fifteen," Mary thought, when Sharon and Alex together boarded the bus in Traverse City that would take them to Chicago. They'd spend two nights with Grandma and Tony and then take the Empire Builder west to Seattle. Across Montana and through the Rocky Mountains—how she envied them. And there, Sharon would board the first airplane of her life, any of their lives, making three hops to get all the way to Fairbanks, at latitude 65 degrees.

Becky was an athlete and Mary hoped that there might be some kind of scholarship to ski or skate or swim or something like that in Becky's future, but there didn't seem to be very many such things available for girls. Plus Becky was so accident prone! She carried a big, star-shaped scar on her shoulder blade from that time the propeller attacked her, but it wasn't the first or last injury. She rocked back in her chair at the dinner table too vigorously one night, tipped over backward, and knocked herself out. She needed five stitches in her scalp that time.

She sat out a month of the ski season with a torn ligament, and field hockey ended when she broke her arm.

Mary was pleased with the school's new emphasis on physical education. That was one more wonderful thing President Kennedy had done. Becky worked as a swimming counselor at the YMCA camp up the lake between her junior and senior years, and after that Mary was certain she could teach physical education in a school; she was so skilled and responsible, and sympathetic to the shyest kids; it would be a natural fit. Maybe there was an education scholarship out there. But it was better if kids thought of these things on their own. The slightest conversational suggestion from Mom could be remembered forever as cruel and constant pressure!

Becky had become stoic, whether from repeated injuries or natural temperament, Mary didn't know. She never fought with Sean the way

Alex had. Because she dated a lot, because she made it her business to get along with boys about whom she'd been so curious for a long time, she made allowances for Sean. He was a boy, and boys just did things differently, and she didn't mind one bit. If Sean got up from the table after polishing off two plates of Becky's creamed-tuna-on-rice and went straight to the refrigerator to get something to eat, Becky didn't burst into tears or argue with him. Now that she found herself in what had been the position of her older sisters, she dutifully put her casserole or fried rice or pigs-in-blankets on the table if Mary couldn't make it home, cleaned up afterward, gave her homework a desperate lick to the sound of the Byrds or some other loud and hairy musicians, then spent the bulk of winter evenings on the telephone.

She would lie down on Mary's pallet to talk to her friends, and one winter night, admiring her toned and perfectly shaven legs as she talked, she put one foot right through the window above her. Just raised a leg and sent it through the window. Glass fell around her.

"Oh my God, I have to get off the phone! I kicked out Mom's window!" she shrieked and hung up. Sean and Mary and Mel came running. At first it seemed there was blood everywhere, but only one of the lacerations required stitches, where a shard of glass went right into Becky's knee. She gritted her teeth and squeezed her eyes shut and gasped but did not cry when Mary removed it. Dr. Bodamer put in ten stitches that later healed into a scar shaped, they discovered later, like an *R* for Rebecca.

Sean taped plastic over the window until they could get a glazier to come. Mary thought, as she often did, of Chris. But there was no Chris to call, and the window man charged a bundle. That was the end of the invading vine from the rosebush, too, of which she'd grown fond. It was gone just like that.

"I could've fixed it," Sean said.

"Glass is very heavy," said Mary.

"I could do it."

"Next time."

It was true; Sean could figure things out. So many things he had learned on his own—how to change a tire, how to re-solder wires in the radio, how to fix drips and leaks and clogged pipes, how to scrape and repaint the windowsills and door trim that suffered the full force of the summer sun off the lake. Mr. Wilgosch might have advised him about the tools he needed and how to use them, and Chris had taught him a few things—besides how to carve away from your own femoral artery—but many skills he'd taught himself.

Somehow the kids had their private lives. Learned things independent of her. She was away too much. Or maybe just enough—maybe the combination was pretty good, a hawk's eye when she was at home, a good imagination as to what kids get into and some healthy distance when she was at work—but never more than a phone call away, never.

Civil rights legislation was upsetting people in Northern Michigan, and most of them wanted to solve the problem by electing Barry Goldwater. We got our protections in the Bill of Rights, groused the administrator of nursing. We don't need this Civil Rights Act! It's not that anyone's prejudiced, it's excess government! Even Mr. Wilgosch muttered, "Government does too much already. Coloreds got to do some a these things for themselves."

Mary liked Mr. Wilgosch, so she kept her mouth shut. But she thought, don't need civil rights?

How about that time, years ago, his neighbor on the far side of Hebron needed money and wanted to sell Mr. Wilgosch a corner parcel with a small, scummy pond. Mr. Wilgosch said he couldn't even consider the asking price, and the man said, "You don't buy it I'll sell it to a nigger. One a those people Mary Leader rents to. You want it to turn into Nigger Heaven 'round here?"

When Mr. Wilgosch reported this to Mary, he added, "I told him, go ahead and sell it to whoever. Black, red, yellow, sell it to another stupid Polack like me thinks he can make a living farming on sand, but don't threaten me. But I know he'll do no such thing."

Mrs. Wilgosch, an unhappy woman, had left him years ago, for another man, Mary heard. Mary never forgot how once, the first summer the Duquesnes arrived, she had called Mary on the phone just a minute after the Duquesnes drove in, just as Mary was greeting them.

"Everything all right down there?" Rose Wilgosch hollered through the phone. "You want me to call the cops?" The Duquesnes had been observed by Rose as they slowed down in front of her house, looking for the Pinestead sign. Rose had run straight to the phone at the sight of colored people on Achill Drive. Mary actually said, "Thank you for checking up on us," before she hung up. You had to maintain good relations with your neighbors, encourage them to watch out for you—those were important things to do. Maybe in her crude and confusing way, the secretly unhappy Rose thought she was doing a neighborly duty.

Rose was long gone, but Mr. Wilgosch was a reliable and kind neighbor. Sean helped out around the farm, on and off, every summer. It was one more place he learned how to do things. He loved it up there, on the heights of the farm, just as much as he loved the lake. He liked Mr. Wilgosch and his old handyman who had mined gold in Alaska, Clint Geoghan.

"Nurse, my rocks hurt," the man in the examining room said. He looked as unhappy as his words. The lower buttons of his shirt wouldn't fasten over an enormous, squared-off gut. From his pallid skin she guessed he hadn't left the house in a long time. Not unexpectedly, his blood pressure was elevated.

"Dr. B. has got two patients ahead of you, so you go ahead and take off your things and put on this gown," she said. "Tell me about the pain."

"It's on the outside and inside both," he mumbled. "They just plain hurt."

"Any rash?"

"Oh no, ma'am. This isn't that kinda thing. I don't fool around."

"I'll leave you alone to put on that gown," she said.

When she checked back a minute later, he was still standing there, gazing sadly at the wall. Two ends of his unbuckled belt swung out from under the belly. But he had made no other progress.

"Go ahead now and get ready for the doctor," she said. "You got to take off those pants so he can examine you." The man stared at her as though her words made no sense. "Come on, now," she said and busied herself at the sink. When she turned back he had unzipped his fly, but that was all. He gazed helplessly forward. Such passivity, she thought, no wonder you're sick! She put her hands into his belt loops and pulled his pants down, hard. "Like this," she said. She pulled them halfway down his thighs. "Take off your pants, take off your underwear, take off your shirt, put on this gown, wait on that table, and the doctor will be right in to see you."

She walked out to the waiting room and went behind the nurses' desk and put her head in her hands. A boy in the waiting room coughed vigorously. She had given him a package of tissues earlier. His nostrils were plugged with green, and his thick, endless coughing and snorting rattled like a peck basket half full of wet corncobs. No wonder people get sick in hospitals, she thought. Last week she had almost lost her temper when a kid wouldn't sit still for Dr. Bodamer's tongue depressor. She wanted to slap the kid hard right across his face, something she'd never done to anyone.

Just like she wanted to call the cops on the frantic mother who wouldn't wait another twenty minutes to pick up a prescription for codeine for her twelve-year-old boy's fractured jaw. He had fallen off a horse. Dr. Bodamer gave him some medication right there in the office, but the mom wouldn't wait for him to finish up another exam and write a prescription. She was wild in her anxiety to leave the hospital, and Mary knew why. The boy's injuries were perfectly consistent with the story, but there was something else going on with this family. They were both, mother and son, going to catch hell from Dad if his dinner wasn't ready, if they were late meeting his expectations. Mary had seen this behavior before.

"He'll have to make do with aspirin," she was shouting, hauling her son out by the arm. The poor boy, dazed, bandaged, couldn't speak a word in protest.

People do so much harm to their own selves. If I see one more gunshot wound, ever, she thought, one more leg ripped open by a chainsaw.

Dr. Bodamer finished examining the man with the painful testicles and pulled the curtain behind him. "That poor fella needs testing for a malignancy," he said softly, and Mary stood up, ashamed of her impatience and yet not ashamed. Is there anything else I can do for a living? she wondered. What else can I do?

Waiting for Melina in the public library, she picked up a *Saturday Evening Post* and read a story about a black farmer in Mississippi letting civil rights workers stay in his home. Eight children of his own, but he cleared out a room for these white and black kids from the North. She looked closely at the pictures of his unpainted house with a breezeway between its two sides and a lean-to kitchen.

Mary remembered asking her mother, "How can darkies stand to live like this?" But she didn't really know how they lived. Had never been inside a black family's home. Whites back then just looked right past Negroes half the time. Once she drove the women at the Bee Laundry home after work, and when they said, "You can let us out here," so she wouldn't have to drive right up to their shabby homes if she didn't want, Mary did just that. Pulled over and let them out, and how far from their own homes? Why did she do that? What was so wrong about giving them a ride directly to their own doors?

That time her mother told her never to eat lunch with the help again. She didn't question what her mom said, she obeyed her.

A man who worked for her father over the years came to his funeral mass in 1944. They all knew him as Sonny Boy. After mass they said, "Thank you so much for coming," but didn't invite him back to the house to eat. What was his real name? What did his wife call him? Probably not Sonny Boy.

She picked up a two-week-old Sunday *New York Times*. On the editorial page she read about the migration of Canada geese, and something inside her exulted. It was a short essay about the beauties of autumn in New England. The turning globe and the mysteries of migration, right on the same page as civil rights and the tax revolt and Barry Goldwater's snowball's chance in hell. It was a very short editorial right at the bottom of the page.

Mary herself wrote things like this sometimes, in kids' spiral-bound notebooks she bought at the grocery store. Well, what she wrote wasn't so well formed, not so cogent. Just paragraphs, not real essays, not by a long shot. It made her feel good, just like paddling the canoe. To write a bit cleared her head and sort of jumped her forward to the next observation. She liked getting it out of her system, and sometimes even reading it later, asking herself what was happening last year at this time and letting her own journal remind her of the cycle of seasons.

It was never impossible to contact that other reality, the world of the animals and birds. You just put down what you were doing and went outside, any time of year. This past spring Mary had asked Sean to take down the old tree house in a red pine that flung out its long twisted limbs over the lake. The tree house was beginning to seem like an attractive nuisance, its layers of disintegrating plywood tempting the children of summer guests. Sean ripped off a few boards, then came and found her.

"A surprise for you," he said, smiling. He wouldn't say more.

They climbed into the tree house, and he said, look up, right in front of you.

It was a vireo's nest, a basket dripping with long fibers near the end of the limb over the water. Her face was almost even with it, yet she wouldn't have known it for a nest except for the three creamy, freckled eggs. The outside was all camouflaged with old leaves, bark chips, moss, and seedy fluff. From the outside it was just a lump of dun-colored forest litter. Peering at the inside, those eggs were safe as if they were in a silk-lined jewelry box.

She watched them all summer, listened to their sweet, early-morning cry. Here I am, Here-ee-o, here-ee-o. Vi-re-o, vi-re-o. A plain gray bird, it inhabited—no, it created—a universe apart from the ER, the resort business, politics, a universe more sacred than anything inside a church. If you ask me, Mary thought.

Melina stopped in front of her with a tower of library books in her arms.

"Soon's I check these out we can go," she said.

"I might get one or two books myself," said Mary.

"Unnh, I have to get home," complained Melina. "I have so much to do."

You mean so much that you've left to the last minute, as usual, Mary thought with a smile.

Because she had skipped first grade, Melina was eleven years old in the seventh grade, flat chested inside her hand-me-down plaid blouse, safety pins holding up the hem of a wool skirt. Hemming was slow, monotonous labor, and Melina couldn't be bothered, despite the fact that in junior high she sometimes experimented with her appearance. She tried out pink lipstick from the five-and-dime that looked and smelled like cake frosting. Her thick, dark-honey hair fell unbraided halfway down her back, and Becky had cut a new style of bangs for her, straight and long, like the Beatles'. But her grades were surprisingly uneven, except in English class. Maybe by second grade the damage had been done. Maybe she had stopped paying attention to things that bored her long before that. She drew odd cartoons in the margins of all her math papers. She couldn't keep her mind free of stories. Those habits a teacher had warned Mary against crept up on her after all.

Mary smiled. Better not retire just yet. I still have a baby at home. Just wish there was a way to change what I do every day.

"I'll be a fraction of a minute," she said and went into the book stacks. There were some books about how to write that she had looked at before. She grabbed *How to Write for Homemakers* and two others and took them to the checkout desk.

A *Miltonia Gazette* was lying on the counter next to the checkout desk, and Melina touched her finger to a picture on the front page.

"We went to that last year," she said.

Right on the front page was a photograph advertising the Miltonia Lions Club Minstrel Show. Four men in black face leered at the camera, and one taller, unpainted Negro man stood behind them.

"No, you've never been to that," Mary said promptly. She wouldn't let her kids go to that kind of thing!

"Alex took me," Melina said.

Mary had never seen a photograph of the show before. It looked to be as awful as she had always imagined. If Alex was with Melina, then it had to have been all right. But why?

"Did you like it?"

"No, I didn't, but the music. I liked the music a lot. I liked that guy." She touched the Negro man's face. "He plays the banjo."

Mary didn't like banjo music growing up, it seemed like pellets thrown at you. Have fun or else! And it seemed peculiar indeed for the newspaper to run this picture of a minstrel show in 1964, while the whole country was in a paroxysm of change. That's a little town for you. That's country. Maybe I haven't come so far from Carolina after all.

"He played so fast you couldn't see his fingers," Melina was saying.

"That's what it is, moving your fingers fast?"

Melina stared up at her mother, her feelings hurt, Mary could see. Mary didn't mean to disparage an interest. She had been about to add "Ptssh," but she stopped herself. What just happened? she thought. Could she take it back?

"Do you want to learn to play an instrument?" she said. "Would you like that?"

"Could I?"

"We'll go to Traverse City and look for a banjo. Maybe someone there could teach you to play."

"Could I really?"

"Well I don't see why not, if you want to."

"But aren't they expensive?"

Mary smiled. It could be a lot worse. Melina could want to play the piano. She held her tongue: no smart remarks.

"Not terribly," she said, thinking of people who played the banjo back in Gastonia. "I think we could try to find one that's more or less affordable. I mean, a banjo—it's for everybody. Isn't it?"

17

The summer of 1968 Alex telephoned from her work at a mental hospital, thrilled because an inmate had tried to set her hair on fire. It's a sign from God, she told Mary.

"How is that?" Mary asked.

"Like the tongues of flame on the Pentecost!"

"Ah," said Mary.

A summer internship for theology students at the state hospital in Sedro Wooley, Washington, with her living expenses paid by the Jesuits at Seattle University, seemed to be reconciling Alex somehow to the faith, after years of anguish over the denial of women's vocations.

"Am I not made in God's image?" she had cried to Tony last year in Chicago.

"Oh dear," said Tony, putting her hand over her heart. "We're all made in his image, they say, but I don't think a man would want to confess his sins to a woman." As if that should settle it.

Alex, flabbergasted, refrained from arguing. She was always loving toward her Chicago relatives. But her first few years at Seattle University she almost changed religions over her desire to become a priest. Preparing to become a professor of theology so that she could explain to young seminarians why there was in fact no theological reason that she could not join them at the altar— the confusion of it, she told Mary, threatened her soul. "The church wants me to become complicit in its own hypocrisy," she said, "or something," a little startled at her own bold words.

But experiences at Sedro Wooley changed her thinking. When her hair nearly caught fire, she recognized her true calling, to become a psychiatrist.

"Take up your pallet and walk," she said over the phone. "That's what I'm called to do, to help people move, to get on with it, rise from the paralysis of disease!"

Mary was so relieved. Even though this would mean medical school and phenomenal quantities of money. Dean Holbus rewrote her life insurance policy and from the dividends managed to extract a few thousand dollars cash.

In the fall of 1968, with Alex in premed in Seattle, Sharon in Fairbanks, Becky up at Marquette, Michigan, and Sean heading off to Ann Arbor, Mary would have only one child left at home, her banjo-picking, daydreaming, tall-as-a-pine-tree baby girl. Melina at fifteen, a junior in high school, appeared to be on her way to a self-determined future just like her sisters. She had shot up in the past two years, the tallest by far of Mary's daughters; she was outspoken and talented, as far as Mary could see. Her grades were ragged, her report card always brought a couple of unpleasant surprises, but there was still time to improve if she could stick to a plan. If she wanted a scholarship bad enough.

In mid-August Melina joined Sean and Becky on a field trip to the UP, to deliver Becky back to Northern Michigan University in Marquette, via the Whitefish lighthouse—Melina was mad for lighthouses—and they spent two nights camping, just the three of them, on the shore of Lake Superior. After they returned home, Mary, Sean, and Melina packed up again and headed south for a quick visit to Chicago before school started.

Mary imagined browsing with Melina through Marshall Field's, choosing skirts and jumpers, fussing a little, having a rare bit of time just for the two of them to celebrate Melina's becoming a young woman, but instead Melina wanted to find the navy surplus store. She wanted corduroy jeans and a blue denim shirt and a sailor's peacoat that didn't show off her pretty figure at all. You can't argue with adolescent girls about clothing, it's not worth it, Mary reminded herself, disappointed.

Nor with boys about the length of their hair. She wouldn't even have been tempted. Sean's sun-bleached hair, which turned banana yellow every summer, fell down his neck. Men snarled at him in Miltonia, but Mary thought his hair was pretty. Jim had never grown his much longer than his U.S. Army Medical Corps brush cut. Would his hair have been like Sean's? What would it have felt like, long and soft?

Once, to steady a young black woman's head while tending a laceration, she'd put her hand into her amazing natural Afro, and she was delighted by the softness of it, the way the cloud of it rose up to her wrist. So different from the shellacked-looking hairdos of the Negro women years ago in Gastonia and Chicago.

Heading north again from Chicago, they took Sean to the university in Ann Arbor. He had no idea how Mary's heart pounded to leave him in the town where she had met his father twenty-eight years ago. Sean's big hands and his shoulders were like Jim's. When Sean hugged her goodbye she wanted to linger there in his arms for just a minute.

Melina didn't have the repertoire of casseroles that her sisters had, but it didn't matter. She and Mom were happy with broiled chicken or toasted sandwiches or English muffin pizzas those nights they managed to be home and eating at the same time. One Friday evening in August Melina bicycled home from town by six and put chicken in the oven with rosemary and lemon slices on top the way Becky used to. When the sun set she turned on the outdoor floodlight. Mom was working late, she guessed, subbing for another nurse up at the hospital. Melina was the only one who used the floodlight any more. Mom liked the darkness.

As the chicken broiled she picked at her banjo, a tune that haunted and pleased her—"what a field day for the heat, a thousand people in the street." She had discovered how to do the extra sixteenth-notes by pulling off a fret. "Singin' songs and a-carryin' signs . . ." She turned on the news and waited for radio coverage of the Democratic convention in Chicago. She didn't care what the newspapers said; maybe Humphrey didn't have it sewn up after all. Why couldn't the delegates surprise everybody and vote their own minds? Vote what we keep saying we need, what the people want? Vote what's right?

She took the chicken out of the oven just as a reporter stepped outside the Hilton Hotel and caught the Chicago police moving into a line of demonstrators. She set the heavy pan on the top of the stove and lingered in the doorway between the kitchen and dining room, staring at the lake. A reporter began to scream: "They are hitting the kids! They are beating these kids on the streets of Chicago!"

Under the floodlight the lake water trembled. A brisk wind was pulling at the surface.

"These children—" shouted the reporter. "Oh my God, they've

been pushed into the plate-glass window! The police are beating a reporter! Oh my God, is this America?"

Melina saw the green light on the front of a boat coming from the south. It rode up and down with the chop on the lake, moving into the path of Pinestead's floodlight. The Flecks' Chris Craft. They'd be leaving this weekend, going home to Chicago. Were they listening to the convention on their radio, out on the water? She couldn't believe anyone would not be listening to this.

The chicken cooled, and she picked at a piece, standing in the dining room. The coverage went back and forth between the streets and the convention hall. A politician inside the hall shouted about Gestapo tactics in the streets, and the vote count began. State after state was caving in, and with a lot of glorious preamble, voting for Humphrey like none of this was happening, the war, the riots—why? How could they? How could they?

A friend at school had shown her a photograph last year of a Vietnamese soldier being stabbed, and just like that, Melina was antiwar. That was all it took. Most of the kids she knew were hawks, but the doves at Miltonia High School found each other. The doves were in the minority, but they flashed a sense of solidarity. They wore corduroys and listened to Cream and David Crosby. Girls no longer wore matching outfits but took bold aesthetic chances. Matching colors on a shirt and skirt made you cringe. Melina's clothes had never matched. Now she had a pair of doeskin boots with fringes and soft, moccasin soles that Mom's Ojibwa friend Mr. Olivet had given her.

A senior named Prew with blue eyes and blond hair sometimes watched her in the hallway. He rode a motorcycle to school. Wait till it got colder, and she could wear her brown cords with her Ojibwa boots and her new peacoat to school.

The broadcast cut out of the amphitheater again and went back to Michigan Avenue, where police and protesters were still battling. Someone in the background shouted, "Stop, I'm a doctor!" A reporter attempted to describe the smell of tear gas, the people gagging and running, frenzied cops spilling into the lobby of the Hilton Hotel.

When she and mom and Sean were in Chicago last week, Grandma and Tony had been extra fussy, kept warning them about which line of the El to ride, which taxi to take just in case, as if Mom had never lived there herself. They just stayed close to home these days, refusing to talk about half of what they saw on television. Grandma pretended some things just weren't happening. "I don't believe it," she said whenever the evening news came on. "Turn that right off," she would say when they showed anything like chaos in the streets.

"But Grandma."

"Just turn it off."

Melina wiped her fingers and her mouth on a dish towel. The broadcast returned to the vote count at the convention. She hesitated before reaching out for a third piece of chicken. She could manage four or five, probably, but she ought to slow down. She had grown five inches this year and was five-nine now, taller than her sisters. Her shins hurt from growing so fast, and her knees swelled up. Osgood-Schlatter's disease, just like Sean had, Dr. Bodamer said.

They had to go clothes shopping in Chicago this last trip, after they put Sharon on the train, because the hand-me-downs from Becky had completely run out and the Sears catalog was positively revolting. Mom took her to Marshall Field's to look for a nice winter coat, but instead Melina talked her into buying these fabulous new cords, two pairs on sale. At the navy surplus store, she found a peacoat for four dollars. She couldn't believe her good luck. School had started last week, and this was going to be an interesting year. She could tell by the way heads turned last time she walked through the IGA in Miltonia. By the way Prew Hatch's head turned in the hallway, the second day of school.

But McCarthy wasn't going to be the candidate for president. How could it be, that everyone could see what a terrible job Johnson and Humphrey had done and no one wanted Humphrey, and yet he was sailing through the vote count? State after state! Sailing through!

She ate a fourth piece of chicken and wondered where Mom was. It was pitch dark now. She studied the pool of light cast over the water and the dock, and she looked into the edges, into the blackness. Was anything moving in those edges? No, everything looked the same, as it always did. No—wait. Something was missing. Where's the canoe? she thought.

The battered green Grumman should have been on the grass near the dock.

Had someone taken it?

Was Mom out canoeing, in the dark?

Melina hadn't thought to check the garage for the car. When she found the house empty at six o'clock, she thought nothing of it, assumed her mother would be home soon enough.

The dogs had given up begging for chicken and were lying down in the living room. She called them and stepped outside.

She looked in the garage and saw the station wagon, and she felt sick. Something unpleasant and scary was going on. Who needs it? Not again.

She looked in all the bedrooms, in case Mom had fallen asleep on someone else's bed. Sometimes she did that.

"Come on guys," Melina said to the dogs, and they went down to the dock and walked out to the end. She aimed a flashlight out to the raft, swung it in a big half circle.

"Mom!" she called. "Mom! Are you out there?"

She almost felt something behind her, coming from the land. She turned around and looked at the pitch dark that pressed against the floodlight's beam. Something in that blackness was soft and beckoning, if you could just relax into it, she told herself. Soft and filled with creatures that wouldn't hurt you, mice and raccoons and harmless insects and deer with their huge eyes and sweet grazing muzzles. Why did she have to fear it? Why couldn't she ever let down her guard?

"Oh, Mom, PLEASE, where are you?" she screamed.

School had started in Michigan this week, and there were no guests at Pinestead. The five cabins were quiet, black, and deserted behind the floodlight.

She swung the light beam up the shore. To her astonishment she saw something. North of the dock the canoe rode on the water, about ten feet out, drifting in with every small wave, then drifting out again. The shoreline made a shallow cove there, and the empty canoe wasn't going anywhere fast; the current pulled it gently down the lake, but the wind kept trying to beach it. She walked down the dock to the shore and headed through the trees toward the canoe. She heard herself whimper, like a lost child. She didn't like leaving the floodlight.

"Damn it!" she cried. "Mom! Mom! Where are you?"

She scrambled down the steep bank above the canoe and took off her shoes. She waded out into water to her hips and grabbed the bow. She wanted her mom to be slumped inside, sleeping, anything, but the canoe was empty. Empty, even, of paddles and lifejackets.

She pulled it back to shore. They were always careful, hauling the canoe over the pebbles and rocks, but Melina wasn't careful now. She jerked and scraped it across the rocky beach and tied the towrope around a shrub. She stood in the water and cried out again, as loudly as she could, "MOM! Are you out there?" and swung the flashlight. "I'm here, Mom! Where are you!"

I have to call the police, she thought.

She waited and tried to listen. "Go find Mom," she said to Klondike and Yukon. "Go on, you stupid dogs, go! Where's Mom?" They barked, ears alert and tails wagging, as if to signal willingness despite complete incompetence. Ungrateful, useless, decrepit old dogs.

She put her shoes back on and walked up the beach, waving the flashlight, shouting.

"Here," came a frail voice.

"Mom?"

"Here I am, Melina. What's going on?"

There, way up the shore, by the big drift log, her mother was getting to her feet.

"Mom!" Melina ran toward her. The dogs began to leap and bark as though they had found her, as though if they showed enough excitement Melina would forget the sequence of events and give them all the credit.

She threw her arms around her mother to discover that Mary was sopping wet and reeked of gin.

"Mom, are you hurt?"

"No, honey, what are you all upset about?" and Mary gave one of her horribly familiar drunken chuckles.

"Oh, Ma."

"Where's the canoe? I'm looking for the canoe. it got away from me."

"Oh, forget the canoe! You're drunk, Mom. Come on home. What the hell you think you're doing out here? Come on!"

"Melina, don't be like that."

"The canoe is tied up down there. Come up the bank. You're coming home."

"But I need to find the paddles. They got away."

There were two Moms, and they did not connect. There was Mary Leader who could do anything, and there was this child, who came out of nowhere to surprise and horrify you. Out of nowhere.

Melina shone the light on her mother's body, over her head, looking for an injury. Mary brushed it away, wincing. "Honey, please don't shine that on me."

"What happened, Mom?"

"Nothing. I was just out for a canoe ride and it got away from me, and I don't know where the paddles are. They're right out there somewhere. Shine the light out there."

"No, we're going home. The paddles don't matter." Melina put her body between her mother and the lake and pushed her toward the bank. Mary capitulated, took a few steps, reached for a branch. It was a struggle for her, and Melina gave her an angry shove on the bottom. "Grab the branch, Mom, for Pete's sake!"

"I want to find the paddles."

"No."

"Melina, you're being silly. I'm all right."

"No, you're drunk. What the hell did you think you were doing? Paddling the canoe drunk! Jesus Christ! Here, turn this way, come on, we're going home."

One evening last year Mary had come into the kitchen with a glass of gin, and Melina, standing at the sink, without thinking, immediately reached for the Bon Ami scouring powder and upended it into Mom's glass, just to have her mother sober for a little while longer. "Oh, Melina!" Mary said, disgusted and embarrassed both. But she stayed sober that night.

But this. This was sacrosanct. You didn't drink and go out on the water, that was one of Mary's own many criticisms of weekend boaters. Christ, Christ, Christ, Melina thought when they got home and she took a good look at her mother. Even her hair was wet. When Mary took off her jacket and sweatshirt, Melina shrieked. A lump the size of a pear bulged from her upper arm.

"What is that! What happened?"

"It's just a bump."

"I should call an ambulance."

"Don't you dare, honey. This is called a hematoma, and it's nothing, absolutely nothing but a bump. There was some bleeding inside. The gunwale just came down on me, it's going to disappear all on its own. I can use my arm fine."

"Your head is bleeding, too."

"A scratch. I still think I should go get those paddles." Mary wrapped her hair in a towel and lay down on her pallet and turned her back on Melina. Sulking. She was embarrassed now. Melina knelt over her and moved the towel away from the scratch on Mary's temple. It didn't look so bad, an abrasion where she'd scraped against something. Superficial, Mary Leader called scratches like this. She never even used iodine or Band-Aids. She'd washed it good in the lake.

Melina put another blanket over her mother, left the room, and sat down with her back against the bedroom door so her mom couldn't leave. The way she felt about those paddles, she really would go after them.

As angry as Melina felt, the abrasion and the hematoma made her nervous. She felt useless, forced into a decision she didn't understand. I wish I was a doctor, she thought. I wish I knew something. How could she do this to me? Aw, fuck it!

Melina hugged her knees and doubled down on her anger. Without even realizing it, she knew that fury was on her side, fury would keep the hurt away.

She sat with her back against the door until she heard snoring from the bedroom. Good, loud snoring. Mom would sleep it off now.

The next morning Melina slept late and woke in the upstairs bedroom she had taken over, next to the peeling wallpaper covered with yellow bows, in the bath of sunlight coming off the lake. She had the whole upstairs to herself this year, though everyone's stuff was still here, including all of Alex's used paperbacks. You could find almost anything among Alex's books. *Life against Death* next to *Plays of Bernard Shaw* next to *Fanny Hill.* Melina had read the plays once and *Fanny Hill* several times.

She put on a pot of coffee and saw that the canoe had been hauled back to the dock and lay upside-down in its usual spot. Mom had been up early, no doubt looking for the paddles, and then she must have gone to work. She was herself again. Everything was back to normal, except for the country, which now faced a contest between Hubert Humphrey and Richard Nixon. It could not be believed.

She was halfway up the stairs after breakfast when she heard a knock at the door. Melina did not like answering the door when she was home alone. She crept softly up to her bedroom and looked out the window, behind the house. No car. There was another knock; she waited, and then she saw Marty Fleck below her, heading back to the driveway. He must have just walked over. He carried some papers under his arm. Her heart warmed to his familiar gait and shining light brown hair. She ran downstairs and out the back door.

"Marty! I couldn't get down in time!"

"Hey, Mel. How you doing?"

"Oh, fine, how 'bout you?" Then she remembered the convention. She shouldn't act too happy; Marty was from Chicago. "Except for that convention last night. Did you listen to it?"

"We saw some of it on TV. Not very nice."

"I didn't get it," she said. "No one wants Humphrey, but now he's the candidate. How did that happen?"

He smiled, but in a way she couldn't read. Like she amused him.

"I came over to say goodbye," he said. "The folks'll be here another week, but I'm off. Your mom home?"

"No." She always found herself dancing around Marty like he was a maypole or something. He was eight years older, practically of a different generation, but usually so sweet, funny, and somehow so—alive. There was always a candle burning behind his eyes.

"I left a flyer on the front door. There's a meeting about the new bridge and a new golf resort some people want to build, up there above the road."

"But that's Mr. Wilgosch's farm!"

"That's how we found out. These builders tried to buy some land from him."

"What? How could they?"

"The lakeshore property owners are going to meet about it this weekend. Maybe your mom would be interested."

"Where you going, Marty?"

"Me? . . . Back to school, I guess, reluctantly. Things are so crazy these days."

That seemed to be a reference to Chicago and the convention. "Yeah," she said, trying to show her understanding.

"You did good waterskiing this summer," he said. They were walking up the driveway now. It looked like she was going to walk him back to his property. Why not?

"One ski, for a whole minute. Finally."

"You're a natural."

"Aw, come on, I can stay upright and that's it."

"Naa, you're great. You're gonna be a junior this year?"

His summer tan was dark, and light brown hairs rose above his bare, brown arm like fur. Startlingly beautiful fur. She kicked a crab apple across the driveway at him, and he kicked it back.

"Yes I am, and what about you, really?" she persisted.

"I'll send you a postcard," he said after a minute, with a grin. "So everyone's off to college, and Mel's holding the fort. That'll be different."

Hold the fort? She had bigger plans! She sent him a sturdier crab apple, and he kicked it back.

"Take care of yourself, Mel," he said at the old fence that marked the property line and let his long brown hand drop on her arm for a moment. "See you next summer."

His hand on her arm startled her. She stared at him, and her reaction caught him off-guard. He hadn't meant anything. Startled, too, he backed away, waved, and smiled.

She walked back to the empty house slowly, holding on to the surprising sensation of his hot, strong fingers. She passed a blackberry bush and remembered the dense thickets across the road. Maybe I'll go hunt up some blackberries, she thought, stay out all afternoon and come back tonight hot and scratched and stained, and laden down with berries. I could make blackberry ice cream. Mom'll be tickled at that. I'll show her we'll be fine together. I can do the right things. She doesn't have to get all sad and depressed and drunk; the two of us can have some fun.

18

One night in October Mary came home to the smell of scorched cheese sandwiches. Melina's schoolwork was strewn across the dining room table. Next to a geometry textbook a three-ring binder, flung open, showed cartoon figures filling the margins of the notebook paper. Faces and bodies, and meaningless stray words—*peregrine, eggplant, nymph, candidacy*—dominated the space around some geometry formulas. Where did Melina's attention go during math class? Straight to the margins, not the teacher's lecture. No wonder she was getting a C-minus. These odd words, she pulled them out of the air like they were dust motes floating by, and she wrote them down, apropos of nothing. Eggplant? And good Lord, why nymph?

Mary turned a few pages and found drawings of male arms emerging from rolled-up shirts almost like the arm on the baking soda box, big and faceted. Some of the arms were at rest, not ending in fists but in handsome male hands with tapered fingers, and sure enough the bicep would be relaxed and extended too. Melina was really interested in the body, it looked like. She drew these over and over again because she wanted to get it right. But couldn't she wait until after math class? Couldn't she do her math problems over and over, instead of masculine forearms?

"Hi, Mom!" Melina called from the stairs. "That you?"

"Yes 'tis!"

"I had cheese sandwiches," Melina announced, and as she came into the room she gave her mother that look. Mary hated and dreaded that look. Melina's wide, sea-green eyes, one of them half brown, inspected her mother with a question in them: are you sober? For a second her eyes held no welcome, only that question. Mary knew that she had put that look into her daughter's eyes, that anxiety into her daughter's life, and she hated it. But tonight Melina's face relaxed, and she became a child again, Mary's fifteen-year-old roomie, happy to see her mother home from work.

They never talked about that night in August when the canoe got away and the paddles disappeared. Mary could not even remember exactly what happened. Sometimes she wondered what might have happened if Melina had not found her . . . how bad would it have been? She knew she had taken her pint of Seagram's out into the canoe with her and couldn't stop tipping it back, pouring it down. She hadn't meant to. A whole pint always did that.

She needed to pour half of it down the sink, soon as she got it home, before she even took a sip, because a whole pint was too much.

What am I thinking? I need to not drink at all, no pints at all! I'm lucky I wasn't sick to death the next day. I must not have drunk all of it. It must have fallen into the water. Where will the bottle end up, the Flecks' beach? Or maybe a summer guest will find it next year. Oh God. Be on the lookout again.

She looked for the paddles for a few days, then bought replacements at an end-of-season sale. They weren't as nice as the old ones.

They didn't have those green handles the exact color of a mallard's head. She could hear the questions now coming at her next summer: Hey, Mom, what happened to the ones with green handles?

And yet, unbelievably, she stopped at the liquor store after a couple of weeks. Just last week Melina came to fetch her for dinner, only to take a good look at her mother and yelp in disgust: "Oh, never mind! Eat whenever you like!" It seemed like Mary couldn't get away with it anymore, couldn't hide that she'd taken a sip or two.

Knowing she'd be found out didn't help one bit; she still wanted to drink. Only now, when she drove past the liquor store, she might think: is it worth it, to risk more disappointment and anger in the house? In order to answer yes—because she wanted so much to answer yes—she had to tell herself tales. How hard her life was, maybe she'd feel better in a couple of days, Melina was resilient and independent and the two of them were coping pretty well most of the time, learning to make allowances for each other . . . A crazy embroidery of outright lies. Yet she'd believe it, 150 percent, for as long as it took to buy the bottle of gin and take a few sips. Then she didn't care what she believed anymore; she just rode the warmth of the booze into nightfall on her pallet under the window.

Every morning she got up and went to work. A few times she was unable to eat breakfast, couldn't even drink coffee, and when her blood sugar fell midmorning she almost fainted at work. But that could be because she was in her fifties, too, after all. When you came down to it, it wasn't that she was drinking very much. The equivalent of going to a cocktail party once or twice a week. It was just that Melina was so sensitive now. And maybe that Mary's system was sensitive, too. Or am I lying again, she thought.

Melina had stopped going to mass, but Mary sometimes went by herself to the fisherman's mass on Sunday morning while Melina slept. A Sunday that began with the mass and included a ramble along the lakeshore sometimes took the worst out of her for a few days. Pity it didn't last. She didn't pay too much attention to the often worthless sermon, but the dark quiet church with mass in progress became a place where she could drop her guard and implore with her head bent to her tightly meshed fingers, "Only say the word, and I shall be healed." Over and over again. As if a loving presence would come right down off that cross with hands out to take the misery from her. Don't give up on me, she whispered.

Now she looked in the kitchen. "Is there another one of those sandwiches lying around? They smell good." That was a lie too, but a happy lie, a gift lie. At best the house smelled of grease and burned, blackened cheddar and ketchup. Melina even dipped her salted carrot sticks into ketchup; she said they tasted like French fries, without the fuss.

"I'll make you one."

"Thank you! That will hit the spot. Tonight's another meeting about the new development up above the lake. Shall we put in an appearance?"

"Of course," said Melina. "Of course of course!" She loved fighting the good fight against the mainstream, paddling into the waves.

"Lemme get out of these stockin's," said Mary. She went into her bedroom to take off her uniform and her control-top panty hose, a great improvement over a girdle. Progress was being made. How could she ever have worn that thing all these years! How easy it was to give it up! Her dress and slip both were spotted with a patient's blood. She let them drop to the floor.

What would Jim think of this body of hers. Her skin thickening, breasts and bottom fallen. Her legs were as slim as ever, and her triceps didn't flap like a shower curtain, thank God, and yet her skin wasn't like before. Her knees used to be faceted like gems. Now, when she stood, they thickened up with sagging material. Mary wasn't fat, just carrying too much material—thigh material, side material, softening her outline. She'd lost her crispness. She missed it. Better not look too hard. Thirteen years without the touch of Jim's hand.

How terribly important it had been for her, years ago, to be touched by Jim's big square hands every single day. How she hungered for it. And yet, for thirteen years, she'd done without, and she didn't even care anymore, not about sex, and that was the truth. Most of the time. But something else was hard to live with. This drinking. This internal combustion engine inside her that sucked down room-temperature gin.

She pulled a cotton skirt and blouse out of her closet, and instead of dressing herself, she bundled them together and put her face into their soft, clean cotton. Her favorite thing now. Soft, clean cloth against the wound of being a human being who hurts.

"Mary, Mary, don't you weep. You're a good person."

"Am I?" Mary said aloud, into the cloth.

"What, Mom?" said Melina, putting her head in the room.

Mary turned and looked at her. It certainly had not been Melina's voice. She wouldn't have said that. Did someone speak? she thought.

"Nothing, honey. I'm talking to myself."

"You want ketchup or tomatoes or both on your sandwich?"

"No ketchup! Do we have any sliced tomatoes?"

"Grilled cheese, tomato, and dill pickle comin' at you," and Melina disappeared.

Mary shook out the fresh clothes, got dressed, then picked up the bloody uniform and soiled slip, held them, and waited. A presence like someone else's breath was still with her in the room.

"I do want to stop," she told someone. "Help me. There's no need for all this extra pain. This isn't life causing it. I'm causing it."

"You're a good person."

What was happening in the room, a visitation to a middle-aged woman changing her clothes? No, don't be irreverent. Don't turn your back on love this time. Someone loves me.

"Please help," she whispered.

The presence was gone, leaving no plan with her. Leaving only an empty Mary. She carried her bloody nurse's uniform to the washing machine. Someone spoke to me, she thought. Someone loves me and wants nothing from me except my own well-being. Is that possible?

She was hungry, too. Had she even eaten today? She said to Melina, "You know, this is the best cheese sandwich I have ever had. Bar none. It really doesn't need ketchup."

The lakeshore property owners' association became a different animal in winter than in summer. Most of the members were summer people who were plenty comfortable and were easy to be with. There was no doubt they wanted politely and firmly to oppose the new golf resort with every tool they had. But by early fall, when they'd left for their homes in the cities, the remaining members of the association were exposed as being at odds with one another. Many of these year-round residents who made their living with boat rentals, marinas, rental cabins, fruit stands, rock shops, and realty offices crowded to the microphone to announce that the new resort would bring opportunities to Achill, and it was the American way. Locals from Miltonia, Itara, Spawn, and all the farms and hamlets nearby filled the hall and found themselves at odds.

Antidevelopment people were outshouted. Mr. Wilgosch, who had refused to sell any of his own land and had fought against the golf resort, growled into the microphone, "I'm afraid some of you all are throwin' away what makes your life here better'n it could be anywhere else, what you live here for in the first place, and you don't even know it. Listen to an old apple grower, it ain't easy, but it's worth it. Or you could just hand Achill County over on a platter to the guys with money, and pretty soon you won't know this place from Racine, Wisconsin."

A scattering of applause, but hostile cries as well.

Melina was the only young person there. In her Ojibwa boots and corduroy jeans, hair shining down to her waist, her appearance alone encouraged half the crowd to dismiss her words in advance as coming from a hippie, but they listened politely, anyway, because she was young and pretty. And serious. Mary doubted that anyone understood what Melina was talking about, but she herself filled up with pride and trembling. That's my daughter, she wanted to say. That's my kid!

"I grew up on Achill Lake, and the new resort will change it forever," Melina read from a piece of notebook paper. "There should be a place where we can all go to hear the sounds of nature and also places where we can honor those who came before us, especially the Indians who were here before us without destroying the land. Here everyone is rich in what matters, and visitors can find solitude that restores them. We shouldn't give all of this up without a fight to the first person with money who comes along. Michigan is just now recovering from the way that lumbering changed the country. But the land is still here, the lakes and the solitude and the loons are still here. We are already rich."

Mr. Wilgosch had received a few hostile shouts, but Melina walked back to her seat to light applause and polite silence. But Mary heard the man behind her mumble, "Who needs work long as you can live on a commune?"

"Sssh," said the man's wife.

"Doesn't know what she's talking about. Doesn't have the sense that God gave geese."

Mary turned in her seat and gave him her coldest look, and he fell silent when Melina came down the row. Mary squeezed her hand.

They left shortly after. "We did our part," she said to Melina as they walked out to the car, and Melina said, "Yeah, we sure did!" Mary had never seen her look so intense, so possessed by an idea; this was not her usual trance of daydreamy creativity. The sheet of paper on which Melina had written out her short testimony was not decorated with cartoon bodies and odd words. Not yet, anyway.

Mr. Wilgosch walked out behind them.

"This one's goin' through. We can't stop it, Mary," he said. "But it's not gonna be all bad." He looked at Melina, getting into the passenger seat, and then said, more softly, "You would not believe what they offered me. I don't like this, but on the brighter side maybe years from now retirement'll be easier. Maybe down the road it'll be to your advantage."

"Oh, Caz," she said, unexpectedly using his first name, feeling closer to him then ever before, "that's hardly a bright side, is it?"

"You got four kids in college, pretty soon five, might be you'll need it. All's I know is we're sittin' on top of land that's worth a fortune. Worth a lot more than any Christmas trees and potatoes that come out of it. Just gonna have to keep starin' west, at the lake. You turn and look east at the resort you might bawl your eyes out."

"You think you'd sell someday?"

"Never. But you're still a young woman, and now you have a cushion. That land's going to go sky high someday. Just case you need it, young lady. Don't think I can't be happy on your behalf. It's not all bad, even though these people cryin' out for development wouldn't know their ass—well, I better watch my language. Our land'll be worth something. Doubt most people 'round here will see a lot of money. It comes in with the rich folks, and they take it home with 'em too."

It was going to be a tragedy, she thought. But how much money did she have in the bank? Practically nothing. And now, with increased summer development back from the lake, as Mr. Wilgosch described it, she had a cushion. What an interesting idea. Used to be a sawmill, a woodworker, a bottler, and a factory in Miltonia, half a dozen chicken farms, all gone now. What else was there for people to do?

The next morning, though, driving Melina into school over the ridge, looking down at the crystalline stretch of Achill Lake through the bare trees, she suddenly wanted to cry out with sadness and anger at those who would change this landscape. Under her breastbone everything felt like waves under crosswinds. Her feelings blew every which way.

At the hospital they were practicing triage all afternoon. Takes your mind off things to run around rescuing the injured, even the mock-injured. She was pleased to see that Adelaide and another black nurse, feigning chest and head wounds, were not overlooked but were ferried into the ER on the very first stretchers, even though the mayor of Miltonia lay moaning nearby with a leg injury.

She drove right on past the liquor store after work and savored a moment of odd joy, almost like victory—then a mocking voice started in: Who are you kidding? You didn't have a visitation! Don't believe it for a minute. Booze is real, and booze is you. One good sip, and you'll be back on solid ground. Better a bottle of gin than pretending to be something you're not.

She wrenched the station wagon over to the shoulder and stopped. What is wrong with me? What is this? Where, oh where, is any help at all? She put a hand on her old woman's empty abdomen. I am out of ideas. I am plumb out. What the hell does it mean to think that booze is solid ground?

She'd read about Alcoholics Anonymous in nursing journals and "Dear Abby," but the thought of exposing herself to such a grim and gloomy crowd gave her the heebie-jeebies. The public library had a copy of their book. She looked at the spine, big and blue on a bottom shelf, and she didn't even have the nerve to bend down and pick it up. She couldn't be going to AA meetings. People talk. God almighty, they already talk their heads off about Mary Leader renting to black people and trying to keep tabs on five children and succeeding, too, thank you very much. Except maybe not quite, if it turns out she's an alcoholic. What if someone tries to take Melina away? Two more years. I need to hang on. Two more years. I didn't come this far to be called incompetent, unqualified to raise my own kids.

But she called the number listed in the *Miltonia Gazette* anyway, just to find out. The person on the other end, speaking in a calm, pleasant, matter-of-fact way, as though alcoholics called him every day—and I guess they do, she thought—told her that there was a meeting once a week in Traverse City that was only for women.

I'm not that keen on women, either, she thought. A walk in the woods is way better for me than a drive to Traverse City could possibly be, just to sit in a gloomy circle of, ugh, women alcoholics. Like me. She almost laughed at herself. But really, more time outside, reading the woods—it was like reading another text, another score, unassuming and secret and life-giving, barely known and not interested in making converts—that was the wilderness, that was where she should be spending her free time.

And then she slapped herself on the thigh. Or you could try it. Just try AA sometime. It's there for you. You could just try it.

19

In August of 1969 Alex came home for the first time in a year and a half. She pulled out of her suitcase a huge pink bucket of Almond Roca candy, a frozen chunk of smoked salmon thickly wrapped in newspaper and bread bags, and three birthday presents for her youngest sister—a Clancy Brothers album, a refillable Rapidograph pen, and a used hardback copy of *To the Lighthouse* which she had found in the dark recesses of the Bookworm on University Avenue in Seattle. Melina loved the way words and pictures flowed out of that pen. Alex made a heavenly creamy sauce with the salmon which they poured over wide, curly noodles.

"First-rate," said Sean, home for the summer from Ann Arbor.

But within days Alex was thinking to herself, something is wrong. Something is very wrong around here.

For starters the Pinestead lawn was all crabgrass and dandelions, though Sean kept it trimmed to the ground with Mr. Wilgosch's little tractor mower. Other people had deep green lawns, like you were supposed to have. Your bare feet wanted to sink into other people's lawns. At Pinestead it hurt to cross that prickly dead stuff.

And the five cabins were so plain, so shabby. The cupboards still had those battered cheap pots and percolators, and the bedsheets were so worn people ripped them with their toenails. Who would stay in these pathetic shacks but long-time renters and oddball fishermen who liked Mom's prices?

The main house was worse, grimy and dusty. Wallpaper peeling off the bow wall in her old bedroom, the carpets worn thin, black holes in front of the fireplace from flying sparks, scum on the stove hood so thick you could write messages in it. The same old dinner plates were yellow from decades of hard water. Old Yukon, their gentler dog, had died, and Mel had put a cross over his grave near the end of the driveway; Alex didn't say anything, but a tip-tilted cross on a dog's grave seemed a poor way to welcome guests to a summer resort.

As for Mel. You could not say from one day to another what that girl would be doing, what kind of mood she'd be in, what kind of progress she'd be making on her own future. She was going to be a senior in high school, but she was always walking around in a fog. Everything was doodled on, even the margins of the phone book! Her pale green eyes, one half brown, startled you, the way she stared into space. She played "Camptown Races" and "Shady Grove" and "Oh! Susanna" and a couple of protest anthems over and over again on that banjo, just because she could play them so fast, but she didn't learn new songs. She hadn't kept up with her lessons. One afternoon she smelled like cigarette smoke, and Alex did not know what to say.

Sean was working all day around the place, at this or that—he single-handedly replaced two rotted beams in the garage—and he was working up at Wilgosch's, and he refused to sit and discuss things. He acted like he was working too hard to afford the luxury of looking for problems. It made him angry when Alex pointed things out, as though her alarm was a criticism of him. Sharon was up in Alaska saving money to marry a seismologist next summer, and Becky was working at a summer camp, and Mom was just not paying attention. Mom was like a kid: she wanted to spend every minute doing something fun—canoeing, berry picking, sometimes consulting with Sean about a few things he might want from the new Ace Hardware out on the highway. She let the renters fend for themselves! If Melina slept in till noon, Mom let her be.

Entropy was no joke.

Was there something else wrong? Alex couldn't put her finger on it, but it was there—the three of them, Mom and Mel and Sean, it was like they weren't a team. They were off doing their own things and not taking part in each other's lives. Glue was missing.

Alex wanted so badly to goof off a little bit with Sean, like they used to way back when. She wanted to poke fun at this and that, without anyone thinking she was being mean. She was just astute and perceptive, that's all, not mean and critical. But he wouldn't do it. In his free time he'd be canoeing or swimming with that empty-headed Yolanda Quillen he'd been friends with forever or heading out to the movies. Yolanda wore a bikini these days. It was the color of the chicory blossoms that lined the driveway and not much more substantial, Mom said, with a chuckle, out of Sean's hearing.

Every night he wasn't out with Yolanda, Sean would swim though the black water in and out of the beam of the floodlight, cooling off after the heat of the day, or he'd argue with her, and that was the worst. It was almost like he was trying to stamp out what she had to say. To stamp her out.

That's how it felt, anyway, though Mom didn't think it was a big deal. "Quibble," Mom would say if she heard Sean and Alex arguing. "Quibble, quibble, quibble." Like it was nothing. Like they could just stop it, if they wanted.

Then, shopping in Miltonia one afternoon, Alex spotted Melina on the back of a motorcycle. Clinging to the driver. Melina wore a helmet, but he didn't. Alex stared at her little sister, and their eyes met before the bike roared off.

"Mom know you're doing that?" she said softly, as they set up to make blackberry jam in the kitchen the next day.

"No, and you just drop it, please."

"That and smoking cigarettes—I think those are the only two things she's asked us not to do, ever. I can't think of another thing, can you?"

"I don't know."

"She's seen things at the ER. That's why she's concerned, you know—one time a boy in a coma for six months after a motorcycle accident. A person on a motorcycle is helpless if there's an accident."

"Yeah, I know, Alex. I just do it a little bit."

Melina should have gone to Interlochen. Why did they all drop that ball? Mom was saving every penny for college tuitions, probably, but college depended on a sensible performance in high school. College-bound kids kept themselves busy! Melina—you could hardly describe her as busy. In her private world, maybe, in the recesses of her own imagination, there was something going on. She finished *To the Lighthouse* in a week and managed to say intelligent things about it. She devoured J. D. Salinger and Herman Hesse. But she couldn't be bothered to scoop the spiders out of the bathtubs, let alone do any of the extras that made a place habitable.

"Look out at the lake, Alex," Mom said when she caught Alex murmuring some discontent. "My goodness. I know the lawn's trouble, and the house isn't up to old standards. But long as we keep the grass shorn, we'll be all right. This isn't Oak Park, and there's something to be said for the way the woods keep creeping up on us."

"But Mom. Look how the flowers are failing. That hydrangea bush—this is the wrong climate for hydrangea and lilacs. No one remembers to water them. They do better in a place like Seattle, not here. Sometimes a ground cover works better, don't you think? You ever thought of getting a new look around here?"

They were talking while Mary leaned against the doorjamb, looking into the cramped kitchen where the two girls were sterilizing jars and lids and stirring a pot of simmering blackberries. Now she pulled a chair up to the door between the kitchen and dining room and sat down with a cup of coffee.

"Let me tell you a story, Alex. Last spring I had that very thought. But what could I do? I went to the Goodwill store in Traverse City where they keep a day laborer pool, and I said I need you to send up a man to do some digging and planting for me. And so one morning, there he was. A warm May morning. We were all heading out, and I didn't really want him coming in and out of the house with no one here, so I made him a big pitcher of lemonade and put it in the cooler in the garage and told him just what to do. I sliced a whole extra lemon and put the slices in. It looked so good!

"I came home early, four o'clock, to see how things were. And what did I find? He was sound asleep on the lawn with a paper bag and a bottle next to him. The lemonade," and here Mary began to laugh, "the lemonade wasn't even touched!"

The two girls stared at her as she chuckled. "So I decided then, keep it simple. I am going to keep it simple around here. Can you imagine if the Flecks had seen that, a man passed out on my lawn?"

"I never knew that, Ma," said Melina.

"Honey, I've wanted the place to look decent. And it does. It looks okay. Look out at the lake, go into the forest. When you get up early enough, you can hear the birds playing their flutes like they own the place. And they do, first thing in the morning. It's a parallel universe." She laughed. "Ptssh, a person could spend every free minute shopping for lime and peat and compost at the hardware, but I can't compete with the garden ladies or the summer people, and I don't want to. That's not why I live here."

Alex didn't argue with her mother, but later she rolled her eyes for Melina's benefit. "Things could be nicer around here with a little more effort."

"Mmmm," said Melina, sampling the jam. She almost never argued with Alex.

But it wasn't the house and the yard that really concerned Alex. Those were only symptoms. It was this other thing, she couldn't put her finger on. The house was a symptom. Mom, Sean, and Melina weren't a team; they weren't watching out for each other. Melina just wasn't . . . just wasn't where Alex thought she'd be, at sixteen. She seemed a little bit lost. Capable of intelligent thought when challenged, but actions? Decisions? Where was the progress?

Sean took a thin paperback out of his back pocket. While Alex crouched a few feet away, burying new daylily bulbs around the house, he sat down on the porch step, reading. It was such an odd sight and almost an invitation to her. Books were her thing. They could talk about books. But she could feel the prickliness coming off of him like a porcupine just about to strike.

"How was your year at UM?" she said at last. "Like it down there?"

"Not much."

"What do you mean?"

Wrong question. He shook his head. She was forcing him to search for words and to explain things, to begin out of whole cloth, not his strength.

"Did you have a favorite teacher?" she tried again.

"Chemistry was good," he said, "but I'm thinking of taking a year off, anyway."

Squatted on her heels below him, she kept planting. Better not to look directly at him, too challenging. Give them both space.

"Take off and do what?"

"It's crazy, all this college, marching forward to some kind of career. I already know what I'd like to do, and it's not finishing up this stupid incomplete I have on the Catholic novel." He waved the book at her. *Bread and Wine*, by Ignazio Silone. She smiled, she couldn't help it.

"Yeah, I thought so," he said. "You could write this term paper before breakfast. You want to do that for me?"

"You're taking a course on the Catholic novel? How interesting!"

"You'd say so. I just thought it'd be easy. Maybe I'd have an advantage. But I been reading this book for the second time all summer long. Listen." He opened it and folded it back on itself, like a peanut butter sandwich. "'Spring passed and summer came, cherries were over and the corn was ripening. Don Paolo's health was much better so he made efforts to escape the boredom of the female atmosphere that surrounded him.' Every time I get to that sentence, I can't go on. I want to escape the boredom of this book. These characters bore the shit out of me. They go here, they go there. It started out good, but they just keep going places."

"You want some help with it?"

"What I really want is to turn Wilgosch's place into an organic farm."

Now Alex fell back on her bottom and stared up at him.

"You're kidding."

"It's just a thought, don't get all . . . Up there on the farm, I can't think of a nicer spot to hang out, to spend the time. I been reading about it. What you do, you improve the soil. It takes time. I did a little soils project last year at school."

He had two incompletes and a D and two Bs. The incompletes were turning to Fs.

"That's a terrible waste of money," escaped her mouth, and as he jerked in anger she instantly tried to call the words back. "But it's okay, it's part of finding out what you want to be doing. It isn't a waste. That's what college is for, to find out."

Sean flipped the book out into the grass and gazed at the lake.

"I don't want to be there," he said at last. "You don't know what it's like."

"You talk to Mom?"

"She's got no . . . she leaves things up to us, you know that."

"You could ask her advice."

"I'm asking yours, for a change."

She wondered if he saw his own life in those words, "he made efforts to escape the boredom of the female atmosphere of this house." Funny, that had never occurred to her before. Escape it for what—Yolanda Quillen in her blue bikini or Wilgosch's farm? Not very ambitious, was he? But did he have to be?

Or would organic farming next door turn out to be as bold and arduous as anything the rest of them might try? Did it matter? What would a psychiatrist advise him to do?

"A year off? You can't farm during the winter."

"I could get a job with this cabinetmaker I know and make some money and take an ag class in Traverse City."

Home, she thought suddenly. Is that it? To be rootless means you're still looking, like that boll weevil. So what if Sean's found his home sooner than anyone else? What's it to you, Alex? Let him be. Maybe he knows what he wants.

"You could try it," she said, thoughtfully, not looking at him. "I mean, you have plenty of time for trying new things." He shook his head.

"So you don't really have an opinion."

"I don't," she agreed. Not quite true, but true enough.

They stared at each other, mildly puzzled, disappointed. Becalmed. Well, at least they weren't fighting.

Last day but one of her three weeks home, Alex drove into Miltonia to mail two boxes of odds and ends to herself in Seattle and afterward, walking back to the car, successfully fought off the urge for a Dairy Twist. She had lost thirty pounds her freshman year in college and never gained it back, but those fat cells lurked in her tissue still, waiting to be refilled, she just knew it. Ten minutes of slurping sweet, soft, cold ice cream was almost worth the empty calories. But not quite.

On the asphalt it was grotesquely hot, still, like an oven. The wooden buildings of Main Street were nothing but crummy three-story apartments behind their storefronts. It was the kind of still day when it seemed like the universe was encouraging you to stop worrying so much, nothing could be worth all the worry. It was too hot to worry. Just be glad you're crossing a parking lot, and somewhere down to your right, in the slow ditch of a creek, there's life, turtles and bugs and crawdads trying to keep cool. Holding out.

A door on the top floor of one of the apartments opened, and three young people came out on the balcony above the parking lot, then started down the rickety steps. Two boys and a girl, smiling at each other. That tall, lean girl with the wild loose hair was Melina.

Alex stopped and stared. She had never been so certain of anything as that those three kids had a secret. Had been up to no good at all. It was in the smile and the way they moved. They had done something, but they were without care.

Melina recognized her sister. At the foot of the steps she waved at Alex, then spoke to the boys. She left them and crossed the hot parking lot.

"Hi," she said.

"What are you doing?"

"Nothing. Talking to you." Melina looked utterly blank. There was no guilt in her face. It was the face of the ten-year-old getting lost at the Lions Club Minstrel Show.

One of the boys had gone around the corner of the building, but the other one lurked, gazing sideways, as if curious about who Alex was or what Melina might do next. Unexpectedly, Alex felt revolted—by the scene, by the boy's presence, by Melina's passivity.

"Well, suit yourself," she snapped. "I'm going home. Coming or not?"

"Well . . . yeah, sure. Aren't we going to have a party tonight? It's your last day."

"I thought it would be nice to do something."

"Just a minute. I'll be right back."

Melina walked back to the lurking boy, and the two of them went around the building, no doubt in search of the third culprit.

Alex got into the station wagon, reversed it to face the street, and when she drove forward, saw the three of them standing around a motorcycle. The two boys mounted it, and the driver booted the kickstand. They took off, and Melina came walking back. She was pulling her thick, honey-colored hair into a ponytail. She wore a striped, sleeveless tank top, and her bony shoulders were so badly sunburned they were blistered and peeling. When she climbed in, she slouched down in the passenger seat and pulled a leg up onto the seat so that she could hug her own knee.

"Owww," she complained, twisting a little bit as her bare skin touched hot spots. Alex thought there was a faint, unholy smell to her. Was she neglecting to bathe, because they were all swimming almost every day?

"Is that marijuana?" she ventured, astounding herself with her own boldness.

“Maybe,” said Melina, with a lack of concern. “Oh, don’t worry, Alex. Truth is I don’t like it myself, so I don’t use it. It doesn’t do anything for me. Does it smell? Hnh.”

“Oh, Melina.”

“What?”

“Are you looking forward to school?”

“Jesus, no. I hate it. What’s the point?” She flung one arm out the window and waved to someone as they passed the drugstore. “I dread it, Alex. I absolutely despise it.”

“Maybe you shouldn’t finish up here. Maybe you should . . . you could come out to Seattle.”

“Hnnh.”

“I’m serious. Though it might be hard on Mom, to be alone. But it’s gotta happen sometime. Or Alaska, you could move up to Alaska for a year. That would look nice on a college application—experience living in Alaska, that frontier lifestyle. You could learn to . . . to hunt and fish, to kill and clean a caribou . . .” What was she getting at? You could learn to live, Melina, to be part of the world around you!

Melina lifted her long, heavy ponytail and draped it over the seat and leaned her head back. She closed her eyes.

“Christ, it’s hot. I am so covered with sweat and ick. And if I wanted to hunt and fish I could do it in Northern Michigan, Alex.”

“I guess so.”

They drove in silence until they reached the long, dusty Pinestead driveway.

“What do you want to do, Mel?”

“I don’t know. Write. Be a college professor or a lawyer. Sometimes I think, maybe a movie actress. It seems like that would be really neat. You could be in story after story.”

“Really.”

“Or maybe I’d like to be a lighthouse keeper.”

“You can’t keep house.” Alex snickered at her own joke.

“A lighthouse, Al.”

“Why?”

“All the obvious reasons. It would be such a neat place to live, and you’d be so, so useful. That’s what I’d like.”

“To be useful?”

“In a way. Yes.”

Alex felt hope for this conversation, which vanished with Melina's next announcement. "I'm going straight into the lake. If you take time to put on a suit you cool down, and it doesn't feel as good. I'm going straight in. You come, too."

Typical. She veered toward something interesting, and then she drifted away again.

"You go ahead," Alex said as they got out of the car. "I'm going to put on a suit."

From an upstairs window she watched as Melina was true to her word, swimming straight toward the dock. Alex thought of the seagull droppings on that dock, despite the tubular flag that was supposed to scare them away, despite people hurling the occasional rock out over the water. It just never used to be this way around here . . . or did it? Was she a victim of nostalgia, casting a spell on herself for some reason?

She walked across the upstairs hall and went into her old room, now Melina's. The bow room. Books, clothes everywhere. Next to the bed, piles of books. The poetry of Dylan Thomas open, face down. Alex picked it up to see what Mel had been reading.

> Light, I know, treads the ten million stars,
> and blooms in the Hesperides. Light stirs
> out of the heavenly sea onto the moon's shores . . .

And just like that, hope returned again. Yes, thoughts were stirring, after all, in Melina's head, her imagination was seeking sustenance after all. Alex sat down on the bed and read to the last line. I must learn night's light or go mad.

Don't go mad, Mel, she thought. It gets better. This is just youth, I promise.

She looked around and saw the corner of a sheaf of papers, poking out of the lowest shelf of the crowded, cluttered, brick and board bookcase. She reached for them, thinking, drawings?

Charcoal drawings of a nude young woman, with long rippling hair. Something familiar about her. Lying on her stomach, posing on one hip, standing with one leg bent up and gripping the ankle like she was a flamingo, crouched and hugging her knee, all moody and introspective. Her face, her hair, her bony hips and shoulders, her long legs, her breasts like tulips, her backbone, were Melina's.

20

For Alex's last night at Pinestead, Sean built a campfire on the level tongue of shore to the north of the main house and stuck foil-wrapped potatoes and ears of corn into the coals. He invited the last renters, a family of four, to share the picnic of potatoes, corn, kielbasa, and marshmallows. After they ate Sean built up the fire again, almost into a bonfire, and they watched the sparks fly up from it to disappear into the darkness. Melina hammered out her repertoire of Stephen Foster at a gentler-than-usual speed.

"You're awful quiet," Mary murmured to Alex. "Is everything all right?"

Alex was still in shock at those pictures. Someone else's troubling reality, on top of Sean dropping out of college, hit her deep inside. She was sobered up inside, not that she'd been the least bit intoxicated at any point. She couldn't have said anything about them, to her mother or to Melina.

"I'm sorry to be leaving," she said softly.

Mary squeezed her hand. Melina set down her banjo against the arm of the lawn chair in which she slouched. One arm propped on the chair, bent, so that she could rest her head in her hand, she stared into the fire. She did pose, Alex realized. She posed all the time, without even knowing it. She draped her long body around things. Hiding her height, or was it an interior fatigue? Lassitude. There's a word for you. Melina suffered from lassitude. But what's with taking off her clothes for some artist? And who could it be?

They were amateurish, for sure, though the artist was talented. A friend or young person, not a teacher. Was that more acceptable? Alex wanted to weep for her little sister's loss of innocence.

Melina's bare knees glowed in the firelight. She began chatting with the daughters of the renters. Drawing them out, getting them to tell her about their ballet classes in Detroit. She could do that, she had some skills. All was not lost. Sean stayed on his feet, tracking down embers that escaped the fire. Occasionally a knot full of pitch exploded, and a spray of sparks flew above their heads and disappeared in the blackness. Alex tried to withdraw her hand from her mother's, but Mary wouldn't have it. She squeezed until Alex's fingers hurt and held on.

"Melina." Alex knocked and then poked her head into the bow room.

"Hnnh?" She was lying on her bed scribbling. She rolled over and gracefully flipped the book or papers she was working on down behind the bed, against the wall. But she still held the pen in her fingers and said, "I love this pen. It's unbelievable. It's so cool. Thank you."

"You're welcome."

Alex walked over to the bookcase and pretended to study the books. Jesus, there was a coverless paperback copy of *Fanny Hill* that had made the rounds at Interlochen, ages ago. Good Lord, she'd forgotten all about that. How did it end up here? Did I bring it home?

She let her eyes wander to the sheaf of drawings that she had crammed back onto the lower shelf of the bookcase, between *Paddle to the Sea* and *Treasures of the Art Institute.* She looked up at Melina, who gazed at her steadily with those unnerving, sea-green eyes, one multicolored. With her pale eyes in a sunburned face, she looked like a photo negative.

"Are you going to have a good year, sweetie?" Alex said abruptly.

"I hope."

"This thing about lighthouses."

"Oh, don't laugh at me. Don't say it's a fantasy. I just like them."

"Thing is, they're all automated now. Almost all. Remember when we went to the UP when we were kids and saw the light at Whitefish Point? There was a family that lived there then. But they were the last ones to operate that light."

"I loved it."

"It's like the Swiss Family Robinson, except for that other thing you said."

"What other thing?"

"Well, that lighthouses were really needed. It was a needful thing."

"Yeah. I like that, and also I like things that are possible," Melina said, surprising Alex. She sat up and crossed her legs in the lotus position. "I like to imagine things that could really happen."

"I know you do. You used to get so scared of things you saw in movies or heard on the radio, or of Russia sending atomic bombs over here, and it was so hard to reassure you it wouldn't happen. Because you always said, it could happen, couldn't it? Your mind just couldn't get off the plausibility of it."

Melina beamed as if she liked this conversation.

"So I won't be a lighthouse keeper."

"But you can . . . you can still do a needful thing. Useful things. You can still shine. You do shine, you know, Mel. You are beautiful and smart and talented. It gets kind of . . . kind of . . ."

"What?"

Hard, Alex wanted to say. Confusing. "A person has to have some inner . . . well, it's like the gospel. Jesus just walked around reminding people that they were strong and powerful and to shine. To feed each other and things like that. He walked around, and whoever he met—if you remember the stories—he said, get up, you're well, get up and get to work on the kingdom. Pretty much that's what he did."

"Are you lecturing me?"

"No." In a rush of feeling Alex sat down on the bed. "I haven't had as much time with you as I'd like. You and me, I've often thought, we have something in common. An intellectual curiosity maybe. But you're so pretty and talented, you can do so many things."

"You're not helping."

"What do you mean?"

"I don't need to hear all this. About being pretty and talented. It doesn't help me make decisions or pull out of things."

"Pull out of what, Mel?"

"Nothing."

"What do you want? What would you like most this year?"

Melina looked into Alex's eyes, and her own showed emotion. She opened her mouth to speak and closed it again.

"This is the year to start thinking about what you want," Alex said.

"I want to get through it."

Alex wanted to say, is that all? but that would be hurtful. Maybe Mel was telling the truth. Her expectations had plummeted for some reason. Survival would mean just coming out alive and free on the other side. That's all she wanted.

Maybe that's what she was supposed to want at this age. Maybe Melina was normal, and Alexandra Leader—the odd-looking woman with outsized mental energy and outsized ambitions—was the freak. And outsized righteousness, someone said to her at Seattle U. Even at Seattle U, they tried to tamp her down. If they almost succeeded with Alex, how could she inspire Melina?

She put her arms around Melina, and they hugged, resting their heads against each other.

"Alex, do you have a boyfriend?" Melina said.

Alex sat back. "There was a boy at Seattle U, but that didn't last. That went nowhere. Now—well, I have a friend, and he's a boy, but it's not romantic. He is a very good friend, we like some of the same things. We take walks and go to concerts, and once we rented a canoe, but it made him nervous. He wasn't used to it. The lake was windy and full of boats, it was his first time."

"What's his name?"

"His name is Harry."

"Harry!" Melina smiled and drew back.

"Don't laugh. It's an old-fashioned name, I know."

"Why aren't you and Harry romantic?"

Alex felt pinned. It wasn't romantic because it wasn't romantic yet. Because for some reason they were shy with each other. She didn't know. She knew that the thought of seeing Harry in a few days made her happy, and that's all she wanted to know. She twisted a little under Melina's gaze and shrugged, and Melina laughed.

"It is romantic, Al! Aha! But you don't . . . yet . . . ?"

"I don't want to say too much. Come on now. It's private."

"Do you have a picture?"

"No. Do you have a boyfriend, Melina?"

"A few too many."

"Oh!"

"Well, they aren't really boyfriends either. Guys to be with. I have to wonder sometimes, whatever do I want to be with them for? But I do. You asked what I want."

"Yes? What do you want?"

"I want to get rid of all this, be free of all this."

"All this what?"

"All this . . . all this boring . . ." she was waving her hands around her body, as if it were her own skin she despised. "All this nye-eevitay I want to get past it. I want to be French-fried. I don't want to dream about going to a lighthouse forever. I want to be there and back, and to talk with some authority about my own life."

They both sat in shock at that one, cogent, declarative sentence.

"Well, there you are," said Alex. "That's a start. Who else would talk for you?"

"I don't know." Melina had burst forth; now she withdrew again. "I'll miss you so much, Allie. I really will."

"And you'll take care of Mom?"

"Mmnh."

"Why don't you come out to Seattle in the spring?"

"We're all going to Alaska, aren't we, for Sharon's wedding?"

"Yes, but you can come out before then."

"Where did you meet Harry?"

"We met at a concert. We were sitting next to each other in the back row, and I had binoculars, so I let him use them. Then when we left we walked together, and he said, how about a cup of coffee?"

"What was the concert?"

"The Clancy Brothers. I gave you their record."

"Aha."

"What do you mean aha?"

"You want to share that experience! It is special, isn't it?"

"Yes, maybe. I don't know."

When they hugged good night, Alex patted Melina's back and was startled at the way her backbone stuck out, like the Andes almost. It came from being long waisted; her legs were plenty sturdy.

"You're so skinny," she whispered, thinking of those drawings.

"Naw," said Melina.

Alex thought, suddenly, maybe Mel drew them herself. Self-portraits, they could be. People did odd things in the privacy of their own home. She wouldn't put it past Mel to do something like that. There could be a reasonably innocent explanation. But embarrassing to Mel. Best not to pry.

The next morning she wanted to talk to Mom a little bit about Mel, but there wasn't time alone. Sean made blueberry pancakes, and then they were all together until Alex walked up the stairs to the rear door of a plane in Traverse City, turned around at the door, and waved and bowed and performed a little Irish jig to their three waving silhouettes in the window of the terminal. It hurt to leave them. She couldn't stop staring at them until the stewardess, with kind insistence, told her to take a seat.

Letting Prew sketch her didn't trouble Melina half as much as this thing with the camera. Taking pictures of her with the camera.

Melina didn't like sex 100 percent. But she did like hugging and kissing, and she liked Prew's body, the heat and the strength of him.

When he fucked her Prew's hunger became hers, became all that there was in the world. Maybe someday she would like it too, as much as he did, all of it.

And she liked what happened in Prew's face when he sketched her—that detachment, that scrutiny, that sense of something going on. To possess and be possessed by a need to study something, some body, some one. She understood that feeling.

His drawings included parts of her body you couldn't especially admire, the way her bottom spread when she sat down, the way the rung of a ladder cut into the fat part of her thigh, the slight S-twist in her long bony spine. And she was getting better at sketching his body, too, which was hard because a man's body didn't flow like a song.

But when he took pictures—that was different. It was exciting and scary and felt kind of wonderful and definitely kind of horrible at the same time. You didn't know how it would end up. He did that in June.

And then he wanted her to let his friend Del take pictures of the two of them, Melina and Prew, together on the bed in Del's apartment. And he just talked her into it. Somehow. Oh God. And they went to Del's place in town. She hated it, and yet she needed to see what it was like. She said she wouldn't screw in front of the camera, but once the idea was there, once the image was in their minds—it was inevitable, wasn't it? They all three wanted it to happen. Prew put himself inside her, and she gasped, and Del was taking pictures. Melina only gave him a minute before she pulled away and sat back. She went laughing nervously over to Del and took the camera from him.

"No," she said. "No way, really, you guys!" She tried to laugh, tried to make it seem more carefree. She pretended that she was going to open the camera.

"Don't do that! We'll stop. I'll give you the films and the negatives," Prew said. "I just want to see them once."

He stepped off the bed and reached for the camera.

For just one thin slice of a second, Melina understood that Prew and Del could do whatever they wanted. Like some kind of shifting undersea presence, their greater strength flashed into her awareness. She laughed and backed against the door.

"No more. No more pictures today. I'm getting out of here, it's too hot."

She tossed the camera on the bed and grabbed her shorts and top.

And it was such a hot day, and so hot in Del's place, that it just didn't seem like the regular rules of life could apply. But when she walked out on Del's balcony and saw Alex there in the parking lot, staring up at her, something happened. Seeing Alex changed it.

You don't have to be doing this, Melina told herself.

Instantly she propelled herself away from what she had done.

Just get away from it. Get distance! Drive away in another direction, and don't think about it again, ever ever again.

A couple of weeks later, when she got the film from Prew, she didn't even look at it; she took it down the lake and drowned it and then put the shreds of film into a bag and into the trash. Thank God Prew and Del had graduated, they wouldn't be at Miltonia High this year.

But she saved his drawings of her. It was not okay, what she had done, but she didn't hate the memory of those first afternoons alone with him. Something nice back there, she had let get out of hand, and she had wrecked. Prew Hatch wasn't like other boys at Miltonia; he wasn't college bound, but he wasn't a dolt, either. They had met in art class, and it seemed like their relationship was an art project, too, from the very beginning. They came from different worlds. His dad worked in auto body repair, and Prew said those fumes had wrecked the old man's brain. Prew took shop, pilot ground school, algebra, and art his senior year, the same algebra class she had taken as a freshman. She stared at him for three weeks in art class, and one day he offered her a ride home on his bike, and it was glorious. Utterly glorious, in every way. Over another month of rides and small talk, they created a way to be with one another—a set of unspoken rules, a certain attitude. It was like creating a work of art. And that was that.

At first it was life changing. But now the true character of the relationship hit her in the face: it was trivial and sordid and done with.

How could she have done this?

The more she tried not to think of it, the more it grew into a grotesque shadow, a fracture in her life. It took all her energy to keep her back turned to it. And she couldn't leave Achill Lake for a whole year. Another year of this place!

She froze him out when he called. She wrote him a letter and said in capital letters, IT'S OVER. But when she saw him once in town the magnetism was there, so strong and hot they both were speechless for two or three minutes, until he said, softly, "What do you want? Do you want anything from me?"

And she said, "No," and moved away.

21

Burnout. Mary read about it in a nursing journal.

It happened to drug users whose brains became like spent shell cases, but this author used it to describe worker fatigue that could strike almost anyone in middle age. Those of us in the service professions who are required to give, give, give, are particularly at risk of this moral exhaustion. To be sustainable, service work has to promise something new, and if it doesn't . . . the creeping symptoms mirror those of depression and occur at a particularly dangerous time of life, the transition to the middle years. Jesus Mary and Joseph, she said to herself. An occupational risk of depression—I've been there, when Jim died; I refused it when Chris died. I will go anywhere else, but not back there.

She went to Traverse City to find the AA meeting but let herself wander through the Goodwill store instead. She bought curtains, percolators, and a few books, including *How to Write for Homemakers*—the same title she'd checked out from the library several times and never found time to read. She could try something new and risky. Take that, burnout!

But within half an hour of opening *How to Write for Homemakers* she had thrown it across the room. To think she had wasted the price of a hamburger on advice like this: "Father Knows Best . . . it's well to get a man's comment on what you write. His direct way of stating facts will help you to put strength into your copy."

What terrible advice—rather than study the way writing succeeds, run to Father for approval. And yet that advice came back to her in the following days. Crummy advice but with sticking power, like a caterpillar or stinkbug on your shoulder after a walk in the woods.

So what if there was no "father" handy who knew best (what a way to refer to your own husband!). I am the kind of person who learns from experience, she thought, and being Jim's wife for twelve years was not wasted on me. I want to learn to convey information—I want to test my own perceptions. This isn't about just being happy in the woods, it's about looking for information about how to live. So, information—movement—has got to come across, with salt for flavor and room to breathe.

What is it about the way men talk to each other? They don't repeat themselves, she thought. They don't go on. They don't even check for understanding, they just assume that if they said something, the other person heard it. Not all men, but quite a few. Dean Holbus, for instance. Chris Olivet and his uncle. Jim. Certainly Caz Wilgosch. Sean, too. I happen to like repeating things, but maybe . . . I don't have to do it quite so much.

Instead of throwing it out, she put the little book on a shelf above her desk, spine against the wall, in case she needed it again. I should be open to accepting even backhanded advice, she thought. But is it really like this in the publishing world?

> *Q.* What shall I do if an editor asks me to make changes in my copy?
> *A.* Make them cheerfully . . .
> *Q.* What shall I do if an editor changes my copy?
> *A.* Nothing. That's her privilege.
> *Q.* If I do not hear from an editor within a month, shall I write her?
> *A.* No. Be patient a little longer. She may be on a trip . . .

Without a doubt, the book helped too by making her so angry that she determined to plunge ahead without dependence on guidebooks after all. Like her own father told her once, the best way to stretch eggs is to use more eggs. Have at it. Crack some eggs. Waste your time, if it comes to that. Make mistakes. Do it without anyone breathing down your neck!

How to Write for Homemakers suggested you take a little stack of your little essays—that word, "little," she didn't care for it—to the proposed market. So that's what she did: took four earthy little essays into the *Miltonia Gazette* on a red-letter day in January 1970 after just about the worst Christmas of her life.

Becky and Sean had come home for Christmas, but no one could pull Melina out of the funk she'd been in for a couple of months. She slept late every weekend, mooning about the house, neglecting herself, was barely scraping through her senior year. Some days she didn't even comb her hair. This angst of hers was the worst yet of all the kids, Mary was thinking, and then Sean informed her that he wasn't going back to Ann Arbor. He was done with the university. Mary herself went into a week's despond.

She didn't thrill to Becky's news either. She was dating a professional skipper—a young man who made a living moving rich people's yachts around on the Great Lakes. Mary hadn't even met him, and she already disliked him; something about that job of his irritated her. To think that her Becky, strong and stoic and with such a lust for life, had been put in a position of waiting for her man to return from the water. Not to mention waiting, vicariously, on rich people.

They cut a Christmas tree and went through their traditional rituals, but a certain hollowness dogged them. The kids gave her a new pair of snowshoes, which touched and horrified her at the same time. Her army surplus bear claws were good enough. These new ones were genuine trapper's snowshoes handmade, by someone Mr. Olivet knew, of birch sapling and sinew. The kids must have spent a fortune, all of them together, just to wow her. She made a huge fuss of thanks, but inside she was mixed up, until the first weekend after Christmas when she tried them out. Floating above a heavy snowfall up at the point, she was transported.

Christmas was over, the returning light of the new year was sparkling off the snow, Becky was back at school, and Sean had found part-time work building kitchen cabinets in Traverse City. Living at home, Sean at least provided some company for Melina. She even seemed to have given up friends. She had ridden her bike compulsively everywhere until the snow fell, but after that she wouldn't go out, except to school. She snacked and left food out on the counters; she lay on the couch and read books with only one eye, half of her face pressed into a couch cushion.

"Don't read that way. It's bad for your eyes!" Mary would call out.

"Mmnnh." Which meant, leave me alone. Disturb me at your peril.

One evening when Mary came home, Melina's banjo was lying on the dining room table, surrounded by the detritus of her Dagwood-style sandwiches. Mary plucked a string, and her fingers picked up crud. Jam or honey or mayonnaise had found its way onto the head.

Chuck Schaffhauser, the editor of the *Miltonia Gazette*, astonished Mary first of all by taking her seriously. His face didn't twist in a sneer. He turned his attention equably to the pages she gave him and read with attention, although his hands shook and the papers fluttered. Parkinson's disease or a hangover? she wondered.

"I'll give these a more careful read and get back to you, when I'm off deadline," he said. "Are you proposing a regular submission? A column, something like that?"

Even when he set the papers down and rested his hand on the desk, she noticed the tremor in his fingers. She wanted to indicate complete willingness for whatever he proposed, without seeming greedy or too much like an acquiescent homemaker. She couldn't find the right tone, so she shrugged—no, that was all wrong—then said, "Do you think there's some merit to the idea?"

He smiled.

"A personal column about the seasons and the countryside? Could well be." He was continuing to scan the pages, and something he read made him stop and chuckle. "Thank you, Mrs. Leader. Thanks for coming in."

"You're welcome," she said. She would have liked to sign something, but he made no such offer. Word of mouth would have to do, though she would have spat in her palm and matched it to his if he wanted. Something about the way his hand shook made their agreement seem tenuous or fragile. But she'd have to live with it, just as she had to live with her excitement now, a whole new batch of hope. Once back in her car, she couldn't help herself. "Oh, oh, oh, oh!" she said aloud, slamming a fist into her palm with excitement. Of course she shouldn't expect money. That wasn't going to happen.

But it did.

He called her two days later. "Mrs. Leader," he said, "would you accept twenty-five dollars for each of these three essays?" He said that he'd run the first, about the darkness of winter and the December solstice, within the week. She had called it "Why I Don't Use My Floodlight Anymore." It came to her one day almost fully formed, when she read a quote from the hermit Thomas Merton: "The night is my diocese." With a thrill she thought, "Me too!" And all the thoughts she'd been having for a few weeks, about the comfort of darkness and the sometimes piercing, painful quality of light, poured out in three pages. She had chipped and carved those pages down by a third. She liked that one best herself.

"Will you be making any changes?"

"Why, no. These look to me ready to go. You know we're a chain, got four *Gazettes* north of Cadillac. I'll try one in all four for the Friday edition. Faith and Outdoors, they go together. I never thought of that before, but seems right."

When she offered her hand to the nearest stranger at mass that Sunday, she couldn't help but think, "Do you realize who you're shaking hands with? A columnist for the *Gazette*!" The fourteen-year-old Mary Ashton who still lived inside her wanted to twist and shout, as Becky used to sing. It didn't matter one bit that this was a paper for which she'd had so little respect over the years. When Dr. Bodamer and Mr. Wilgosch congratulated her, both on the same day, she almost felt like she was fielding off a crowd of fans.

A person, a family even, could eat high enough on the hog for twenty-five dollars a week. At least if they remembered to put the mayonnaise away when they finished making a sandwich, she thought, looking into the kitchen that Melina had ravaged and abandoned. And tie up the bread bag! What has gotten into my youngest child? I didn't raise her to live like this.

Maybe that's it—lethargy is her rebellion. Sure. That's what it is. She's found a form of rebellion. How else could she rebel? I don't forbid her to do anything, I don't drag her to mass, I don't ask her to put in two hours of housework every day. Maybe that's my mistake. Especially the housework part.

One evening Mary came home late to the most god-awful, depressed crooning from the hi-fi she'd heard yet. Compared to this sound, the Beatles, the Byrds, the Rolling Stones, really were Beethoven.

Melina slouched in an easy chair facing the black window, her eyes closed.

"I'm home!" Mary called to her.

"Hi, roomie."

"What's that you're listening to?"

"Mmmnh."

The man's voice was so low and guttural you just knew there was nothing he wouldn't do. Subterranean! Like someone willing to crawl under a door. Mary picked up the record jacket. *Songs from a Room* by Leonard Cohen. "I have tried in my way to be free," he groaned, descending on each phrase like a very old man in heavy unlaced boots clumping into a basement. Dear God in heaven.

Mary dropped the record jacket onto the couch and went into her bedroom. She would not criticize her children's taste. She would not. That road led nowhere. You couldn't win.

Sometimes after supper Sean took Melina out for a driving lesson. Tonight Mary scoured the kitchen good while they were out, took the stove pans out from under the burners and attacked the crud with steel wool and Bon Ami. As she was replacing them, the old dog, lying in the door between the kitchen and dining room, lifted his head and growled.

"What is it, Klondy?" she said.

The growl became a bark, and he unfolded and hoisted himself to his feet. Younger, he would have bounded to the front door before the knock. Mary went to the door.

The man looked very familiar, sickeningly so. It took a minute to recall him.

"Mrs. Leader, Douglas Hatch Sr.," he said.

"Yes. I know who you are." That man whose kids dumped manure in her driveway. He seemed much smaller than years ago.

"I saw yer story in the newspaper, and I, a couple things I thought to talk to you about if I could."

"What is that, Mr. Hatch?"

"Wonder if I might—you're lettin' the heat out this way."

"So I am."

"Well . . ."

"Please come in." She stepped back, and he came inside. They stood staring at each other just inside the dining room. She pulled a chair out from the table and offered it to him. When he sat, she sat.

"I know you got no use for us."

"That's not true."

"But I thought I ought to come by anyway, couple things I wanted to pass along."

"And what are they?"

"Ma'am, that time with the manure was a long time ago, and we both raised children, and you learn as you go along. I done my best, but I missed some things, I didn't realize all that was going on."

"Uh-huh."

He seemed to her to be in bad health. His gray mechanics' clothes were thoroughly paint spattered, his head balding, and his pale eyes sad. Incredibly sad.

"Last week I sent my youngest, Prew, off to the Soo. He's goin' be working up there this year anyways. The youngest gone off. You know my youngest, Prew?"

"No. Why should I?"

"Well, I wondered if you might. I got two boys in Vietnam and one boy in the Soo, and that part of my life that was so much trouble to me is outta my hands now, and I can't get over it. I mean, I don't know what to do with myself."

"Yes?"

"Ma'am, this isn't easy for me. I wouldn't tell a person like you a thing. I grew up here, I lived here all my life, I got no education. Kinda work I do isn't good for a person, not really, gives some people bad headaches, though I done all right. The fact is I coulda been a better father to the boys. I missed something important goin' on back then. My wife, she died seven years ago. It's been hard."

"Well, I certainly understand that. Would you like a glass of water, Mr. Hatch?"

"Yes, I would."

She stepped over the dog and got two glasses of water. She was going to feel sorry for this old guy in a minute. She hadn't thought about what had happened back then in ages. Maybe he had come to make amends, truly make amends this time.

"What's on your mind, Mr. Hatch?" she said, sitting back down.

He drank the water. "Well, that time. First of all, that time they dumped the manure. It wasn't like you and I thought. It wasn't just what you call prejudice. We don't care, me and the boys, we don't care anymore about all that. Ain't ruinin' the world to have black people doin' things next door to you. My boy Doug, he's fightin' with black kids in Vietnam. I mean, we have our preferences, maybe, in a free country, but hell."

"Well, you and I see things differently. But is that what you need to tell me?"

"It was like this, Mrs. Leader. Prew and I we had some knockdown battles. I'm the one sent him off to the Soo. You're outta here, I said. See, maybe you knew this. I found out he's dating, I mean he used to date, your youngest girl."

Mary stiffened, moved to the edge of her chair. Ready to throw him out.

He looked up at the dining room ceiling. "My house, we got the kinda ceiling tiles you set in frames; kids sometimes stored their cigarettes up there. I was fixing to try to repair a leak from the upstairs pipes, and I lift the ceiling tiles and find things there all covered with dust. Cigarettes, okay, an empty bottle or two, and I find some pictures of your daughter, the tall pretty one, though all your daughters are pretty. Prew took the pictures." He took a sip of water. "Nice enough pictures, harmless pictures. Kinda pictures that two people goin' out take of each other. Hell, he's got other pictures too. But I'm so mad at him about things, I ask him, this is the Leader girl? What's goin' on? We have a knockdown battle. Thought I'd break my hand on him. An' I tossed everything of his, threw all his stuff in the incinerator along with the week's trash. I mean, it was that booze and his other stuff that got me so mad."

"Oh?"

"So I come over here for two reasons."

"Mr. Hatch, I don't see how any of this . . . You're probably wrong. How did you know it's my daughter?"

"Like I just said, Prew told me. Oh, Mrs. Leader. Your daughters, everyone knows them. That's what I'm trying to say. That time years ago the boys dumped that manure in your driveway. They didn't even know any black people, they was just interested in your girls. Trying to get your girls to pay attention to them. Teenage boys. I didn't get it at the time. Now that they grown out of all that behavior I see it clear as day. Maybe you already knew this even, but I didn't. I didn't know Prew was dating your girl, till I find this stuff in the ceiling. But when we talked, well, it all come out."

"I don't understand."

"But you raised five kids yourself, Mrs. Leader. You know what they do."

Mary drank some water. Douglas Hatch Sr. smelled odd, not of sweat but of cigarettes mixed with something pungent and powerful. Solvent.

"So, well, that's what you want to tell me? That we should have recognized that boys will be boys and to shrug it off? Okay, it was a long time ago, and that's fine with me."

"Well, I myself found comfort in that idea. That they was tryin' to get your girls to notice 'em. I never could understand why they done such a dumb thing. Mostly I wasn't paying attention to them, couldn't remember about bein' that age myself. They'd do anything, boys that age would, not out of prejudice but something else. They don't care about prejudice and society, they jus' want people to notice them. And the youngest, there, she did notice Prew finally, and they went out on a few dates, and then he and I we had this big knockdown fight, and he's gone off to the Soo. He won't be back for a while. And I got to thinkin', the girl should know that he's gone. And maybe she don't care, but I had to let you all know—would you tell her that, for me?"

"How is it your business or mine? If they were dating he probably told her."

"Well, it might matter. Prew's gone, and before he left I done incinerated everything I found in his room because I'm gonna fix up the house, gonna paint maybe. So if she left anything with him, well, it's all gone. There's nothing left."

"Why would she want to know this?"

Douglas Hatch Sr. finished his glass of water and looked at his curled hands as if checking a script. She was being too hard on him, but the more he talked, the colder and more frightened she felt.

"She prob'ly doesn't. I just wanted to pass it along. That's all. 'Cause I didn't give him any time to say goodbye. I threw him out. But about that other thing, the manure. Like I said, they was boys trying to get girls to notice 'em. Oldest story in the book. One of many things I failed to see when they was younger. Do you mind that I come by, Mrs. Leader?"

She couldn't move, she could not unbend. As if, so long as she didn't move, this horror would pass her by. "No. But I think it's best if you leave now."

"Yes I'm goin' to. Like I said, I wasn't the best father ever come down the pike. And you, you was good to us long time ago. Before it ever happened, I remember, you even come out to the house to talk my wife into the polio shots, years ago. You're a nice nurse, Mrs. Leader, and I appreciate your story in the paper."

And with that, he left. He was out the door before she even managed to say, "Good night." His "'Night then" came back to her from the front steps.

Melina and Sean found her sitting in the same chair, motionless, nothing in front of her but a glass of water.

"Mom?"

"Hi, honey," she said.

"What's wrong?"

"Nothing, I . . ."

Mary got up and walked into her bedroom. Melina followed. Mary sat down in her office chair, the chair that had been Jim's so long ago.

"What's the matter, Mom? You look stunned."

"Well, dear. I don't know. While you were out . . ." Mary felt numb. She didn't know how to get up from this baffling news, which way to go. Was he just trying to tell her what a lousy parent she was? She knew that already, she knew that. At least tonight she did.

"What?"

"It's nothing. Are you all right, honey?"

"Why wouldn't I be?"

"You don't seem happy this year."

"Am I supposed to be happy? What happened while we were out?"

"A man named Douglas Hatch came by."

The light went out of Melina's eyes.

"And?" she said after a long moment.

"He wanted to let you know that his son has moved up to the Soo and also that he's thrown his son's stuff in the trash incinerator, in case there was anything you wanted. He told me they'd had a big fight, and then he got to thinking you might wonder where the boy was since you had dated him. Did you date him, Melina? What does that mean?"

Melina came over to Mary's chair and knelt in front of it. She moved in close so she could rest her head against her mother. Mary wrapped her arms around her.

"It means nothing. Nothing. We did a few things after school a few times, and we went out this summer, I liked him for a while. Mom?"

"Yes, honey?"

Melina looked up. Her pale green and half-brown eyes darted around Mary's face. She looked scared and unhappy.

"What is it?" said Mary.

"Well," Melina said and then, "I guess, nothing," and she dropped her head against Mary.

Everything this girl has going for her, Mary thought. Why does she have to suffer like this? She chooses it, but why? Good Lord.

"Do you miss this young man? Is this why you are unhappy?"

"Oh no, God, I do not miss him. But he was fun. He liked to draw."

"Oh!"

"Yeah, he drew me once in a while. I suppose that's what Mr. Hatch burned. Sketches. From art class."

"Oh, I see."

"Anyway." Melina pulled back and stood up. "I had a good night-driving lesson, I think. Sean thought so. He's making popcorn. Do you want some?"

Mary would have preferred a drink. When Melina left the room she continued to sit, as if bound to the chair.

I would not have missed Melina's growing up for the world, and yet I did miss it.

It's not that I've been wandering in the woods. It's because when I was home, I was drinking. Just enough to miss her growing up. I would not have done this, but I did.

So it's true.

Whatever else is going on, I have lost control of things. I have been fooling myself.

22

The weather band crackled in the kitchen, and at the words "tornado watch" Mary and Melina leaped to their feet, raced around the place shutting windows, grabbing at webbed chairs, toys, and towels, hauling the canoe into the boathouse. Mom sent Melina to the cabins to alert the renters to come next door and wait it out in the crawlspace. Only one was home, a photographer from *National Geographic* who was driving to Alaska, and she took Melina's warning with a look of delight.

Mom warmed to all of this. Melina hated it. A tornado alert shot her right back to the panic of an eight-year-old. As if the Russians had just sunk the *Thresher* and stolen its nuclear secrets, finished their hydrogen bomb overnight, targeted Detroit, and that jet you heard was a Russian bomber. The logic of panic was irrefutable.

"Don't worry," Mom always said. "The terrain isn't right for a tornado here. Too hilly! There won't be a tornado, but we're sure going to get a squall. It will come right up from Itara like a movie screen coming at you. Oh, look at those boats!" She aimed her binoculars at a few boaters still heading north across the lake. "Go in, you numbskulls!"

The dark sheet of the storm to the south canceled the sun. It was like a translucent curtain on a stage. Behind it the surface of the water was crumpled and cracked and wild. The squall moved toward Pinestead like a semitruck coming down the highway, eating up the distance. It was steady and irrevocable, and it would hit with a blow. Even so they wouldn't consider going into their makeshift storm shelter in the crawlspace for a squall like this, destructive as it was going to be, except for that yellowish green light in the sky and crackling warnings from the radio.

Sean ran down from Wilgosch's at the last minute. "What needs doing?" he shouted as he burst inside, but Mom called back, with that same energy in her own voice, "I think we have it."

The shelter was always stocked with water, flashlights, blankets, and a first aid kit, none of which they'd ever had to use. Melina carried her banjo and two binders full of poems and scribblings down from upstairs—what if the house lifted off or completely collapsed?—and set them back in a corner. The photographer, a woman in her twenties named Reggie, carried the Leaders' aged Klondy down the ladder and then helped her own dog, a healthy young Lab. She hunched up with her arm around her dog, looking pleased. How could she not be? She was on her way to Alaska with a pickup camper provided by the National Geographic Society.

The Leaders wouldn't be going to Sharon's wedding, after all, because Sharon had ended it with her seismologist, had thrown his engagement ring back at him. Melina had heard Mom talking to her on the phone. But this young woman, Reggie, was heading up there all on her own, to photograph the Alaska Highway.

How do you get to the point in life where you do things like that? Melina wondered. How do you become fearless?

Their storm shelter was full height but did not extend under the entire house. It was only the size of one room, with walls of stone against silt. They had to get down between those walls like they were hunkering into a grave. Melina sang "Wish I Was a Mole in the Ground," trying to outmaneuver her own dark spirit, but she still felt sick with fear. She knew they were going to be buried alive. She would be, at least. She looked up and moved six inches to the right, to be out of the way of the floor joist when it fell.

For forty minutes they listened to the muffled sounds of the storm, the odd creaks and crashes from afar. The storm itself was a little too interesting to feel the need for much conversation, but Reggie rattled on some about her upcoming drive. She'd intended to stay at Achill Lake just one night but had arrived on a day of such incredible calm, heat, and beauty that she couldn't bear to move on. With Sean and

Mary she had canoed across the water the next morning at seven A.M., taking pictures like mad. Later on that day she photographed Melina and Sean waterskiing. When she tried to take a picture of Melina close up in her bathing suit, with the lake in the background, Melina instantly ruined it—waving her hands and then leaping off the raft like an ungainly frog.

"What's wrong with you?" Sean asked her. "Don't you want to be in *National Geographic*?"

"You be in *National Geographic*, you think it's such a good idea," Melina spat at him, surprising herself.

Reggie didn't try that one again, but she had such a good time she decided to stay an extra few days. And now the storm arrived. She was so lucky to see another face of this amazing lake, she said, while the storm raged above them.

"This lake has got to be on anyone's short list for the most beautiful spots in the world! Or at least in the western hemisphere!"

Mom laughed with delight. "How long is the short list?"

"Five, six, eight—three let's say. Where do the colors come from?"

"The clarity and depth of the water," Mary said, beaming at Reggie. "It's very deep in the middle, a V-shaped valley." When it comes to describing lakes, you have to use the language of gems, she wrote once in her newspaper column. She'd probably write about this storm, Melina realized. And people would say to her, "Your mother is something else. Wow. She's an emergency room nurse, and she writes that nice little column in the *Gazette*, and she's so different. You're lucky to have such a cool mom," and Melina would nod. They didn't know about the times the cool mom disappeared into a tipsy child. Sometimes by lunchtime Saturday.

It didn't happen every weekend, but often enough to make Melina sometimes touch the *Gazette*, with Mom's essay in it, and think: Why can't it really be like this? We're just pretending things are this nice. But she knew her mom wasn't pretending. The woods really were her salvation, she really did come alive and happy in the outdoors. So how could it be a lie? And yet what other word was there? This version left too much out. Left her out.

She watched Reggie's sunburned hands resting on her dog's neck. Her knuckles were big and rough, though she was a small, pretty woman. She used those hands. She had even changed her own flat tire, the day she arrived, wouldn't let Sean help.

Klondy didn't like storms. Lying next to Melina he kept his eyes open. From time to time a pathetic shiver went through his frame, and he looked up at Melina as if to say, why are you doing this to me? But Reggie's big, young dog seemed perfectly comfortable. What was all right with his human was all right with him. And it was all right with Reggie to be trapped in a dank cellar with three strangers. She didn't know about the drinking either.

Was there a family in the whole world that really was just as it appeared on the outside? How about the Flecks, next door?

The floor joist above them did not bend or break, and the squall passed in an hour. When they came out, rain was pouring down, and the lawn was strewn with cedar limbs. A table no one had thought to secure earlier had blown up against the front door. The woods on the north shore would be a mess, but for Mary an adventure, no doubt. Picking her way through to describe the destruction would keep her excited for a day or two, Melina knew. It would fill one of her essays.

Melina was just so thoroughly relieved it was over, once again. Makes no sense that I can't enjoy things like other people do.

Mr. Wilgosch came down and told them a small twister had actually touched down on the high, eastern edge of his farm and flattened a swath of his woodlot. It seemed to be jumping the ravines and just lighting on a few ridgetops, he said. The evening news reported that two teenage girls out on the lake in a Panther sailboat were missing, and trees at the YMCA camp had crashed down on the dining hall. No one was hurt at the camp, and it turned out the girls had made it to shore after their boat swamped, and tucked themselves down like hedgehogs behind an empty cottage to wait out the squall. They were terrified.

"But what in the Sam Hill were they doing out on the water?" Mary muttered. "I tell you. When teenagers push away from the parental brain that's been thinking for them, they don't always make it." She was just grousing aloud, but after she said that she shot Melina a strange look. Then she said, "Not you, honey. Not any of my kids. Thank heavens, you grew up here. You know what's what."

Melina had failed to graduate from Miltonia High School because she slept through American Government. There had been a tempestuous two weeks of agony when she didn't get a diploma, but the principal promised it by December if she finished a government course at Traverse City Junior College in the fall. The credits would transfer over. She wouldn't have to set foot in Miltonia High again. That was the main thing.

Two days after the storm, the heat returned. Away from the water it was unbearable. Melina wrapped herself in a secondhand sundress, $1.25 from the Nifty Thrifty in Miltonia. Someone must have made it out of old curtains, the cotton was so soft and worn, but the print was delightful, blueberries and green leaves on a pale orange background. In the 40s-style dress she looked like an elegant survivor of the Blitz from one of those great old World War II movies.

Sean was flipping through record albums when she came out of the dressing room with the dress on, and he smiled. "You know what it makes me think of?" he said at the cash register. "The little girl in *Blueberries for Sal,* all grown up." For a minute Melina wanted to cry. She had to take a deep breath, and she knew that her eyes filled with tears. What a nice thing to say. Had Prew ever said anything half that nice? It was always in Prew's eyes, what he wanted. Would any willing girl have served his purpose, or did he really care about Melina Leader? Sometimes, remembering being with him, going to that place in her thoughts, she wanted to stab herself. Why didn't you know better, you dolt? What's inside you, to have let that stuff happen?

She pictured doing something to herself with a knife.

But riding his motorcycle—that was glorious, especially the first couple of times. They had been free, both of them. Not like today, the heat pressing down like the bottom of a cast-iron frying pan, holding you to the ground. Even the wind came warm across the lake, and at times, on days like this in the middle of August, the water had isolated spots almost as warm as bath water. Days like this, people swam around looking for cold springs.

She and Reggie walked up toward the mailboxes and the Flecks' house between lines of blue flowering chicory that straggled along the edges of the long, dry, dusty driveway. It was a pretty weed that Sean especially liked, with flowers that looked like they'd been cut out of paper with pinking shears. The meadow above them, leading up to Wilgosch's farm, was filled with sweetpea, Queen Anne's lace, and black-eyed Susans. Reggie snapped away. Melina loved that solid click of her big camera. It was a satisfying sound, it really felt like she was capturing something. But not me, thanks, she thought. No more.

And there was Marty Fleck, always a delight to see. Worth wearing a sundress for. He offered anyone who wanted a fast ride up the middle of the lake in the Chris Craft, and then Melina found herself next to him, on the warm leather front seat. Reggie sat behind them. Out on the lake, with the throttle open, the wind on their sweaty bodies did the job of cooling them down. The acres of blue water to each side hurt you behind the eyes. You wanted to swallow it whole, and you couldn't. Melina sat with bare feet on the leather seat, her knees up, the wind cooling her legs. The speed and comfort of this boat was a first-class luxury. But you could get used to it.

Riding behind Prew on his bike—you didn't get used to that. Never got enough of it. "Who needs it," Prew had said once about a mansion they drove past on the Lake Michigan shore north of Petoskey. "Right, Mel? In an aquarium, everyone's a fish."

She thought that was true, then, and a clever remark. Rich people stick to their own. Their lives are boring. But Marty Fleck wasn't a fish. His whole family was great, rich or not. They were good neighbors—at least when they met at the mailbox or property owners' meetings or when Marty came down to waterski. They were easy to be around—not pretentious at all. The Flecks' summer house was big and comfortable, but not grand.

Back home in Marty's Chicago, was everyone a fish?

In Marty's eyes and smile she could tell that he liked seeing her in the sundress. It felt great to be sharing this joyride with him. His eyes were mild but lively, his brown and furry arms gorgeous. But she wouldn't have told him one honest thing about herself. She couldn't possibly. She could tell him that Sharon had broken up with her boyfriend. But that would bring up how Sharon used to be his special friend, back when they were fifteen or so, and he would think that Melina and her mom probably wanted him to go to Alaska and rescue Sharon. The Leaders were careful not to want things from the Flecks, ever. Long ago Marty, the youngest in his own family, had wanted someone to play with, and the Leader girls had fawned over him. Now they were all grown up. That was that. He was in his twenties, and Melina was seventeen and a total embarrassment to herself.

When they got back to the Pinestead dock, Reggie climbed out first. Melina stood up and picked her skirt away from the backs of her legs.

"Phew," she said. "Back to the furnace. Maybe I'll just jump right in the lake."

"In that pretty dress?" said Marty.

"This dress is made from old curtains. A buck twenty-five from the Nifty Thrifty."

"Doesn't look it."

"I dare you to jump in, Marty." She climbed out and looked back at him. "Come on, why not? You gotta catch a plane or something?" She walked to the end of the dock, looked back at him, and stepped down the ladder into the lake. Her wraparound dress fanned out like a poppy opening its petals. She turned around, laughing with relief, and saw Marty grinning, his eyes wide. Melina threw herself backward, arms outflung. He ripped off his t-shirt and followed.

They swam out all the way to the dropoff and back again. You had to be careful out that far on an afternoon full of boat traffic. No one would notice your small head on that big water. Melina had been warned about that all her life. Sometimes you could hear a speedboat while you were underwater, like a chainsaw coming at you.

She and Marty climbed up on the raft, stood at opposite ends, and jumped vigorously, making the raft rock, tipping each other into the drink. He looked once but didn't stare at the way the dress clung to her legs. For a few minutes they stretched out head to head, and their feet at opposite corners of the raft.

"Where's college going to be?" Marty asked her.

Melina astounded herself. A plan leaped out. "Sometime, maybe in January, after Christmas, I'm going up to Alaska. Like Sharon. She loves it so much. And we've never gone up there!"

"Wow." He was impressed. "Wish I could do something like that."

"Why can't you?"

"If my draft number comes up, I'll be heading to the deep woods of Canada, but right now it's finish grad school. I'm so fed up with it all. A chemistry grad student and I didn't even have the nerve to picket Dow when they came recruiting. A bunch of kids at school did. Some of them got arrested, got beat up."

Melina was impressed. She rushed to reassure him.

"Oh, Marty, you have nerve. You have plenty of nerve."

He was silent.

"Well, no," he said at last. "I pretty much do what I'm told."

"Really?"

"Yup. Most of the time." He rolled over and smiled at her. She didn't know what to say. A man could do anything. A strong, smart man with Marty's money could do whatever he wanted.

"Who tells you what to do?" she asked.

"The family, of course. Who tells you?"

"No one."

"Ah, well."

A speedboat came past, too close to the raft. They stood and waved their arms to signal that the boat should be farther out. Summer visitors often sabotaged the lake etiquette. The raft rocked almost violently in the wake.

"You're lucky," Marty announced. "And you're sensational in that dress."

He said those few words like he meant them, yet he conveyed something else too. It was in the way he said it. He meant, in that dress or any other, you have value. The moment, completely unexpected, touched her so deeply she shook her head and fell silent. She sat back down on the raft.

Half the time Melina felt like trash, but whoever she was—trash or not—she sensed that Marty was looking at a person of value, he saw something she couldn't see. Because he had no intentions toward her. He wasn't the kind of guy to take things that didn't belong to him. People weren't objects to Marty, was that it?

She observed the two of them—a high school flunkout with dirty secrets and the young man wanting to escape his family. But there was more to each of them.

As if aware of touching on a tender subject, he sat back down, next to her. They looked out at the lake.

"Sure," he said. "No question about it."

"Race you back," she said at last.

They slipped off the raft without another word. The water embraced her. I don't want to be easy, she thought, as her arms churned. I could throw myself at him, but he wouldn't do it, he wouldn't trash me or this place he loves. He wouldn't ever do what I always do, wreck things.

The dress was old and worn, and when she unpeeled it that night, letting it drop to the floor of her room, she saw that it was freshly torn along the sideseam. She might never wear it again. That might be it.

Don't be a cocktease, Prew had told her once. How that had

shocked her, at sixteen. She was suddenly horribly to blame for something she'd never even heard of, couldn't imagine. She hated him for naming her that. Marty wouldn't use a word like that, she knew. That was wrong of Prew, horrible of him, and she'd never realized that until now. How dare he!

She picked up the dress, smoothed it, and hung it up. The cloth was too worn and frail to hold a repair, most likely. But maybe a patch from the inside would hold. Maybe she'd try that.

23

In a dented Falcon he bought for four hundred dollars, Sean drove her twice a week in the fall to Traverse City, for American Government, creative writing, and private banjo lessons. Sean worked at a cabinet shop and took one chemistry class, and sometimes they stopped for donuts or groceries on the way home. Sean liked shopping. He was frugal, but he always bought some kind of treat or a new food to try, and a half gallon of whole milk. Mom would shake her head at the fat in it, but he didn't care.

"The best thing about UM was drinking fresh milk," he told Melina. "I can smell that powdered stuff we always drank just by thinking about it. You know I've never met anyone else who had to drink that shit?"

She laughed; it felt like a good time, to stop for groceries or twenty-nine-cent hamburgers with Sean, unless he had something on his mind. A date with Yolanda Quillen, maybe, in which case he'd be toxic, trying to get home, because Yolanda didn't winter at the lake. Time was short. The Quillens returned to Cincinnati and their other life in September.

The banjo lessons turned out to be a mistake. In his stuffy, soundproof room at the back of a music store, the banjo teacher sat too close to her, with his legs wide. She wanted to say, why are you sitting like that? And at the same time she wanted to put a hand on his heavy, jeans-clad thigh. He wasn't her type at all, no Marty Fleck, but sometimes she couldn't help but enjoy his overheated physicality next to her. Yet she hated herself for this thing happening, the space between them supposed to be filled with banjo music now contaminated with sexual possibility. Even with Marty this could have happened. It would have been easy. But Marty let something else into the space, instead. Something good. What was it?

The banjo teacher favored bluegrass. He wanted her to peg the resonator back onto her banjo.

"It's so much lighter this way, easier to hold," she said.

"Bluegrass has to ring out!"

"I just want to learn a few new songs."

"We need to move on, try new things. You can do more contemporary stuff with the banjo than you realize."

After six weeks she stopped going to the lessons, just quit one day.

What if she bought an old used car herself sometime and drove south, instead of back home? To Luddington and the ferry across Lake Michigan, before it shut down for the winter. Drove west with a sleeping bag in the back of the car. To wild Montana, the Rockies, the Pacific Ocean. Wild, upon a peak in Darien.

Miss Gloom and Doom, a classmate called her. Dee, another student in creative writing. They bummed cigarettes from one another, even though this girl was a Jesus freak in embroidered overalls. A smart Jesus freak who read widely. She gave Melina a nickname: Seff, short for Persephone.

"Because you like wandering in the dark places," Dee said. "Six months in the underworld, nibbling pomegranate seeds? Other people would have been planning to escape, but Persephone says, 'Oooh, what's this place? What is this strange feeling of grief and stagnation that possesses me?' and she hangs around."

Melina laughed.

"Or maybe she really liked that attention from what's his name, Pluto," said Dee.

Melina actually thought the picture of a woman held captive by powerful, almost deadly forces had a certain attraction.

"I'll call you Dora," she said to Dee. "For Pandora. Because you just let it all out! Fearless you!" And they both laughed at that, pleased to share mythological references.

It felt odd to have someone recognize bits of her. Like Marty did. Not like Prew, no. Or yes, even Prew, sometimes. In an aquarium, everyone's a fish, but not you, Melina.

Another morning when coffee didn't sit well, and all Mary wanted to do was get through to one o'clock or so, when her stomach would feel strong again. When she'd forget all about this discomfort, this fragile, shaky, barely-holding-on aftermath of maybe too much to drink, again.

But a morning when coffee didn't go down was like a Sunday without mass or a newspaper without the crossword. Making the coffee and carrying the first cup around the house or through the woods—that hour or so set Mary's day up like nothing else. Pure pleasure on a clean slate.

Day like today, she just wanted the queasiness to stop. Too many of these days.

She had called in sick only once in these past fifteen years, on account of the flu. She'd manage today, too. Get me through to one o'clock. Get me through, dear God.

Her shift began at ten. Dr. Bodamer told her some story about getting ready to open his own practice in Traverse City, and she ought to care terribly, but she could hardly pay attention. She had to sit down and rest her head in her hand.

"Are you all right, Mary?"

"I'm fine, fine."

At noon a Sprite filled with chopped ice from the hospital canteen restored her. By four, driving home, she couldn't even remember feeling bad. But she did remember that she had nothing to drink at Pinestead. Nothing hidden in her room, no cases of beer in the garage either.

How could you even think about drinking, Mary?

So rather than invite mental debate, rather than subject herself to the eternal round robin of rationalization, she slammed down the door on thought and made a quick turn into the IGA off the highway. Didn't signal the turn in time, and the guy behind her honked.

She bought eggs, pickles, hot dogs, several packages of day-old sweet cinnamon rolls, a jug of Chianti, and a pint of Seagram's. And a six-pack of Fresca for Melina.

There were several coffee cups rolling about on the floor behind the driver's seat. At the top of Hebron Road, above the Lake—she wasn't at her own driveway yet, but all she had to do was drive down steep Hebron Road and cross the road at the cluster of mailboxes—she stopped and poured a half inch of gin into a coffee cup. She swirled it and gulped the dusty, coffee-flavored, warm gin and very quickly felt better. Alive again. She deserved another half inch in the now-clean cup.

A pickup approaching behind her. Someone might be curious.

She set her cup on the floor of the car and grabbed the binoculars off the passenger seat. Everyone around here knew Mary Leader was a sucker for views. She gazed at the lake through her binocs and raised a hand to the truck as it passed. If you looked over your right shoulder you saw the country club, the new golf course, and the grounds all manicured like the top of a rich lady's dresser, but if you looked straight ahead, or to the south, all was as it should be. As God and old farmers had left it.

After that ordeal, she refreshed what was in the coffee cup and sipped it down more slowly. Something rose in her stomach, a discomfort, a warning. She wondered if she had eaten today; suddenly she couldn't remember. She'd better have something.

She opened a can of Fresca and a package of cinnamon rolls, nibbled at a corner of roll and sipped the Fresca. When the can was about a third emptied, she poured a bit of gin into it, shook it gently to mix her drink. Took a good long swallow.

About twenty minutes later she started her station wagon and came down Hebron Road toward the mailboxes, perhaps a bit too fast. She looked to the right and saw no one coming. She began to look toward her left, but by that time she was out in the road, and the school bus was coming out of nowhere, from the south, from behind the trees. She didn't know what to do for a second, then her foot slammed on the gas, and she shot across the road, gripping the steering wheel. Her station wagon veered wildly, missed her own driveway, leaped the runoff ditch, and then slammed into the woods, into the alder bushes and a beech tree. Her head flung up and forward and met the rearview mirror.

Behind her, the school bus wrenched violently to the right, took out the six mailboxes on posts, and plunged down into the runoff ditch behind them. The bus seemed to sigh and even quiver as it sought a balance, and after what the driver remembered later as a small eternity, it tipped and crashed down on its right side.

Inside the bus a six-year-old girl named Vicky Tolling fell from her front, left bench, right behind the driver, and her forehead hit the brass corner of a boy's trumpet case. Her forehead broke open.

Because the bus had paused before its fall, the children fell on top of one another, rather than being thrown a distance. They screamed and fought to disentangle themselves, and the eighth-graders at the back got the emergency door open. The bus driver struggled through the bus, exhorting them to get out, herding them toward the open door with Vicky Tolling a silent white doll in his arms.

A passing car turned down into Pinestead Resort to call an ambulance. Melina, reading *Miracle at Philadelphia* on the living room couch, gave the driver the telephone and then accompanied him back up the long driveway to the road. For some reason she thought not to go empty-handed, and as she ran past the kitchen she grabbed a stack of clean cotton dishtowels. Something Mom had always said about clean soft cloths being useful for an injury.

24

Melina saw the school bus on its side across the road, a crowd of children huddled in the meadow above it, before she turned her head as if in slow motion and saw her mother's car against the tree. The driver's side door was open, and Mary sat inside, facing out, her legs on the ground, her head bowed.

When Melina reached her and cried out, Mary raised her head. Her face was covered in blood. Melina knelt next to her, touched her shoulder.

"Mom."

"Melina, honey. Am I . . .? What about the others?" Mary moaned softly, touched her face and then looked down at her bloody hand. "Oh shit, oh shit," she whispered. "What's happening?"

"Can you walk with me?"

It seemed important to get away from the car. Mary took Melina's hand and stood. They walked a few feet and sank down on the driveway near the Pinestead sign. Melina dabbed her mother's face with a towel. Blood ran from a gash in the ridge of her eye socket. Apply pressure on the wound, she remembered her mother saying.

Despite the horror of an overturned school bus across the road, Melina wanted to laugh with relief that Mary could walk and speak.

But now Mary started babbling; she wanted to cross the road and examine the children sitting stunned in the brown grass of the meadow.

"No, Mom, stay here. You're all bleeding, you'll frighten them. People are looking after them, and the ambulance is coming."

"An ambulance? Oh no."

"Where does it hurt?"

"I don't hurt, I'm fine. Is anyone doing triage? Let go of me. I need to find out."

Her eye socket kept filling up with blood. Melina held her mother in her arms, trying to keep her still. She wondered if she herself was going to make some injury even worse. "Sit Mom, just sit now. Do just as I ask. Let's hold this cloth to your forehead. You're bleeding a little, so let's hold this towel here, Mom. I hear the ambulance. See, here it is."

A medic helped Mary onto a wheeled stretcher and to Melina's surprise belted her in. He laid two ridges of plastic next to her face so she couldn't turn her head.

"Can you tell me your date of birth, Mrs. Leader? And who is this young lady with us?"

"That's my beautiful daughter Melina, she is seventeen years old. Help those children first! I was born on April 4, 1916, in North Carolina. The president is . . . the president is Nixon. I didn't vote for him! Please tell me if anyone is hurt!"

"Can I ride with you?" Melina asked the medic. "Please."

"If there's room," he said.

When they lifted Vicky Tolling into the ambulance, she opened her eyes and whimpered.

"Hello miss!" one of the drivers cried. "Thatta girl. What a trooper! Mommy's on the way!"

"Oh, thank God," Mary said, forced to stare straight up because of the supports against her head. "Oh, thank God. Melina, is she all right? Tell me if she's all right. How bad is it, tell me!"

Melina had not looked inside her mother's crushed station wagon, but she knew the smell of gin. The babbling that the medics said was due to shock might have another source.

"Oh," she said to herself. Anger and mockery, her usual response to Mary's drinking, were right there inside her, along with the dread and confusion and relief. "Oh, for Christ's sake," she said. "Hang on, Mom, just hang on." She climbed into the ambulance, crouched behind the gurney, and took her mother's hand. "I'm with you."

The medic leaned over Mary's face for a minute and waited, and Melina knew he was smelling it, too. He sat up and gave Melina a quick look. She looked back at him. It's out of our hands. But love is still here. Melina closed her eyes in amazement as the bizarre sequence of emotions rushed through her. Oh, Mom. How could you do this, I'm here for you, no one will hurt you, you crazy idiot you've done it this time.

Dr. Bodamer was on his way home, but he rushed back to the ER to help examine the shocked and bruised children and to examine Mary. From inside the curtain, Melina could hear her continue to babble.

"I'm all right," she moaned. "Go help the children. Please."

"They're being looked after, Mary, they're being looked after."

"That's all I want. Look after them."

"I know, dear. But I think you've got a concussion and a severe laceration. You want to hold onto your daughter while I sew you up?" He pulled open the curtain and signaled to Melina.

Melina perched on a stool, and Mary's hand closed over hers so hard that Melina immediately gasped in pain. Dr. Bodamer leaned over Mary's forehead with his needle and thread. Despite the urgency all around them, a dreamy intensity came over him like men always got when they studied trout flies in a tackle box. Mary's grip was like iron, forcing Melina to pant and grit her teeth.

"Eeeegh," she whispered. "Mom, I need this hand."

The grip didn't lessen. Melina glanced at Dr. Bodamer's needle going into the thin flesh above Mary's eyebrow. He ignored the two of them and stitched away, peering through extended magnifying glasses.

"Mary, you are not even going to have a scar," he announced after a few minutes. "Ann Arbor has nothing on this country doc." Melina chuckled; she liked the sound of that. When he finished she extricated her fingers from her mother's and was amazed to find them unbroken.

He left them alone. Mary closed her eyes at last, but not to sleep.

"I made some big mistakes, Melina," she whispered. "I didn't eat. That was bad. And something else. Something else. I thought I would have a sip to take the edge off. That's all. But I was wrong."

"I know, Mom."

Dr. Bodamer looked in.

"Mary, your son Sean is here. Can you talk to him? The little girl,

Vicky, she's had twenty stitches at her hairline. She'll be here overnight, but we think that she's going to be just fine. The X-ray looks just fine."

"She's all right?"

"The two of you will stay a night for observation, but no one else even has to stick around this hotel."

"Oh, Dr. B., thank you. Thank you. Oh thank you, God."

She couldn't stop babbling. Adrenalin, shock, Dr. Bodamer told Melina, and perhaps alcohol?

"Could she have been drinking?"

"Yes," said Melina. "I think so."

"You're not surprised."

"Yes and no."

His expression, as he studied Melina, was neither pitying nor alarmed.

"A trooper out there is getting bits and pieces of the story. I don't think Mary is ready to talk to him, frankly. She is gonna sleep good with what I gave her. You and your brother, sit with your mom for a while. He can come back tomorrow."

He went out to the waiting room.

Melina and Sean sat on opposite sides of Mary's bed and stared at her and at each other. True to Dr. Bodamer's words, she was dozing within minutes. Melina noticed that Sean was worse off than she was. There was something wild in his eyes, like he had to do something and he didn't know what.

Thinking you have to do something, not knowing what. That's bad. But she was feeling better, to her surprise. The weird emotions had assailed her, but moved on. They blew threw her like storms and then exited. She knew that she herself had done what she could. She wanted to console Sean with her newfound wisdom. It's all right. When there's something to do, you'll know. Till then, love. Why, it's a verb. That's what it is.

When they left the hospital, the two of them went to the Dairy Twist, where they could eat in the car, and they ate in silence. With her sisters, by now, there would have been some joking, some sardonic or rueful laughter. Some connecting with each other. They'd have been trying everything to connect. But Sean, whatever was spinning round in his head—he couldn't share it, and he couldn't seem to acknowledge Melina. Or that it could have been much worse. They were well off, turns out, didn't he see that?

She didn't know how to talk to her brother. If she tried to tell him how it was with her, he'd argue. He'd tell her what she wasn't seeing. He'd come down hard. So she said nothing.

Dean Holbus, the insurance man, was in Mom's room the next morning when they came to get her. The babbling child was gone. Mary Leader was back in control, somber yet vigorous, waiting for the clothes that Melina brought. But her face was yellow and blue and swollen like a lumpy basketball, with cartoon X's of black thread curving above her left eye. Dean Holbus smiled at Melina and Sean. The three of them sat awkwardly for a few minutes, and then he rose and said, "Mary, we'll continue this conversation later on."

"I'm fine with what I've said, Dean. I know what I'm doing."

"If you're fine with it today, Mary, we'll wait a day or so, and you'll be fine with it then, too. Please don't move too quickly."

"Oh, but I will."

He nodded, briefly, just to end the conversation, but Sean followed him out into the hall.

Melina kissed Mary on the unswollen part of her face. "What's that all about, Mom?"

"Vicky, the little girl, she's okay," said Mom. "No skull fracture. I don't know if I have ever been so relieved in my life. Now I have to do something about this."

"What can you do?"

"We'll see, Mel, we'll see. I'm going to do what I can. The trooper was in here this morning, too."

"And?"

"He has to cite someone. In a traffic accident someone has to be cited. So . . . I'm being cited, which is the correct thing in this case. I wonder if the story will be in the newspaper."

"Oh, Mom."

"I'm sorry to have done this to you."

"You didn't do anything to me." Melina liked the sound of that. Was it true? "Everyone's all right. What matters to me is the same thing that matters to you, Mom."

"I didn't eat, I made some big mistakes, I had something to drink at the top of Hebron Road. Never let this happen to you, Mel. Eat regular meals, and only drink at home. Give every ounce of alcohol an hour to metabolize."

"Yes, Mom," said Melina, laughing.

"The worst thing in the world, I guess I must have thought, was . . . well . . . people finding out. Exposure. Losing my privacy. I was wrong. The worst thing is hurting a child, and that didn't happen this time. I can take anything else."

"Yeah."

"But . . ." Mary looked at her daughter. "There's more."

"Let's go home, Mom. Let's go home and settle down."

"For one thing, I'm going to need you and Sean to drive me places for the next year."

"Really?"

"Yes. The trooper took my license."

"We can manage that. Hey, Mom, let's not solve all these problems now. Let's take it easy for a day or two, okay? Play it cool, man, real cool." Melina hummed the tune from *West Side Story*. "Why'nt you get dressed? Sean's all keyed up. We'd just like to go home now."

"I need to stop up front and pay some bills."

"Sure, okay."

It was the Tollings' bill she wanted to pay, of course, but that was not to be the end of it.

Dean Holbus told Sean, "If anything could have made your mom less stubborn, you'd think this would be it. But I guess there's no hope for the lady after all. She is never going to fall in line." Sean heard the affection in his words.

"Is she going to let the needs of others run over her, run over all of us, again?" Sean said to Melina, thinking aloud.

"What do you mean?" said Melina.

"I don't know. I really don't know why I said that. It just feels—like she has no resistance when people need something, sometimes. No matter what Dean Holbus says. Always heading off to the ER, always inviting people to the lake. What do I mean?"

"I don't know either."

"I wish there was someone to talk to."

"You can talk to me, Sean."

Sean looked at her.

"I know," he said. But still he didn't act on it.

Chuck Schaffhauser, editor-owner of the four small Northern Michigan newspapers that ran Mary's Leader's column, "A Spell on the Water," went on extended leave for health purposes, and his wife, Bett, was taking over their newspapers. The announcement, short on hard information, had appeared in the paper a few weeks earlier. Mary had not yet met the new editor. She was instantly relieved at the sight of the younger woman behind the huge, cluttered desk.

Bett Schaffhauser looked up from her paperwork at Mary's entrance and gave an automatic, apologetic smile. She leaped to her feet and sat down again. Not as secure and easy in this job as her husband had seemed to be. But what woman, starting out in a man's world, ever is? We're always a bit jittery, Mary thought. Terrified to be found incompetent, unable to relax with the reins yet afraid to surrender them. There are so many hands ready to grab them away.

Bett was in her forties. A pretty woman with a cap of shining brown hair, hair like a coffee bean. Maybe that's what they mean by nut brown hair, Mary thought.

In her husband's wheeled office chair, Bett pushed back a little too hard and fast from the desk that had been her husband's for twenty years and sailed back into a filing cabinet behind her. She startled herself, snorted with laughter, recovered, and reached for the three pages that Mary announced would be her last submission to the paper.

"Oh, we'll see about that!" Bett said. "Let me take a look."

A SPELL ON THE WATER
By Mary Leader

When I first spent summers on Achill, in the 1940s and 1950s, the expanse of water would cast a spell on me.

We ran around after our five small children, trying to keep a low-budget resort in operation, and eager ourselves to do so many fun things on the water—we sure didn't look like we were under a spell. No one would have pointed at us and said, "Look at those people, are they in some kind of trance?" It was more a matter of being in touch with congenial rhythms. Despite the unpredictable squalls from the southwest, the world made sense. We were under the best kind of spell, God's own, nature's own.

Nature's pace is congenial to human beings. We ought to stay hitched to these connections, not defy them. We forget our natural pace when we detach ourselves from nature in order to plug into modern-day consumerism: we rush into town to buy the latest do-dad, the biggest outboard, another labor-saving device. We keep up with the news as if our lives depend on having the latest news about winners and losers in the big cities!

When the vireo sings, we're too busy to hear. When the loon calls, we're excited, but when the loons fall silent we forget their existence.

But when I first came to the lake I did the opposite of forget: I remembered who I was. I replenished. I got to refill my pitcher.

I learned to do a thousand new things, by trying to learn them, at my own pace.

When my husband died in 1955, I thought I would give up, but the lake refilled me again. The woods were full of their own sounds, and those sounds comforted me even more than a choir in a church. The lake water lapped over the rocks in 1955 as it does today—that very same sound, like a best friend who didn't die, didn't even get older.

Ojibwa friends in Northern Michigan have a philosophy that I admire. They understand that at the end of every day, the light fails and the darkness comes—no matter who rules the country, no matter how bad things get, the light goes out and the darkness comes upon us. No matter what is causing your own heart to break, night comes to all of us. Next morning, the sun rises on the rich and poor, the powerful and the troubled alike. I also took comfort in that cycle of things.

I got through some hard times.

I could always turn to the water and rest my eyes, no matter what happened behind me.

And I thought I could protect my five kids all by myself from some of life's ugliest moments, simply by refusing such things entry into our lives here at the lake.

But now, I think I was wrong about that. Like one of those mythic kings who learned that his own son was predestined to kill him, and so he ordered his baby son banished or slaughtered . . . well, it never worked. To expunge what you fear, just like that—it never works.

There are spells and there are spells. The good spell I was

telling you about, and then a wrong spell—which is anything, anything at all, that keeps you from seeing and thinking clearly. It may not be all bad, all the time, but it sure can be wrong, inappropriate, and dangerous.

My daughter, who is studying writing at Traverse City Junior College, suggested that I should look at the history of the word "spell" itself. We found out that "spell" is from Old English, and has the same root as the "spel" in Gospel. The spell you're under could be God's own good news. It also means recital, or tale, and that's when you can see how easy it is to fall "under" a spell, or victim to it. Who ever left a story easily? Scheherazade in *The Arabian Nights* saved her life by casting a spell on the sultan with story after story. He fell under the influence. Lucky for her.

I've been under the influence some in my own life. Of Anne Morrow Lindbergh's stories, of Achill Lake's changing face—those seem like very good influences. But some influences we don't want to acknowledge.

"Spell" has even more meanings. How about the idea of doing things in shifts as in, would you take a spell at this ice cream crank, please? Now where does that meaning of "spell" come from?

Same thing: it comes from the letter by letter way we have of creating a story, or a chant, or a curse, or a parable. To spell out the letters is to begin.

Here's a lesson I've learned, maybe not from the woods of Northern Michigan, so much as from a hard look at my own life. I need to take a spell at starting over. I need to start raw. I need to begin a new direction. It's never too late.

Bett Schaffhauser looked up at Mary with eyes the same shining brown as her hair.

"Boy," she said at last, "I sure do understand about starting over."

"It's difficult."

"But I'm not inclined to accept the conditions that you attached to this column," Bett said slowly. "Calling it your goodbye column. I don't want to run a final column, Mary. Couple of reasons," she continued, as Mary frowned. "I'm feeling my way here, so I may be making the wrong decisions ten times a day. Chuck sure liked your column, he gave you free rein. He'd publish it. And he'd understand if you wanted to take a break from it, too. If you want to consider a hiatus, fine, but for me, this sort of goodbye dear reader . . ." She set the pages Mary had given her down on the desk. "Sorry about that; I don't mean to dismiss it. I mean, this is . . . too good, on the one hand, and on the other hand . . . do you really want to lay yourself out like this?"

"Yes, I do," Mary said, thinking, *goodbye dear reader*? That hurt.

Bett flattened her hand over the papers. "It's a kind of, you know, personal philosophy or, uh, mental pilgrimage, beautifully put."

"I suppose it's about trying to get my life back in order."

"You have a right to do that in privacy and safety, seems to me," Bett rushed on, as if finding the point she wanted to make. "Chuck's illness has taught me that. We all, we each, have a right to our private, you know, journey. We need some privacy for what we go through. But signing off? I don't want to give you up. It would certainly be okay, you know, to try other magazines, other places, too. Are you maybe ready for that?"

"But haven't I given that right to privacy away, by what happened? I've gone and let the wide world in."

"No," said Bett, with the disciplined wisdom of a woman who had been taking care of a desperately ill husband for years. Wise before her time. Mary had seen this before. "It's been, what, six weeks since that accident. Is it possible that you're moving too fast?"

"Lord no, isn't it too late?"

"Who else do you talk to about things like this?"

"What do you mean?"

"Maybe it's not necessary to be deciding this all on your own."

Mary gazed at the younger woman. Bett had a surprising steadiness to her, despite the initial look she had offered when Mary came into her office—a beleaguered person out of her depth, slightly wild-eyed at her new responsibility. Mary remembered Chuck Schaffhauser's tremor. Hard and painful experiences are not lost on some people. This woman has lived some, she realized, and yet has the spirit to tackle a new life. Sometimes hard times work like a baptism. Or a fiery furnace.

"Dear Abby would say to talk to a clergyman. Is that what you mean?"

"It's possible." Bett sat back. "You know, you've had a really interesting life."

"Ptssh."

"Seriously," said Bett. "And in my own way, I have too. Talking to my peers is what's helped me. Other people who have been through similar things."

But that's just what they recommended down at the AA meetings in Traverse City. Mary had gone to her first one swollen face and all. She clung to their promises like someone clinging to a raft with her fingers. She had been going every week; maybe she could learn something from those people now. This was no time to start thinking. This was no time to second-guess herself.

To Bett Schaffhauser, she said, "Telling my story, yes, well maybe I'm getting there."

In AA it seemed like a recurring topic. My last day drunk. The women in Traverse City talked about that one a lot. The day you finally get it, and the new thing now was that Mary could connect with that one, too. That first rung on the ladder: I agreed before that I shouldn't drink, but now I believe it. Now I get it.

I get it. That means, not at odds with myself about that particular step anymore. No more of those arguments with myself! I receive.

"Well. I really do feel like a hiatus, like taking a break and coming back in a few months, maybe," she ventured. "Is that what you suggest?"

"Yes, Mary, yes. But make it weeks, not months. Look, if you're a writer, you have to write. Don't cut your life rope. Chuck . . . As Chuck would say, writing didn't cause any of this grief and confusion. Writing might help you get through it. That is, if you're a writer, not just pulling teeth when you do this. And I think you are." She smiled. She stood up and reached for Mary's hand.

"My best to Mr. Schaffhauser," said Mary.

"I will tell him." It seemed that Bett's eyes then filled with tears. Mary hesitated.

"I'm terribly sorry for his illness, and I hope and pray he does well," she said.

"Thank you, Mary."

"Can I do anything?"

"We both have our plates really full," Bett said. "That's how it is."

"I would loan you my guardian angel, if I could."

At that Bett laughed.

Mary put half of Pinestead Resort up for sale to settle the damages claims from the school district and the Tollings out of court, against Dean Holbus's advice. The south half on the other side of the cedars: a stretch of crabgrass, five small, run-down tourist cabins, and two acres of sugar maples, red pines, and white ash trees. The white ash turned red in the fall, bending over the rocky shore. She would miss those trees.

Her kids were horrified and angry and made noises about fighting the suit. The ladies in AA said to wait a year before making drastic changes, Dean Holbus said to wait; but Mary had waited too many years already.

She wasn't making a change. She was acknowledging changes that had already occurred.

She owed the Tollings more than their medical bill. And she owed her own children help with their far-flung adventures, medical school for Alex, graduate school in anthropology for Sharon, Sean's dream of buying Wilgosch's farm. Becky was talking about teacher certification, and Melina needed to get on with her own life. This hanging onto a dream of the lakeshore when people dear to her needed help, needed their freedom? Never again. And Mr. Wilgosch was right: she couldn't believe what the real estate agent offered her.

She would always keep the quarter mile of woods to the north. Unbroken mixed forest. She could put up a tent there if the house ever got too crowded. She'd just put up a wall tent and lie down on her pallet and listen all night to the strange rustlings on the other side of the canvas. Long as the new owners to the south didn't make too much noise. That'd be all right.

She would have liked to handpick the buyers, but you couldn't do that anymore, thanks to the open housing law she had supported so fiercely years ago. At least she could hold out for a bundle, no need to bargain down. And she did hold out. The new owners paid full price and immediately razed the cabins, and the Leaders that summer tried not to look past the row of cedar trees at the new border of their property. It was strange and assaultive to have these strangers next to them, doing whatever they liked. The builders mowed down the pines and brought in a backhoe to carve a new driveway down from the road. Mary knew that she would never get used to it. Even the wind sounded different, lost its music when there were no trees. They poured riprap against the lake shore and probably buried the loons' nest without even seeing it.

But the loons would find a new place. They'd find a new place.

Get up, let's go. Time to move, they'd call to one another. Time to quit this place. We've dallied long enough. There have gotta be pockets of quiet out there for a loon family. North of here. Let's go.

25

November might be an off time to take the ferry to Alaska, but Melina discovered the MV *Taku* to be deliciously uncrowded.

Long before she stepped aboard Melina floated above the ground with excitement; she had been above the ground for weeks. This entire expedition north was charmed, from the day she had first discussed it with her mother. To her astonishment Mary had immediately encouraged her adventure.

"The geographic cure, they call it in AA," Mary chuckled.

"Is that bad?"

"It's exactly right for an eighteen-year-old. It worked for me in 1941 and in 1955, and in a way, it's working now, but my geographic cure is to stay put. Yours is to move on. Discover your country! I'm so glad I didn't stay put in North Carolina when I was young. Imagine!"

"You wouldn't have met Daddy, and I wouldn't be here."

"That too."

"Maybe you ought to come with me, Mom. It's so horrible to have that house next door and the golf course up the hill! There's fifty miles of elbow room in Alaska."

"I might do that in a couple of years. Who knows? At least the golfers aren't here most of the year. A few more years with the health service, and then who knows?" Mary hadn't gone back to Miltonia Hospital's emergency room after the accident; instead she taught home health care to public health nurses and aides, down at the junior college.

"You can teach in Alaska," Melina said. "They need nurses and nature writers, I'm sure they do."

"I might do that. I just might," Mary repeated. "But for now I think I'll just stay right here. I need to learn patience." And for some reason, she chuckled again.

It had been so difficult at first. She had the resiliency of a windowpane; she flew into a tirade when plans went awry, as they always did. Her mouth went into a permanent upside-down U, like a croquet wicket, when the backhoe came next door and the cabins were razed, the new driveway bulldozed, and the pine trees cut. But then she began to find a new rhythm. They went on picnics farther north, and camping up on Lake Superior, and they all baked a lot more. They filled the freezer with jam and pies, and starting in July they wolfed berry cobbler almost every night, with ice cream that Sean and Melina cranked melting into it.

And with Alex's and Sharon's encouragement, via phone calls and letters, Melina made plans for a trip. She would take the fall semester off and start at the University of Alaska in January. And someday, soon, Mary would follow.

Melina took the bus to Chicago, spent two days with Grandma and Tony, then boarded the train to Seattle for a week with Alex. The Alaska ferry would take her up the Inside Passage, starting right from downtown Seattle all the way to Skagway, and there she'd get on another train to Whitehorse, Yukon Territory, Canada. Those words, Skagway, Yukon, trailed clouds of romantic lore. She could see the Mounties in her mind's eye, behind them the endless Northern woods. She could imagine the rivers . . . And from Whitehorse, a cross-country bus would deliver her in another two days to Fairbanks!

From her seat in the Empire Builder, Melina not only had a view of the country but was held in a congenial, distanced relationship with a dozen other passengers who could study each other over a few days. They were an amazing collection. A thin woman in her thirties dressed all in macramé—dress and sandals—created more macramé items as the train rocked and shifted and sighed toward Seattle. Yarn rose and fell in her fingers.

A huge young man with long greasy hair, in a suede jacket bordered with fringe, came on the train drunk, fell asleep in the facing seats at the front of the car, and cursed the conductor who woke him and tried to move him from the "family seats" to another seat back in the car.

"When I worked for Southern Railway we called this the Medicare

Run, because all the conductors between here and Seattle are over sixty-five!" he announced to the car at large. The conductor and the passengers ignored him. The next day, sober, he was a different person, mild, quiet, and lonely. Melina heard him talking about his Vietnam tour in the club car. The "facing seats" from which he was expelled were taken by a family of Hutterites, going home to Montana, two women in long skirts, their hair hidden in scarves, and two young, handsome men in square-cut wool pants with suspenders. One of the couples carried a year-old baby. From her seat Melina could steal a look at the baby's hands pressing and pulling at the father's shirt, while the man smiled and held a necklace of teething beads. The baby's hands dug into the cloth of his shirt. What would that be like, Melina thought, to be held by a father? How big a father is, to a child, big and gentle. The whole family seemed so pure, so homegrown, she was astonished to see them eating potato chips out of a Tupperware bowl one afternoon. The Leader household had never owned Tupperware. They used potato chip boxes to carry their picnics.

One night the baby's cry woke Melina. She opened her eyes to see the young mother standing in the aisle, letting the motion of the train rock her and the baby. Her scarf was off, and long dark hair fell down to her waist. Her hem swung just above her boots. The isolation and intimacy of their life cast a bit of magic into the car, seemed to fill all of the passengers with an unexpected desire for something that rich with simplicity.

Melina felt like a sponge; everything she saw mattered. Her own responses interested her, too: her lust for the Hutterites' simplicity, a strange automatic recoil from the veteran, once she heard him say those self-incriminating words, so filled with compromise and sorrow and trauma: "When I was in Vietnam . . ." The incredible sense of well-being as twilight fell outside the west-bound train. She opened her new journal and wrote pages every day, describing them all—the Hutterites, the Vietnam vet, and the woman producing macramé like a noiseless patient spider.

Alex's apartment in Seattle was two blocks up from Lake Union. They went to concerts and took walks and ate pizza or fish-and-chips every night. They shopped at the Bookworm, at St. Vincent de Paul, and at the Recreational Equipment Co-op for Alaskan clothes—a checked red-and-black wool shirt like Sharon had and a down vest. Alex wanted to rush right by the hippie head shops on University Avenue, but Melina took her inside and bought them both jewelry—long earrings for herself, and an agate on a string for Alex. They crossed a tiny bridge over a canal and ate hamburgers the size of plates at a tavern under Queen Anne Hill. Melina had not had such a good time with Alex in years.

"I'm so sorry," Alex said, when they talked about Mom's drinking, and Melina stared at her. "I had no idea." For the first time in her life, Melina sensed the progression of it, of Mom's drinking, the changes over the years in her own mother. That her sisters had not known the extent of it amazed her. That it had gotten worse. Melina ended up bearing witness alone. No, Sean was there too, the last year.

"She wanted to protect us, but she ran out of energy. It got away from her." They walked along the waterfront with arms linked. "She wanted to keep us from . . . from elements in society that she thought she had escaped, that she thought were sordid, and wrong. And you know what, Mel? She couldn't."

Melina would get on the ferry in a few minutes. They walked back and forth, holding each other close. Their family was a package they were just now unwrapping together. Partly unwrapping; they couldn't fathom the entirety of it.

Alex said, carefully, experimentally, "Maybe when Mom did that . . . when she had that accident—it's as if she found out herself, that she was one of the very people that she tried to keep us safe from. She was the bad people." Arms linked, they stared at each other, amazed at the logic of it. "I can say this to you because you don't take things literally," Alex went on. "That's why she sold the land. If thine eye offend thee, pluck it out. She always did overdo things."

"Oh, now. I'm so relieved that we have a little money," Melina said. "Aren't you?" She thought about the two thousand dollars that Mom had sent to a bank in Alaska for Melina. She held her sister tightly, saving some of what Alex had said to think about later. When she would be alone on the ferry boat.

Because sometimes, even though Alex spoke with a magnificent sureness, she was speaking out of her own mix of dilemmas. Even with her sharp vision she couldn't possibly escape the special colors of her own point of view. She didn't know the extent of Mom's drinking. That continued to amaze Melina.

"It's way different back home," Melina said, "but she's getting more relaxed. She was grief stricken about the sale, but she's getting over it. I'm amazed that she—given everything, that she—didn't pack up and flee. She just stuck it out, just inhaled the humiliation of it, and it has kind of dissipated now. It's not so bad. She says maybe she will come up to Alaska sometime."

"I hope so."

"She was grim all the time last winter, but now she's funny again. It's wonderful that she doesn't have to worry about that damned resort business anymore. I couldn't believe it at first but we'll . . . get used to it. Which is kind of awful, isn't it. But Jesus, it was nice not having to look after renters this summer. Oh, you have no idea."

"Yes, I do," Alex laughed.

They did a U-turn at Ivar's Fish Bar and walked back toward the ferry terminal. Departure time was getting closer. Alex clung to her sister.

"Here's something that helped me once," she said. "Years ago, when I wanted to be a priest . . ." She laughed again, at the memory of believing in the impossible. "Years ago. Do you know the story of Abraham and Isaac?"

Instantly Melina recalled the colored plate in her children's Bible of a mountainous, white-bearded Abraham raising a knife just like Sean's buck knife over his teenage son. A blond angel with an impassive face reaches out to pluck at the sleeve of his raised arm. The teenage boy Isaac is no child, he has muscles of his own, and big knees like Sean's, but he is overpowered and tied up.

"Yes."

"Well, I read a book about it by Soren Kierkegaard, and he says the reason Abraham was willing to do it was his faith. It's hard to explain, and that's not what made me happy. What happened was, I was standing in the Bookworm reading this, just before I bought the book, and Kierkegaard says that great grief, suffering, can kill some people. For some people, it's too much. But other people, other strong people, can force themselves back on track after great grief. Like tacking, they manage to get their sails pointed the right way in the wind. Only, as a result of the effort, they become slightly odd. Those were his exact words. And I remember looking up from that book and thinking about our mother. That she was slightly odd. And in a way, despite everything, it's kind of a badge of honor. Oddness, in other words, it's all right. It's there on account of a great story."

Melina thought about that picture of Abraham. How did she do it, how did Alex find understanding in the most unlikely places?

As if there were so many things still to be said, Alex stuck around the boat dock as long as possible after Melina went on board. At the rail, Melina fixed her eyes on Alex where she stood waving, until the boat, with a tremendous blast, began to move away from the pier. Melina stared back at her until her sister's form disappeared into the rainy jumble of receding docks and piers and warehouses. Then she was on her own, bound for Alaska.

For a minute she was terrified. She wanted to retreat, be something, anyone, different from Melina Leader. Then she thought, no one knows who I am. Just do this. Just make some motions, and see what happens. What else can I do?

She laid her sleeping bag on a chaise lounge on an upper deck, under the orange heat lamps. A few other passengers were doing the same thing. It was dark, and the boat groaned comfortably.

Within twenty-four hours the passengers without cabins, who were sleeping on chairs in the lounge, or on the covered deck, fairly quickly assessed one another. She recoiled at first from a young man with a guitar, just as she had tried to keep distance between herself and the lonely vet on the Empire Builder. But despite several initial glances and smiles, the young man didn't come after her. She began to get interested in him. He acknowledged her banjo case with a smile rather than an invitation to play together, thank God.

After two days they crossed some open water, a rough passage of about six hours, which she spent inside, armed with Saltines and Sprite, trying to keep her stomach calm. And then they entered the quiet, dark green waters of the Panhandle, where nearly vertical ridges covered with rainforest sloped right into the water at isolated rocky beaches. You wanted to get off the boat and claim a cove for your own, abandon school and society, live on ferns and crabs and inside the rhythm of the tide and the seasons.

She hung over the rail and stared and daydreamed.

On the fourth and last morning it began to snow.

The flakes settled on the steps of the gangway and covered the white rails of the boat. They melted into the slate-gray deck, disappeared into the deep green water. Melina and the guitar player were the only ones lingering on the deck that afternoon. He offered peanut butter, hardtack, and dried apricots; she opened a jar of Michigan blueberry jam. He had grown up in Fairbanks, spent the last five years "outside," he said. He was going home. He played Woody Guthrie tunes and sang so softly, she could hardly make out the words. It didn't matter. His name was Denali, a perfect name. His parents had actually named him after a mountain!

"Inside, outside, Morningside," he said now, standing near her as she stared down at the water and the tempting, half-hidden beaches.

"What's that?" she said.

"In territorial days those were your choices. Where you could be: inside Alaska; outside, in the states; or if things got really bad, down at Morningside Hospital for the mentally ill in Oregon. Alaska didn't have a mental hospital, so crazy folks who got committed had to go to Oregon. Inside, outside, Morningside. That's what they used to say, when I was a kid growing up in Fairbanks."

She laughed. "I like that. Inside, outside . . . if you can keep moving or at least not get stuck, you can stay out of Morningside. Is that it? The geographic cure?"

"Could be."

He had long, very dark brown hair, thick and curly, almost to his shoulders, and warm, lively, dark eyes. She could see him note her varicolored irises, but he didn't say anything. She liked that he was her own height, and she liked the simplicity and grace of his kit, of his routine. She liked the distance they were keeping from each other. Behind her he picked up his guitar again.

"Ain't nobody that can sing like me, way over yonder in the minor key . . ."

Not many people knew that one, but she did. It was Woody Guthrie's, too. Not an anthem for a generation, just something Woody wrote for himself. For the moment it was the perfect tune. She didn't have to throw herself away on one of these tempting beaches, she could let Denali's music get under her skin instead. Where it disturbed her a little, in a not unpleasant way. A background song to this solitude, this adventure.

Funny, people talked about the spirit of adventure that Alaska called forth, but her sister Sharon, eight years ago, was the least adventurous of them all, not the energetic lover of risk you'd expect to go to Alaska. Sharon set her hair in curlers every night, followed recipes to the letter, stayed home reading on winter afternoons rather than learn to ski. But she was the one who decided to fling herself to the top of the planet.

Melina folded her arms on the deck rail, leaned over, and looked down at the water parting for the slow-moving, northbound *Taku.* She loved this great, hollow, groaning boat. She leaned forward onto the rail, put her weight on her elbows, and lifted her feet off the ground. Let her arms on the rail take her weight. She swung her legs in the air. How free she felt, out-traveling the ties that hurt. The decision she had made, to go north, sang inside her with Denali's little song. Not much to that song, but there wasn't one word that wasn't true enough, and good enough, to get her to Alaska.

She said it's hard for me to see
how one little boy got so ugly
Yes my little girly that might be
But there ain't nobody that can sing like me . . .

THE END

Acknowledgments

Writer friends in Fairbanks carefully read selected chapters; my thanks to Jean Anderson, Burns Cooper, Kim Cornwall, Susheila Khera, John Kooistra, John Morgan, and Linda Schandelmeier. I am enormously grateful to Barbara Kingsolver for her careful reading of the entire manuscript, her words of encouragement and fine advice. Thank you to other sharp readers of the book: Marie Boudreaux, Dixon Jones, Marion Avrilyn Jones, Paul Kowalski, and Pat Lambert. Thanks to Ellen Moore, as always, for her reading and her ideas. And thank you Sandra Boatwright for stepping forward at the right minute with a clear vision which saved the day.

Everything I know about banjo lore and banjo playing, I learned from Fairbanks recording artist Robin Dale Ford, who is an amazing musician, teacher, singer, songwriter, storyteller, businesswoman, and good friend.

Set in the years from 1955 to the early 70s, this book required considerable research with the help of Jeanie Williamson of the Noel Wien Library Van Delivery Service in Fairbanks. Interlibrary loans, especially on the history of minstrel shows in America, were indispensable. I thank Jeanie for these and other books and magazines that she provided in quantity and at the right time. Thanks also to the city clerk's office in Mancelona, Michigan, for providing hard copies of newspapers back to the 1950s and to the staff of public libraries in Alden, Bellaire, Central Lake, Traverse City, and Mancelona, Michigan.

Members of the extended family of Joseph A. and Mary Elizabeth Lambert in Northern Michigan have made me welcome in their home year after year since 1996 and shared without stinting all that they love about this beautiful landscape. Without their hospitality this book could not have been written. I thank them with all my heart.

My sons, Henry and Desmond, could not know all that they do for me. Their encouragement is steady and indispensable, and their comments always right on. Thank you to my beloved husband, Pat Lambert, who carried so much of this one on his shoulders.